Juno Rushdan is the award-winning author of steamy, action-packed romantic thrillers that keep readers on the edge of their seats. She writes about kick-ass heroes and strong heroines fighting for their lives as well as their happily-ever-afters. As a veteran air force intelligence officer, she uses her background supporting Special Forces to craft realistic stories that make readers sweat and swoon. Juno currently lives in the DC area with her patient husband, two rambunctious kids and a spoiled rescue dog. To receive a free book from Juno, sign up for her newsletter at junorushdan.com/mailing-list. Also be sure to follow Juno on BookBub for the latest on sales at bit.ly/bookbubjuno

Linda O. Johnston loves to write. While honing her writing skills, she worked in advertising and public relations, then became a lawyer...and enjoyed writing contracts. Linda's first published fiction appeared in *Ellery Queen's Mystery Magazine* and won a Robert L. Fish Memorial Award for Best First Mystery Short Story of the Year. Linda now spends most of her time creating memorable tales of romance, romantic suspense and mystery. Visit her on the web atlindaojohnston.com

Also by Juno Rushdan

Fugitive Heroes: Topaz Unit
Rogue Christmas Operation
Alaskan Christmas Escape
Disavowed in Wyoming
An Operative's Last Stand

A Hard Core Justice Thriller
Hostile Pursuit
Witness Security Breach
High-Priority Asset
Innocent Hostage
Unsuspecting Target

Tracing a Kidnapper

Also by Linda O. Johnston

Her Undercover Refuge
Guardian K-9 on Call
Uncovering Colton's Family Secret
Colton First Responder
Second Chance Soldier
Trained to Protect

Discover more at millsandboon.co.uk

WYOMING WINTER RESCUE

JUNO RUSHDAN

SHIELDING COLTON'S WITNESS

LINDA O. JOHNSTON

MILLS & BOON

First Published in Great Britain 2022
by Mills & Boon, an imprint of HarperCollins*Publishers* Ltd
1 London Bridge Street, London, SE1 9GF

www.harpercollins.co.uk

HarperCollins*Publishers*
1st Floor, Watermarque Building,
Ringsend Road, Dublin 4, Ireland

Wyoming Winter Rescue © 2022 Juno Rushdan
Shielding Colton's Witness © 2022 Harlequin Enterprises ULC

Special thanks and acknowledgement are given to Linda O. Johnston for her contribution to The Coltons of Colorado miniseries.

ISBN: 978-0-263-30364-3

1022

WYOMING WINTER RESCUE

JUNO RUSHDAN

For JBR. Thank you for your unwavering
support and love.

Chapter One

"Nash, don't bother coming." Lourdes Lynn Delgado cradled her cell phone between her ear and shoulder as she locked her computer screen and grabbed her purse. "There's nothing left to say. Besides, I'm already leaving the office." She should've left an hour ago.

"I'm sorry I'm running late, Lynn."

To her, Lourdes was her grandmother, so almost everyone called Lynn by her middle name, which she preferred since she was the namesake of someone still living. Although her family affectionately called her Lola for as long as she could remember. For some reason, Nash had never taken to it.

"Running late is ten minutes. Not sixty." Nonetheless, here she was with a grumbling stomach at 8:00 p.m., waiting on him. Like an idiot.

"I got hung up at work," Nash said, "and before you say it, *yes*, as usual."

He was an FBI agent, saving lives and stopping bad guys. She admired him for it, but his tardiness only scratched the surface of a much deeper problem in their relationship.

"Wait for me." The entreaty in his voice tugged at her, but she braced against it, refusing to get sucked back in. "I'll be there in five minutes," he said, which she'd learned meant twenty. "Wait, okay? We need to talk."

She didn't believe it. He wasn't going to shed the military stoicism from his former army ranger days any time soon and suddenly open up.

"You haven't changed." Lynn turned off her office lights. "What we need is a clean break."

As a psychotherapist she knew that seeing one another after a breakup while being attracted to each other and still having feelings wasn't advisable. Studies suggested time apart was best. Six months without any interaction. Without speaking on the phone. Without letting the good memories cloud judgment and convince her that separating was a mistake.

Lynn stepped into the hallway. "I'm leaving now." She locked her office door. "Don't come to my house, either. We're done." Saying the words out loud made her heart ache. She'd once envisioned building a life with him, but if they were wrong for each other, it was better to end things now before they got in any deeper. "It's for the best. Good night."

After she disconnected, she put her phone in her purse and turned to leave.

Movement at the end of the hall stopped her cold. The cozy waiting room near the front door was dimly lit by one lamp and the plugged-in glowing jack-o'-lantern on the side table. She hesitated a minute but didn't see anyone, didn't hear anything. With Halloween coming up and all the horror movies she'd been watching, her subconscious was probably playing tricks on her.

Yet the warning hairs on the nape of her neck rose. "Hello."

Maybe it was her colleague, Dr. Richard Jennings, whose practice she had joined last year. Or perhaps one of his clients. She couldn't recall if he'd mentioned any late appointments.

Lynn strode down the hall, treading lightly on the carpet until she could see the entire waiting room and the front door.

She saw something. Or rather someone. Standing in the corner, in the shadows.

A woman?

No…a man. Definitely a man.

"Rich, is that you?" Even as she asked the question, she could now tell it wasn't. The height and build were wrong. Too short, too slim to be Rich.

The man stepped into the light.

It was Andy Crombie. One of her clients she'd been concerned about since their last session.

Lynn tamped down her rising fear. "Andy? What are you doing here? It's very late and we don't have an appointment." She stepped closer. "Is everything okay?"

Shaking his head, he burrowed his hands in his pockets. His shaggy black hair was disheveled, with inky strands clinging to his pale face. His brown eyes were watery, his nose swollen and red, his beard shabby. He was wearing a dirty, stained T-shirt and a ragged jacket.

"No," Andy said, with another sharp shake of his head, his voice hoarse. "Everything's not okay." His hand slipped from his pocket. Metal glinted in the amber light.

He had a gun.

Lynn stiffened, but her mind was racing. She'd gone through a course to prepare for a situation like this. Ninety percent of the scenarios from her training hadn't ended well. That was the reason she had decided to stop treating severe psychological pathologies and hadn't opened a practice alone.

She shifted her stance to an angle, allowing her a glimpse of Rich's office without turning her back on Andy. Rich might still there. If so, the door would be unlocked. She hoped.

It was closer than hers, only a few feet away.

As long as Andy kept the gun lowered, down by his side, she might be able to make it.

Slowly, very slowly, Lynn raised her palms. "Stay calm." Her tone was steady and soft despite the fact that her nerves were pinging. "Whatever the problem is, we can find a solution. We can get through this. Together." She crept backward, inch by inch. "But having a gun pointed at me makes me very uncomfortable. Can you put the gun away so we can work through this peacefully?"

He rubbed the side of his face and yanked at his hair. "No."

A knot of tension tightened in her stomach. "Okay, okay. How about putting the gun on the floor or the side table next to you so no one gets hurt by accident."

"I said no," he spat through gritted teeth.

Lynn drew in a strained breath. "Then talk to me. Tell me what the problem is."

"The problem is you." Andy lifted the automatic weapon.

Lynn's heart dropped as a sickening dread washed over her. She stared at the muzzle of the gun.

Silver.

Lethal.

Aimed dead center at her chest.

A scream started in the back of her throat, but Rich wouldn't be able to hear her. The therapy rooms were soundproofed to safeguard the privacy of their clients. As well as to keep outside noise from disrupting a patient's train of thought.

Lynn swallowed back any useless cries for help. "You don't want to hurt me." She took another small step. Another and another. "You don't want to hurt anyone."

"But I do. I really do," he said, jabbing the gun in her direction. "I want to hurt you, the way you hurt me."

Heart thudding, she licked her lips. *Don't panic. Do not panic!* "What's wrong, Andy?"

His gaze roamed while he pinched his lips together. Tears welled in his eyes. The gun shook in his hand. But he didn't answer.

"Please tell me what's wrong." Lynn eased her back up to the door. "I want to help you." She reached for the knob.

"Liar." Andy's gaze flickered up and homed in on her. "It's all your fault." He cocked the hammer of the gun.

Oh, no.

Lynn twisted the doorknob, hopeful it was unlocked.

The cool metal in her hand turned, and scant relief whispered through her. She ducked inside the office, closed the door and engaged the lock.

Spinning around, she faced Rich and his client, Cindy Morris.

Rich's hand fell from Cindy's cheek, and the two of them jumped apart on the sofa like a couple of teenagers caught making out.

Wide-eyed and flushed, Rich hopped to his feet. "Sorry. Uh, I thought you'd already left. We were just, uh…"

Lynn glanced past Cindy, who lowered her head and was adjusting her blouse, and she hustled around behind Rich's desk. She pressed the red panic button that would notify the police. Both offices had one in case of emergencies.

"What are you doing in here?" Rich asked, his tone sliding from apologetic to indignant. "How dare you barge in on a counseling session."

"Andy Crombie is here."

"At this hour?" Rich's puffed-up chest deflated, and he rubbed his trim powder-white beard. For a man in his late fifties, he looked a decade older. "I thought you decided to stop seeing him and referred him to a different therapist."

"He's got a gun."

"What?" Rich blanched.

Cindy bolted up from the sofa and ran to him. The young

woman, half his age, grabbed Rich's arm and clung to his side. "Do you think it's loaded?"

Lynn grimaced at the question. "I didn't ask." The odds weren't in their favor. When did anyone in the Cowboy State deliberately carry an *unloaded* firearm?

A gunshot cracked, blasting a hole in the door as bullet-split wood fractured the air.

Cindy shrieked.

Rich dragged her behind the desk beside Lynn, where the three of them huddled together.

The cops would be there soon. They had to be. And Nash was on the way.

Where was he?

Then she remembered their conversation. Telling him not to come because it was pointless.

She gritted her teeth in bitter regret.

Two more rounds were fired into the wood jamb.

"He's going to make it inside before the police get here," Rich said. "We've got to buy time, do anything to stall him, so he doesn't kill us all."

Time was something they didn't have. It would take the sheriff's department seven to ten minutes to respond.

Another bullet hit the metal doorknob. The shrill sound echoed through Lynn, reverberating down to her bones.

The guts of the latch rattled when Andy kicked the door. On a second kick, the frame splintered, and the door burst open.

Andy stormed inside the office, brandishing the weapon. "You're a liar! If you wanted to help me, you wouldn't have gotten rid of me!" He swung the gun in Lynn's direction.

She cringed, her spine pressed to the wall, grabbing her purse tight against her stomach. Through the soft leather of her handbag, she felt the hard outline of the Ruger LCR .38 revolver that Nash had given her.

The compact gun was simple to operate. She didn't have

to think about anything, not even racking a slide. There was no safety, and it had a hammerless design. She'd regarded it as a hazard that could do more harm than good, but when her FBI agent boyfriend prodded her to carry it, she hadn't argued. But she doubted she could ever bring herself to use it.

"Why did you pawn me off on that psychiatrist?" Andy asked, drawing closer.

"I'm sorry." Tightening her grip on her purse with one hand, Lynn slid the other inside. "You need specialized treatment. I thought with his expertise that he'd be a better match for you."

"A better match?" Andy's voice was a fierce whisper. "I thought you cared about me."

"I do." Lynn nodded as her fingers skimmed the cold steel of the Ruger. "Very much." She gripped the handle. "I'm deeply invested in all my clients." It was true. She had struggled with the referral, worried it might affect the progress that had been made. She didn't want him to feel emotionally stranded. And right now, Andy needed her help more than ever. She let go of the gun. They just had to buy time. "I only want what's best for you."

"Liar!" Andy's face twisted in anger. The gun shook in his hand as he leveled it at her chest. "I hate you for lying."

This wasn't happening. Not to her.

"She isn't lying," Rich said. "Don't blame Dr. Delgado. No one is to blame." He stepped forward with his hands at his sides, palms facing forward in a nonthreatening manner.

Cindy clawed at Rich's sleeve, urging him not to move any farther. "What are you doing?" she asked in a frantic whisper, staying behind him. "Don't be a hero."

"It wasn't an easy decision for Dr. Delgado," Rich said. "She consulted me about your case. There were many factors to take into consideration. Her top concern was always your well-being. I advised her to refer you to—"

Pivoting, Andy swung the gun at Rich and pulled the trigger.

The gunshot was like a thunderclap in Lynn's soul. Her knees buckled, and she fell to the floor.

Time slowed. It was as if everything was happening at a distance. Someone else's living nightmare that she was being forced to watch.

Rich was writhing on the carpet, gasping for air. Blood pooled on the carpet beside him.

Screaming, Cindy dropped to her knees, lowered her face to the floor and covered her head with her hands.

Everything inside Lynn went numb. She was disconnected, reeling in disbelief.

Rich's legs stopped twitching. He was no longer moving. *Oh God. Is he dead?*

"I was warned not to trust you," Andy said. "I should've listened." He stalked around the desk.

Lynn couldn't breathe, couldn't think. She looked up, her gaze not making it to his face, locked on the sight of the pistol in his hand. Pressure built in her chest. Her ears filled with the roar of white noise as Andy lowered the gun, pointing it straight at her head.

Chapter Two

It was his lucky night.

Nash Garner pulled his truck into the parking lot across the street from the small one-story clinic. Lynn's SUV was still there, along with three other vehicles. He hadn't missed her. After a horrendous week at work, finally something was going his way. She must've decided to wait five extra minutes. Not that it had taken him that long. He'd made it in four, but it wouldn't smooth over the fact he was an hour late.

On top of that, he had to convince Lynn to give him another chance. He was usually the one to bail on a casual fling after a couple of months. Figures, this was the first *relationship* he wanted to last, and he was the one getting kicked to the curb.

Second time was the charm. At least for him. He'd failed ranger school on the first try, but he hadn't given up and had gotten in on his next attempt. Same with the FBI. He'd neglected to properly study for the initial exam. A miscalculation he didn't repeat. Getting things right the first time wasn't his forte, but he was a quick learner and never made the same mistake twice.

He hopped out of his truck and headed across the street. Then he remembered the flowers sitting on the passenger seat that he'd picked up to help lower Lynn's defenses. Going back to get the bouquet of camellias and roses, her favorites, he decided he wasn't going to leave the clinic until they had talked, again. The first time, he'd listened, mumbled a bit and shut down.

This time would be different. No matter how long it took, and it might be a while considering he had no idea where to begin, he was going to put his all into trying.

He clutched the door handle of his truck, the sight of the flowers on the seat making him smile.

Gunshots rang out, piercing his thoughts. Three in close succession.

They had come from inside the clinic.

Adrenaline sparked inside him. Dashing across the street, he whipped out his cell phone and dialed 911.

The line rang. An operator answered. "Laramie 911, police, fire and—?"

"This is Special Agent Nash Garner. Shots fired at the Turning Point clinic," he said, reaching the entrance. He couldn't see inside, because the glass of the front door was tinted. "I need backup now."

A fourth shot was fired.

Without waiting for a response from the operator, he hung up, drew his sidearm from his holster and swept inside in the building.

After a quick scan of the waiting room, he cleared it.

Light spilled out from the first office. Voices carried down the hall: Lynn's, a man's—one he didn't recognize— and Rich's.

Another shot boomed.

A scream punctured the air.

Nash's heartbeat kicked up a fraction. Everything around him sharpened, his senses going into battle mode. He moved on silent feet down the hall until he reached Rich's office.

He took in the busted side jamb and bullet holes in the door.

From the hall, his gaze landed on Rich, on the floor, wounded. Not moving. A woman was screaming. She was crouched in a corner, head pressed to the floor near Rich's feet.

Not Lynn.

"I was warned not to trust you. I should've listened," said a man, who was out of his line of sight.

Easing inside the office with his weapon at the ready, Nash spotted the man holding a gun. The guy stood on the other side of the desk, his back to the shrieking blonde, his focus on somebody else. His weapon was pointed at the individual hidden from Nash's view by the desk.

It could only be one person. Lynn.

His training usually kicked in without hesitation, but for a frozen heartbeat, Nash feared Lynn was a dead woman. The nanosecond ticked on. Everything happened all at once, bleeding together.

Weapon trained on the gunman, the words rose in his throat—*FBI, drop your gun*—but not fast enough. Nash got out the first syllable. "Eff—"

The man's gaze whipped to him as another gunshot exploded in the room.

The guy jerked backward. A red stain blossomed on his chest, center mass. His weapon fell from his hands, and he slumped to the floor in a crumpled heap.

Relief flooded Nash along with regret. Lynn was alive. She had been his main concern. But she'd killed someone because he'd been seconds too late.

Nash raced around the desk. Lynn was sitting on her heels, still as stone, arm still raised, hand concealed inside her purse. Wisps of smoke rose from a hole in the leather.

"Lynn, are you okay?" He kicked the perpetrator's weapon away and holstered his own.

She didn't move, didn't look at him. Only stared at the

space where the gunman had stood. She didn't even seem to be breathing.

Nash knelt in front of her. "Lynn." He brushed her long, dark brown hair from her face and put a gentle hand on her shoulder. Her olive skin was pale, almost ashen, her lips pinched until they were colorless. Her amber eyes, usually so full of life, were glazed and dull. "Lynn," he said again, this time giving her a slight shake.

Drawing in a sudden breath, she blinked. Briefly her gaze was lost as if coming out of a trance, then realization chased off the expression. She looked at him, and her raised arm began to shake.

"Are you hurt?" He slowly took the purse from around her hand and put it on the floor. Then he pried the gun from her trembling fingers.

"Y-y-you shot him." She looked down at the man who had threatened her life but quickly shuddered and glanced away back to Nash.

"No," he said, shaking his head. "I didn't. You did." The trauma of what'd happened must've been too much for her. Nash looked over at the dead body. He could only begin to imagine what she and the other two had gone through.

"Me?" A sob caught in her throat.

"You did what you had to do." She must have acted on pure instinct. "It's going to be okay." He glanced back at her. "I need to check on the others. All right?"

She gave a weak nod.

Nash hurried over to Rich and put two fingers to his carotid artery in his neck. There was a pulse. A strong one. The wound was in his shoulder. He was probably in shock, but it was also possible a main artery had been hit and he was bleeding out. Nash grabbed a handkerchief from the inner pocket of his blazer and applied pressure to the gunshot wound to slow the bleeding.

He glanced at the woman, who was now sobbing as she

rocked back and forth with her arms wrapped around herself. "Hey, what's your name?"

"Cindy. Cindy Morris."

Despite the screaming and crying, she looked to be in better shape than Lynn. "Are you injured?"

"No. But Rich. Oh God. You have to help him."

Nash was doing his best to stanch the blood flow.

Two men swept into the office, wearing black uniforms, weapons at the ready. Nash hadn't heard any sirens. If Rich or Lynn had triggered the silent alarm earlier, then it was law enforcement's protocol to approach without alerting the offender that they were on the scene.

"Sheriff." Nash tipped his head at Daniel Clark. They were well acquainted. Not only from working cases, but his best friend was the chief deputy. Nash was known to pop into the office for professional as well as personal reasons.

"An ambulance is on the way," Daniel said, surveying the room while the other deputy went to check on the women and verify the culprit was dead. He pulled down the radio attached to his shoulder and notified the EMTs en route of the gunshot wound. "What happened here?" He took out a notepad and pen.

Nash gave a quick rundown of what little he knew, with one modification. He neglected to mention that the assailant had acknowledged him with a look, even though his head had been in motion, and he'd kept his weapon pointed at Lynn. This was a case of self-defense. The gunman had already shot one person. Nash didn't want to say anything that might cast a shadow of the slightest doubt on the situation, or on Lynn. He'd do anything to protect her. Cindy's head had been down, making it unlikely she'd say anything to contradict his version of events, and Lynn was too confused to say something that might hurt herself.

The thought of how close he had come to losing her burned his gut.

"Rich has a strong pulse," Nash said. "If there aren't any internal complications, he should pull through. Lynn and Cindy will have to fill you in on what led up to all this."

Two EMTs hustled into the room, carrying a medical bag and a stretcher. Once they signaled to Nash that he could take pressure off the wound, he stood and moved out of their way. The techs worked quickly, but thoroughly, patching up the gunshot wound, transferring Rich to the stretcher and getting him out of the building.

That could've been Lynn. Injured and bleeding, being rushed to the hospital. The other alternative, her in a body bag, was something he couldn't bear.

"Just to be clear," Daniel said to Nash, "after you identified yourself, the assailant didn't drop his weapon?"

"Everything happened fast, almost simultaneously. I was in the process of identifying myself." Then he would've told the man to stop and throw down his weapon. None of which he'd had the chance to get out of his mouth, because it had all gone to hell in a handbasket. "But he didn't drop his weapon until after Lynn shot him."

"Bag up the gun that was used," Daniel said to the deputy.

"Already done," the deputy responded, wearing gloves and holding up an evidence bag.

"Once we officially close the case, we'll return it to Lynn," Daniel said. "Should be a day or two if everything checks out." He perused his notes and gave a low whistle. "They all got pretty lucky. Provided Dr. Jennings pulls through."

Across the room, the deputy finished taking Cindy's statement.

"She saved us," Cindy said, tears streaming down her cheeks. "He was going to kill her and then he probably would've killed me, too."

The deputy patted Cindy on the back. "Okay. Try to

calm down." He turned to Lynn and helped her up into Rich's chair.

She was still out of it, suffering from a different kind of shock. Nash wanted to go to her, be at her side, hold her hand through this.

"You should probably go get cleaned up first," Daniel said, as if reading his mind.

Nash's gaze dropped to his bloody palms. "I'll be right back. Would you mind getting Lynn a water, or..." His voice trailed off as he returned his attention to Lynn.

She was in desperate need of something. He doubted water would cut it, but it would be a start.

"Sure." He tipped the edge of his felt cattleman hat up with a knuckle. It wasn't often he wore the cowboy hat in uniform. He gave his deputies the option of wearing one or a ball cap with a sheriff's logo, and he usually sported the latter. "I'll look after her. Go on."

Most folks were aware they'd been a couple since last year. Law enforcement looked out for everyone, but they took special care of their own and by extension loved ones.

His last glimpse as he walked out of the office was Lynn trembling all over while she gave her statement, explaining how she'd found Andy lurking in the waiting room.

Nash strode down the hall, passing Lynn's office. In the bathroom, he scrubbed his hands twice with soap and warm water. His only thought was getting back to her as quickly as possible. She was going to need help through this. Not answering questions about what happened. That part would be fine.

But what would come later, processing everything, coming to terms with it, that would be tough. Especially for someone like Lynn who felt deeply about everything and everyone.

He made his way back to Rich's office. Lynn was holding a glass of amber liquid. There was a half-full bottle of liquor on the desk.

"I didn't hear Nash announce himself." Lynn sipped from the glass and winced as she swallowed. "Like I told you, it was like static in my ears. I didn't hear the Ruger either." Anxiety tightened her voice.

Not wanting to disturb her train of thought, Nash approached slowly.

"I found Jennings's scotch in the desk." Daniel stepped aside to make room for him to get by. "Figured she needed something stronger than water."

Nash clasped his shoulder as a *thank you*. He crouched beside Lynn, taking her free hand between his.

Almost as a reflex, she pulled away from his touch and pressed her palm to her stomach like she was fighting the urge to retch.

Crowding her, making her uncomfortable, wasn't his intent. He didn't want to take her withdrawal personally and even worse, he hated the helpless feeling crawling over him.

Daniel motioned for Nash to move to the side of the room with him and leaned in. "This sort of thing, killing someone, hits everyone differently. For us," he said, gesturing between the two of them, "it's one thing, a possibility that comes with the job. Still…" Daniel blew out a slow, deep breath.

Nodding, Nash understood what hadn't been said because there wasn't a need. Taking someone's life, regardless of the circumstances, was never easy. He'd know.

It took a toll on law enforcement, too. Just a different kind.

"Civilians have no idea what we face, what we have to go through," Daniel continued, his brown skin pulling taut over the sharp slashes of his cheekbones. "But for them, this type of experience can be significantly harder to deal with."

Once again, Nash nodded. Lynn's world had flipped

upside down tonight. Although she had defended herself and survived without any visible wounds, of course she would need to heal from this ordeal. "Yeah, I suppose you're right."

"When she's ready to be held and to talk, she'll let you know. Until then, be patient. She might need a little space."

It was sound advice.

Patience he had in spades. Space he could give. Anything Lynn needed, he'd do for her.

No problem.

Chapter Three

Five weeks later

Drumming fingers on the table was the only sound in the room. The cursor flashed on the blank laptop screen. A cold, dark fury swelled, a storm building inside that would be unleashed.

Soon.

Very soon.

This letter had to be short. Concise but clever. To the point but at the same time puzzling. In case the police ever read it, they'd have nothing to go on.

This one had to be the best, standing out from all the other letters.

At last, it became clear what needed to be written.

Tense fingers clacked out the message with enraged strokes of the keys. Taunting words that concealed the bitter anger behind them exploded across the page in all caps.

Once finished, the lines were centered, the fonts and sizes varied to emphasize certain words. Everything was highlighted in bold.

It had taken an hour to think of the right thing to say, seconds to type.

With one final keystroke, the printer hummed, warming up. The paper chugged and spewed out onto the table. Latex snapped and crackled as gloves were pulled on. There'd be no clues that could be traced back. Only then was the page picked up. After one final check, it was ready to go.

Perfection. This would do the trick.

That woman brought this on herself and deserved what was coming.

The paper was folded with precision, ensuring even, sharp lines, and then stuffed into an envelope that had been stamped and addressed:

Dr. Lynn Delgado
Turning Point Therapy and Wellness Clinic
Laramie, Wyoming

This would be the last letter sent to the high and mighty doctor, but this was far from over. This wouldn't end until Lynn Delgado was no longer breathing.

NASH SLOWED HIS truck in front of the Underground Self-Defense school on Third Street, catching a glimpse of Lynn inside. The sight of her had his heart melting in his chest.

He could stare at her all day. It was the same every time he saw her, which hadn't been much recently.

What he wouldn't give for her to answer one of his calls.

What he wouldn't give to talk to her.

She was in pain, suffering from what had happened with Andrew Crombie. Although she wouldn't admit it, he sensed that she was in trouble. Trapped in a personal hell of her own making.

He could help her through it. If only she'd let him, trust him.

Right after the shooting, she'd taken off to Fort Collins, where she had family, and had refused to take his calls. He had to hear from someone else when she came back to Laramie a month ago.

Then he'd waited, kept giving her space, thinking sooner or later she had to talk to him.

At this point, his patience was threadbare and on the brink of snapping.

A car honked behind Nash.

With a rueful shake of his head, he held up an apologetic hand in his rearview mirror to the inconvenienced driver. He pulled off but decided to circle the block. If he lingered long enough, he'd be able to nab one of the few parking spots on Third Street near the USD school.

After working sixteen hours, he was exhausted and wanted nothing more than to eat dinner and crash, but now that he'd seen Lynn, she was all he could think about.

For some reason, she had been avoiding him, but this torment of dodge and evade that she was putting them both through had gone on long enough.

LYNN NEEDED THIS. BADLY.

She parried the incoming blow from her opponent. Then countering, she struck back with a vertical hit at his shoulder. The punch connected, but it didn't slow him down. He attacked with a quick thrust to her midsection that knocked the wind from her lungs, and she fell onto her backside.

He lunged and was on top of her with his hands around her throat. Lynn grabbed his forearms, struggling to break free of his hold.

"Stop," said Charlotte Sharp, the owner and main instructor at USD, Underground Self-Defense.

Her cousin, Rocco, released Lynn's throat and stood.

"Stay down on the mat, Lynn." Charlie turned to the other ladies standing in a circle around the edge of the mat. "What did she do wrong?"

After a long, awkward moment, the only person to raise their hand was Becca Hammond. FBI agent extraordinaire, according to Nash.

Charlie sighed. "Anyone else?" She looked around, but there were no other volunteers. "All right, share with the group."

Becca lit up like a star pupil who had all the answers. "She never should've let him get on top of her."

"Exactly." Charlie nodded and took a knee beside Lynn. "How do you feel being down here on the mat?"

Lynn shrugged. "I don't know."

"We don't lie to each other," Charlie said. "At least, not in here. How do you feel?"

The same as she did that fateful night in Rich's office when she was down on the floor, cowering, cornered, certain she was going to die. "Weak. Helpless," Lynn admitted.

"Believe it or not," Charlie said, "in a fight, this is the best position for you to be in. Your most powerful weapon is your legs. Next time, use them like we've practiced." Charlie looked around at the group. "You all know what to do."

Charlie was a thorough instructor who had run them through countless drills, but when the moment came and Rocco had lunged, Lynn had failed to do the right thing. Again.

"I reacted," Lynn said. "I didn't think."

"Fear is natural, but don't let it stop you from thinking." Charlie gave her a hard glance but put a supportive hand on her shoulder. "If you do, you won't survive. ATOB, ladies." Always Think Outside the Box. "That's why you're here. To learn, to practice until these self-defense moves become instinctive. Until ATOB becomes instinctive. We're out of time tonight, but Rocco will be back next week. I'll have him come at you again, Lynn. When he does, I want you to kick him with all your strength. Don't forget to vocalize, to harness your power."

"But I might hurt him," Lynn said, not wanting to injure anyone.

"Don't worry about me." Rocco folded his buff arms across his solid chest. "I can handle it."

There was no doubt in Lynn's mind that he could handle himself. The Alcohol, Tobacco and Firearms agent worked on the same joint task force as Nash and Becca. So far, he'd participated in three of the eight women's self-defense classes she'd taken. Charlie wanted the ladies to have a feel for what it was like to go up against a man in a practical scenario.

Lynn climbed to her feet and tugged down her sweatshirt. "When will we learn how to disarm someone who's holding a gun?"

Rocco arched an eyebrow. "Wow, someone wants to sprint ahead a few classes."

"That'll come *much* later." Charlie propped her fists on her slim hips. "First, I need to make sure you have a solid foundation with the basics. My goal is to prepare you to survive. Not endanger any of you. Got it?"

"Yep." Lynn got it, even if she didn't like it.

Charlie put an arm around her shoulder and guided her away from the group. "Are you okay?"

"Sure, sure, I'm fine," Lynn said. She was living a lie. Telling everyone she was fine and that she was coping when in reality she was slowly unraveling. Part of her was embarrassed. She was the trained professional who was supposed to have the answers, but for the first time, she was lost.

"What's up?" Charlie asked. "Is this about those threatening letters you've been getting?"

Lynn made a noncommittal gesture. The truth was, *no* and *yes*.

She'd come here to learn how to protect herself without needing a weapon. For her, the point of this was to survive without anyone losing their life.

"I received another one today," Lynn said. It had been

delivered with the late-afternoon mail before she left the office.

"Have you taken them to the sheriff's office?" Charlie asked.

Going to the sheriff meant the chief deputy, who happened to be Nash's best friend, would also know. One quick phone call to Nash, and her ex would know, too.

No, thanks. Anything that would drag Nash back into her mess of a life wasn't a viable option. She thought about him all the time, which only brought her pain. She needed the full six months of no contact to flush him out of her system. Based on the numerous voice mail messages that he'd left for her, he needed the time apart as well to move on.

"I went to the Laramie police," Lynn said. The situation fell in the sheriff's jurisdiction, but the female police chief was willing to advise her. "I was told that law enforcement couldn't do anything about it since the letters are more ominous than outright threatening and couldn't be traced. Once someone acted on them, then the police or the sheriff would be able to do something."

Waiting for someone to try to hurt her sounded far too late in Lynn's opinion.

"Don't worry," Charlie said. "Whoever is sending those letters is a sick coward, only looking to scare you. But it's my job to prepare you just in case. Okay?"

Lynn nodded, though her stomach roiled. If scaring her was their objective, mission accomplished. Those letters had her on edge day and night, living in a perpetual state of anxiety and fear. Thinking about the haunting words had goose bumps prickling her skin.

"I'll see you next time," Charlie said, walking away. "Try to have a good night."

She'd try. Inevitably, she'd also fail.

Swallowing her disappointment at not having mastered

the skills she needed to learn, Lynn grabbed her coat, purse and gym bag.

Her body was sore from the workout and her soul leaden. Guilt clung to her, weighing her down like sandbags. Nothing lightened the load, not jogging, not a glass of wine, not a pint of gooey ice cream, not a hot bath. Nothing, except these classes. Even then, they only helped a little.

"Hold on." Becca came up to her. "If you want extra practice," she said, and then lowered her voice, "*free of charge*, I'd be happy to help you on my days off."

That was a generous offer. Unfortunately, Lynn questioned the motivation behind it. "Thanks, but I'll get the hang of it eventually. Can I ask you something?"

"Sure." Becca flashed a bright smile. With her auburn curls pulled back in a ponytail, makeup-free skin showing a dusting of freckles across her face, she looked devoid of ulterior motives, but Lynn knew firsthand that looks could be deceiving. "Ask me anything."

"Why do you come here? You're obviously proficient at this and don't need the classes." Becca didn't strike Lynn as the type who needed to show off to feel better about herself. The woman was the epitome of the four *C*s: cordial, confident, competent and capable.

That left one alternative. Nash had sent her to spy on Lynn.

Becca's mouth hitched into a half grin. "My motto is never stop. Learning. Practicing. Preparing. I come here so I don't get rusty. After every class, I spar one-on-one with either Charlie or Rocco."

"That's smart." Made sense for someone in her line of work. Lynn's suspicion was in overdrive and misplaced. She needed to decompress. Her vacation with her bestie starting tomorrow couldn't come soon enough.

"I won't be at the next class," Becca said, "but will I see

you at my office holiday party with Nash? It's the one time of year we let our hair down with civilians."

"Oh, um…" The question caught her off guard, making Lynn's stomach twist into a pretzel. She thought everyone was well aware of their status. News spread in this small town quicker than pink eye in a preschool. It was hard to keep your personal affairs private. "No. Nash and I broke up."

A poker face replaced Becca's smile, dimming the light in her eyes. "Really? I hadn't heard. Not that Nash is into sharing. But a breakup would explain a lot."

A lot?

Two little words that held so much meaning.

Lynn was tempted to ask, but the answer would only lead to more questions about Nash. The last person she wanted to think about, much less discuss.

"Well," Becca said, "if you change your mind about the extra practice, let me know."

"Will do."

Lynn slipped on her down parka, slung the straps of her purse and gym bag on her shoulder. Forcing herself to push past the soul-deep ache that never left her, she shoved through the front door out onto Third Street. The freezing wind hit her like a hard slap, but she shuffled through it. Her SUV was parked in the lot of the grocery store. It was in the opposite direction of her family's restaurant, Delgado's Bar & Grill, where Nash often had dinner.

Parking two blocks away might seem excessive, but she didn't want to risk running into him. Besides, the extra walk helped her get in her daily steps.

Christmas wreaths and white string lights adorned the lampposts lining the busy street. Every shop window she passed was decorated. Each time a store's front door opened, holiday music flowed from inside.

She used to love this time of year. It had once been her

favorite. In fact, she'd met Nash early December last year. This Saturday would've marked their one-year anniversary if they'd still been a couple.

Now, the sparkling decorations, the twinkling lights, the saccharine music, all made her think of Nash.

Which in turn made her think of that awful night.

The two were inexorably linked.

Lynn sidestepped a woman fumbling with her bags, to keep from bumping into her, and when she looked up, she spotted him.

Tall and broad and brooding. Nash Garner.

Her breath froze and then burned in her lungs as her feet faltered to a halt. He strode down the sidewalk, making a beeline in her direction.

His gaze locked with hers, and it all came back to her in a sickening rush.

ANDY CROMBIE.

Locking herself inside Rich's office. Gunfire. Rich being shot. Lynn crouched on the floor behind the desk. Paralyzed in fear. Andy pointed the gun at her head.

The feel of the Ruger in her hand.

The next thing she knew, Nash was rushing around the desk and then kneeling in front of her. He was speaking, but it took a moment for things to come back into focus. For his words to penetrate as he took the gun from her fingers.

She didn't remember pulling the trigger. She didn't hear the last gunshot, but the Ruger had gone off. She'd felt its kick, the sensation almost filtered, as though it were someone else's memory.

But it was hers.

She'd killed Andy Crombie.

THE MEMORY BURNED like acid.

Maybe it wasn't too late to avoid a run-in with him. She

spun around and took five steps before the sound of his gruff voice made her hesitate.

"Lynn! Lynn, please wait."

A strong hand clasped her shoulder, turning her around.

It took only an instant for her to absorb every detail about him. Granite features. Hard, square jaw. Collar-length dark hair that was longer than she remembered. Two-day old stubble that formed a barely-there beard and mustache. He wore a black cowboy hat—his usual cutter—a sheepskin jacket, jeans and boots. His muscular six-four build blocked out the rest of the world, or maybe it was the sheer power of his presence.

She gritted her teeth against the punch of attraction coiling through her.

His face wasn't pretty but definitely striking in a wounded, fallen angel sort of way. Exactly her type. Unfortunately.

His leather-gloved hand left her shoulder and glided down her arm, caressing along the way, conjuring a flutter in her chest—a wave of jumbled emotions so strong and unsettling she wanted to break free and bolt.

But his piercing gray eyes pinned her to the spot.

She should've taken one of his many calls and gotten through this over the phone, where she didn't have to see him and be under the microscope of his laser-like focus. Instead, for the first time in five weeks, they were face-to-face.

Chapter Four

Nash silently thanked Becca for cluing him in that Lynn was taking a class every Thursday evening at USD. He'd played it off as though he'd already been aware. Without that tidbit of essential information, who knows how much longer he would've been forced to go without talking to her, unless he'd resorted to stalking her at home. Something he'd been extremely tempted yet prudently reluctant to do.

A "happenstance" encounter in public was far better.

"Finally." He was thrilled to see her. His spirits instantly lifted and just as quickly dampened. He was burning with too much frustration to muster a smile. "I've been trying to reach you."

Sliding his hand down her arm to cup her elbow, he desperately tried to ignore how his body instantly came alive when touching her.

Lynn stiffened and shrugged free of his grasp. "I got your messages."

He waited for her to continue, to give him a damn explanation for not returning a single phone call. "And?"

"And what?" she asked, looking genuinely confounded.

"I've been worried sick about you."

Biting her bottom lip, she lowered her eyes. "No need to worry. I'm fine."

Now she was lying to his face. Everything about her, from the dark circles under her eyes, the tension in her posture, the noticeable pounds she'd dropped from her already-lean figure, to taking self-defense classes at USD told him she was anything but fine.

"What's going on with you?" he demanded.

She crossed her arms, defiance flashing in her whiskey-brown eyes. "Nothing."

This was so foreign to him. Lynn had always been eager to communicate, the one pressing him to open up and share. Well, the tables had turned, and he didn't like it one little bit.

"I can tell when you're lying," he snapped.

Lynn shook her head, her patience visibly wearing thin. "Go to the grill and have dinner. Don't worry about me. My problems are no longer any of your concern."

The matter-of-fact words were like a knife in his heart.

"I know how precious your time is," she added, without a hint of sarcasm, "and I'm sure you have better things to do." From her tone and expression, she honestly believed that.

They might not be a couple anymore, but if Lynn had a problem, it would always be cause for concern to him. There was nothing he wouldn't do for her.

That would never change.

"I can't bear the thought of you hating me." He had no idea where the admission came from, but he was glad the truth had slipped out, because she softened.

Sadness snuffed out the fire in her eyes. "I don't hate you." Even her voice softened.

As he looked into her beautiful face, all he wanted was to be closer to her, pull her against his chest and wrap his arms around her. But he had to keep his distance or else she might take off like a jackrabbit. "Feels like it. You won't take my calls. You run from me on the street." He swept an errant lock of hair that had gotten loose from her bun back behind her ear.

So much for keeping his distance.

His gaze fell to her lips. Those full lips he could kiss for hours. She was wearing the berry-colored gloss he liked. It tasted as good as it looked.

He tore his focus from her mouth and met her eyes.

"I didn't run, and I don't hate you. Honestly. I never could." Tightening her grip on her gym bag, she shuffled backward until his fingers, which were still caressing her soft skin, fell from her face.

At least she hadn't slapped his hand away, but she was making it clear she'd rather not be touched. Not by him, anyway.

Lynn took another step. "I need to go home and get cleaned up. Have a good—"

"Can I walk you to your car?" he asked, and she looked back at him, as if unsure what to say or do. This was an opportunity to get answers to his questions. He had to seize it. "Where are you parked?"

She frowned. "The grocery store."

Not surprising. Parking at Delgado's would've been closer to USD, but he frequented the bar and grill ever since he'd met her there, and it was painfully obvious Lynn was doing her best to steer clear of him.

If only he knew why.

"You can walk me on one condition," she said.

He drew closer, keen to have more time with her, even if it was mere minutes. She was talking to him, sort of, letting him escort her. Baby steps he'd have to accept. "Name it."

"You don't ask me any more questions."

Nash had a laundry list of those clogging his brain, which she'd rightfully expected and didn't want. If he was going to be in her presence, it had to be on her terms. For now.

He nodded, and his breath crystallized in the air as he said, "Deal."

A snowflake drifted down as they walked, followed by

another. He longed to take her hand the way he used to when they'd stroll together, but instead he clenched his gloved fingers. He didn't want to push it and completely blow it tonight.

"I'm worried about you," he said. "I get the sense that you're not coping well with what you've been through. It can be difficult."

She shoved her hands in her pockets. Silence stretched between them until it became awkward. Tense. He was beginning to think that she wasn't going to respond.

Then she looked at him, her eyes haunted. "We all cope, in our own way." A quiet desperation deepened the lines in Lynn's forehead and around her mouth. "I'm doing my best."

He didn't doubt it. "Keeping things bottled up inside isn't healthy."

She gave him a baleful look for throwing her own words back at her. "Thanks for the sage words, Dr. Garner."

"All I'm saying is that you don't have to go through this alone. I'm here for you, to listen, any time." The good doctor obviously needed to start taking her own advice and talk to someone. "Even as just a friend, if that's what you want." *Friend.* He wasn't sure he'd ever really be able to think of her that way, but to help Lynn, he was willing to give anything a try.

Shaking her head, she avoided his gaze. "We can't be friends."

"Wh—" He swallowed the question burning his tongue, remembering his promise and not wanting to break it.

Time evaporated in the short distance of two blocks. The parking lot was in sight, across the street. It was now or never to clear the air.

"I think about you," he blurted out. "About us. All the time." He'd never felt more vulnerable. Exposed.

He'd been raised to believe there was no need to spill

your guts. The proof was in the pudding so to speak, and the pudding was a man's actions. It was better to show those closest to you how much they meant.

Lynn shivered. He hoped from the cold and not from his confession.

"That's why we can't be friends." Emotion he couldn't name flickered across her face, and she glanced away. "Give it a few months. By then, our relationship will be a memory and you'll have moved on to someone new."

He didn't want to move on, to be with someone new, for their relationship to become nothing more than a fading memory.

He wanted Lynn. A few months, heck, a few years, wasn't going to change that.

But her theory registered, sinking beneath the surface like an itch he couldn't scratch.

Had Lynn been avoiding him to give herself time to move on? Had she already found someone new?

She stopped at the corner. "I'm okay here. Good night." She gave him a tense grin before looking both ways and darting across the street.

He couldn't shake the sense that he was going to lose her forever if he didn't say something. Anything.

"Lynn," he called out, "I'm sorry."

She glanced back at him across the street. The wind whipped stray locks of hair in her face. "For what?"

For not wearing his heart on his sleeve the way she had wanted. For not being an open book. For getting caught up at work and being late that night. For not getting to her sooner. For not being the one to shoot Andrew Crombie, so she didn't have to.

"For everything I did wrong."

Flashing him a smile so sad it damn near broke his heart, she held up a hand goodbye.

An apology didn't mean a thing to her. Not that he blamed her.

Nash cursed himself for his endless capacity to destroy any good in his life. All he had left was the FBI. Although he was great at his job, it was sucking his soul dry. At his core he was a lawman, like his father before him and his brothers. He couldn't fathom being anything else.

There was a time when he'd been quicker to smile, to joke around, to share his thoughts. A time when he'd been an easier man to get along with. Eight years in the army and four with the FBI had worn off any boyhood charm. At thirty-four, he was not a man who engaged in small talk, wasted time on pleasantries or pretended that a situation was anything other than what it was.

Lynn had liked him anyway until she broke things off.

One more thing he'd ruined.

A gust of icy wind sliced through him as he stood there, unable to take his gaze off her. Crossing the well-lit lot over to her SUV, she pressed her key fob, and the lights flashed on her two-door Land Rover Defender.

Lynn threw her purse and gym bag in the passenger's seat, climbed in and closed the door. After cranking the engine, she pulled off and made a right out of the lot. A left turn and taking Third Street would've been the faster route for her to get home, but she probably wanted to avoid passing her pining ex, who was standing on the corner, watching her like a stalker.

Way to go, Nash.

This was shaping up to be a banner evening. Maybe after dinner and a beer with his buddy Holden Powell over at Delgado's and then some solid shut-eye, he'd feel better, though he doubted it.

As he was about to walk away, she passed a lamppost—the light from the streetlamp washing inside the SUV—

and he glimpsed a dark blur emerge from the back seat behind Lynn.

Nash's gut clenched as he doubted his eyes.

Was someone inside her vehicle?

Chapter Five

I'm sorry.

Two words Nash Garner rarely used. Certainly not lightly. Perhaps that was the reason they carried so much weight with Lynn.

If only what had been the problem between them could be fixed with an apology.

Glancing at the corner of Third Street, Lynn didn't want to pass by Nash, who stood watching her. Or worse, get caught at the traffic light beside him and have to force a smile and give another wave bye. It had been hard enough seeing him, talking to him, being so close she could've reached out and touched him.

When he'd tucked her hair behind her ear, brushing her skin with his fingers, all she wanted was to curl up in his arms, where she'd always felt safe. Her face heated thinking about it. Nash was all male and more enticing than any man she'd ever met. She desperately wanted to lose herself in him. Only guilt had made her pull away. She didn't want to use him for comfort. No matter how much she needed it. She couldn't let herself off the hook, to allow herself to feel better. Especially not with Nash.

Theirs was a complicated relationship with a capital *C*.

A pang of loneliness howled through her like the wind outside.

Instead of going toward Third, she turned right onto

Lewis Street, away from Nash. The easier choice albeit not the fastest.

Something hard jabbed into the back of her head.

"Make a left at the corner," a male voice said from behind her.

Lynn's chest convulsed. She looked up into the rearview mirror.

In the back seat was a man. She couldn't see what he was holding in the darkness, but she assumed it was a gun. If it had been a knife, she would've felt the sharpness of the blade.

"I said to turn." The man nudged her head with what she guessed was the muzzle of a pistol.

The command snapped her attention back to the road. Her heart pounded wildly against her sternum as adrenaline flooded her veins, but her thoughts were clear.

Stay calm. Stay alive. Breathe.

Drawing air into her lungs, deep and steady, she forced herself to comply, doing as he instructed. The left turn kept her on a side street with limited traffic, two other cars ahead, no pedestrians. Even if she passed someone on the road, she had no idea what she could do. Signaling a passerby was out of the question so long as he held that gun.

Her mind flooded with terrifying possibilities of what could happen, but she shoved them all to the side. Imagining the worst wasn't going to help her get out of this. She hadn't survived that horrendous night with Andy to die today.

Not today, she told herself. *Not today.* "What do you want? Where are we going?"

"Keep driving," he said, his mouth close to her ear.

That voice. It was familiar. One she'd heard somewhere before.

Her gaze flashed up to the mirror again for another look at him. A full-face black ski mask covered his head. It was made of a smooth material. A skeleton skull pattern was printed over the face. Only his eyes were visible. Cold. Dark. Steely.

Those she didn't recognize.

"Turn here. Another left."

She rolled through the intersection, ignoring the stop sign, hoping someone might notice as she made the turn.

"Do that again, and I'll hurt you." With his other hand, he reached over the front of her seat and seized her throat in a savage grip, pinning her head back against the seat, and squeezed her windpipe. "Do you understand?"

Panic erupted alongside pain. Lynn gasped, struggling for air. She nodded as best she could. "Yes."

His fingers loosened from around her throat until he released her.

She coughed and sucked in a deep lungful of oxygen. Her hands clutched the steering wheel in a death grip. Her stomach tightened, but she kept herself from succumbing to the fear.

"We can do this the easy way, or the painful way. You decide." His voice was harsh, but his tone was controlled.

This man wasn't unhinged, acting on emotion. He was completely self-possessed. Aware of what he was doing. Calculating his responses.

Somehow that made the situation far more chilling.

As she approached the next intersection, she glanced around, searching for one of the sheriff's telltale white SUVs, a pedestrian whose eye she might catch, anything. But her captor had her sticking to the more isolated pockets of town, away from the two main veins of activity, Third Street and Grand Avenue.

Heading down Russell, she tried to remember if anything would be open down here. What was located on this street?

An elementary school. A taxidermy. What else?

"There." He pointed, reaching over the seat, and she followed the direction of his leather-clad finger to a small building that was dark with no cars in the lot. "The Plainsman Bank. Pull up to the ATM drive-through."

Lynn exhaled, relieved. He wanted money, and once he got it, this could be over. But her relief quickly soured. She was aware how often robberies went wrong. How easily a life could be taken over a couple hundred bucks. A few grams of meth. A pair of sneakers. Or far less. Sometimes there was no explanation at all as to why the victim had been murdered. Just a senseless loss of life. She'd heard countless stories from Nash and the chief deputy, Holden. Not to mention from her own brother, who was also law enforcement back in Denver, Colorado.

After she entered her code in the machine, he could decide to kill her.

Tears pricked the backs of her eyes. If she wasn't careful, she might not leave that drive-through alive.

Come up with a plan.

"Do it, slowly," he said.

She pulled into the lot and maneuvered her Defender between the concrete pillar and the wall as she drew close to the teller machine. Too late, it occurred to her that there had been a chance for her to leave a gap large enough for her to open the door and squeeze through. Now there was no room to get out while they waited for the cash. She'd blocked herself in.

Reaching for her purse to get her debit card, she wondered if she'd be able to find the small canister of pepper spray inside her handbag before he realized what she was doing. Ever since Andy, she stopped carrying the Ruger in favor of a nonlethal deterrent. Maybe, if she was fast enough, she could spray him, press on the gas pedal to clear the pillar and make a break for it. Could she do it all without him getting off a shot first?

"Give it to me." He snatched the purse from her hands, extinguishing what little hope she had for the flimsy idea, and scrounged through her handbag. The weapon lifted from the back of her head, but not long enough for her take any action. Finding the wallet, he tossed her purse up front into the passenger's footwell. "Which card is it?"

"The light blue one. Cowboy State Credit Union." In front of the passenger's seat, her handbag sat open. The pink top of the pepper spray was visible. She'd have to reach pretty far over to grab it from the footwell. Doing so with her seat belt on would be tough and even if she made it, her timing had to be just right.

"Here." He handed her the card while keeping a hold of her wallet.

"How much should I take out?" Her voice wavered and cracked like she was about to cry. Something she refused to do. Not here. Not now.

The cold hardness of steel returned to the back of her head. "Withdraw the max."

Closing her eyes, she swallowed and tried to think, but she didn't have any other choice besides doing what he demanded. All she could do was pray for the best, that he'd take the cash and leave her alone, and not shoot her, dump her body on the side of the street and steal her car.

With trembling fingers, she hit the button on the door, rolling down the window, and inserted her card. Quickly, she punched in the PIN and scanned the words on the screen.

"The ATM limit is three hundred at this machine," she said. That gave her a slim opening, something to work with. She had to give him a reason to keep her alive. "But my daily limit is a thousand." A renewed sense of determination surged in her veins. "I can get you the rest if we go to different machines." Somewhere more populated. There weren't many ATMs like this one, located off the beaten path. She'd forgotten it even existed. "We can go to the one next to the big-box store off Grand." The superstore was open until eleven and thanks to the well-populated area stayed busy until it closed. That was her best chance. "It's not far and the limit at that one is five hundred."

The promise of a thousand dollars in one night had to be a decent score for robbing one person.

She had plenty of money—almost a hundred grand. Granted, it was split between her solo 401(k) and brokerage investment account for a down payment on a house. Not that she had access to either pool of funds at an ATM. Her checking account on the other hand had nowhere near five hundred left in it after this withdrawal since she'd already paid her bills. But this guy didn't know that, and she'd figure a way out of this before the transaction was declined.

"It'll only take a few minutes to get there," she said. Once in the active lot, a whole world of possibilities would open. Honk her horn to attract attention. Dive for the pepper spray. Simply jump from the vehicle and run for it.

"Shut up." He whacked the cold steel against her cheek. Not hard enough to break bone, but plenty to silence her.

Tomorrow she'd have a bruise. If she was lucky enough to live that long.

"When I want your suggestion, I'll ask for it," he growled.

Turning to the machine, she entered in the max amount of three hundred. Seconds ticked by as the machine hummed. She pressed against the seat while rubbing her face and looked back at him. He'd slid over behind the passenger's seat, probably positioning himself to avoid being captured on the ATM's camera. From this angle, he wouldn't be seen, but she now had a clear view of his weapon.

An automatic 9mm. With an attached sound suppressor.

Her blood turned to ice.

Ordinary criminals didn't use silencers, though they were easy enough to come by. Nelson's Gun and Outdoor Sports shop sold them. Could probably get one used that cost even less than the amount she was being forced to withdraw from the ATM over at a pawnshop.

But what kind of lowlife robber used one?

Maybe a smart one. A serious guy who meant business and didn't want to draw unwanted attention when he fired his weapon.

She gulped. Cold sweat beaded along her forehead. Her stomach twisted.

The machine spat out the bills. She took them and handed him the wad of twenties. Out of habit, she reached a shaking hand back to get the receipt.

"Leave it." The command was sharp. "Drive. Now."

Not bothering to roll up the window, she pulled off.

"Hang a right," he said.

Doing as he instructed was taking them in the general direction of the big-box store. Hope spurted inside her. The plan could work. She wouldn't know for certain if that's where they might be headed until this road came to a three-way intersection, when she would be forced to make another turn. She was too afraid to ask him any questions, not wanting to tick this guy off again.

Despite the frosty air flowing in from the open window, sweat trickled down her spine. She clenched the steering wheel, holding her breath as they came to the T-intersection across from the park.

At the stop sign, she cranked the wheel, preparing to go to the left, toward the lights and activity about a half mile away.

"Don't even think about it," he said. "We're heading the other way. Go." He waved the gun at the windshield.

Why didn't he want the rest of the money? She had promised him a thousand dollars.

Her fingers tingled as cold set in. Lynn turned the SUV to the right. Toward the darkness. She caught a glimpse of the street sign, South Corthell Road, and it occurred to her where it led.

Panic tightened in her throat. *No, no, no.*

Traffic didn't come this way. The lights on the utility poles didn't even work on the isolated stretch of road. There would be no stores. No houses. No sidewalks. Not a sole pedestrian. No possibility of help.

There was nothing down that way, besides a barren field and a dead end, and no *good* reason to take her down this dark road.

Her racing heart dropped into the pit of her stomach. She looked up into the rearview mirror. Their gazes met. His unflinching stare was so cruel it sent a chill through her. He held the gun rock-steady in his grip. His body language was rigid in coiled readiness, a cobra measuring its prey.

In the faint gleam of his eyes, his intent was clear. Pure malice.

He was going to rape her. Or kill her.

Or worse, do both.

Her mind went to Nash. Whatever happened, Lynn had to live through this. She couldn't die with him thinking she hated him. So many things she hadn't told him. He deserved an explanation as to why she'd been avoiding him these past weeks. She owed him better than the silent treatment. Nash had endured his fair share of hardship, but having her ripped from his life in a brutal way might break him.

The full moon cast light on the grim, stark landscape surrounding her. It was quiet. No one nearby for miles. She glanced around desperately, trying to think of something to do. The pepper spray sat at the top of her purse but was out of reach. Attempting to negotiate, to talk her way out of this, would be a waste of her energy.

With each utility pole she passed, Lynn's dread swelled.

Farther and farther, they went into the darkness. Closer and closer to her last breath.

The next time he told her to pull over and stop the vehicle that would be it. The end of her.

Headlights glimmered in the rearview mirror. In the distance. Not too far behind. Another vehicle had turned down the same road and was headed their way.

One more spark of fight burned through her. Maybe it was just adrenaline. Either way, she wasn't giving in.

Not today. Not ever.

She eased off the gas, slowing down to let the other car catch up to them.

This was her last chance. She sensed it. Time was running out for her. She had to act before he noticed the car that was quickly closing the distance and panicked, doing something rash, like shooting her and taking off.

What would Charlie do?

Her experienced instructor would be able to get out of this situation in a cinch with her martial arts skills. But what would she tell Lynn, a terrified novice, to do right now?

All her training at USD came back to her. Not the fight moves and evasive maneuvers. She heard Charlie's voice in her head, reminding her of the different ways to survive. How to use everything around her to her advantage.

Always Think Outside the Box.

Sucking in a deep, steadying breath, she tightened her grip on the steering wheel. The man in the back seat had a gun trained on her, but she wasn't helpless, and she wasn't unarmed.

She was in the driver's seat of a one-and-a-half-ton weapon. In full control of it.

People were injured and killed in car crashes every day. And she was the only one wearing a seat belt. The rear seat could be as deadly as the front when someone was unbuckled.

Her pulse thundered in her ears, but she was focused on what she needed to do.

Headlights from the other car blazed up behind them.

Twisting around, the man looked back through the rear windshield, moving the gun away from her head. "Speed up." He swore, banging the gun on the back seat. "Go faster!"

Her thoughts precisely. Lynn pressed her foot down on the gas pedal. She jerked the wheel to the right. As soon as the tires skidded off the asphalt and hit dirt, she straightened, lining her vehicle up with the utility pole looming dead ahead of them.

"What are you doing?" He grabbed her shoulder and squeezed.

Nausea gripped her. A scream welled up inside her, scraping her throat raw. At almost the last second, fear made her lift her foot off the gas, not wanting to kill anyone else, especially herself, but she didn't dare hit the brakes.

"Stop, damn you!"

Go to hell. Throwing her arms up in front of her face, Lynn looked away as they slammed into the pole.

Chapter Six

Lynn!

With his heart in his throat, Nash zoomed up behind her SUV. Dust whipped around his truck when he screeched to a halt.

In the distance were sirens. Holden would be the first one on the scene. As soon as Nash had suspected Lynn was in danger, he called his buddy. Then he had sprinted to his truck and searched for her vehicle. Found her on Russell Street and observed from a position close to the bank parking lot. He had to be sure that fatigue hadn't been making him see things. Once he'd verified the guy in the back of her car was real and had spotted the gun the man had on her while she withdrew money from the ATM, proceeding with caution became a necessity. As did vigilance. There was no way he was going to take his eyes off her vehicle.

He threw the gear into Park, leaped from his truck and drew his weapon. Worry gripped his chest as he raced up to her SUV. The front end was totaled, twisted around the utility pole. The damage was serious. He yanked open her door and stared down at her.

His terror washed into relief.

The driver's-side airbag had deployed and was already deflating. She was alive, *thank goodness*; conscious, but a little woozy. His gaze snapped to the rear seat as he trained his weapon in the same direction.

Empty. The passenger's seat had been shoved forward and the back door was flung open. Her assailant was gone.

But he was out there. Somewhere in the darkness. Hiding. Possibly running. Not that Nash could tell either way with the sound of the sirens drawing closer, masking any noise in the vicinity.

He holstered his weapon and unbuckled Lynn's seat belt.

"Nash?" Her wide, frantic eyes locked onto his. "What are you doing here?"

Watching out for you. Something he'd do for as long as he was able. He didn't know how to stop. It was the way he was wired.

"What the hell happened?" He cupped her cheeks in his hands and looked her over. No scrapes on her face. No bloody nose. She was fortunate.

"Wait." She twisted in her seat as if remembering something, her gaze flying to the back. "Where is he?"

"Gone. He took off. The back seat was empty by the time I got to your car." It hadn't taken Nash long. His guess was her assailant wasn't badly injured if he'd been able to get out of the car so quickly and disappear. That didn't mean he was unscathed from the crash. Nash hoped like hell he was in pain. "Did he hurt you?"

She shook her head *no*, but the expression on her face said otherwise.

Flashing lights zipped down the street, illuminating the dark road. A white deputy's vehicle led the way, followed by an ambulance.

Good thinking, Holden.

"What about in the crash?" Nash asked. "Any injuries? Did you hit your head?"

"I don't think so."

It was still possible she might have whiplash or a concussion. "Can you move?"

Nodding, she said, "Yeah."

He helped her climb out of the SUV as the first-responder vehicles pulled up to a stop. She took a couple of steps, and her legs gave way.

Nash scooped her up before she fell. She was shaking uncontrollably in his arms.

"I'm a little dizzy and nauseous, but I can walk," she said, her voice low yet her tone insistent. "You don't have to carry me."

His only response was a grunt. Fighting with her wasn't going to help, so the fewer words he used the better.

"I don't want you to hurt your back," she added, softly.

Unbelievable. She was the one who'd crashed her vehicle after being robbed at gunpoint. Now she was more concerned about him than herself.

But that was the kind of woman Lynn was. Considerate. Caring. Always putting others first.

"You're light," he said. "I'm fine."

Sometimes his back ached. Old injuries from the military flaring up, reminding him they existed. All rangers had to be airborne qualified. Aches, occasional inflammation, sometimes arthritis were typical consequences after being required to jump out of airplanes on a regular basis. But not a stitch of pain bothered him at the moment.

All he felt was adrenaline and worry for Lynn.

Nash made his way to the back of the ambulance where the EMTs had already opened the rear doors. He sat her down inside. "She was in a head-on collision in the driver's seat. Airbag deployed."

The EMTs put her on a gurney and began checking her out.

Holden hopped out of his vehicle, slammed the door and hurried over. "What happened to her vehicle?"

Nash stepped out of Lynn's earshot but stayed where he could keep an eye on her. "She crashed it. On purpose."

"What in the hell?" Holden looked as baffled as Nash felt.

One paramedic took Lynn's blood pressure while the other flashed a light in her eyes and had Lynn track her finger.

"I haven't had a chance to ask her why," Nash said. But Lynn never acted without a good reason. Same applied to her breaking up with him. She analyzed all the factors, weighed her choices and decided accordingly. "Must've had something to do with the armed guy in her car."

"Is he dead?"

If only they could be so lucky to have this resolved with a corpse in the back seat. "No. He got away. Took off out that way somewhere."

"Did you get a look at him?"

"He was gone by the time I got to her."

Holden keyed his radio. "Dispatch, this is Chief Deputy Powell. Where's my helicopter? Is Mitch in the air yet?"

Mitch Cody was a maverick the new sheriff, Daniel, recruited after procuring additional funding for a law enforcement helicopter. Mitch used to fly Black Hawks for the army. Nash liked him. Sometimes he'd join him and Holden for dinner at Delgado's.

"He's in the air," dispatch responded. "As soon as I notified him of your call, he hustled over as quickly as he could."

Good man. Not a slacker.

"I need him over the barren field off South Corthell Road," Holden said. "We're searching for a fleeing suspect, male, on foot. Dark clothing. That's all I've got for now."

"Roger that," said the dispatcher.

The radio went silent.

"We might spot him," Holden said to Nash. "It's worked before, and Mitch is pretty fast."

Nonetheless, Mitch's response time wouldn't be fast enough. Nash sensed it in his gut, despite his desire for this to go in their favor. Spot the guy, vector to his position and arrest him—end of story.

"Two close calls for Lynn in less than two months." Holden clasped Nash's shoulder. "My mom would say these things come in threes."

Nash clenched his jaw. Ever since that night at Turning Point, it had been lurking at the edge of his mind, the dark possibility of *the next time*. He was grateful she wasn't dead behind the wheel of her car or lying on this dark road in the freezing cold with a team of crime-scene techs surrounding her.

"Let's hope Mrs. Powell is wrong." Nash didn't know how much more Lynn could handle.

She was a strong woman, but this wasn't a matter of strength. Everyone had their breaking point. All he knew was he couldn't take it if anything happened to her.

That was the secret fear of everyone in law enforcement. Being unable to prevent something horrible from happening to their loved ones.

"All right, go be with Lynn." Holden pulled out a pair of latex gloves and tugged them on. "I'll take a look around her car. Once the paramedics clear her, I can ask her a few questions."

"Okay."

Unhooking a flashlight from his utility belt, his friend trekked toward the crash site, and he went to check on Lynn.

HOLDEN POWELL EXAMINED the driver's-side door first. Taking a good look at the window and door handle, he found several small scratches near the lock and along the base of the window frame. That's where the guy had gotten in.

But her car alarm should've gone off. It would've drawn

a lot of attention. Once that happened, most perps grabbed whatever they could, any high-value items in the car, and bolted.

Flashing his light inside, he crouched down and peeked in, up under the dash. Powder from the deflated airbag lingered in the air, itching his throat. He spotted what he was looking for. Wires for the alarm had been pulled, sliced and tucked out of the way so Lynn wouldn't notice when she first got into her vehicle.

This wasn't an impromptu job of someone like a junkie, desperate for some quick cash to get their next fix. Whoever did this had taken the time to prepare and plan and had the patience to wait for Lynn.

A good thing Nash had spotted the man in her back seat, or this night could've ended much differently.

He pushed her seat forward and flashed the light around the back. Maybe the robber had dropped something, slipped up and left behind a clue that might help identify him.

Nothing on the rear seat or the floor. The inside was tidy. He checked the seam at the very back of the seat to be sure. No loose change, no papers, no keys. There wasn't even a gum wrapper.

Holden climbed out and went around to the front of the vehicle and inspected the damage from the collision. The impact had crushed the front. From the looks of it, he guessed it was mainly the frame and that the engine was probably intact. Still, her vehicle was an older model. The insurance company would consider it a complete loss and cut her a check rather than pay to have it repaired. Good insurance would even pay for a rental.

The sound of the helicopter he noticed first, followed by the bright spotlight washing over the adjacent barren field. It had taken a little longer than he would've preferred for Mitch to get out there, but considering the guy hadn't been on duty, his response time was impressive. The circumstances that brought Daniel Clark to the Albany County Sheriff's Department weren't pleasant, and Holden would rather not think on it at all, but Daniel had been a good fit for the department, even managing to get them their first law enforcement helicopter.

Moving to the other side of the Defender, he swept the beam of his flashlight over the passenger's door. His suspicion was confirmed that the suspect had gotten in on the driver's side when there weren't marks or scratches on this door.

A dark spot on the frame caught his attention. Under the light, he made it out. Blood. The man's hand had touched blood and it was smeared on the side frame as he pressed his palm there for leverage when getting out of the car.

It was the same on the back of the seat that had been shoved forward as well as the inner door handle.

No other apparent traces had been left behind, but this was the next best thing to the guy dropping his ID.

In the front, he spotted Lynn's purse and larger bag. He shone his light on both as he went through the contents. Next, he checked her glove box and the inside of her center console.

A couple of things worried him. Hopefully, Lynn would erase at least one of those concerns when she answered his questions.

After he contacted dispatch to have a crime-scene tech come out, he grabbed both bags and did a cursory once-over of the rear of the car.

An etching on the bumper, where the paint had been scraped off, glinted in the light. He got down low, balancing on the balls of his feet, for a closer look.

He cursed under his breath.

It can't be.

Holden wanted to be mistaken about the engraving that had been keyed into her car, but the longer he stared at it the more certain he was of what it meant.

Lynn was in grave danger.

Chapter Seven

The wind gusted, sending a spray of ice crystals over Nash. He shivered from the cold, his back now starting to ache. The brisk chill made him feel all his thirty-four years on the planet and then some. Standing at the rear of the ambulance in between the open doors, he shielded himself as best he could from the cold. His black Stetson was clamped on tight against the wind. He stayed out of the way of the EMTs and listened as they finished examining her.

"How fast were you going when you hit the pole?" the slim, lanky paramedic asked.

"I can't be sure." Lynn laced her fingers together and squeezed, like she was trying to stop them from shaking. "But I eased off the gas at the last minute. I think the speedometer dropped somewhere below fifty."

"It's a good thing you slowed down," he said, charting the patient care report on a tablet. "If you hadn't, you might be in worse condition."

From the looks of her vehicle, if she had been going any faster when she'd hit the utility pole, the impact harder, she might not have survived. "So, how is she?" Nash asked.

"No concussion," the other paramedic said, kneeling beside the gurney. She was a petite blonde, with her hair in a braid down her back. "No internal injuries. Whiplash is still a possibility. Symptoms don't always present immediately."

Lynn leaned forward, holding on to her knees, and

winced. "Ouch." She held up her left arm, taking the pressure off it.

"Let's have a look." Her coat was already off, and the tech pulled up the sleeve of her sweatshirt gingerly. There was a cut on her forearm, the skin split, angry red and bleeding. "Did you hit your arm against anything in the crash?"

Lynn thought for a moment. "Only the airbag. I threw my arms up in front of my face, instinctively, right before the collision."

The two EMTs exchanged a look. Then the one standing said, "That explains why you don't have a single mark on your face. Those airbags can do a number on a person."

Nash knew firsthand how true that was. He'd once been in a car chase with a suspect that had ended with the perpetrator crashing. The force exerted on a person's face when there was a collision caused you to smash into the airbag. It could easily fracture your nose, dislocate your jaw, damage the eyes. The perp hadn't walked away from the accident.

"Will she need stitches?" Nash wondered.

"No. The cut isn't deep. I can take care of it." The paramedic cleaned the wound and applied a series of butterfly bandages to the slash on her arm. "Tomorrow don't be alarmed in the event you have any pain or soreness in other places. It's common, but if you experience anything severe, you should see a doctor. Tonight, be sure to ice the arm."

"I will, along with my cheek." She pressed a palm to the right side of her face.

Nash stepped closer, noticing the pink mark on her skin. A bruise was forming. "I thought you said you didn't hit your head?"

"I didn't. The guy smacked my cheek with his gun."

He inwardly winced, though anger burned through him. If he ever got his hands on that man, Nash would make him regret the night he climbed into Lynn's car.

She must have read the intent on his face. "I'll be fine, really. Whatever you're thinking, Nash, you can forget about it."

He tilted his head up to the night sky and sighed. All he was doing was reaffirming the reasons why Lynn thought they wouldn't work as a couple and had ended things between them. His propensity for violence. His use of compartmentalization, which made him emotionally unavailable. The fact that he was a workaholic control freak.

She had even said that they didn't speak the same love language. Whatever that meant.

There was uncomfortable truth to the things she'd brought up months ago. So much so that he had been unable to deny any of it, but that wasn't his whole story.

"Well, ice both and take an NSAID," said the paramedic. "You should feel better in the morning."

"I hope so." Lynn put on her coat. "I'm going on vacation tomorrow."

Nash thrust his hands into the pockets of his parka. That was news to him. He had no idea what was going on with her since she shut him out. He also had no right to ask the question at the forefront of his mind. Instead, he decided to bide his time and bit his tongue.

The EMT lowered the tablet. "Where are you going?"

"Mountain cabin retreat."

Maybe there was a new guy in her life after all. Lynn wasn't the type to go away alone.

"You deserve a vacation after this. Somewhere special," one of the EMTs said.

"It's nothing fancy." Lynn clutched her hands as a small smile graced her lips. "We're staying in state. But I think it'll be special."

He caught the "we're." She definitely wasn't going alone. An unwanted surge of jealousy sent a sharp pain through him. The only thing worse than that awful feeling was the fear that had gripped him when Lynn's car crashed. He wanted her to be healthy, happy and safe, even if it wasn't with him.

"Hope you two enjoy the trip." The paramedics looked at Nash.

"Oh, I'm not going with him," Lynn said, dropping her gaze and drawing everyone's attention once again. "I'm, uh, going with my best friend."

Yvonne Lamber. She moved to Cheyenne this past summer after she got a big promotion to executive manager for a local hotel chain. The two women had gotten close quickly when Lynn relocated to Laramie to help out her aunt. Miriam Delgado had Alzheimer's and could no longer handle things at the bar and grill. The first to pitch in whenever family needed assistance, Lynn uprooted herself from Colorado, put her real job on hold and worked sixteen-hour days managing the restaurant until she found a stable replacement. Eventually she got her aunt settled in the Silver Springs senior living center, where Lynn visited her as much as possible.

Laramie was a close-knit community full of good people willing to lend a hand. Everyone did what they could to help. Even if it was something as small as patronizing the living heck out of Delgado's the way he and Holden did.

That's how he had met Lynn. Over the Wednesday special plate of meat loaf with garlic mashed potatoes and green beans.

Lynn was tireless, working nonstop. Caring for her aunt. Volunteering at the community center. Keeping an eye on Delgado's, filling in when they were short on staff. As well as treating clients.

A vacation would do her good, especially after tonight. If anybody deserved one, it was her. He regretted that they'd never been able to take one together. They'd both been too busy.

Holden approached them. "Are you going to be okay, Lynn?"

She nodded and slid down to the end of the gurney. "Besides a cut on my arm and a sore cheek, I was given a clean bill of health."

The EMTs moved toward the front of the ambulance and started putting away supplies and equipment.

"That's good to hear." Holden gave a tight smile. "I'm happy to say the perpetrator didn't get away uninjured."

"What do you mean?" Nash asked.

"I found a bloody handprint on the seat that he shoved forward to get out, on the inside door handle, and side of the car. My guess is that he hit his face, probably got a bloody nose and wiped it with his hand."

"You won't be able to pull any fingerprints," Lynn said. "He was wearing gloves."

"But now we've got his DNA. If we're lucky, we'll get a hit on a match in the system," Holden said, meaning the FBI's CODIS—Combined DNA Index System—which was used by law enforcement labs nationwide.

The database linked unknown DNA left during the commission of a crime to offenders who were legally required to provide samples. The hitch was they'd only learn his identity if the guy was a previously convicted criminal or had a DNA swab upon arrest in one of the states that allowed taking it without a conviction.

"A crime-scene tech is on the way. In the meantime, Lynn, can you run me through precisely what happened?" Holden asked.

"Sure. I left USD, like I do every Thursday. Ran into Nash. He walked me to where my car was parked."

"Actually, she stopped me at the corner of Third and Lewis," Nash said. "I watched her walk the rest of the way to the grocery store lot by herself." If he had been less pushy, she might've let him walk her up to her vehicle and this whole mess might've been avoided.

"When I got in my car, I was wrapped up in my own thoughts, distracted." She glanced at Nash. "I didn't realize the man was in my back seat until I had turned out of the lot."

Not only had he been too aggressive in his approach with her, but he'd also been the source of her distraction. "That's when I thought I saw someone and called you."

Holden nodded slowly, taking in the details. "Did you get a look at him?"

"No." Lynn shook her head. "He wore a black ski mask with a skull face painted on it. All I could see were his eyes, but it was too dark to make out the color."

"Go on," Holden said.

"He forced me to drive to the bank at gunpoint and withdraw the max."

"How did you end up on this road with your car wrapped around that pole?" Holden hiked a thumb back at the crashed vehicle.

"He made me turn this way at the intersection," Lynn said. "I had offered to go to another ATM to get him more money, but he didn't go for it. That's when he hit me and told me to shut up. When he demanded that I drive down here, where there were no lights, complete isolation, I realized he intended to kill me. I saw Nash's headlights behind us, but I didn't know it was him. That's when I had the *brilliant* idea to crash my SUV." Sarcasm dripped from her voice. "I figured it would stop the guy in the back seat. At the very least, slow him down long enough for the other driver to intervene."

Quick thinking for certain, albeit reckless.

"Was there anything distinctive about him?" Holden asked. "Did he speak with an accent, a lisp, a stutter?"

"No, nothing I can think of."

"What about his build?"

"I'd say about your height." Lynn gestured to Holden. "Around six feet. Not as lean as you. Slightly more muscular, like Nash, but not as wide-shouldered."

"Did he mention or say anything that stood out? Give any indication why he targeted you?"

"Not that I can recall."

"Did he say outright that he was going to kill you?" Holden asked.

Squeezing her eyes shut a moment, she shook her head. "No, but I could tell. I felt it. His intention to do me harm."

Maybe it had been the nature of the situation, like when you're walking down a dark street and you feel someone getting too close. Maybe it had been that Lynn was sensitive and good at reading people. Either way, Nash believed her when she said that man had intended to kill her.

"Okay. That gives us something to go on." Holden handed Lynn her purse and gym bag. "I do have a couple of immediate concerns. The first being that your gun wasn't in your purse or anywhere in your car."

Nash had shared with Holden when he'd given Lynn the handgun as a gift and had advised her to keep it on her person. After the incident at Turning Point, everyone in the sheriff's department was aware that Lynn was packing.

"Is it possible the suspect stole it?" Holden continued.

Lynn hesitated. "No." She clenched her hands around her bags. "I don't carry it anymore."

"Why not?" Nash asked, the question coming out harsher than he'd intended. "I told you to carry it with you at all times." He'd insisted until she had agreed. Having that gun on her saved her life that night when he'd been too late and too slow to do it.

Lynn straightened and fixed him with a direct gaze. "Because I got rid of it."

"You did what?" he snapped. "Why?"

"I have my reasons," she said.

"It's always better to be the person holding the gun than the one running from the gunman," Nash said. *Or rather the one crashing into a pole.*

"Amen to that," Holden mumbled under his breath while scrubbing a hand over his jaw.

"Of course you would agree with him." Lynn threw a hand up in resignation.

"What's that supposed to mean?" Holden asked, looking between them.

"Let's just say you two share a similar philosophy about life," she said, making it sound like that was a bad thing. She lifted her chin and stared at Nash. "Can we discuss this at a more appropriate time so your buddy can get on with his job?"

As much as he hated to admit it, she was right. This was not the time or the place for this discussion. "What was your second concern, Holden?"

"Lynn's wallet is missing from her handbag."

Damn it. Credit and debit cards could be frozen with a simple phone call, but that man now had her driver's license, which meant he had her home address.

The impact of the news was visible on Lynn in the shrinking of her shoulders and the slight hunching of her posture, as if she'd taken a blow. "He took it from my purse and handed me my debit card but held on to the wallet." She quickly straightened, recovering, and inhaled a deep though shaky breath. "I forgot that he'd kept it."

"There's one more thing." Holden's tone implied he was reluctant to mention it. "I found a symbol scratched onto your rear bumper." His gaze flew to Nash. "The symbol for a female. A circle with a cross at the bottom."

"That's no big deal, right?" Lynn said. "Some kid must've keyed my car."

But if this was going in the direction that Nash was dreading, then the significance was major.

"It also had a box drawn around it," Holden said to Nash, "with an *X* marked through it."

A sinking sensation dropped in the pit of his stomach. Things just went from bad to a whole helluva lot worse. It also confirmed why that man had brought her down this particular road.

"What does it mean?" Lynn asked.

"Nash, I figured you might want to be the one to tell her."

Lynn scooted to the edge of the gurney. "To tell me what?"

Nash didn't want to alarm her, driving her stress levels any higher, but this situation might not be over. She needed to know. "We've received updates from the Colorado field offices about three cases spanning from Denver to Fort Collins. Women who were stalked and murdered. Each had the symbol Holden described drawn on their rear bumpers. We believe it's the killer's calling card." Nash's office brought the information to the attention of the local police and sheriff's department once a pattern emerged, and it appeared as though the killer might be preparing to cross the border into Wyoming.

"A serial killer?" Another blow. This time blanching the color from her face.

Nash scanned the area. Killers preferred remote locations such as this. It gave them the privacy and time they needed to torture and murder their victims.

Anger slithered through him, but he was careful not to show it.

Holden folded his arms. "Since this guy knows where you live, I have to strongly advise you not to go home tonight. In fact, it's best if you don't go home for a few days," Holden said. "Give us a chance to apprehend him."

Lynn lowered her head and exhaled a harsh breath. "I was planning to spend a long weekend up in the mountains with Yvonne, but we aren't meeting up there until tomorrow afternoon and I haven't even packed. I have to go home to get some things."

"Not alone," Holden said. "And you can't spend the night there."

If this was the same serial killer, then he'd been watching Lynn for a while and knew where she lived long before he'd stolen her wallet. Although she lived across the street from the University of Wyoming Police Department, it gave her a false sense of security. She never even had an alarm system installed. It would be easy enough for someone to break in on the back side of her house, which was shrouded in darkness and tall bushes.

The last place she could stay was at her home.

"I'll take you to your house," Nash offered, "so you can get what you need. You're welcome to stay the night with me. In my guest room," he quickly added. "If that doesn't suit you, I'll drive you to Yvonne's in Cheyenne." It was an hour drive one way. He'd rather not spend two on the road when he was bone-tired and starving, but he'd learned his lesson about being pushy.

Weighing her options, Lynn frowned. "I don't want to inconvenience you, put you through any extra trouble, considering everything you've already done for me. Once I grab my things, you can drop me off at a hotel. I need to go to Turning Point in the morning, and I can make arrangements to have Yvonne pick me up there in the afternoon."

Nash cut his gaze to Holden, who met his exasperated glance. This decision was up to Lynn, but he expected her to make the right one.

"That's not a good idea," Holden said, without Nash needing to utter a word. "You shouldn't be alone tonight. Not just from an emotional perspective, but what if you suddenly get dizzy or a headache or something? It's better to have someone look after you tonight."

Holden had practically read his mind. This was why they were tight. They were cut from the same cloth. Understood each other. Shared a *similar philosophy about life* for sure.

"I can see I'm not going to win this fight," Lynn said. "I know what it takes to challenge one of you, let alone both, and I'm not up for it right now. So I concede. We'll do it your way, Nash. But I have one request."

"Whatever you need."

"Let's not discuss anything else tonight." Weariness clouded her face. "I don't have the energy."

She needed to rest, and he'd see to it that she did. Safely, without interruption.

"You'll have peace and quiet tonight," he promised. "But tomorrow, we'll talk?" His question surprised Holden, who arched his eyebrows in response.

Nash was normally a reticent man. Listening, observing, digging around, made him good at his job. Not chitchatting. He most certainly didn't request to have conversations.

Things had to be different with Lynn, as she had already made abundantly clear. He was prepared to try to give her what she wanted. One day, one discussion at a time.

First, she had to give him a chance.

"Yes," she said. "Tomorrow, we'll talk. A proper discussion is long overdue."

Good. He couldn't agree more.

They'd wasted too many weeks as it was, and if the man who'd set his sights on Lynn was indeed the serial killer the FBI was hunting in Colorado, better known as TRK, an abbreviated form of *torture, rape, kill*, then he wasn't going to squander any more time. TRK had murdered three women, moving progressively north. Nash wasn't going to let Lynn become the fourth victim.

Chapter Eight

For the past twelve hours, Nash had been the epitome of patience. Considerate beyond belief. Lynn was grateful to him for it. Truth be told, she had needed the quiet, safe space he'd provided. No prodding her to eat dinner when she wasn't hungry last night. No crowding her space. He'd given her a couple of ice packs, some medicine for the pain, ensured she was tucked into his guest room with plenty of water and had bid her good-night.

It was strange, being at his place and not in his bed with him wrapped around her. She missed the feel of him, the smell of him. She missed the comfort mingled with pleasure that he brought. Not that she deserved either from him.

It had taken a while, but once the adrenaline had faded, she'd gotten her first peaceful night's rest in weeks without any nightmares and had even slept in.

Nash had called into work, letting his office know he'd be in late. Made her a home-cooked breakfast of scrambled eggs, bacon and toast. Rather than bombarding her with questions and criticisms while she ate, he'd been silent, pensive. Watching her with those eyes that seemed to see straight into her soul.

Sitting in the passenger's seat of his truck, she rubbed her arm. More than the laceration on her forearm hurt. Her whole body was sore, but spending time with Nash made her heart ache.

As he pulled into the parking lot across the street from the Turning Point clinic, she realized she couldn't put off the discussion any longer. She feared the prospect of saying something that might hurt him, especially since she was still processing her own emotions over the shooting. She had even begun to tackle how she felt about what happened last night. More so, she dreaded stepping inside the clinic. Every time she crossed the threshold, the building came alive with horrible memories.

Sometimes it took a couple of hours for her anxiety to subside, sometimes most of the day, but it never went away completely.

It hadn't been so long ago when she'd been thankful to work at Turning Point. Once Rich had learned about her aunt, Miriam, a pillar in the community suffering from a neurological disorder, he had graciously offered to let Lynn join his practice. Even helped her build a list of clients. If only she had known where it would lead.

Working at Delgado's and waiting for a position to open at the hospital would have been better.

She peered out the window. From this part of town, there was a view of both the Laramie Mountains and the Snowy Range.

Today was overcast, a leaden sky hanging over Laramie. The temperature was freezing, and the forecast called for heavy snow. Flurries had already started and were sticking to the ground. She couldn't wait to get up to the cabin with Yvonne before the roads got bad and simply relax. Forget about the lethal criminal, a possible serial killer, who had her wallet and knew where she lived. She'd canceled her cards, and would have to rely on Yvonne for money until they were all sorted.

A massive shiver moved through her. She felt sick again, thinking about last night.

As she often told her clients, avoidance didn't solve problems. It often only made a situation worse.

Lynn turned to Nash.

His face was stoic, with no hint as to what he was thinking. His gaze was diffuse, eyes scanning the street all around them, like he was looking for something. Large hands weren't clenched at his sides but were still primed to curl into fists in the blink of an eye if he needed to leap into action. It was as if he was always ready to tackle a threat. His muscled body was still as stone.

"I can understand you wanting to talk to me here," Nash said, indicating the clinic with a nod of his head. "On your turf. Instead of at my place. Whatever is more comfortable for you."

Actually, she had planned to hash over things in *his* truck. She didn't need any perceived position of power. It was sweet of him to worry about her and give up the seeming advantage.

"Before we go inside," he said, "I need you to know something." The intensity of the look he gave her, dark and mysterious as a forest and yet as sharp and cutting as a blade of saw grass, sent a flutter through her chest. "No matter how our conversation ends, I want you to remain in my life. Even if that means only as friends." He offered his hand.

"Nash." She said his name like a curse, her voice thick with emotion.

"No more avoiding me. We started as friends. We can be that again. If it comes to that. Promise me."

She glanced down at his extended hand. The last thing she wanted to do was touch him. Once she got started it would be hard to stop. But if she rebuked this small gesture, then he'd certainly believe she hated him.

"Okay." She put her palm in his.

Brow creased, he looked down at their joined hands. He

rubbed the inside of her wrist with his thumb in light, tender circles, the way she used to love.

Those flutters slid from her chest down to her belly.

Damn him.

It was hard to resist a man like Nash. The one area of their relationship where they'd never had a problem and had been a perfect match was in the bedroom. When they had first taken things to an intimate level, they'd spent two straight days between the sheets. Over time, any issue that popped up between them, instead of talking, he sought to resolve by making love to her—sometimes slow, sometimes desperate, always leaving her moved, spent, shaken. She'd succumbed to his seduction so many times, so easily, so eagerly, it had become an unhealthy habit.

Still rubbing those soft circles on the inside of her wrist, he cupped her face with his other hand, sending a rush of uncertainty through her. His touch was warm, careful not to aggravate the bruise on her cheek. "Thank you." His voice was astonishingly gentle.

Gentleness was not something Nash often showed. But it was there, in the touch of his hand on her cheek, in the softness of his voice.

Their gazes locked, and a spark of heat flashed between them hot enough to start a wildfire. Every time she got close to him, there was an underlying current of sexual awareness.

If she didn't get out of this truck and away from him, he'd have her thighs quivering next.

"Nash," she said, this time in a half whisper, not certain if she was asking him to stop or continue.

His gray eyes were stripped of all their usual cool hardness. They were as clear as glass and full of desire. And more. A tenderness she had never seen in them before.

As he leaned in, she realized she was in trouble. Because she wasn't pulling away.

The front door of Turning Point flew open, drawing their attention. Rich staggered outside, fumbling to hold on to a box with a sling around his bad arm that looked like a broken wing.

Nash swore under his breath. He dropped his hands, turned off the engine and hopped out of the truck.

Lynn sighed with relief. Her body was attuned to Nash's, responding with the slightest contact, pushing her to draw closer. At the same time, her head was a conflicting jumble that screamed for her to keep her distance.

Given a few more minutes, seconds if she were being honest with herself, and they would've kissed.

So much for being friends.

She watched Nash hustle across the street to provide assistance.

Saved by Richard Jennings.

TALK ABOUT BAD TIMING. This couldn't have been any worse. Why couldn't Rich have waited two minutes before shoving through the front door?

All Nash had really needed was one, and Lynn would've been in his arms with her lips pressed to his. That would've been a much better way to start their discussion. He always lacked the right words but had no difficulty showing her how he felt about her.

He jogged over and scooped up the cardboard box as it was about to tumble out of the doctor's grasp. A frame tipped over the side, but Nash managed to grab it in midair before it smashed to the ground.

"Thank you," Rich said, looking flustered as he took the frame from Nash's hand. "I'm glad it didn't break. Custom frame. That's my son."

Nash looked down at a magazine cover. It featured a man in his thirties wearing a suit with his arms crossed.

The subheading read "Five Minutes with Devin Jennings: Mitigating Artificial Intelligence Concerns."

"He's the cofounder and vice president of Trident Security." Rich beamed as he spoke. "The company has become a real powerhouse. They're based in California. Los Angeles."

"You must be proud."

"I am. Wish his mother had lived to see it. He favors her. Fortunate for him." Rich laughed, moving his bad arm. Wincing, he hissed with pain.

The bullet had struck the bone, fracturing it and complicating his recovery. If it had passed straight through, not hitting anything important, he would've been out of the sling weeks ago.

"Let me help you with this," Nash offered, and they started across the street, where Lynn was waiting next to Rich's car. As they walked, he scanned the contents of the box. It was filled with personal items. A coffee mug, two plants—succulents—a framed PhD, some files, books and a bottle of scotch. "What's all this? Are you leaving the clinic?"

Rich stepped onto the sidewalk near Lynn. "Yes." He glanced at her with a sad smile. "It's time."

Lynn nodded with a sympathetic expression.

"I thought you'd be there providing counseling for another ten years," Nash said. Perhaps longer.

"So did I, but that night...the shooting." Rich adjusted his arm in the sling and winced. "It changed everything for me."

"For both of us," Lynn said, her light brown eyes somber beneath their long black lashes.

"I'm afraid I can't do this anymore," Rich said, "no matter how much a part of me would like to. This is for the best."

"What are you going to do with yourself?" Nash wondered. Rich was middle-aged, but still full of life.

"My son wants me to move out to LA, to be close to him and his kids. I've put my house up for sale. Once it's sold, I'm going to try retirement on the West Coast. Devin is going to buy me a condo with a great view. Walking distance to his place. There'll be plenty to keep me busy, with three grandkids all under the age of five." Rich unlocked his trunk and opened it.

"Sounds like you'll have your hands full." Nash set the box down in the car and closed the trunk. "When is the retirement party?"

"I don't want to make a fuss."

Rich was the first to throw a party for any reason and invite half the town. There were probably a lot of folks who would've liked the opportunity to say goodbye to him, but then he'd have to rehash the trauma, explaining why he was retiring early.

Nash didn't blame him for not wanting to go through that repeatedly during a party that was supposed to be fun. The man had almost lost his life. His recovery was long and painful. Based on the way Lynn was handling the situation, he imagined Rich was healing not only physically, but mentally, too.

"I thought you'd be here at nine," Rich said to Lynn. "When you didn't show, I packed up my stuff and left my keys in the top drawer of my desk."

"I'm sorry I'm late." Lynn tensed. "I had an incident last night. I was mugged and my car was totaled. It was a long, difficult night."

"My word!" Rich exclaimed. "Are you all right?"

"I got lucky. Thankfully, I am." Not that she looked the least bit all right. Makeup covered the bruise on her cheek, but her deepest wounds were on the inside. It wasn't unexpected that she didn't get into details; still it surprised him how much she downplayed what had happened. She'd come close to being killed. Not to mention there might very well be a serial killer stalking her. "I ended up staying at Nash's place and overslept. It was the first time I've had more than a few hours of solid rest in weeks."

"Is there anything I can do?" Rich asked. "Would you like me to spend the day here while you see your clients? The place feels a bit creepy when I'm in there alone these days. I can only imagine what it's like for you."

A look of embarrassment crossed her face, and she hung her head. "That's kind of you, but no. I don't have any clients coming in today. I came to see you off and to get the keys. I'm only hanging out until Yvonne drives down. Then we're off on our vacation."

"Oh, I forgot about that. I guess starting today it's a vacation for both of us. Only mine is permanent." Rich exhaled heavily.

Lynn put a hand on his good shoulder. "I'm sorry for how things turned out," she said, and Nash saw the weight she was carrying, how she blamed herself for everything surrounding Andy Crombie. "But you're making the right choice."

Nodding, Rich took a deep breath. He opened his door, slipped into the car and waved to them.

"It seems like this wasn't an easy decision for him," Nash said.

"No, it wasn't." Lynn turned, heading for the building. "He agonized over what to do. In the end, he made the right choice. This is the best thing for him. He gets to start the next chapter of his life in sunny California, close to his family."

As they entered the building, Lynn faltered to a stop and stiffened.

He put a hand on her arm. To remind her she wasn't alone. That he was there, ready to help in any way.

"I'm fine." She nodded as if trying to convince herself. "Really, I'm fine."

"Sure."

"Is it okay if we talk in my office, instead of the waiting room?"

She was in charge of how this happened. Not him. "Yep."

He flipped the latch on the front door, locking it since she wasn't expecting any clients and Yvonne wouldn't arrive until later. Then he followed her down the hall.

"Could you write down for me where you're going to be staying with Yvonne?" They were no longer a couple, and she had every right to refuse, but it would put his mind at ease.

"I'll be fine out of town. Safer than staying here."

He hoped that was true. "Still, if you wouldn't mind and call me, too, once you get there."

"Sure," she said reluctantly.

Lynn unlocked the door and traipsed inside, taking off her coat.

Entering her office, he realized how remarkable she was. Day after day she came back here and did her job regardless of how challenging it might be for her. Rich was retiring while Lynn was sticking it out, choosing to sacrifice her personal comfort to help others. He admired her so much he didn't have the words for it.

As she grabbed a notepad and pen and looked up something on her phone, he realized there were also things about her that he couldn't wrap his head around. For instance, how she could return to a place where she'd been the most vulnerable without any protection.

"Where's the gun I gave you?" he asked. Better to cut straight to it, push through the messy bits, and hopefully find a way back to each other.

Sighing, she set down the pad and pen and leaned against the edge of her desk. "I don't carry it anymore."

"Heard that part last night." He removed his jacket, tossing it into a chair. "Why?"

Lynn clasped her hands in her lap. "You won't understand."

She was probably right.

He looked around her office, his gaze going to the Sierra Club calendar, her Ivy League degree hanging on the wall, the Montblanc pen on her desk that cost as much as her designer handbag. The differences between them were stark. Growing up in a big city, with well-to-do parents, she had wanted for nothing. While he had lived on his family's ranch under his father's iron fist until he was thrown into the foster care system, where he learned to fight for everything if he wanted to have anything.

Sure, there were times he didn't get her perspective, her preferences. But it was their differences as much as their similarities—love of family, a strong work ethic, service before self—that attracted him to her.

"After what you went through here, I would've sworn you'd be inclined to carry it."

"It's because of what happened that I don't," she said.

"Having that gun saved your life."

"With that gun, I took a life." Her expression was determined, but she didn't look the least bit tough.

"You had no choice. Andy Crombie was going to shoot you. He was crazy."

"Don't use that word with me," she said, wagging a finger at him. "Not ever. Andy wasn't some violent criminal. He was suffering from severe mental illness. He was in crisis and needed help. It was my job to protect him." Shadows swam in her eyes, and he saw the scar that night had left. A scar that marred the soul rather than the body. "Instead, I failed him." The self-condemnation in her voice ripped at Nash's guts.

Why couldn't she see that she had been in an impossible situation?

"If you hadn't shot him," he said, slowly, carefully, "you'd be dead."

"You don't know that for certain, but the conclusion you jump to is that killing him was the right thing."

"Why would you say that?"

"Taking a life sometimes comes with the territory of your job. I get that, but I think you might've gotten to a point where you've normalized it, so you don't feel the gravity anymore."

Is that what she thought of him? That he didn't feel the gravity of taking a life?

"You should know better than that about law enforcement." He crossed his arms over his chest. "Your brother is an FBI agent the same as me."

"I'm not talking about all law enforcement. I'm talking about you."

He swallowed, stricken, not knowing what to say. How to defend against such an accusation. He opted for his default setting, silence.

"Jake isn't like you," she said, mentioning her brother, who worked down in Denver. "Or maybe it's that I know him so much better. I've seen how deeply things affect him."

Clenching his jaw, Nash breathed through it. This unfair comparison of him to someone she'd known and loved her whole life.

Again, his instinct was to stay quiet, but that was how the conversation had turned out before. One-sided and not going in his favor.

"Give me time." He pushed down the frustration and the ugly sense of desperation swelling in his chest. "To show you."

"Once Jake found out we were dating, he told me some things about you."

And that unfair scale tipped even further against him.

Nash cleared his throat. "What things?"

"That you consistently get the job done. No matter how tough," she said, but the compliment had him bracing for what was to come next. Lynn liked to soften the blow of the bad by starting out with something good. "That you have a reputation for being decisive...to the point of unfeeling. That you've been reprimanded for using excessive force."

His brain snagged on the one word ringing in his ears. *Unfeeling.*

For some reason, this felt like a betrayal by one of his own. He and Jake weren't friends. Still, on something like this he'd expected the guy to have his back. Not stab him in it. They were colleagues after all, working in a dangerous line of work that required tough choices.

Lynn pushed off the desk and eased closer to him. "I didn't break up with you because of what Jake said. I form my own opinions, but it did make me look closer. Then there was the incident when you got hurt in the line of duty and a suspect died."

The man had been a violent repeat offender and had attacked Nash, resisting arrest with a deadly weapon. They'd fought on the roof of a building. The guy had gone over the edge. An accident.

If he could've brought the guy in alive, he would've.

"You wouldn't talk to me about it." Lynn's gaze lingered on him, her eyes searching his for he didn't know what. "You shut down whenever I brought it up, or anything deep for that matter. You've never even said more than ten words to me about your childhood."

"Try living your entire life keeping your thoughts to yourself, your feelings bottled up, and then one day being asked to spill your guts on demand about everything."

Served him right for falling for a therapist. When they'd met at Delgado's, he hadn't known what she was. A keep-your-distance, avoid-at-all-costs shrink. That was a head-ache he didn't need. He had intimacy issues, possibly trust issues, too. But there had been something about her, right from the get-go, that had hooked him.

"I found it alarming the way you'd withdraw from me," she said, "when all I wanted was to get closer to you. Quite frankly, it scared me."

"You fear me?" He rubbed his forehead. This kept get-ting worse. For months, his woman had been scared of him. No wonder she'd ended things.

"I don't fear you, Nash. I fear *for* you." She closed the gap between them and put her hand on his chest.

He flinched at the contact. Not because he didn't want her to touch him. On the contrary, he wanted it too much. He ached for her. Weeks of hoping they'd work it out, and now she was touching him, yet at the same time, keeping him at a distance.

"I can't be with someone who won't talk to me," she said. "Who hides their past and their emotions. I told you it was a deal breaker and you didn't care."

It wasn't that he didn't care. "Compared to everything else going on," he said, thinking about his job, putting away criminals, "it didn't seem like a big deal." He watched a different kind of pain fill her eyes, and he regretted the words. "I mean I thought I had more time to work on it."

"Maybe we view everything too differently. Take the situation with Andy. I read the police report. You were in the process of identifying yourself when I pulled the trig-ger. If I had waited, ten seconds, maybe just two, then I might've registered that you were there. You might've been able to talk him down. How can you, of all people, say I didn't have any other option?"

How could he say anything else?

To do so would condemn her to live with this guilt for the rest of her life. It wouldn't be right. Not after what Andy had done, shooting Rich and turning the gun on Lynn.

Nash wanted to protect her, wanted her to heal and move on. Not suffer.

"Everything happened really fast," he said. "You could've been gone in the blink of an eye. Sometimes the only choice is the hardest one, and you have to forgive yourself for it."

"That's easier said than done."

He could help her through this. If only she'd let him. "Why have you been avoiding me?"

"Because when I listen to your voice messages," she said, "when I see you in the street, the first thing I think of is Andy. I think of what I did, and I can't bear it."

He turned, putting his back to her.

It would've been easy to leave the conversation there, with their relationship diminished to nothing more than friendship, and her stuck, unable to forgive herself.

Nash never chose easy. He was a fighter. Born and bred. He spun back around, meeting her tortured gaze. "Did you ever stop to ask yourself what's the second thing you think of when you see me? Or the third? I refuse to believe it's all death and darkness." Her amber eyes softened. Big, liquid eyes you'd see on a fawn. The same way she had softened in his truck earlier. On some level, she wanted to be near him, to get closer, and if he had kissed her, he was willing to bet everything he owned that she would've kissed him back. "You must think of Andy when you're in this office. But you still come here, every day. You haven't run from your job. Don't run from me, either."

"Continuing to work here has been a serious struggle. I've been thinking about moving back home to Fort Collins."

The statement hit him like a physical blow, and he stilled.

"My family thinks it would be good for me to go back, now that Aunt Miriam is settled in a nice place, like Silver Springs, and Delgado's is thriving. But I have an obligation to the Turning Point clients. I can't simply abandon them."

What about abandoning him?

"Running down the street to get away from me isn't good enough. You have to leave the state?"

"It's only a forty-five-minute drive."

He clasped her shoulders, and she stared up at him. "I think you've been avoiding me to punish yourself. When we're together, it's like we're in this bubble, where the outside world disappears. You said yourself that being at my place helped you get the first decent night's sleep in weeks. It's okay to be with me. To let me hold you. It's okay to feel better."

"I'm not sure I'll ever feel better here. In Laramie."

"Why not?"

Tears welled in her eyes as she lowered her head. "Because of the letters I keep getting. I don't think they'll ever stop coming unless I leave."

"What letters?"

Chapter Nine

Tension coiled so tight through Lynn she could barely breathe. She pulled out the letters from her desk drawer and gave the bundle of them to Nash with a shaking hand. "They're in chronological order. The most recent one I received was yesterday." On a wave of nausea, she sank into her leather chair and dropped her head into her hands.

This was humiliating. Being reduced to a trembling heap. Forced to drag Nash deeper into her troubles, after doing her best to cut him out of her life. He might be the only one capable of keeping her alive through this.

The panic that lived beneath her skin, burned through to the surface, paralyzing her where she sat. A tremor racked her entire body.

Five weeks ago, Sheriff Clark had done her a kindness by keeping most of the details of what had happened to Andy quiet, issuing a simple statement to the media. A nosy reporter, dissatisfied with the lack of information and sensing a story, kept digging. The day she returned to Laramie from Fort Collins a sensational article broke, announcing to everyone that she had shot Andy Crombie. The words *self-defense* had not been used, though subtly implied, right along with a dereliction of duty on her part. That as a therapist she had been culpably inefficient.

Four days later the first letter arrived. It had been a total blindside.

Her mind stumbled over images of it. She remembered the message vividly.

She had them all memorized, down to the disturbing fonts.

**YOU WERE TRUSTED AND VIOLATED
THAT SACRED CONVENANT
IN THE WORST WAY IMAGINABLE.**

The second was equally unnerving.

**HOW CAN YOU LOOK AT YOURSELF
IN THE MIRROR?
HOW CAN YOU SLEEP AT NIGHT AFTER
WHAT YOU'VE DONE?**

Every time a new one appeared in the mail, she wanted to retch. She considered burning it. Never opening it. Tearing it to shreds instead of reading it. But each time she'd been compelled to see what horrible, nasty things the note would say.

**YOU SHOULD BE ASHAMED.
WHERE IS YOUR HANGDOG FACE?
MAYBE YOU SHOULD JUST HANG.**

Then she became scared. Terrified that maybe someone wanted to do more than shame her. Perhaps hurt her.

**YOU HAVE BECOME DEATH,
THE DESTROYER OF WORLDS.
SOMEONE SHOULD STOP YOU.**

Or kill her.

YOUR TIME IS AT HAND.
BUT WHICH WILL GET YOU FIRST?
KARMA? OR ME?
BELIEVE.
YOU'LL GET WHAT YOU DESERVE!

Dread slithered over her at recalling the harsh words, so cruel and insidious.

The police had given her sympathetic looks when she'd shown them the letters but had done nothing. If they couldn't help, then no one could.

But Nash would do his best to try, using all the tools in his box. Ironically, some of the qualities that made an effective FBI agent were also the same characteristics that had eroded their relationship, driving her to end things.

She looked up at him.

There was a sharp intelligence in those gray eyes that missed little. He studied the letters with a silent, deliberate resolve.

When he had suggested that she was avoiding him to punish herself, she had thought the idea ridiculous.

Nightmares plagued her. Guilt was consuming her. Someone was terrorizing her with those cringe-inducing letters. The one man who'd ever brought her solace had become a constant reminder of her biggest regret. As if that weren't enough, now a serial killer was targeting her.

She didn't need to punish herself, not when the universe was doing such an excellent job of it. Was karma giving her what she deserved?

Staring at Nash as he examined those wretched notes gave her a surprising sense of hope that had her reconsidering his suggestion.

He looked up, his eyes flashing to hers, making her skin tingle and her heart twinge.

Besides his good looks and muscular build, there was something about him that she couldn't ignore. An aura of strength and determination, like he'd find a way to tackle any problem. Whatever it was, a little kick of awareness shot through her whenever she sensed his eyes on her.

Although her first thought when she looked at him was of Andy, Nash was right that it most certainly wasn't the only one. Part of her had longed to escape all of this with him in their bubble. He still owned her heart, and she didn't know what to do about it. Legitimate excuses always arose as to why she needed to keep her distance—like she'd only be encouraging the unhealthy habit they'd formed, and sex wasn't going to get him to open up, really let her in the way she had always hoped he would—but perhaps he had realized something she had missed.

That she was punishing herself by pushing him away. Because deep down she knew that in his arms she might find some absolution.

Even if it was only temporary.

GRITTING HIS TEETH, Nash fumed over the letters. There was no way he could imagine the toll they were taking on Lynn, and he wasn't going to pretend to. "I'm sorry someone has been harassing you like this."

One more form of torture she didn't need.

Not only was Lynn as beautiful on the inside as she was on the outside, but she also had a powerful intellect and even more powerful compassionate spirit. It burned his gut that someone would have the vicious audacity to send her such heinous letters.

Lynn had been wise to save them, keeping each in a separate plastic resealable bag along with the envelopes. It would preserve any possible fingerprints while minimizing the addition of others.

"Have you taken these to the sheriff's office?" He doubted it because surely Holden would've told him about it, but he needed to ask.

"No. But I did take them to the Laramie PD. There was nothing they could do about it until something happened as a result."

"Why'd you go there instead of the sheriff's?"

She stared up at him and frowned. There was no need for her to say it. Because she hadn't wanted him to find out what was going on.

"Right." He set the letters down on the desk, side by side, in the order she'd received them.

All printed on the same plain white sheets. No watermarks. Nothing special about them in terms of thickness or weight to distinguish the pages from regular printing paper. The ominous words had been typed in different fonts and sizes. All of them in bold letters, all caps.

A letter sent snail mail was fairly old-school for the twenty-first century. Then again, email was a lot easier to trace if you didn't know what you were doing.

First thing first, he was going to have the notes checked for prints. He looked over the envelopes again.

"What is it?" she asked. "Did you notice something?"

"The postmarks vary in terms of location. They were all mailed from different post offices. The first in Jackson, next Riverton, Casper, then Cheyenne. The last one was here."

"Does it mean something? Is there a pattern of some kind?"

Taking out his cell phone, he pulled up a map. He had his suspicions but wanted to be sure. "Jackson is the farthest away. Then each location draws closer to Laramie if you look at it, taking Route 26 to I-25 over to I-80." He turned his phone so she could see the screen and pointed out the route.

"What do you think it means that the last one was post-marked here?"

"I'm not sure yet." It wasn't a good thing, but he didn't need to pile more stress on her. "There are a lot of moving pieces to consider."

Lynn stood and came around the desk to where he was. "Tell me what you're thinking. Please. You've got that look in your eye."

"And what look is that?"

"The one where I can tell that you've flipped that switch in your head. Everything personal gets locked away in a vault and you disconnect. It's only stone-cold business."

Pushing everything else to the side so he could focus with a clear head was how he performed at his best. Over the years, he'd learned to suppress his personal feelings while working a case. One of his greatest strengths was his complete control over his emotions. It had served him well. But now it was impossible to disconnect, as she called it, since this concerned her.

"Don't sugarcoat it," Lynn prodded when he remained silent. "Just give it to me straight."

"It's possible that you might have more than one prob-lem to contend with. Based on the marking Holden found on your bumper, it looks like the guy in your car last night is the TRK serial killer."

He'd given it a great deal of thought last night as he read over old news articles. Each of the three victims in Colorado had been single females, between the ages of twenty-five and thirty-five, who had stood out publicly in some way. One had been given an award for community service. Another had won a special scholarship for excel-lence in STEM for a master's program. The last victim had been the focus of a scandal surrounding embezzlement of company funds.

Lynn fit the profile down to the unflattering article that had been printed about her. Each had even made ATM withdrawals the night of their murder. The FBI believed it was the killer's way of psychologically tormenting the women before he moved on to the physical aspects.

After the women had been tortured and raped, they were stabbed to death. Never shot. Maybe TRK only used a gun to intimidate and coerce.

Nash had to wait until he got into the office to read over the details that hadn't been released to the media. His boss planned to update the Denver field office regarding what happened to Lynn and see if they had any new information. He also thought that Special Agent Becca Hammond might be useful providing support on this. Nash didn't have a problem with any assistance, so long as no one got in his way.

"As far as I'm aware," he continued, "TRK didn't send letters to his victims beforehand. Which means a different person, one with a grudge against you, wrote them. Mailing them from different post offices, moving strategically closer, could indicate they are preparing to take action." Almost like a countdown. "Or at least they want you to think that they are. Perhaps to scare you."

It was one horrendous thing after another for Lynn, but something about this bothered him beyond the fact that she was the target.

The letters combined with the assault last night could be a coincidence. A big one, possibly where the article about Lynn had set two different things in motion around the same time.

He believed in coincidences. They happened every day. The trick was being able to discern when something was more than coincidence.

"Well, it's working." She exhaled a shaky breath. "I'm downright terrified." Trembling, she wrapped her arms around herself protectively and cast a despondent look at him.

If he were working a case, this was where he'd step away, giving the civilian space to emotionally gather themself.

Although Lynn needed him to do his job, she also needed the things she'd asked for from him in the past.

Nash reached out and brought Lynn close, pressing her to his chest. She shivered harder, burying her face in the crook of his neck and slipping her arms around him. Caressing a hand up and down her back, he vowed to find a way to keep her safe.

"You're going to be okay. I won't let anyone hurt you."

Part of him was glad Lynn was leaving town for a few days and wouldn't be alone. He needed her safely out of the way so he wouldn't be distracted worrying about her.

Before she headed out of town, he did have a few questions for her, but it was probably best for him to wait until he showed Holden the letters. That way she wouldn't have to go through it twice.

His cell phone rang.

They pulled apart. She wiped at her eyes as he took his phone from his pocket. The number was to the sheriff's office, Holden's extension.

They must be on the same wavelength.

"Hey," Nash said. He'd spoken to Holden earlier that morning to coordinate. While Nash was with Lynn, Holden was going to begin investigating. "Did you find anything?"

"As a matter of fact, I did. You and Lynn should both get over here as soon as possible."

HOLDEN WAS EAGER to share what he'd discovered. As soon as Nash and Lynn arrived, he beckoned to them through the glass window of the chief deputy's office that overlooked the reception area.

"How are you feeling today, Lynn?" he asked as they entered the office.

"As well as can be expected, I suppose."

The two removed their coats and were about to sit.

"Actually," Holden said, "why don't you come around the desk. I've got something to show you."

Nash came to his right side and Lynn over to his left.

"After you mentioned that TRK surveilled his victims for days before striking—" he said to Nash, and a small gasp from Lynn cut him short.

Her face was pale and pinched.

Immediately Holden realized Nash had neglected to tell her, most likely due to its alarming nature, but he hadn't been told to censor anything. "Sorry about that." He looked from Lynn to Nash on guidance about how to proceed. He didn't want to step on any toes.

"It might be better if you got a cup of coffee," Nash said, "while I go over this stuff with Holden. Most of it will be boring."

Lynn straightened. Pushing her long brown hair behind one ear, she turned on him. "Do you think I'm too weak to handle this?"

"No." A nerve pulsed in Nash's jaw.

"Then why is this the first I'm hearing about this?"

Nash shoved his hands in his pockets. "It's just that you've already been through so much. I thought it best to do whatever I could to lessen the strain."

"I was shocked to hear that a serial killer has been watching me for days, but that doesn't mean I need to be protected from the truth." Strength flowed in her voice and gleamed in her eyes. "I need to hear everything. I'm staying."

Holden braced for Nash's response. His buddy tended

to take a hard stance when he believed his actions were in the right. Considering they were talking about protecting Lynn from troubling information, he expected Nash to double down.

"You heard the lady," Nash said. "Let's get on with it."

That was surprisingly easy, but Holden wasn't complaining. He gave a curt nod. "As I was saying, Lynn mentioned that she'd left USD the same as she had every Thursday. I figured the guy might have been captured on camera while learning her routine." The good news was the grocery store had an outdoor camera mounted on the southwest corner of the building trained on the parking lot. He typed on his keyboard and brought up the security camera footage he'd obtained earlier from the store. "First, I looked at last night's feed to see when he got into her car, so I had something to go on to identify him."

He hit Play.

The video showed Lynn pulling into the lot and parking. She grabbed her stuff, got out, locking the door as the lights flashed, and hurried off to her class.

"There," Holden said, pointing at the screen. "Watch." Seconds later a man with a dark hood pulled over his head, dressed in dark clothing but without a big, bulky coat, as if to stay light and limber, strolled past the lot and headed in the same direction. The use of a winter vest and lack of a heavy winter coat made him stick out. "How long would you say to walk to USD?" he asked, pausing the video.

Lynn shrugged. "I don't know. Six to seven minutes."

"Four and a half," Nash said.

That was eerily precise.

"Note the time." He restarted the footage and fast-forwarded to the part he wanted them to see. "Less than ten minutes later, the same guy is back. Long enough for him to make sure you went inside USD and return to the lot."

"Why is he lurking in that corner?" Lynn asked.

The man stood in the shadows observing his surroundings.

"To stay out of the direct view of the camera," Holden explained. "Unfortunately, in every shot of him we can't see his face clearly but can tell he's not yet wearing the ski mask you described." Her assailant had shielded himself, either by luck or by intention. After rewinding and replaying the clip on the computer umpteen times, Holden banked on the latter. "All we know about his identity so far is that he's a white male, six foot, medium build. Any hits we might get in the database on his DNA will take a little time."

Lynn leaned in toward the screen. "What is he doing? Why is he just standing there?"

"Waiting for the lot to clear of foot traffic," Nash said. "So no one will notice him when he breaks into your car."

As soon as the lot was clear, with no one walking to the store or their car, the man leaped into action. He moved quickly, purposefully straight to Lynn's car. Taking out a slim jim, a universal lockout tool, he looked around, ensuring the coast was still clear. He used the tool to jimmy open the door.

Lights flashed on the car and the alarm must've sounded.

The man slipped inside the front seat. He bent over, disabling the alarm, and the lights stopped flashing. Then he climbed into the back seat.

"Goodness," Lynn said, sounding astonished. "I had no idea it could be done so fast, so easily."

Provided you knew what you were doing, it was shockingly simple. People were more vulnerable than they realized, particularly if they drove an older model that lacked a decent anti-theft system.

It was a good thing Lynn's car was totaled. Knowing her, the next one would be an upgrade in terms of it being something new. Some of the latest modern cars were almost impossible to steal.

"So, he stayed cramped in my back seat for almost an hour?"

Holden nodded. "Sure did." Incredible patience. "This was a week ago." He rewound the footage back to the previous Thursday and hit Play again once Lynn's vehicle came into view. "Same guy appears." Holden pointed. "He never parks in the grocery store lot. Must be somewhere down the street, but I couldn't find any cameras that might have picked him up. This time, he doesn't return until you do." He advanced the footage, showing them.

"What do you think he was doing while I was in class?" Lynn asked.

"Watching," Nash said. "From someplace that allowed him to keep an eye on you."

Holden nodded in agreement. "My thoughts precisely. I checked security cam footage and caught him going into the coffee shop across the street."

"That's more good news. The angle of the camera in there would cover the registers as well as most of the shop."

"It does," Holden said, in a flat tone.

"But?" Nash said, waiting for the other shoe to drop.

"They suffered a power outage a couple of days ago that wiped their stored security footage."

"Do you think that's a coincidence?" Lynn asked. "Or do you think he had something to do with it?"

"My guess is that he was covering his tracks," Holden said.

"This guy is meticulous." Nash's gaze bored into his. He didn't like this scenario, and Holden understood why.

One, it suggested that the assailant was a thorough planner who was thinking two to three steps ahead. Better to have a hothead, someone who acted impulsively. That type was far easier to catch. Two, it suggested that the guy could still be out there, watching and waiting for his next opportunity since he'd gone to the trouble of covering his tracks.

"I hate this." Nash took off his Stetson and raked a hand through his hair before putting it back on.

Holden hated it, too. Lynn had come very close, within a razor's edge, of losing her life last night. And they were no closer to neutralizing the threat.

"There's more," Nash said. He took out resealable bags that contained what appeared to be correspondence and set it on the desk. "Someone has been sending these to Lynn over the past several weeks."

Holden perused them while Nash explained what he'd ascertained thus far. The third letter made his gut clench, and it only got worse from there.

"Do you know anyone who might have a grudge against you over what happened with Crombie?" Nash asked her.

"Enough to send those dreadful letters?" She shook her head. "But it could be anybody from Jackson to Laramie."

"My gut says it's closer to home," Nash said.

"Best place to start looking," Holden agreed, "and then widen our search from there."

Lynn crossed the room and sat in one of the two chairs facing the desk. "The reason I left town for Fort Collins weeks ago for a few days was because Mrs. Crombie tracked me down at Delgado's. She screamed at me. Said horrible things. She even threw a glass of water in my face."

Holden leaned forward. "Mrs. Crombie was initially quite vocal around town about her feelings toward you." The woman had just lost a son and was grieving. She had needed someone to blame. Lynn fit the bill. "But after that news article came out," he said, and Lynn cringed, "she seemed satisfied."

She had stopped ranting and raving to anyone who'd listen, stayed home, stayed quiet.

"Or perhaps justified. To continue in a more vicious way," Nash suggested. "With those letters."

Holden glanced down at them again. His heart went out

to Lynn. "Only one way to find out." He stood and put on his jacket.

"I'm coming with you," Nash said, then he turned to Lynn. "I'll grab the bag you packed from the truck. Call Yvonne. Have her pick you up here. Don't leave. Don't forget to write down your travel details and don't go anywhere alone. Got it?"

Lynn nodded. "I understand."

Chapter Ten

On the drive, Nash couldn't stop worrying about Lynn.

TRK had attacked his previous victims while they were unsuspecting and alone. Lynn was no longer either, and she was leaving town. The methodical killer presumably had opportunities to corner the women at their homes, or even to strike while they had slept. Instead, TRK had always waited until the women were in public, where they thought they were safe, to show them otherwise.

All those things should've lessened Nash's concern, but it did nothing to bring him peace of mind.

As they pulled up to the Crombie property, Nash wished he'd driven his truck to give him a better sense of control over the situation. On most cases, he preferred to work alone, do things his way. At Holden's suggestion, they'd taken his sheriff's vehicle to eliminate any confusion on the part of the Crombies as to the nature of the visit.

Holden pulled up the driveway and parked in front of the one-story log house that sat on ten acres of land on the outskirts of town. The place had gorgeous views but looked as if it was in much need of repairs.

"Let me do most of the talking in there," Holden said, killing the engine.

"Why is that?" Nash asked as they climbed out of the vehicle and headed for the house.

"Shirley Crombie is not what I'd call a pleasant woman.

This is a sensitive area for her, as well as for you. A cooler head asking the questions might be prudent."

The curtains moved aside in one of the front windows. Someone was watching them. From the way the light hit the window, casting shadows, it was impossible to discern male or female.

Nash got his badge ready to show, moving it from his back pocket to one in his coat. "I'm capable of conducting an investigation that centers on Lynn."

They walked up the porch steps. The wood groaned beneath their weight.

"This isn't a matter of capability," Holden said. "Only practicality."

"Fine." He'd do his best to let Holden take the lead, but he'd step in if and when he felt it necessary.

Holden opened the screen door and knocked. "Albany County Sheriff's Department."

There was movement inside, close by. Something heavy was set down on the floor near the doorjamb. Possibly a shotgun.

The door opened. A woman in her late sixties or early seventies with weathered skin covered in liver spots and scraggly white hair framing her face stood in the doorway. She was slim but with a sturdy look about her. "What do you want?"

"Afternoon, ma'am." Holden tipped his hat at her. "I'm Chief Deputy Powell and this is Special Agent Garner."

Nash flashed his badge, giving her a chance to properly see it.

"We'd like to ask you a few questions," Holden said.

Her gaze bounced between them. "About what?"

"Do you mind if we step inside out of the cold?" Holden asked.

"As a matter of fact, I do." She closed the front of her sweater and folded her arms.

Most folks would've been more hospitable, inviting them in, offering them a cup of coffee.

Not Mrs. Crombie.

Nash took a step to the side for a better view inside the doorway on the other side of her. He glimpsed the distinctive outline of a double-barrel shotgun.

Catching Nash's eye, Mrs. Crombie leaned forward, snatched the screen door and slammed it shut. "Ask your questions right here."

"All right, ma'am." Holden took out his pad and a pen. "When was the last time you've seen Dr. Lynn Delgado?"

"I don't know. I suppose it was when I threw water in her no-good face over at Delgado's."

"I imagine you must still harbor a lot of resentment toward her," Holden said.

"Then you imagine correct. What's this about? Did something happen to her? Did she get her just deserts?"

As if the self-inflicted suffering Lynn was putting herself through wasn't enough.

"Do you wish her any ill will?" Nash asked, unable to stay silent.

Holden sighed heavily and flashed him an annoyed glance, making his disapproval known.

In a relationship, keeping quiet was no problem, but Nash wasn't used to sitting on the sidelines when it came to working a case. Holden was reminding him why he preferred to work alone, without interference or judgment, like he was getting now.

Mrs. Crombie cocked a bitter, lopsided grin. "I wish someone would blow a hole in her the way she did my boy. Do you consider that ill will?"

Nash clenched his hand, keeping it at his side. "Yes, ma'am, I do."

She sucked her teeth. "I don't turn the other cheek. I believe in an eye for an eye."

"Would you take it upon yourself to carry out such judgment?" Holden asked.

"Please." She waved a wrinkled hand at them. "If I was going to do it, it would've already been done. Before my boy was cold in the ground. First, that woman ruined the life of my oldest and then took the life of my youngest. Shameful, I tell you." Mrs. Crombie sneered. "And shame on both of you for coming here, disturbing my peace about her."

"Who's your eldest?" Nash asked.

"Phil."

"Philip Pace," Holden clarified.

"He's the only good thing to come from my first marriage," she said. "But I wouldn't let those boys call each other half brothers. No sirree. Blood is blood. And they loved each other. Phil tried to warn Andy about that Delgado woman after what happened to Phil. Andy should've listened to his big brother."

Nash braced against a gust of frigid wind. "What happened to Phil?"

"The court ordered him to take mandatory anger management classes with her as a condition of his bail. Twelve one-hour sessions. As if he needed even one. He wanted to get through it faster. Double up in a week. Dr. Delgado told him no. Then when he missed a couple of classes, she reported him to the court. Phil begged her not to. He swore he'd make it up. But she did it anyway. The court threw Phil in jail for a month. Because of her, being so cold-blooded, he missed the start of a great new job and the beginning of a semester of classes over at LCCC," she said, referring to the Laramie County Community College. "To make matters worse, the court told him that he was going to have to start those pointless classes all over again from the start. Can you believe that?"

"Why was he ordered to anger management in the first place?" Nash asked.

"Phil got into a bar fight. Broke someone's jaw. Boys are going to be boys."

"That wasn't his first offense if the court was making him take classes," Holden said.

"He's got a little bit of a temper. That's true," she said with a nod. "Got it from his father. Not his fault."

Nash bet that Shirley Crombie was the kind of mother who absolved her sons of their responsibilities as citizens, as decent people, and rushed to bail them out of difficult situations rather than holding them accountable. Such actions would only make a person worse, not better.

Behind Mrs. Crombie, a man, slightly older than her, in his midseventies, plodded by, slowing as he peered their way to see who was at the door.

"Mr. Crombie," Holden called out, with a wave, "can we speak with you for a minute?"

"He don't got nothing to say to you. Either of you." She looked over her shoulder at him. "Go watch your program, George. I'm handling this. Go on."

The old man kept shuffling forward, disappearing out of sight.

"Where can we find Phil?" Nash asked.

"Beats me," she said with a shrug. "Have you tried his apartment?"

"I doubt he's sitting in his apartment waiting for us to arrest him," Holden said. "When was the last time you saw him?"

"After the court issued a warrant for his arrest for not taking those classes all over again." She rolled her eyes. "Since then, we haven't seen hide nor hair of him."

Holden wrote in his notebook. "When? What month? What day?"

"I don't remember the day. It was sometime back in October."

Around the same time something or someone had set Andy off.

The TV blared to life in the next room.

"Turn it down!" she called out, spinning around. "George! It's too loud! I can barely hear myself think." The volume lowered. "He needs to watch his shows. Loves his daily programs. Probably more than he loves me."

For some reason, that wasn't hard to believe.

"Do you have any relatives around here Phil might turn to for assistance?" Holden asked.

"Not no more. My kin's gone. George doesn't have anybody else. Phil's father, Terry, has people in Idaho, but we don't talk to them."

"What about family friends?" Holden asked.

"Nope."

Nash gritted his teeth, his patience beginning to wear thin. "Do you know anyone in Jackson, Cheyenne, maybe Riverton or Casper?"

She shook her head. "We don't know nobody in any of those places. We've done for ourselves. Relied on ourselves. We don't need nobody else," she said with pride.

"Have you sent Dr. Delgado any harassing letters?" Nash asked.

"Letters?" A perplexed look crossed her face like she genuinely had no idea what he was talking about. "Why would I waste the money on a stamp to send her a letter when I can throw another glass of ice water in her face? Or better yet, a cup of piping hot coffee."

Was she sure Phil got his temper from his father? If so, the man was cursed with two sets of bad genes.

"One more thing," Nash said, "does *hangdog* mean anything to you?"

"Hang what?" She reeled back with a grimace. "Did somebody hang her dog? Is that what this is about? I would never hurt a defenseless animal."

Well, that was good to know.

"Delgado wronged this family, that's a fact, but I guarantee you we ain't the only ones she's angered. Ask around, you'll see. And if her dog got hung," she added, the features of her face contorting in a nasty expression, "and it broke her heart, made her cry for days on end, then good for her."

Grief notwithstanding, that was a spiteful woman.

"We won't take up any more of your time," Holden said. "If you hear from Phil—"

Mrs. Crombie slammed the door in their faces.

They turned into the icy wind, headed for the steps. The air was bitter cold. Snowflakes were falling heavily. The roads would be blanketed with a couple of inches within the hour.

"What do you think?" Holden asked him.

Shirley Crombie didn't have the intelligence or the patience for a snail-mail campaign. "I don't think she's behind the letters."

"Neither do I. But Phil on the other hand…" Holden gave a one-shouldered shrug. "A man who was taking classes at LCCC and has nothing except time on his hands while he's in hiding might."

"You think he'd take the risk, making the drive to Jackson and the other cities when there's a bench warrant out for him?"

"Not much risk," Holden said, "if he's doing it at two a.m. and doesn't commit any traffic violations to cause him to get pulled over. A weekly road trip to mail a threatening letter might be his only outlet."

Nash opened the car door and got in. "Mind if you focus on finding him while I concentrate on TRK?" He couldn't wait to get into the office and dig into a couple of things that had been bugging him.

"Divide and conquer sounds good." Holden hopped in. "Mrs. Crombie might be onto something about someone else in town having an axe to grind with Lynn. I'll look into it, but first, I think I need to get a warrant."

Nash climbed in and shut the cold out. "For what?"

"To search that house." He hiked his chin up at the Crombie place. "I'm pretty sure Phil is hiding in there somewhere. Like she said, they rely on themselves and don't need anyone else."

"How long to get the warrant?" Nash asked.

"All depends on the judge."

As Holden backed out of the driveway, Nash's cell phone rang. He pulled it from his pocket. The number was for the Denver field office.

"Special Agent Garner," he said, answering it.

"I would have at the very least," snapped the male voice on the other end, "expected a call from you considering this involves my sister."

Jake Delgado. Fellow agent who trash-talked his colleagues for a hobby.

"I followed procedure." Nash kept his tone level and his temper in check. He'd notified his boss late last night that Lynn appeared to be the target of TRK. His boss had said that he would update the Denver office in the morning.

"To hell with procedure. How about a little common courtesy?" Jake asked.

"If Lynn thought you needed to be notified, she would've picked up the phone and called you herself."

"I just got off the phone with her," Jake said. "Thank goodness she's on the road, on her way out of town. Otherwise, I'd be in the car, headed there now." Denver was an easy two-and-a-half-hour drive from Laramie. "My sister gets a pass, considering she was the one who was attacked and in a car crash. It's understandable if *she* wasn't thinking clearly. But *you*? What's your excuse?"

Nash didn't need one, and he didn't bother to offer any.

"Garner, you should know better. How would you feel if it was your sister?"

He didn't have any sisters, but if this was happening to one of his brothers, he would've appreciated a phone call. In hindsight, he would've handled things differently. Not as if he needed to give Jake any additional reasons to dislike him. "I'm a little busy investigating, trying to make sure a serial killer doesn't get your sister. So if there isn't anything else—"

"I hope you're not going rogue, doing this by yourself."

"Rogue would imply that I'm breaking the rules. This might be personal, but I'm doing it by the book."

"We have partners for a reason on cases like this. I doubt you can be objective considering this involves your *ex*."

Throw salt in the wound. "Could you be objective? Would you let someone else head up the investigation?"

"I wouldn't do it alone. That's my point."

"I've coordinated with local law enforcement and I'm working with the chief deputy of the sheriff's office closely on this. My boss has also brought Special Agent Hammond up to speed." Becca was staking out Lynn's place in case TRK went there looking for her. "If I need her assistance, I've got her number on speed dial. Provided that's your only concern, let that put your mind at ease."

"When you're involved, my concerns are endless."

"I'm the first to admit that my record isn't spotless." He'd been written up for insubordination, once, as well as excessive use of force. Also a onetime offense. Never the same mistake twice. "But my success rate is above reproach." Every scumbag he'd gone after, he'd nailed.

A loud exhale on the other end of the line. "I didn't only mean professionally. Look, I don't think you're a good match for my little sister. She needs someone softhearted with a PhD or MD. Someone who's going to make her laugh and take her dancing. Not someone like you or even me, for that matter," Jake said.

As far as Nash was concerned, all of that might be true, but it was up to Lynn to decide those things for herself. "None of that is any of your business."

"You're right, and it's not important right now. My only priority is keeping her safe. Okay. I don't want anything to happen to Lola."

Hearing the nickname her family called her with such affection made Nash think how it might be true that he'd always held back in his relationship with her. For one, he had never used the moniker. To him, calling her *Lola* would've indicated he wanted to take things to the next level. Something he hadn't been ready for.

Nash took a deep breath, realizing Jake's current hostility was more about his worry for his sister than his dislike of him, the ex. Fighting with him was a waste of both their energy. "I'll do everything in my power to make sure nothing happens to her." He'd risk his life to protect hers in a heartbeat. "We're going to find this guy. And stop him. You've got my word."

Snowbound

Chapter Eleven

Snow fell in big, thick flakes so dense that the wipers struggled to clear arcs across the windshield. Rounding the last bend, the tires of Yvonne's four-wheel-drive scrabbled for purchase on the slick surface as the Red Tail Lodge came into view.

The log cabin sat perched on a hilltop in the Snowy Range, surrounded by the Medicine Bow-Routt National Forests. Smoke wafted from the chimney. On the front door was a modestly decorated wreath.

They pulled in front of the wide wooden staircase and came to a stop. Lynn gave a silent sigh of relief that they'd made it there safely.

"Finally," Yvonne said, sounding as relieved as Lynn felt.

They got out of the Jeep, and snow crunched underfoot. Lynn took in a deep breath of clean mountain air. Nothing in the world smelled better.

She looked around at their remote surroundings.

Clouds darkened the late-afternoon sun, bringing an early twilight. A heavy layer of snow blanketed everything, turning the landscape into a picturesque winter wonderland. The small lodge rented rustic cabins for those looking to unplug and unwind surrounded by the splendor of nature.

Down the hill behind the main house, she spotted four cabins spaced far apart to give guests their privacy.

They hurried up the steps and pushed through the front door, which had a welcome sign hanging in the middle of the wreath. The heavenly scent of cedar and pine enveloped them. An enormous Christmas tree that looked professionally decorated stood twenty feet tall beside a roaring fire. The main house was deceptively large on the inside.

They stomped off the snow from their boots on the mat before stepping onto the hardwood floors.

Wearing a faux-fur zebra-print headband, fuchsia parka that somehow didn't clash, slim-fitting winter pants that highlighted her svelte figure, and with her dark blond hair pulled into a sleek ponytail, Yvonne looked ready to hit the slopes in Aspen instead of lying low in a rustic cabin. It was a shame some hot single guy would miss seeing her in that sexy outfit.

They both headed for the front desk where a man in his seventies rose to his feet.

"Welcome to the Red Tail Lodge. You two must be Ms. Lamber and Ms. Delgado. I'm Earl Epling, the owner. Please call me Earl."

"Hello. I'm Yvonne."

"Nice to meet you. I'm Lynn."

"Glad you two made it with the storm that's rolling in."

"Storm?" Lynn asked, taking off her gloves. "I thought we were just getting some snow."

"The most recent weather report mentioned something about the pressure center shifting, becoming so low that it increased the wind and intensity of things out there, turning it into a deadly storm. Heavy snow, freezing temperatures, possible ice. But not to worry. Now that you're here, this is the best possible place to be in a storm. Your cabin has plenty of firewood and your fridge is stocked per Ms. Lamber's instructions."

"Drop the 'Ms.' Call me Yvonne." Her best friend flashed

a smile at Earl. "Thank you for helping me out on that front. You saved us a trip to the grocery store."

Lynn thought it would be a horrible inconvenience to ask someone at the lodge to pick up groceries for them if they were willing to do it at all. Yvonne had disagreed. Working in hospitality, she was confident that almost any accommodation could be met, especially if you were willing to pay a little extra to make it happen.

"Not a problem," Earl said. "My son, Ryan, got everything in town. He brought it up the mountain, loaded it in your cabin and then hightailed it out of here before the storm."

"Thank you," Lynn said to the kind owner, but she also patted her friend's arm in thanks as well. Yvonne was a great planner who prepared for everything. Lynn never should've doubted the idea that had saved them time and made the start of their vacation much easier.

Easy was what she needed right now.

"We usually provide breakfast and dinner up here at the main house," Earl said, "but with it being so close to Christmas and you two being our only guests, my wife, who does all the cooking, is visiting with the kids and grandbabies. So I didn't charge you anything extra for the grocery run."

"We had no idea we were the only guests. I'm sorry we're keeping you from your family," Lynn said, hating to be an intrusion.

"Don't be silly. That's why we're here." Earl gave a smile so warm it turned his affable features ruddy. "To help folks get away from it all. There was another couple scheduled to come tomorrow, but they've pushed their arrival back a day to be sure the storm has passed and the roads have been cleared. Better safe than sorry. That's what I always say." He set a brochure down on the counter. "We've got a variety of movies and a ton of books you're free to borrow. The VHS cassettes and DVDs are all listed in there," he said, and she exchanged a look with Yvonne that screamed *who owns a VCR anymore?* "Also there's a map of trails in the area if you're interested once the storm dies down. Now I just need a credit card. Should I run the same one on file that the reservation was made under?"

"Yes, that would be fine," Yvonne said since she had booked the place.

Lynn had planned to cover half the expenses before she'd canceled all her cards after her wallet had been stolen. "I'll pay you back my share."

"Are you kidding me? Not a chance. This is my treat."

Yvonne had been horrified as Lynn had recapped everything she'd been going through on their ride up the mountain. She only wished she had shared the threatening letters sooner with Yvonne and Nash. Trying to deal with this nightmare on her own hadn't been working. She'd always considered herself a strong, independent woman, but there came a point where everyone needed help.

"Thanks," Lynn said, trying to hide her embarrassment. She'd make it up to Yvonne on her birthday next year.

Earl turned and grabbed a key from one of the hooks on the wall behind him. "You're in cabin number two. It's the first one on the right. You can drive down the hill and park in front of your cabin, if you want, but with the heavy amount of snow we're about to get, it'll be difficult to get out. I recommend leaving your vehicle parked where it is and carrying your bags down."

Yvonne sighed. "I hope you're up for a workout."

"We can handle it." They both were thirty years old, made it a point to stay fit and had packed lightly for their five-day getaway. Both of them only had overnight bags that they could sling on their shoulders. No heavy wheeled luggage to trudge through the snow.

"Would you like snowshoes?" Earl bent down, grabbing a pair from under the counter, and held them up.

Lynn and Yvonne exchanged a questioning look, debating whether to take them.

"I think we'll pass," Yvonne said. "There's only three or four inches of snow."

"Suit yourself. If you need anything else, give me a ring," Earl said. "Your cell phones won't work around here, but the cabins have landlines."

Lynn took her phone from her pocket. There was a *no service* message in the top right corner of her screen. "What about Wi-Fi?"

"Sure, here in the main house. Afraid not in the cabins though."

When the Red Tail Lodge website had mentioned *unplugging* from the world, Lynn hadn't realized that they'd meant it literally.

"Your Honor, with all due respect, this is unacceptable." Standing in front of the massive mahogany desk that ate up most of the square footage in the judge's chambers, Holden put a fist on his hip. "I don't think you understand the urgency of the situation."

"First," Judge Don Rumpke said, lifting a finger, "when anyone prefaces a statement as you did 'with all due respect,' it means whatever follows is most assuredly not respectful." Don unzipped his black robe, hung it on a hook and put on his suit jacket. All bad signs. "Second, there is nothing wrong with my comprehension of the situation. You've simply failed to convince me of this sudden supposed urgency."

"As I've already explained, there is an outstanding bench warrant for Phil Pace. Dr. Delgado is being harassed. She's received five threatening letters, and I suspect Phil may be behind it. There's no reason to deny the warrant to search the Crombies'."

"Repeating yourself without adding any new information does nothing to persuade me." Don began packing up his briefcase. "The Crombie residence was searched by—" he paused as he leafed through some pages "—Deputy Livingston in your department when the bench warrant was first issued."

Holden must've been out that day, because he would not have let Livingston go to the Crombies' alone. Not only was Livingston constantly slipping up, making inexcusable mistakes, even for a rookie, but Shirley would've pushed him around, preventing him from doing his job properly. The new sheriff, Daniel, had still been getting to know everyone, feeling out personalities and assessing capabilities.

"Phil Pace was not found on the premises," Don continued.

"Mrs. Crombie probably assumed the house would be searched within the first forty-eight hours and that afterward they'd be in the clear. I have reason to believe that he's hiding in that house."

"I don't doubt you. Phil is most likely squirreled away in a closet somewhere. That's why I've agreed to issue the warrant *tomorrow*."

Holden gritted his teeth. "It has to be today, Your Honor. It can't wait."

"Oh, really?" Don slipped on his wool coat and put his fedora on his head. "Look outside and tell me what you see."

Holden didn't bother looking. "Snow, sir."

"Know what I see? A blizzard. That storm is going to shut down roads, knock out power for some, the unfortunate ones with no generators. Every time we get one of these major snowstorms, emergency services will get flooded with calls. Now, you're asking me to tap vital resources to search the Crombies in this." Don waved a hand toward the snowstorm outside. "If Phil is hiding somewhere in that house, as he probably has been for the past two months, he'll still be there tomorrow. He's not running out to mail any letters and make a great escape in that wicked weather. As I've said, I don't see the urgency. It can wait. As for me, I'm going home to snuggle with my wife in front of the fire and enjoy a cup of hot cocoa."

"If Phil is responsible and he does get away, this will be on your head, Your Honor. I would hate to have to file a complaint to the Commission on Judicial Conduct and Ethics. Neither of us would have to worry about it coming to that if you just issued me the warrant. Today."

"You of all people are threatening me?" Don exhaled with a look of exhaustion. "You are on thin ice as far as I'm concerned, Holden James Powell," Don said, and Holden took it as another bad sign when one's elder called them by their full name. "The previous sheriff, your boss, turned out to not only be corrupt but also in cahoots with your former fiancée." Don paused for effect, letting the wretched but truthful statement hang in the air like a bad odor. "And you claim to have had no idea."

"That's true." To his shame, when the scandal broke, he had been as shocked as everyone else, but also humiliated. How could he have not known? Had he been too trusting? Too naive?

Too obtuse?

The worst part wasn't that he'd become the laughing-stock of Laramie. No, what was even worse was that it had been a bigger blow to his pride than his heart. It made him realize that he hadn't been in love. The engagement had been her idea, and he'd agreed because the relationship had been easy, effortless. Turns out that it had been without any problems, as if they were a match made in heaven, because she had been using him the entire time.

"The whole town has heard some cockamamie story of how you, Mr. Smart-as-a-Whip, were suddenly clueless when it came to the two people you were closest to, who were doing dirty business right under your nose." Don neglected to mention the fact that one of his fellow judges had been less than honorable—corrupt—and also embroiled in the scandal. "They may buy it. Part of me wants to as well because I know your parents and I know they raised you right. But had it been up to me, you would've been fired to clear out the stink from the sheriff's department and to let it have a fresh start."

The declaration was like a cold, hard slap in Holden's face.

He straightened and stood his ground. "Good thing then that it wasn't up to you."

"Be grateful you still have your position as chief deputy sheriff. Be grateful I'm going to give you your warrant. Tomorrow. Be grateful you're free to accomplish other important tasks instead of utilizing precious resources that'll be needed elsewhere," Don said.

His plate was full at the moment. He had Mitch compiling a list of other individuals enrolled in the anger management program that Lynn had been running. Once that was done, he'd have to start knocking on doors and asking questions.

"Before I leave," Don said, "I'd like to hear your gratitude, if you'd like me to sign your warrant."

Holden swallowed the anger rising in his throat. "I earned my position as chief deputy. I'm not proud of what happened with the previous sheriff and my fiancée. In fact, I'm embarrassed by it. But I didn't break the law. I've done nothing but uphold it and I deserved to keep my position." Despite what everyone in town thought to the contrary. "Thank you for your time, Your Honor. But I will no longer be needing your warrant."

Frowning, Don rocked back on his heels. "What are you going to do without it?"

"There's more than one way to skin a cat." He knew a

bail bondsman itching to get his hands on Phil Pace. If Phil had listed his parents' place as an address he frequented on the bail agreement, then the bail bonds agent had statutory authority to search the premises without a warrant. Knowing Phil, not planning to jump bail, he'd put the Crombies' residence down on that agreement.

"Well, if your clever little plan falls through, I'll be here tomorrow, waiting for you to come back to me with hat in hand."

Holden hoped with every fiber of his being it wouldn't come to that. "Enjoy your cocoa and give Mrs. Rumpke my regards."

THE ONE THING niggling at the back of Nash's mind was when TRK marked Lynn's car. Living across the street from the University of Wyoming Police Department meant that the front of her house along with the garage where she kept her car were covered by security cameras. Still, he'd followed protocol and reviewed the footage to be sure he hadn't overlooked anything.

Her car hadn't been marked at her home. Of that he'd been certain.

As far as he knew, she hadn't resumed any of her volunteer activities. The only other places she went regularly were USD, Turning Point and the Silver Springs senior living center.

One phone call had given him access to the surveillance footage of the nursing home, and according to their logs, Lynn had most recently visited last Saturday, six days ago, between one and three in the afternoon.

Nash rewound the footage to twelve fifty-five. Two minutes later Lynn pulled into the lot adjacent to the living center and parked. From the way she grabbed her purse and hopped out of the vehicle, she seemed to be in a hurry.

Hair hanging loose around her face and wearing a dress and heels, she walked at a brisk clip and disappeared inside.

Not long after, a man with a black hoodie over his head, same lightweight vest as worn in the previous video of the supermarket, crossed the street and entered the parking lot. His head was lowered and canted away from the camera. He was aware they were there, once again, deliberately trying to avoid getting his face captured.

Taking out a pocketknife, the man knelt at the back of Lynn's vehicle and began scraping a mark on her bumper. His head was on a constant swivel to the left and right, staying aware of his surroundings.

Nash's attention shifted across the screen. Lynn shoved through the front door of the center, headed back for her car.

But the man was still there.

She pressed the key fob and her lights flashed.

He crouched lower for a second, and, timing it just right so as not to be seen, he scurried around to the right side behind another vehicle as Lynn reached hers. She ducked inside, grabbed something from the back seat, and emerged holding a bag from the bakery that was down the street from Delgado's. Her aunt Miriam loved their pastries.

The man could've stayed low, hiding until she went back inside. Instead, the son of a gun stood, strode around the other car, pushing his hood back to reveal his face, and approached Lynn. He stopped her in the middle of the parking lot, keeping his back to the camera, and spoke to her.

A chill danced across Nash's skin watching Lynn smile and nod as she pointed to the facility. The jerk even made her laugh right before she gestured for him to come into the center.

He shook his head no and glanced at his watch. Then he said something else to which she nodded again and waved goodbye.

Four minutes and twelve seconds. That's how long TRK had spoken to Lynn.

She'd been open and engaged, with no hint of wariness. She'd seen his face, heard his voice, laughed at his joke, invited him inside, waved to him as though…

As though TRK had passed himself off as a concerned family member contemplating putting a loved one in Silver Spring. That had to be it. The only reason Lynn wouldn't have been more guarded talking to a random stranger.

All this time he'd been tracking her, getting up close and personal, and she'd been none the wiser. But now she could identify him. With a physical description, they would be able to have a forensic artist draw an image of him. Then they could plaster his face everywhere.

Nash took out his cell and dialed Lynn. It went to voice mail without ringing.

Why would she turn off her phone? What if he needed to reach her with updates?

He tried once more. Straight to voice mail again. "Hey, Lynn. It's me. Give me a call as soon as you get this message. It's urgent."

As he disconnected, he had a bad feeling in the pit of his stomach.

This time he tried Yvonne. He still had her number saved in his contacts.

Same thing. Not a single ring, and voice mail picked up.

Maybe they had both deliberately shut off their phones for the weekend. But what were the odds of that? Lynn and Yvonne treated their phones like they were appendages. Always connected to them. One of them might have turned it off, but not both.

Cold dread was a sick knot in his gut.

There could be an acceptable explanation. Perhaps they were out of range of service.

Or…

Nash blocked the horrible thought that sprang to mind before it could sprout roots and germinate. Overreacting and jumping to the worst conclusion would get him nowhere. Only talking to Lynn would calm his fears.

He turned back to his computer to look up the number to the mountain retreat and call the front desk.

His chest tightened. The only problem was he'd never gotten the name of the place. All he knew was that it was a lodge somewhere in the state that rented cabins. He'd pressed her for the details, and she'd finally agreed to give them to him. Back at the clinic, she'd had the notepad in her hand and was about to write everything down until he had sidetracked her by getting into their relationship. Then she'd told him about the letters and had focused on the new threat.

Before heading out with Yvonne, maybe she had still written it down.

He made a quick check with Holden to see if she'd passed along anything to the people in his office, where he'd left Lynn to wait for her girlfriend.

No one had seen her leave any info for him, no notes.

He checked his phone messages. Nothing.

Had she deliberately kept it from him—was she that desperate to be out of his sphere?

Due to the theft of her wallet, he had authorization to monitor her credit cards in case the guy was stupid enough to use one. So far, he hadn't been. But that permission also allowed him to dig through recent credit card authorizations.

He brought up her transactions and perused the last two months when she would have booked the cabin.

Dead end. Yvonne must have reserved it. Getting access to her credit card transactions would require a warrant.

Tamping down anxiety, he needed to tackle this logically. There was no reason for them to drive three hours or longer. Not when there were mountain ranges offering stunning vistas so much closer to home.

Maybe she'd told Jake the name of the place when they'd spoken earlier. Not that he was looking forward to another chat with her brother.

Nash went to recent calls in his cell and dialed him.

"Agent Delgado."

"This is Nash."

An exasperated sigh. "I'm in the middle of something urgent, can this wait?"

"I'll make it quick," Nash said. "Did Lynn happen to tell you the name of the place where she's staying?"

"Um," Jake hesitated. "I thought she had, but thinking back on it, no. It's some lodge in the mountains. I was so upset about her getting attacked and neither of you calling me that I didn't focus on it."

At least Nash wasn't alone there. "Did she mention their driving time?"

"A couple of hours," Jake said, confirming Nash's best guess. "Why? Did something happen?"

"She can identify the man we're looking for, but she doesn't realize it. I found a video of him talking to her." Nash withheld the part about it happening outside of Silver Spring because he didn't want to unnecessarily upset her brother. Seeing the playback had made Nash's blood boil. "Her cell goes straight to voice mail."

"Did you try Yvonne?"

"Of course. Same thing."

"The service connection can be dodgy up in the mountains."

"Yeah, I realize. That's why I wanted to call the place. Reach her via landline. I'll make a list of the possible retreats and start checking with them."

"One sec." The line sounded muffled, like Jake had put his hand over the phone. "Hey, I've got to go. Something urgent has come up. If you haven't been able to reach her by morning, let me know."

"Sure." Nash stabbed the end call icon.

Damn it. He banged his fist on the desk in his cubicle, drawing a few looks from the others on the task force.

Drawing a breath, he faced his computer.

Beginning his search with retreats around Laramie Mountain, Medicine Bow Mountain and Snowy Range were his best bets. He'd make a list of all of them in the area and going in alphabetical order, call them one by one until he reached her.

Chapter Twelve

"This is perfect." Lynn set down the map of trails she'd been looking at and took the filled champagne flute Yvonne handed her. "Just what the doctor ordered." Her body ached all over, but she decided to forgo taking any more NSAIDs in lieu of some medicinal bubbly.

Yvonne poured a second glass of ice-cold champagne and sat on the bearskin rug beside her in front of the fire. "I can't believe we planned this vacation to distract you from the fact that it would've been your anniversary with Nash and it turned into a much-needed great escape from town. Never in a million years would I have imagined you being targeted by a homicidal maniac."

That made two of them.

Lynn hadn't mustered the courage to go into detail about the threatening letters and had kept the description of them vague. A serial killer was enough to flatten the vacay vibe. Plus, she didn't want Yvonne giving her any more pity looks.

"Speaking of which, I should probably call Nash and let him know that I got here safely."

"A little worry can do wonders to make the heart grow fonder. You're safe. You're with your bestie. Let him wait until the morning. Trust me."

Maybe Yvonne was right.

Lynn had left the details of where she was staying with

Deputy Livingston. If Nash really needed to hear her voice, he'd call the Red Tail Lodge.

"So, you spent the night with Nash." Yvonne flashed a coy smile. "I want to hear all the juicy details."

Sipping her bubbly, Lynn leaned back against the sofa. "Nothing juicy to tell. I spent the night at his place. Not in his bed." Although there had been a part of her that had longed to curl up beside him, absorb his warmth, his comfort. "He only offered because he's the kind of man who does the right thing."

"Oh, please." Yvonne waved a dismissive hand at her. "He's the kind of man who'll seduce you out of your knickers given the chance." They both laughed. "There's nothing wrong with that, and yes, he's also a good guy. Very loyal *and* he likes to snuggle. That's really hard to find."

"Not if I get a dog. They're loyal and the right breed will cuddle with me."

More laughter as they clinked their glasses together.

"Seriously, I was rooting for you two," Yvonne said. "I like him. You were so relaxed around him. You always looked happy. Practically glowed around him, like you radiated joy from the inside out."

"Yeah." Lynn sighed with disappointment. "When things were good, they were the best. But he won't talk to me. How am I supposed to know who he really is? How he feels about things? About me?" She set her glass on an end table. "The entire time we were together he never said the three words."

"I. Love. You." Yvonne's voice was singsongy and playful.

The words had slipped from Lynn's mouth one night at dinner. Nash had looked like a june bug caught in a zapper. Immediately, she'd taken it back, claiming the timing was wrong. Then he'd gotten a work call and left.

She hadn't brought it up again. Neither had he.

"Ten months," Lynn said. No declarations of love. No

letting her in behind his emotional bulwark. No sharing his past. It was too much.

"I've had a lot of guys say it to me, usually after I've rocked their world in bed, and do you know how many of them meant it?" Yvonne formed a zero with her fingers. "Talk is cheap. When you were with him, did you feel loved?"

Lynn shrugged. "I think so." She had felt adored, sexy, safe. Seen, like he knew her, but she wanted to know him in the same way.

"Are you sure that he won't eventually open up under the pressure of your superhero therapist skills given enough time?"

Time was what he had asked for. "But how much?" Shouldn't she follow the same advice she gave her clients? Express your expectations. Set a deadline to see results and stick to it. She was done with dating around and was ready to settle down. Start a family. "Aren't we here to talk about anything but this?"

"I'm sorry." Yvonne topped off her glass of champagne. "You're absolutely right. How does steak and a rom-com sound?" She patted the thick stack of chunky VHS tapes on the floor next to the DVDs they'd also picked out. "Nothing sappy. Something to make us laugh out loud until our stomachs hurt."

"Sounds like you're reading my mind."

Yvonne wrapped an arm around her shoulder and pressed their temples together. "It's all going to work out. You'll see. In the meantime, I'll do my job and keep you distracted without a care in the world. I'm even going to do all the cooking. You won't have to lift a finger since you wouldn't let me take you to that magnificent ranch at Elk Creek. The one with the luxurious spa."

The ranch with cabins looked like heaven. But paradise was pricey. A hundred and fifty dollars for a manicure, three hundred for a facial, four for a massage. None of which included the cost for the cabin. She'd rather put that money toward her down payment for a house or shoes or purses. All of which would last a lot longer than a few hours of pampering.

"This is what I really needed," Lynn said. "Quality time with you away from the real world." Not thinking about anything serious. Forgetting her troubles.

"No better way for us to continue our escapism than with a movie and more champagne."

"ARE YOU SURE there's no way I can persuade you to do it today?" Holden asked, speaking into his cell phone as he walked down the hall of the Albany County Courthouse toward the sheriff's department.

"Sorry, man. No can do," Trevor said. "I'm in Cheyenne, visiting my mother, and there is no way I'm driving back to Laramie in this weather."

Holden turned left down the next hall. "But it's Phil Pace we're talking about." Just as he'd suspected, Phil had listed the Crombie residence on the bail agreement.

"I'd love nothing more than to get my hands on that weasel and wring his neck, but I can't do it today. No one in their right mind would in this weather. I'll be back the day after tomorrow."

Two doors down another corridor, he came to the open set of double doors with Sheriff's Department stenciled on the front and waltzed inside.

"That's too late." Holden would have his warrant before then.

"I don't know what else to tell you. Sorry."

He pushed through the half door at the reception counter and acknowledged Mitch Cody with a nod. "Yep. Thanks anyway." He hung up and put away his cell.

Mitch got up from his desk and cut across the room, headed toward him.

Holding up a hand in greeting to the sheriff, who was on the phone across the hall in the larger office, Holden traipsed into his own office with Mitch close on his heels.

"Who burst your bubble?" Mitch asked.

Holden must've looked as defeated as he felt. Even his bail bondsman wasn't willing to venture out in this storm. "The Honorable Judge Don Rumpke." The judge was going to love seeing Holden with hat in hand tomorrow morning. Not wanting to rehash everything with Mitch since he'd have to do so when he updated the sheriff, he changed the subject. "What did you find?"

"I have ten names for you," Mitch said.

Jeez, that sounded like a lot. Holden had expected five, tops. He took the list from Mitch and looked it over. "Why are people divided into two columns? What's AM and DV?"

"Anger management and domestic violence."

Weren't they both about anger? "What's the difference?"

"I don't know. One's about beating up people in bars and throwing a fit at work while the other is about beating your spouse?"

"We should probably ask a professional." The distinction seemed important. He picked up the phone and called Dr. Jennings over at the Turning Point clinic. His voice mail picked up, stating that he was retiring and referring all calls to Lynn. *Great.* Holden looked up his cell phone number and tried that.

The call was answered on the second ring. "Hello."

"Dr. Jennings, this is Chief Deputy Holden Powell. I had a quick question. I'm going to put you on speaker. I have Deputy Mitch Cody with me."

"All right."

He hit the speaker button and put down the receiver.

"We know Lynn was treating people in the anger management and domestic violence programs. What's the difference between the two?"

"Well, in the former, the program focuses on anger as a misunderstood and misaligned emotion, which often follows fear, depression, stress, or a perceived threat or personal attack."

"Like starting a bar fight after you feel verbally provoked or threatened?" Holden asked.

"Yes. It could even be something like a supervisor demotes someone and that person lashes out in response. Domestic violence on the other hand is about power and control. That program deals with male and female socialization, male domination, interrupting the cycle of violence. It doesn't focus on saving relationships, but rather on ending abusive and violent behavior."

"So if a husband felt that the program was a threat to his marriage," Holden said, thinking out loud, "because it might result in his wife leaving him, could he in turn view Lynn as a threat?"

"Oh, yes, definitely," Dr. Jennings said. "That's why I handed off both programs to Lynn. It was one of the conditions of her joining my practice."

Rather than taking the heat, Jennings had thrown Lynn into the fire. "Is there anyone in particular who stands out in your mind as being likely to go so far as to harass her, but anonymously?" He wasn't sure if Jennings was aware of the letters and didn't think it was a good idea to unnecessarily share that information.

"Sure," Dr. Jennings said. "Any of the people in the domestic violence program. Take your pick."

Holden stared down at the seven names in the DV column. One woman. Six men.

But only one person concerned him. Todd Burk. He belonged to a motorcycle gang called the Iron Warriors. The club had suspected ties to illicit activity. Nothing they'd been able to prove so far. At least half of the members were rotten apples, real dregs of society. Todd was one of the worst. He wasn't married but had a girlfriend who lived with him. She always refused to press charges against him, no matter how badly he had hurt her. Once Todd had beaten her in public, in front of witnesses willing to make sworn statements.

Unfortunately, the corrupt judge who had been on the Iron Warriors' payroll had ordered Todd to take the domestic violence program instead of jail time.

Getting to Todd meant going through the Iron Warriors. A bridge he didn't want to have to cross.

"I also remember Phil Pace getting quite irate with Lynn one day in the waiting room," Jennings said, "because she wouldn't let him circumvent the rules of the program. He's the type who wouldn't threaten an authority figure outright and would prefer an anonymous method."

"Thank you for speaking with us, Dr. Jennings."

"Happy to help in any way that I can."

"Stay safe in this storm." Holden disconnected. The perspective was insightful, but it also brought him back to square one. He needed to find Phil Pace.

Then, if necessary, he'd talk to Todd Burk.

NASH HAD CONTACTED almost every cabin retreat within a two-hour driving range of Laramie. Twenty-two so far. Everyone he had talked to didn't have Lynn or Yvonne listed as guests. He had thought for sure the lodge at the Elk Creek Ranch with the fancy spa would have been the one he was looking for. Yoga, massages, facials and gourmet meals were right up Lynn and Yvonne's alley. But no such luck.

There were only three others left on his list. All in the Snowy Range. The Moosehead Dude Ranch, Painted Cup Cabins and the Red Tail Lodge.

THE LANDLINE RANG in the kitchen.

Yvonne paused the '80s movie that neither of them had seen before, starring Melanie Griffith, Harrison Ford and Sigourney Weaver.

"I'll get the phone." Lynn stood and crossed the open space to the counter. Like everything else at the lodge, the phone was old school. It was lime green, attached to the wall and had a long, coiled cord. She took the receiver from the hook. "Hello."

"Is this Yvonne or Lynn?" Earl asked. His voice was tight and curt, lacking the cordial tone from earlier.

"This is Lynn. Is everything okay?"

"I need Yvonne to come up here. Her credit card didn't go through."

"Oh. We're sorry about that." Too bad Lynn didn't have one to give over the phone. She couldn't even offer a check that wouldn't bounce. "I can put her on. She probably has another one that—"

"No, no, that won't do," he said, his voice sharpening. "I need to see Yvonne right now. Have her come up to the main house to get this sorted." The line disconnected.

"How rude," Lynn said, staring at the receiver in her hand. "He hung up on me."

"What's going on?"

"Earl said your credit card didn't go through." She hung up the phone. "He wants you to come up to the main house. Apparently taking care of it over the phone isn't good enough."

"That's weird." Yvonne set down her glass, grabbed her boots that were near the fireplace and tugged them on. "There's plenty of room on the card I gave him, but sometimes my bank will decline a large charge until they've checked with me first." She picked up her cell and frowned at the screen. "Of course, they have no way of contacting me." Yvonne took her coat from the hook, slipped it on and grabbed her purse. "I might have to call to get the charge to go through. Worst case, I have another one I can use."

Lynn picked up her boots from beside the hearth. "Do you want me to come with you?"

Yvonne gave her a displeased look that warned her to stay put.

"Okay," Lynn said, raising her palms. "How about I get dinner started?"

"Only if you don't mind. I'm supposed to cook for you."

Her bestie really was the best. "It's no trouble, and I'm willing to let you do all the cooking tomorrow."

Yvonne opened the door, the old wood groaning on the hinges, as she let in a breeze along with thick snow flurries. "Good grief, there's almost a foot of powder. I should've taken the snowshoes." She sighed. "I like my steak medium rare." Then with a wave she was gone.

Exactly the way Nash liked his steaks. Lynn had become a pro at whipping up simple meat-and-vegetable dishes with a baked potato on the side for him. He always gushed over her cooking, proclaiming it better than what was served at Delgado's. She wasn't sure if she had entirely believed that, but it had made her feel good to hear it.

They worked well together on so many levels, but not the most important one.

Maybe she needed to take a leap of faith and have confidence that he would one day give her what she needed. But if she gave him more time and he didn't follow through, could she trust herself to walk away from him again?

It had taken all her strength to do it once before. She wasn't sure she was strong enough do it a second time.

Lynn washed her hands and pulled out the meat. After prepping the boneless rib eyes, liberally sprinkling them with salt, she found a cast-iron pan and put it on the stovetop to get it hot. She washed and chopped the vegetables for a salad and set it all in a large bowl she'd taken from the cabinet. After rummaging through drawers, she found a wine corkscrew to open a bottle of Bordeaux so it could breathe before dinner. It was a 2010 Château Branaire-Ducru. Yvonne had brought the good stuff.

She went to the window adjacent to the door and pulled back the curtain. The sun had set. Moonlight shone on the bright white snow. A pristine landscape.

Since the front of their cabin faced the other cabins a few hundred yards away, it was hard to see the hill that led to the main house and whether Yvonne was on her way back down.

In the kitchen, the oil she'd added to the pan shimmered and moved around fluidly when she tilted it, letting her know it was hot enough to get a crust on the steaks. Just as she was about to put the rib eyes on, she reconsidered. The meat would only take three minutes per side, and she didn't want the food to be cold by the time Yvonne got back.

How long did it take to run a credit card?

The west side of the cabin, where the two bedrooms were, faced the hill. From there, she'd be able to see all the way up to the back door of the lodge. She passed the first, smaller room Yvonne had claimed and went to her bedroom for a better look. Without bothering to turn on a lamp, she peeked through the curtain, hoping for a glimpse of Yvonne.

At the sight of movement headed down the hill, she smiled. "Took long enough," she said to herself.

She focused a little longer on the figure stamping through the snow as it drew closer and into the moonlight. No fuchsia coat. No slim, feminine physique.

Her scalp prickled with foreboding. It wasn't Yvonne.

Black hood pulled up over his head. Dark winter coat and pants. Fists covered in black leather gloves. Moonlight reflected off the white skull face on his ski mask.

It was *him*.

A rush of fear jetted through her veins as she stared, eyes narrowing, fingers curling at the edges of the curtain. The snowy image in front of her wavered and blurred. Her knees weakened, and she forced herself to blink, to breathe, to focus.

How did he find her? Had he followed her there?

On the ride up, it hadn't occurred to her to check the mirrors or keep an eye on the cars behind them. She hadn't imagined he would track her to the lodge.

She'd underestimated him.

Her breath tried to escape on a sob, so she clamped her lips together as she stared out the window.

He moved quickly, effortlessly through the snow down the hill.

Toward her cabin. To torture her. Rape her. Then kill her. That's what he did to his victims.

A scream built in her chest, but she kept her mouth pinched closed. She sucked in shallow, rapid breaths through her nose, trying to think.

What was she going to do? What happened to Yvonne? Did he hurt her? Kill her?

She'd put her best friend and Earl in danger.

Oh God. He was almost there. Any minute, he'd be at the cabin.

Spinning around, she bumped into a nightstand. The lamp on top of it wobbled, but she steadied it before it fell, not wanting to make any loud noises.

She ran back to the kitchen. The pan on the stove was starting to smoke, forming a gray cloud in the room. She grabbed the phone from the hook. Pressing the receiver to her ear, she went to punch in 911 on the keypad, but there was no dial tone. Not even static. She depressed the hook switch several times.

Still, nothing.

The line was dead.

Chapter Thirteen

Pressing a hand to her temple, Lynn whispered to herself, "Think, come on, think…"

A hundred thoughts raced through her head at breakneck speed. But one stuck.

Run! Go, go!

She had to get out of there. Right now.

Pushing aside the suffocating panic, she gathered herself. She threw the phone down, the receiver knocking over the roll of paper towels onto the stove. She flew to the front door and locked it. Turning, she caught sight of the flames.

The paper towels had caught fire. If she went to the kitchen, she could put it out before it really got started. But there was no time to worry about a fire.

She raced to Yvonne's bedroom, engaged the push-lock on the doorknob and shut it from the hall. Once he got inside, he'd reach that bedroom first. If he found the door locked, he'd waste time getting in to look for her. At least she hoped so.

Then she hurried into her room. Locked that door, too. She pushed the heavy, solid oak dresser, shoving it against the door to slow him down.

Now what?

She looked around frantically. For what in particular, she didn't know. Her gaze landed on her purse. She grabbed it from the bed, unzipped it, snatched the pepper spray and stuffed it in the pocket of her jeans.

What if she hid, waiting for him to get close enough, and sprayed his eyes? Then what? Pepper spray would only slow him down. Not stop him.

Maybe she could run to another cabin and hide there. Wait until someone showed up.

But who?

She had no idea what happened to Yvonne or Earl. The landline was down. If the fire in the cabin got big enough, someone would eventually see it and come. But how long would that take? How many hours?

No one knew she was in immediate danger. She hadn't even bothered to call Nash when they'd arrived like she'd promised.

The thought of Nash was like a beacon in the darkness, guiding her. She needed to get out of the cabin and go somewhere with cell reception. But first, she had to find out what happened to Yvonne.

Lynn grabbed her phone and shoved it into her other pocket. Escaping through the front door was out of the question.

Her darting gaze settled on the window, her feet moving toward it before she had consciously made the decision. Up close she noticed the window had a triple track system. One pane on the inside, a storm window on the outside and a half screen in between.

As she unlocked the interior window, there was the unnerving slow groan of the front door.

TRK hadn't kicked it in. He must have picked the lock. Now he was inside.

Terror pulsed through her. For a precious second, she froze before hoisting the screen up out of the way and fumbling with the storm-window fastening. There was a click.

She gave it a good shove, swinging the window out, and braced against the blast of frigid air.

She swung one leg over the sill and then the other, dropping to the ground below. A shock of razor-sharp cold sliced through her as her sock-covered feet sank into the snow.

If only she'd thought to grab her boots and coat before she'd bolted from the other side of the cabin.

She reached up to shut the inside window, hoping TRK would waste a little extra time searching the second bedroom as well for her, giving her an invaluable head start. She would need a big lead to get away from him. He was too fast to outrun.

The snow-covered ground was a lot lower than the floor inside had been. Her clammy fingers slipped on the bottom edge of the window as she tried to pull it closed.

To her left was an old, chunky HVAC unit. She climbed on top of it, giving her the extra height that she needed. The heavy thud of footsteps crossing the floor deeper in the cabin echoed in the bedroom. A second later the smoke detector went off, filling the air with a high-pitched beeping noise.

She slammed the interior window shut, followed by the exterior one, and didn't allow herself to hesitate, taking off up the hill.

In case he glanced out the window, looking for her, she stuck close to the tree line, where she could blend in with some concealment, and stayed off the main pathway that was bathed in moonlight.

Pumping her arms and driving her legs as fast as possible, she plowed through the drift, sinking calf-deep in the snow with every stride. She looked down, noticing her all-too-visible tracks. They might as well have been glowing in neon paint, spelling out: this way to your next victim. As soon as he ventured out to look for her, all he had to do was follow the fresh broken trail of snow.

Maybe she should have forgone the cover of the trees and used Yvonne's tracks. Too late now.

The blustery wind whipped snow around her. The cold gnawed down to her bones.

The slope of the hill, the icy gusts, the freezing snow all slowed her to a nightmarish pace. But she couldn't think about it. Dwelling on it would only impede her further.

Keep moving.

Sweat beading at her hairline, she drove her body harder, willing herself up the hill. Her feet and hands were numb with cold, but she pushed grimly toward the lodge.

She ran four miles every other day. The main house was less than four hundred yards away now. She could do this. She had to.

Snow fell in a dense curtain. One TRK would soon part.

Go, go! Faster, faster!

Her mind was spinning, her body protesting, but she kept running. With each step, she expected to hear footfalls gaining behind her, to feel hands grasping for her, or the excruciating jolt of a bullet ripping through her. But she didn't dare look back, not even a glance over her shoulder. She kept her sights locked on the lodge that was slowly—much too slowly—getting closer.

Ignoring the pain and fatigue settling in her body, she ran onward. Hard. She scrambled from the tree line and sprinted for the house, reaching out for the stair railing like a lifeline.

Her feet slid on ice as she hit the back steps of the lodge, nearly losing her balance. She dashed up the stairs to the back door. It was wide open. The screen door was the only thing partially keeping the snow out. She swung it open and hazarded a quick glance back.

TRK was nowhere in sight.

She slammed the solid door shut and engaged the dead bolt. Whirling around, she ran through the house to the front desk. She stumbled to a stop and gasped at what she saw.

Yvonne was on the floor behind the desk with her hands tied. Earl was a lump beside her, also tied. They weren't moving, but they were gagged—and tied up.

That meant they were alive. He hadn't killed them.

Lynn hurried to Yvonne and put two fingers to her carotid artery to be sure. There was a pulse. *Thank God.* She checked Earl as well and was relieved to find him still breathing.

She looked around for a knife or something to use to cut them loose, but there wasn't anything at the desk.

Hurry up! You can't stay here waiting for him to catch you.

A tear leaked from her eye at having to leave Yvonne, but she was alive. As long as Lynn stayed away from her, she'd be all right.

Lynn unzipped her friend's boots. Moving quickly, she ditched her soaked socks, trading them for Yvonne's, and then put on the warm fur-lined boots. With Yvonne's hands tied, she couldn't take her coat, but Lynn would freeze to death if she didn't find something to put on. Or somewhere warm to hide. She checked Yvonne's pockets and found the car keys.

Yes!

Knowing she didn't have a prayer of outrunning him, couldn't hope to evade him for long, she concentrated on getting to the car. It was her only chance.

She threw open the front door and hustled down the stairs of the lodge. Stumbling down the last two steps, she fell onto her hands and knees into the snow, bringing her eye level with the wheels.

Both tires were flat. She climbed to her feet and pushed around to the other side of the vehicle. The tires on the left side were also flat.

All four had been slashed to the rims.

A chilling, mind-numbing fear seeped through her. He had cut her off from any help and made sure to leave her no way to escape.

She'd have to risk going on foot. In the middle of this blizzard.

Hitting the key fob, she popped the trunk. Yvonne was always prepared for anything. There had to be something in the trunk that she could use.

Her gaze locked onto the blue-and-black winter road-side kit. She had no idea what was inside, but it had to be exactly what she needed. There was nothing else there.

Out in the elements she'd need a coat. With the kit under her arm, she rushed back inside the lodge. Lynn spotted Earl's coat on a hook behind the desk. She hurried over and grabbed the heavyweight hooded parka. Her gaze flew to the snowshoes under the counter. Those would come in handy, allowing her to move faster, so she snagged a set and headed for the door.

A squawk of static stopped her in her tracks.

"Big Bear," a male voice said down the hall. "This is Little Bear again. Over."

A radio. There was a radio.

She dashed back through the house to where she thought the sound had come from into the living room.

"Big Bear, it's been fifteen minutes and you're still not answering. If you're in the commode, drop the newspaper and pick up. Otherwise, Mama is going to have a fit worrying."

Following the sound of the voice, she tracked the radio to a table on the far side of the wall.

She picked up the handset of the CB radio and pressed the button for the microphone. "Hello, hello."

"Who in the tarnation is this?"

"We need help up here. Call the police and the fire department," she said, and once the words left her mouth, she realized that local first responders would have no idea what they were dealing with, and it was too complicated to explain in a matter of minutes. If she had that long.

"Put my father on, Earl Epling. Right this minute."

"He's unconscious, but alive."

"What? Who is this?"

"I'm Lynn Delgado. If this is Ryan, you bought groceries for me and my friend Yvonne Lamber. She's unconscious, too. There isn't time for this. Please, listen to me. Contact FBI agent Nash Garner. In Laramie. Tell him that TRK followed me here. He's trying to kill me."

"Kill you? Is this some kind of sick joke?"

Holding the handset, Lynn walked around the table to the window and pulled the edge of the curtain back for a view of the hill.

Smoke wafted out of the cabin—from the bedroom window. Then she saw him. A streak of black slashing up the white hill.

He was coming. Moving to a jog.

Dread cut to her core.

"Oh God, he's coming back to the lodge," she said into the microphone. "Please, I'm begging you. Contact Special Agent Nash Garner. Laramie. My name is Lynn Delgado. Tell him I have to leave the lodge." But where was she going to go? Her thoughts careered back to the map she had perused earlier. The trails in the area had all been highlighted. One led to help. "I'm going to try to make it to the park ranger station. The tires of our car were slashed. I have to hike there. Remember, Nash Garner. If you don't contact him, TRK is going to kill me. Do you understand?"

"Yeah, okay. I'll do it."

Lynn snapped off the radio, ensuring it wouldn't draw TRK's attention once he got back inside. Turning, she made a beeline for the main door.

By the front desk, her eye caught a glimpse of the maps. She snagged one, disrupting the pile, and rushed out through the front door. The park ranger station was less than six miles away, but she didn't want to have to rely on memory to find it in the middle of a snowstorm.

On the porch, she shoved into the coat, yanked the hood up over her head, fit her boots into the bindings of the snowshoes. Hastily, she wrenched the straps around the toe as well as the heel, tightening them. The width of the snowshoes—oversize tennis racquets—would make getting down the steps tricky.

She hit the stairs at a ninety-degree angle, taking them one at a time at a hurried pace.

At the bottom, she ran. Once she made it to the woods and onto the trailhead she needed, she no longer felt any fear. Only adrenaline and a hard-edged determination to survive. No matter what it took.

Despite how crazy it sounded in her head, she prayed for the snowstorm to worsen. Strong sustained winds and heavier snowfall. It would decrease her visibility, but his as well, making it harder for him to track her, if not impossible.

The only thing that might be able to save her was a whiteout.

Chapter Fourteen

Unable to sit still on the stool at Delgado's, Nash shifted in his seat, tapping his fingers on the bar while he waited. Never before had he felt so useless, so impotent.

Holden sat beside him, nursing a draft beer. "Just because you haven't spoken to Lynn, doesn't mean something has happened to her."

"The only cabin retreat I wasn't able to reach was the Red Tail Lodge in the Snowy Range. The call wouldn't connect. The operator said that their line wasn't operational."

"It could be down because of the storm."

True, but Nash wasn't counting on it. His mind kept circling like a buzzard around one thought. TRK might have followed her up to the retreat.

Earlier on their way from his house headed to the Turning Point clinic, Nash had been wary, ensuring they hadn't been followed, and again, after they had arrived at the clinic, he had surveilled their surroundings.

But his vigilance had faltered once he'd learned about the threatening letters and Holden had called.

If someone had been waiting at the clinic, watching Turning Point in the hopes that Lynn might show up there, and had followed them at a cautious distance to the sheriff's department, it was entirely possible that he might not have noticed. Possible that he had been too preoccupied and in a rush.

"You can't even be certain she's staying at the Red Tail," Holden said.

"I could kick myself for not asking her the name of the place." How stupid could he be? He'd told her to write it all down for him, but he could have just asked for the damn name of the lodgings. With that, he could have gotten the rest of the info on his own.

"You had a lot on your mind. It's understandable."

No, it was inexcusable.

Nash had been somewhat relieved that she would be in a remote place, out of harm's way. Now he couldn't reach her. She might be cut off, with no way to send him or anyone else a message. An easy target. Too easy.

Isolated.

Snowed in.

With no help around for miles.

He hoped to high heaven that Lynn was all right.

But something in his gut told him that she wasn't. He was going to assume the worst until he knew, without a doubt, that she was safe and sound.

There was only one way to find out.

His cell phone rang, vibrating on the polished wood in front of him. He knew who it would be and answered right away. "Tell me you can do it," Nash said without preamble.

"I've got clearance from the sheriff," Mitch said.

Relief washed through Nash, tempered by deeper worries.

"But don't get too excited just yet," Mitch continued.

"What's wrong? Spit it out."

"The snowstorm went from bad to being on steroids. It's not safe to take off in these high winds," Mitch said, and Nash clenched his jaw in frustration. "I checked with the meteorologist over at the news station. In an hour or so, the storm will start to pass. Once the winds die down to fifty-five miles per hour, we can go."

Lynn might not have that long, but he was out of options. Driving there was impossible. The Wyoming Department of Transportation had closed portions of I-80 due to the storm. WDOT wouldn't deploy crews to clear and reopen those parts of the interstate until later tonight. Wyoming Highway 130, also known as the Snowy Range Scenic Byway—a popular "cut-across" for travelers—closed annually every winter because snow lingered late and returned early at the upper elevations. To reach the lodge from Laramie left him one choice. Going by air.

"I have to warn you," Mitch said. "In order to do what you're planning the wind speed needs to be under forty miles per hour. Even at that, you HALO jumping in under these conditions is completely bonkers."

His opinion meant something. Not only had Mitch flown Black Hawks, but he had spent a couple of years as a competitive skydiver before joining the sheriff's department. He understood the risks involved better than most, but there was nowhere suitable around the lodge for Mitch to set down and land.

Once again, Nash had no better option other than strapping on a parachute and jumping.

"I'm always game for a rough, wild ride," Mitch said, "but you could get killed doing this."

"I've done dangerous jumps before."

"From a helicopter?" Mitch asked, sounding like he thought Nash was short one too many brain cells.

"No." Never. The only thing more dangerous than leaping out of a perfectly good airplane was doing so out of a helicopter, much less in the middle of a winter storm. But making sure Lynn wasn't in danger was worth any risk. "This really can't wait any longer than absolutely necessary. I have to get out there."

"Understood. I'm with you all the way. Once a brother-in-arms, always," Mitch said. "I'll run home and grab one of my parachutes and a harness for you." He lived within walking distance of the sheriff's department. In fact, his apartment was right above Delgado's.

"Thanks. What kind of chute?"

"Ram-air."

Self-inflating airfoils, known as parafoils, gave the jumper greater control of speed and direction. They also spread the stress of deployment. He couldn't ask for a better chute. "I appreciate it."

"Since we have to wait a little to take off, I suggest you get something to eat and gather everything else you'll need."

Done. After he'd called Mitch asking for the favor, Nash went home and got his gear together. "I'm at Delgado's as we speak with Holden waiting on some grub."

Before a mission, he always ate. That's what the army had taught him. Once an operation had started, it might run longer than anticipated. The last thing you wanted was to have to fight or hump out a fellow soldier on an empty stomach. If time permitted, it was best to sleep as well. It didn't matter if you weren't hungry or tired or thought yourself too nervous to eat; that was just the way it was done.

"Order me whatever you're having," Mitch said.

"Will do." He disconnected and took a heavy drink of his water. "Once the wind settles so it's safe enough to take off, we're going to head out," Nash said to Holden.

They had both agreed that it was best to let Mitch square away getting clearance without Holden present. The sheriff had already been apprised of the situation, and Nash didn't want Holden putting himself in a precarious situation, where he might look to be showing a bias because they were friends.

The sheriff was a reasonable man, the facts spoke for themselves, and Mitch was the pilot, who had to fly under less-than-desirable conditions. There was no reason for Holden to stick his neck out.

Holden patted his back with a look of relief. "You'll get out there and see that she's fine."

Nash hoped so, but he doubted things were fine.

Holden's head turned and whatever he spotted had a smile spreading across his mouth. Nash followed his gaze to Grace Clark.

She was a natural beauty. Tawny brown complexion. Long dark hair that was more curly than wavy. Petite build. But she was young. Nash guessed twenty-four, twenty-five tops. He wasn't sure how her much older brother would feel about a seven-year age gap between his little sister and Holden, and there was also the scandal to complicate matters.

But whenever his buddy laid eyes on her, he lit up like a football stadium on Super Bowl Sunday.

"Here you go," Grace said. As she went to set down a plate of cheeseburgers and fries in front of each of them, Holden took his directly from her in midair.

It was something his friend always did, but this time Nash noticed the way Holden brushed his hand against hers, like he was using any excuse to touch her.

"Thank you," Holden said. "That was quicker than expected."

"You said you were in a rush, and I aim to please." Grace flashed a dazzling smile.

"You're doing a fine job of pleasing me," Holden said. "I mean, here in the restaurant. You're great at this."

"At serving food and drinks?" she asked, her smile turning coy. "Well, thanks for the high praise."

"I'm sure you're great at plenty of other stuff, too," Holden said, and Nash shook his head, hoping his friend would do himself a favor and talk a little less. "How did you do on your final exams?"

"I aced them."

"See. I knew it. Working here full-time while earning your advanced degree and you make it seem effortless. You'll graduate with honors."

Grace smiled. "Can I get you two anything else?"

"Another order of the same," Nash said. "Mitch is coming."

"I'll go put in a third rush order. Hold the pickles and add mayo."

Holden sat up taller on the stool. "You've got an excellent memory if you remember how he takes his burger."

Grace chuckled. "You guys have been in here every night since…" Her voice trailed off as she looked at Nash, and he wasn't surprised that she was aware of the breakup. Grace cleared her throat. "With customers as frequent as you guys, any waitress-slash-bartender worth her salt would remember. I'll go put that order in." After another smile, this one shaky, less confident, she turned and left, pushing through the left swing door that led to the kitchen.

"Why do I always sound like an idiot when I talk to her?" Holden stared at the double doors like she might reappear any second.

"Why don't you just ask her out?" Nash picked up his burger and took a bite. He wasn't the least bit hungry. Worrying about Lynn had sapped his appetite, but he shoveled a few fries in his mouth, too.

"She's the sheriff's sister," Holden said, as though that explained everything.

"So?"

"So? I know what people think about me."

The scandal happened almost a year ago. The old sheriff was behind bars, right along with Holden's ex-fiancée and a corrupt judge. There was a new sheriff in town. Holden had maintained his position and his dignity. Tongues were still wagging with idle gossip, and the occasional side-eye was still being cast, but that would eventually stop.

"And?" Nash asked around the food in his mouth.

"And?"

"Please stop repeating me." Nash didn't have the patience for it tonight.

Holden took a long draw on his beer. "I can't afford to rock the boat with Daniel. He wasn't one hundred percent sure about me or my judgment, but he's given me a chance. I don't want to blow it by messing around with his sister."

"If your intentions are to mess around, then you'd certainly blow it." Nash took another bite.

"I didn't mean it like that." Holden exhaled, his shoulders sagging. "I need to be careful, is all I'm saying. Dating the sheriff's sister, my boss's sister, isn't what I'd call being *careful*."

"Seems like you're overthinking it. You don't even know if she's interested in you."

Holden scowled. "If I asked her out, you don't think she'd say yes?"

Nash wondered what it was like to be Holden, the golden boy—figuratively and literally. High school quarterback selected all-state. Chief deputy with an unblemished record. Blond hair and baby blues women fawned over. Had been next in line for sheriff. Everything came easily to him on his first time trying until that despicable scandal had cast him under a spotlight of doubt.

The sooner he put it behind him, the sooner others would also.

"Does it matter what she'd say?" Nash asked. "Apparently, you're not planning to ask her anyhow."

Holden's face twisted into an expression that made it crystal clear he was torn about what to do. Grace reemerged from the kitchen and headed to the opposite end of the bar to take someone's order. His attention again fastened to her, the look on his friend's face intensifying.

"Eat," Nash said, hoping to distract him, and gestured to Holden's untouched plate of food.

"Eat?"

He was doing it again. Nash grunted his annoyance.

"You're about to jump out of a helicopter in the middle of a winter storm. How can you stomach all that food?"

"Training." There was plenty of time for his food to digest before they'd be up in the air.

"I just wish I knew that Daniel fully trusted me," Holden said, lowering his voice. "You know?"

Not being fired and kept on as chief deputy might be as good as it was going to get. "You may have to settle for him trusting you *enough* instead of *fully*."

These things took time. Trust had to be earned, and Holden had a lot going for him. He had this way of growing on you, endearing himself to people. Before too long Holden would be in Daniel's good graces without question.

The door to Delgado's opened, letting in a gust of cold air. Daniel Clark walked in.

Speak of the devil.

Their gazes collided, and the sheriff's face tensed.

Nash set his burger down and wiped his hands on a napkin as Daniel made his way over to them. "What is it?" He hoped the sheriff hadn't changed his mind about letting Mitch fly him to the Red Tail Lodge.

Daniel took off his Stetson and clutched the cowboy hat in his hands the way a man often did when he was about to deliver bad news.

"Mitch checked with the meteorologist," Nash said. "We're going to wait until it's safe to leave. You don't have to—"

"That's not why I'm here. It turns out that Lynn left a note with Deputy Livingston that she'll be staying at the

Red Tail Lodge. He was fighting with his girlfriend on the phone when Holden checked with him earlier. He was distracted and forgot. Misplaced the note. Not that there's any excuse for his oversight."

Holden rolled his eyes and shook his head while he muttered something about incompetence.

Nash couldn't deny he was irritated as well, but Lynn hadn't forgotten to leave her contact information for him. She'd followed through.

"It's been one blunder after another with Livingston. I plan to have a stern talk with him." A grave look tightened across Daniel's face. "What jogged his memory was a call we just received from the Carbon County Sheriff's Department," Daniel said, and every muscle in Nash's body tensed. "There's been an incident at the Red Tail Lodge."

Nash's heart seemed to stop, his lungs shriveling in his chest, robbing him of oxygen.

"Lynn made it there. She contacted the owner's son on a CB radio and said that TRK had followed her up to the place. The owner and Yvonne were found unconscious and unharmed. Looks like he used chloroform on them. And," Daniel said, hesitating, "Lynn's cabin was on fire."

Nash's mind whirled, his guts twisting. His intuition that something was wrong was validated. "Was she inside?"

"No. They think the fire started before she made contact on the radio, because she told the son to call the fire department."

"How long ago did she make the call on the radio?"

Daniel's gaze fell a moment, then lifted, meeting Nash's again. "Over an hour ago, possibly longer," was the grim response.

"What?" Slamming away from the bar, Nash shoved to his feet.

"The owner's son wasn't sure how seriously he should take the things Lynn said before contacting the FBI like she asked him to. He did call the local sheriff and drove up to the lodge to see for himself first. It took them a while to make it up there on account of the storm."

Holden swore, taking the words from Nash's mouth.

Precious time was slipping away that could cost Lynn her life.

"Lynn asked the son to contact you, specifically. To let you know that she was going to try to get to the nearest park ranger station. On foot."

Things were worse than Nash feared. He scrubbed a hand through his hair. "How far away is the closest station to the lodge?"

"About six miles."

Nash squeezed his eyes shut, trying to stop the sudden roar in his ears. Time stood still. All he felt was pain. Helplessness. Utter fear for Lynn.

Six miles. In a deadly winter storm. On foot. With a serial killer chasing her.

Opening his eyes, he shut down the white noise in his ears. "She's strong. She's smart. She can make it."

Daniel nodded, though he looked doubtful. "Yeah, she will."

"And you'll be there by the time she arrives," Holden said, his voice also uncertain.

Come hell or high water, regardless of strong winds, he would be.

Chapter Fifteen

Lynn slowed to a slog. She had been switching off between jogging and walking and falling behind to plodding when each heavy, ragged breath began clawing at her lungs. The wind had been brutal, viciously lashing her with persistent gusts. Combined with the heavy snowfall, slippery conditions and diminished visibility, it was taking her forever.

She stopped entirely to rest and leaned against a tree for support. Her breath punched from her mouth in clouds. The ache in her body had deepened, sinking down to her bones. Her limbs felt leaden, and she was growing light-headed.

The first time she had taken a break, she'd rummaged through the winter roadside kit. Inside she'd found a foil blanket, gloves, packets of hand warmers—which she'd used immediately in the gloves and boots, a rope, a phone charger, a utility knife she'd put in her pocket, protein bars, a first aid kit, and a flare gun that came with yellow and red shells.

Glancing over her shoulder, she searched for a glimpse of her assailant, but all she saw were trees and a swirl of white. As if her prayer had been answered after she'd fled the lodge, the bad weather had picked up earlier. The storm had raged, visibility practically nil. She had gotten her whiteout.

For the past two hours, she had been relatively safe.

If she had been unable to see more than a few feet in

front of her, then it would've been the same for him. The flip side of her circumstances was she couldn't be sure she was still going the right way with the path covered and unable to see landmarks in the distance.

Now it seemed as though the storm was passing. The wind had died down. The snow had slowed to flurries. She had no way of knowing if he had picked up her trail, and if he had, how far behind her he might be. Every few minutes she would have to check so he didn't come up on her while she was unaware.

If he did, she would be done for.

On the bright side, she should be able to figure out how far she was from the park ranger station. Lynn took out the map along with a protein bar from the emergency kit. Not having had anything to eat for hours, she was famished and fatigued. Maybe food would restore her strength.

She tore into the wrapper with her chattering teeth. Taking a few bites of the chalky peanut-butter-flavored bar, she used the dark outline of the mountains cutting through the moonlight around her to orient herself.

Medicine Bow Peak was the highest point in the Snowy Range. The summit, at little over 12,000 feet, had only been ten miles from the trailhead she'd taken. The Laramie Mountains were to the northeast. A ridgeline she knew well, having seen it every day.

She pinpointed the Sugarloaf Park Ranger Station on the map next.

It looked as if she was going in the right direction but had veered way off the path during the whiteout. According to the map, the fastest way to get back on it was to trek down to the narrow valley that was mostly treeless. The station was less than a half mile on the other side. Based on her estimates, she had traveled at least four and a half miles, maybe five. Her body protested that she had run a marathon, and, at a minimum, she had more than a mile still to go, factoring in the added distance through the valley to get back on the trail.

Maybe she was able to get a signal here. She took out her cell phone. One bar.

She dialed Nash and waited. The call dropped.

Stupid mountains.

It might go through to emergency services. Her cellular provider might not have coverage here, but if any other company did, they legally had to route it to a 911 call center. She tried again, dialing 911. The same result.

Lynn was tempted to scream in frustration, but it wasn't worth if it might give away her location to the man hunting her.

Putting away her phone, she stared at the frigid landscape. The snow was making this so much harder, compounded by the higher altitude.

The valley would be at a lower elevation. From there it should be much easier, relatively speaking.

Lynn looked back again over her shoulder. No sign of him.

With any luck, she might be in the clear.

FLYING IN BAD weather was nothing new to Nash, but from inside the helicopter, with every vibration and shudder of the aircraft, he felt that today was exceptionally bad.

The weather wasn't nearly as violent as it had been a little while ago. Although he had protested, wanting to ignore the warnings about the wind, to reach Lynn that much sooner, the pilot had been wise to delay takeoff.

Mitch seemed to be using all of his concentration to keep them on course. Not to mention in the air as the potential of icing increased.

"Come on, Sienna Rose, you can do this," Mitch said.

"Are you talking to the helo?"

"Yep. I do that sometimes. Mostly when I'm worried."

"Why Sienna Rose?" Wouldn't one or the other suffice?

"Back in the army, I had a girlfriend with that double-barrel name. She was a looker and sweet on me. Told me she was saving herself for marriage. I was cool with that until I found out she had been sleeping around with everyone but me. I swore to myself that if I ever got to be the only person to pilot a particular chopper, to have her all to myself, I'd name her Sienna Rose."

That sounded like one way to work through your issues. Cheaper than hiring a therapist.

Right about now, Nash was willing to pay everything he had to take Lynn in his arms. To get the chance to make up for the all the ways he had been holding back in their relationship.

He hadn't realized that he had been. Hadn't understood that he'd been afraid.

If the last twenty-four hours had taught him anything, it was what real fear was and how the possibility of forever losing the woman he loved at the hands of TRK would devastate him. There was nothing in the world more terrifying.

The woman you love, Nash, think about it.

But there was nothing to think about. In that moment, he had never been more certain of anything in his life. He loved her.

He ran his hand over the buckles of the harness that held the attached parachute he was wearing. The revised plan was to head to the Sugarloaf Park Ranger Station. There was enough space for Mitch to land safely. From the station, Nash would head out on a snowmobile the rangers had left for him to look for Lynn, and Mitch would continue to search from the air.

Based on the flight plan, they would end up flying near the Red Tail Lodge on their way to the ranger station.

Provided things worked out, Nash wouldn't have any need to use the chute.

But he was well aware that sometimes plans were worthless while planning was always essential. Trying to get into the harness inside the helicopter would have been awkward if not time-consuming. It was easier and simpler to be prepared and discard the pack at the ranger station.

Mitch keyed his microphone that was attached on his headset. "One second, Sheriff, let me patch him in so he can hear you as well." He flipped a switch on the panel intercom, connecting Nash's headset to the radio transmission. "Go ahead," Mitch said. "He can hear you now."

"I reached out to the rangers like we discussed. They were finally able to mobilize," the sheriff said. "Unfortunately, the storm slowed them down. Two of them just headed out to conduct a search-and-rescue for Lynn."

Thank God. Additional help was on the way for her. "Good work."

"If I hear anything else," the sheriff said, "I'll let you know."

"Much appreciated."

Mitch flipped the switch on the panel back down. "Hey, look." He pointed out the windshield.

Below them there was a towering plume of smoke rising skyward from a raging fire.

Lynn's cabin.

There were other small cabins in the vicinity of the one burning. On a hilltop sat a larger main house. Flashing red and blue lights of patrol cars were out front along with a fire truck.

They had reached the Red Tail Lodge. Where a serial killer had stalked Lynn and was hunting her now.

Seeing the fire reminded him they were close, keying him up and putting him on edge.

"Do you want me to circle lower for a closer look?" Mitch asked.

Waste time on a scene that Lynn had fled? "No. The

sooner we get to the ranger station, the better." Then he could get out there and search for her, too.

He looked over the topographical map again, focusing on the trailhead Lynn would have taken. But it would have been easy for her to lose her way, at night and in a snowstorm.

Gripped by emotion, he swallowed hard.

There was also no telling if that psycho had found her, gotten his hands on her. Was she alive? Injured and at the mercy of that man? Was it already too late?

Or was she still doing her best to evade that maniac?

His shoulder muscles bunched as a vast hole opened inside him. An emptiness born of the unknown. Magnified by his deepening fears.

He refused to let this get the better of him and tamped down all the negative, destructive feelings into the pit of his soul. The same way he tuned out the beep and whine of the electronics in the helicopter. If he wanted to help Lynn, he needed a cool head, laser-focused thinking, to be ice-cold with determination.

Nash chose to believe she was still breathing. He had to get to her as soon as possible.

Where there was hope, there was a chance.

TRK liked to take his time with his victims, torturing them for hours before raping and stabbing them to death. Nash needed her to survive. To stay alive, no matter what happened.

With renewed purpose, he looked back at the map.

Hang on, Lynn.

Keep moving. Keep fighting.

Hang on.

CLUTCHING THE EMERGENCY kit to her chest, Lynn finished making her way down an escarpment into the valley. Once she reached flat ground, she bent over, putting a hand on her thigh. As she caught her breath, she cursed the madness that had brought her here.

If only she had stayed out of the newspaper, she never would have captured TRK's sick interest.

It took longer than she expected to recover her breath. Lynn was beyond exhausted. Before this she would've called herself in shape. Although it was so cold that her feet and hands were numb, she was sweating buckets beneath her clothes. As much as she ached, and as tired as she was, she couldn't give up. She had to keep going until she reached help. Then she could rest, once she was safe.

Only a little farther now, and she would be at the ranger station.

She should check the time and see if she could get a signal. Her phone should work here in the valley. She fished it out from her pocket.

The screen was dark and wouldn't wake. Her phone was dead.

She should have thought to charge it earlier, but there was nothing stopping her from doing it now. Digging into the emergency kit, she found the phone charger and connected it to her cell. Zero percent flashed on the screen. Throwing both in the bag, she figured she'd give it until 15 percent. That was usually when her phone became reliable for calls.

Setting her teeth and shivering from the cold, she stood and plodded down the valley.

There were tracks in the snow. Not footprints. But those of a small vehicle. From the width and depth, she guessed a snowmobile. The tracks ran ahead of her toward the station.

That was probably where they had started. Maybe rangers were out looking for her. If they were, then it meant that Ryan had passed along her message.

Had she just missed a ranger? Had the noise of the snowmobile gotten lost in the roar of the wind? She wondered how long ago one had come through here. More importantly, how long until one came back?

Closing her eyes, she listened, but didn't pick up on the whirring motor of a nearby snowmobile. But there was the sound of something else. Far off in the distance she registered a distinct thumping beat. Perhaps a helicopter. Not close enough to see yet to be sure.

Nonetheless, she opened her eyes and looked up. The sound seemed to disappear. Had she been mistaken? Turning around, she searched the night sky. Clouds, stars and flurries. No helicopter. Then her gaze fell to the other end of the valley.

Her heart nose-dived to her stomach as *he* rounded a bend, coming into sight.

That cold-blooded killer must've assumed she would try to get to the ranger station and had probably lost his way as well in the storm. The same as her, he was using the valley to make up time.

He was relentless. A hunter.

And about a hundred yards away. Only the length of a football field separated them.

Cold, horrifying dread thrummed in her veins.

Run, run, run!

Lynn's mind screamed at her. She whirled around and ran. The singular thought repeated in her head—a chant of survival.

One foot in front of the other, she drove herself forward, pushing to the point that she was once again, far too quickly, breathless.

And terrified.

Her lungs burning, fear cutting through every inch of her sharp as razor blades.

Glancing over her shoulder, she freaked at what she saw. He'd also had the prudence to wear snowshoes and was running at a dead sprint, eating away at the distance between them at a startling pace.

She stumbled. Caught herself. Ran.

Beating back the panic that caused the surface threads of her sanity to unravel, she kept moving, tramping through the storm. Only she was too slow. Too tired. Even without the snow and fatigue, there was no way she could ever outrun him.

Under these conditions, his advantage was greatly amplified.

Another glance back confirmed her worst suspicions. Swinging his arms to and fro, pumping his muscular legs, his breath fogging the air, he would overtake her in a matter of minutes.

Sheer terror clawed at her. She was running out of time. It was as if a clock was ticking inside her to the rhythm of her heartbeat. The seconds of her life sliding away with each step that man took.

Keep going, she told herself over the sound of her pulse hammering in her ears.

Don't stop.

Run as fast as you can!

Adrenaline propelling her, she struggled to go faster, racing along the valley floor.

Heart in her throat, she pushed through the snow. She could see the woods and the path that led to the ranger station. But she would never make it to the path, much less the station.

Not like this.

What would Nash do? He, with his Special Forces background and FBI experience. The love of her life, who was most at home in the middle of action, on the job, instead of talking about his feelings.

Stay calm.

Use logic.

Then another voice resonated in her ears—*always think outside the box.*

The words solidified what to do. The last thing the man chasing her would expect. The one thing her instincts warned her not to do.

She stopped running.

Unzipping the emergency kit, Lynn forced herself to stand still to keep from spilling the contents onto the ground. She fumbled around inside. Her fingers closed around the hard plastic of the flare gun.

Looking over her shoulder, she rummaged for a shell as he drew closer and closer. The crunch of his footsteps through the snow bounced off the valley walls, echoing in her ears.

Without looking down and keeping her gaze fixed on that man, she popped the shell inside the flare gun. She turned and aimed, wishing with all her heart and soul that it had been a real gun. The Ruger Nash had given her. Loaded with bullets.

Because for the first time in her life, she wanted to kill someone—that man.

Then she squeezed the trigger, the gun bucking in her hand.

A deafening crack resounded through the valley, making her assailant freeze. Only fifty yards from her. Mere seconds of hesitation before he resumed charging toward her.

Damn it! It must've been the yellow shell. A blank, delivering a loud gunshot-like sound to scare off bears.

She looked in the bag. There were four red shells. Fifty yards shrank to forty. She fished out a red one. Dumped the used cartridge and reloaded.

He was thirty yards away.

She aimed.

Fired.

Once more she felt the recoil. The flare streaked straight

ahead and hit him. He stumbled back, his arms flailing as the flare blazed, burning dead center. With the protective layer of his coat, she had no idea if it would burn through his clothes to cause any real damage.

But with him distracted and focused on something other than her, she started running.

Lynn reloaded another red shell while keeping her feet moving. She looked back to take aim. This time at his head, where she knew it would hurt, if not kill him.

He was throwing snow on his chest, causing the flare to sputter out quickly.

As she squeezed the trigger, his gaze lifted.

The flare hissed forward. But this time he dived, face-down into the snow, and it missed.

Lynn took off again.

The air was so crisp it was brittle. Her lungs were on fire, her legs aching with each jarring step. It was surreal, as though they were the only two people in the world. A gasping, exhausted woman unable to move fast enough and an unrelenting murderer steadily closing the gap between them.

She couldn't let him catch her. She had to find a way to save herself.

In the kit, she snagged another shell. Trying to reload and hold on to the bag at the same time, her feet faltered. Her knees began to buckle, and the cartridge slipped from her fingers into the snow.

Reaching out for a tree, she righted herself.

She couldn't afford to go back for the shell. All she could do was keep moving, even though she had nowhere to go. Nowhere to hide.

Don't think about it! Keep. Going. She was breathing hard, frosty air scorching her throat. If only there was a way to call for help. But the phone wasn't charged and even if it was, how would help get there in time? She was all alone.

No one in sight. Only that man. Only her own ragged breathing, and his, making a sound.

She hazarded another quick glance behind her.

God, he was so close. Less than fifteen yards. Maybe ten. The crunch of snow behind her bit her ears.

One last red cartridge left in the kit. Gasping, her heart threatening to burst, she slowed despite her mind protesting. Unable to keep hold of everything, she grabbed the shell and dropped the bag. Reloaded. Whirled to shoot.

He was right up on her. He lunged, thrusting his body through the air, and tackled her to the ground.

She hit the valley floor hard with him on top of her. He wrenched her hand holding the gun up. Her finger squeezed. The last flare—her last chance—streaked up into the air.

Chapter Sixteen

"Did you see that?" Nash asked, pointing out the windshield.

A flare shot up, cutting through the dark sky.

"Yeah, I did. Hard to miss. I'll circle around to where it came from." Mitch pulled on the cyclic control stick, turning into the wind, taking them east.

Toward the valley.

"Can you get lower?" Nash asked. With the darkness, it was hard to see from the air despite the full moon and its light shining off the snow.

"I'll do my best." Mitch flew over countryside, getting so low that the tips of the trees scraped the underbelly of the helo. "Sorry about that, Sienna Rose. I can do better." He adjusted a bit, taking them slightly higher. Once they reached the valley, he dipped lower but stayed above it. "It's too narrow to fly through it."

That wasn't what Nash wanted to hear, but he said, "Understood."

The flare had been a signal from Lynn. In his gut, he knew it. What were the odds of someone else wandering around in this area, in a blizzard, shooting flares?

His guess was zilch.

A glistening swath of white, sprinkled with trees, ran west to east. At the western end, it was wide, but narrowed the farther east it ran. On the map, the valley looked like a dagger. Not far from the eastern point was the ranger station.

There!

Beyond a cluster of trees were two individuals, both in dark clothing, wrestling on the icy, snow-covered ground.

"It's Lynn," he said, half to himself and partly to Mitch.

"We could head to the ranger station. Drop you in. From there, you could backtrack on a snowmobile," Mitch said, but Lynn was literally fighting for her life and didn't have that kind of time. "The wind is still high. It would be safer for you."

"But not for her. Get us to the minimum altitude for me to deploy a chute."

"I'll take us to two thousand feet AGL," Mitch said, referring to *above ground level*.

"Make it one."

Mitch grimaced. "That's madness. Two is pushing it."

"You know we can do it lower."

"The lowest recorded altitude for someone to open a chute at terminal velocity and survive is eight hundred feet. Even extreme athletes don't go that low."

"I'm not asking for eight hundred. I'm telling you a thousand." Nash glared to convey his seriousness. They did not have time to squabble about his safety. Get him the altitude and he'd get to Lynn. "Do it," he snapped.

"It's your funeral," Mitch said.

Better his than Lynn's. But he wasn't going to die on this jump, because he needed to survive long enough to save her.

Mitch complied, taking them to one thousand feet AGL. "All right. I'll try to hold her steady."

Nash unbuckled his seat belt, removed his headset and got into position at the door.

"I'll have the sheriff contact the rangers," Mitch said, "and I'll keep the light on Lynn."

Nodding his thanks, Nash opened the door. He waited for Mitch to steady the helo as much as he could, and then he jumped.

LYNN'S ASSAILANT YELLED obscenities at her. "First, you run, making me chase you and take care of this in the snow when we could've done it back at the cabin." He was furious. His eyes burned hellfire, and she felt the same as she struggled against him. "Now you want to shoot me with a flare." He smacked her with the back of his fist.

Pain exploded in her face. Her vision swam along with her brain.

"I was going to make it quick," he said. "Instead, I'm going to have some fun."

A helicopter cut overhead, a spotlight washing over them and then moving away, putting them back in the darkness.

The man looked up at the sky.

The chopper stayed close, possibly hovering nearby. She couldn't be certain because her focus wasn't on the helicopter. Or her attacker, who had taken a position on top of her.

She concentrated on the utility knife in her pocket as she gripped it.

Slipping it from her coat pocket, she unfolded it with one hand and it made a slight click.

He glanced down at her, their eyes meeting.

Without hesitation, she jammed the blade into his thigh.

He roared back in pain, and she didn't give that sick SOB a chance to recover, to retaliate.

She rammed her knee up between his legs. When he doubled over, bringing his face closer, she slammed the heel of her palm up into the bridge of his nose.

The impact pushed him far enough back, freeing her hips. And her legs. She kicked him once, her bootheel connecting with his stomach. Twice. The thrust landed in his chest, shoving him farther back.

Lynn flopped onto her stomach and scrambled away. She spotted a dark figure floating from the sky. Parachuting down.

Nash.

It had to be him.

He was almost to the valley floor. But he wasn't close enough to help her.

A whisper of gunshots echoed off the valley walls. She glanced over her shoulder. Her attacker had drawn a gun, silencer attached.

Ping! Ping! A chilling sound that scraped along her nerve endings as bullets struck the helicopter, forcing it to veer off and ascend. The spotlight danced around, not staying focused on any one thing while the chopper zigged and zagged, climbing higher.

The man lowered his gun, redirecting his aim.

Four more muffled pops of gunfire. She turned back to see holes puncturing Nash's parachute. His body jerking as though he'd also been hit. The material of the chute fluttered and crumpled, and he plummeted in free fall.

No! Please, please, no!

BULLETS RIPPED THROUGH the canopy above Nash's head. Parafoils burst with a loud pop-pop-pop. Another bullet struck his Kevlar vest. But the last tore through his arm, shredding muscle. Adrenaline pumping inside him right along with the pain. Refusing to focus on the latter, he let the former fuel him as he braced for what was to come next.

The chute deflated, sending him into a rapid descent. Dread fisted a tight knot in his stomach. In a desperate act, he grasped the chute lines, knowing it wouldn't slow his fall.

There was nothing he could do but steel himself for an ugly impact.

He glimpsed Lynn—staring at him, face contorted in horror. Then he saw that bastard going for her again.

A blind rage consumed him, burning inside him like a piece of hot metal right before he struck the ground a lot harder and faster than he'd hoped. A gust of wind snatched the chute as he tucked into a roll, the way his training had taught him. But the wind dragged the chute across the ground, hauling him with it until he smashed into the side of a tree, his head slamming against the solid bark.

LYNN'S INSIDES TWISTED harder than ever before watching Nash get shot and crash to the ground. Then he had been slammed into a tree. On impact she heard a crack.

She thought she might puke.

He couldn't die. Not like this. Not because of her.

The helicopter changed position, staying high and casting the spotlight on her. She kept moving, crawling forward through the light, trying to will her legs to stand. To run to Nash. To help him. He wasn't moving.

A big hand locked onto her ankle. Then there was a yank on her leg. *Oh no!* He had her. Why wouldn't he just let her go? Another brutal tug and she was wrenched backward through the snow.

Screaming and clawing at the icy ground, she thrashed, struggling to hold on to something. Bitter cold snow slipped through her hands.

He fired the weapon near her head but into the ground. She froze and shuddered. Trying to outrun him was one thing. Trying to outrun a bullet was impossible.

Still, she refused to give in.

Desperation flared hot under her skin. She shoved her hand into her jeans pocket for the only weapon she had left.

Something sharp bit into her calf. She shrieked in agony.

A blade twisted in her flesh, and she could no longer crawl, could no longer run. Groaning through the fog of pain, she pried the pepper spray from her pocket.

He pulled the knife out of her leg and flipped her over as though she was a fish he intended to gut. Grabbing hold of the edge of her coat, he dragged her beneath him, locking her legs with his hips.

Holding the blade, he stabbed down at her. She raised her left arm, blocking him. The knife tore at the coat, down to her arm, drawing blood and searing pain. He kept slashing at her, cutting her shoulder. Her cheek. Intent on killing her. Slicing her to pieces.

Any second, he'd slit her throat.

Determinedly, closing her eyes, holding her breath, she lifted the pepper spray and depressed the release button.

He howled in anger, rearing off her. Dropping on all fours, he rubbed snow in his eyes. She wormed away from him on her back. Fearful that if she took her gaze from him that he would attack her again like some horror movie villain.

Footfalls crunched across the snow behind her.

The man brushed the snow from his face and turned in her direction. Lifted his weapon. But not at her. His aim was higher.

Her heart seized, eyes closing reflexively as a gunshot rang out.

She stilled and realized the sound had been different. Louder. No sound suppressor. Peeling her eyes open, she dared to look. The man had been thrown onto his back from the impact of the bullet.

Nash stormed past her with a slight limp, heading for her attacker, weapon at the ready. He was all right.

She didn't know how that was possible. There was no way any ordinary man could have survived something like that and keep on fighting. But Nash Garner was anything but ordinary.

He was too damn tough and stubborn to die without meeting his objective.

The spotlight from the helicopter followed Nash, bathing his movements in light. Her attacker sat up, also fighting until the end, and raised his gun.

Two more shots fired. Again, like thunderclaps, too loud to have come from a suppressor. The man's gun skittered from his hand, and he squirmed in pain. Wounded, but he was alive.

Nash punched him and tossed him onto his stomach. He threw a knee into her assailant's back and handcuffed his hands behind him. Then Nash put zip ties around his ankles.

Lynn gathered herself, sitting upright, clutching her wounded arm.

Holstering his weapon, Nash ran to her. He knelt in the snow, bringing her into his arms.

Tears prickled her eyes as she burrowed her face into his chest. She clung to him, astonished that he was there. Grateful that he'd found her in time.

The sound of snowmobiles rose above the thump-thump of the helicopter. Rangers were closing in.

"It's over. We've got him," Nash said. He kissed the top of her head, holding her tight. "Are you okay?" His voice was heavy with emotion. He touched her arm gingerly and tried to pull back to look at it, but she kept holding on to him, unable to let go.

She opened her mouth to answer him but all that came out was a sob that was a mix of joy and relief.

"Shh." He stroked her hair. "I've got you, and I'm not going anywhere."

The nightmare was over.

They were both alive.

She was in Nash's arms.

Nothing else mattered.

Chapter Seventeen

A heavy cloud of darkness lifted.

Lynn opened her eyes. The world blurred. Then ceiling tiles with tiny holes came into focus. White walls. Dim fluorescent lights. Antiseptic smell. The faint sound of a machine beeping. An IV in her arm. Hospital bed.

Slowly, it came back to her. Helicopter ride back to Laramie. The surgery for her calf. Tendons had been severed when she was stabbed.

Memories ricocheted in her mind. Running for her life. *Him* catching her. The exhaustion. The blinding pain. Though she felt little now thanks to the drugs pumping in her system.

He had cut her so many times. Would have killed her, too.

If not for Nash.

She swallowed against the dryness in her throat. The stitches in her cheek pulled at her skin. There were more on her shoulder and arm.

A toilet flushed nearby. She turned her head toward the closed bathroom door in her room. Water ran. The faucet shut off.

The door opened. Nash came out, meeting her gaze. Intense gray eyes locked onto her. The smile that spread across his mouth tugged at her heart. All she wanted to do was kiss him.

"You're awake." He came to her side, sat on the edge of the bed and took her hand in his.

"I thought you left. Went home."

"I cleaned up while you were in surgery. But I was back long before it was over."

Tightening her fingers around his, she looked him over. He'd showered and changed. Now he wore a black T-shirt. There was a bandage around his left biceps.

"What happened to you?"

"No big deal. Took a bullet. Got a concussion," he said casually, like it could be remedied with a Band-Aid and aspirin.

She doubted that there was anything that could bring him down. Still, he was human.

Lynn grimaced. "Are you going to be okay?"

"It's nothing for you to worry about."

"If you're hurt, then I'm worried."

A faint smile pulled at his lips. "I've survived worse. No permanent damage. I'll have to do some physical therapy. But so will you."

She moved her injured leg. A slight ache coursed through the wound. Once the drugs wore off it would be a different story. "Maybe we can do it together." She stopped short of saying *as a couple.*

Dr. Lewis came into the room. "Nice to see you awake, Ms. Delgado. The surgery went well. You'll have to use a cane for a few days and you'll have a bit of a limp for a couple of weeks. Then after some physical therapy, it'll be like it never happened. Aside from a small scar."

Glancing at Nash, Lynn wondered if she'd ever be able to forget what happened. He must have read the look on her face.

"You're going to heal," he said, "and you're going to move on from this. I promise."

She swallowed the emotion rising in her throat and nodded because she believed him.

"You have your share of cuts, bruises and abrasions," the doctor said, "But he's right. You'll heal. We ran an IV drip for you because you were also dehydrated. We'd like to keep you overnight. You've been through a very traumatic experience."

"No, I want to go home." She tried to sit up and winced from the protestation of her body. Exhaustion forced her back down to the bed, her head throbbing.

"She'll stay the night," Nash said to the doctor.

"I'd rather be with you."

Never had she thought of herself as someone who would *need* another person. She had spent so many years being independent, never clinging. Yet here she found herself hating the thought of being separated from him. Tonight, she needed him.

"You will be." A grin tipped up the corner of his mouth. His thumb stroked the pulse point in her wrist. Slow, soothing circles. "I'm not going anywhere."

The way he spoke the words flooded her heart with warmth.

"Now that we have that settled," Dr. Lewis said, "I'll let you get some much-needed rest. We can discharge you in the morning."

She nodded. "Thank you."

The doctor left, shutting the door. Nash got up and drew the curtain around the bed, giving them more privacy.

Turning to him as he sat back down, she asked, "How are Yvonne and Earl Epling?" Guilt and remorse coursed through her over endangering them.

"They're both okay other than headaches. TRK used chloroform on them. Mitch will fly back out tomorrow, pick Yvonne up and take her home, where she can recuperate from the ordeal."

"What about her car?"

"We'll figure it out," Nash said. "Easy enough to get tires replaced and have someone drive it over. She knows you're okay and that I'm not leaving your side."

"I feel so bad about everything." She thought about the fire she'd accidentally started. "It's my fault the cabin burned down."

He kissed the back of her hand. "That's what insurance is for. It'll cover the damages." His voice was so soft, reassuring. Deep and so sexy. "You have nothing to feel bad about." He took off his boots. "Scoot over."

She made room for him in the bed and he lay down beside her, wrapping his uninjured arm around her shoulder, bringing her body to rest against his.

This was the best place in the world. In his arms.

Lynn put her head on his chest. "What's going to happen to TRK? And who is he?"

"They patched up his gunshot wounds. I didn't hit anything vital. He's on a different floor. His wrists and ankles are handcuffed to the bed. He's not going anywhere. The Laramie police chief volunteered two of her officers to guard him for the rest of the night when she heard what was happening. The sheriff was happy to accept her offer since his deputies haven't slept. They have instructions not to underestimate that man or lower their guard. We'll transport him to the sheriff's office tomorrow and interrogate him there. So far, no word on his identity, and he's not talking. At least not yet."

She'd been through so much. They'd been through so much, together, to get here. "Are you always like *this* on the job?"

"What do you mean?"

"The way you were out there in the valley." Unstoppable. Unrelenting. Unbelievable. "You really went above and beyond to get a serial killer."

He eased onto his side, so they were face-to-face, and looked down at her, staring into her eyes. "Everything I did was for you." Cupping her face, he caressed her jaw with his thumb, and she loved the feel of his calluses on her skin. "I'll always fight like hell for you, Lynn."

The shadows under his eyes. The injuries he had sustained. Jumping out of a helicopter in a storm...for her. The way he was looking at her right now, with such warmth and passion and tenderness. It all coalesced, making her wonder if there might be a real chance for them.

"I was wrong for thinking that you had a propensity for violence," she said in a whisper, ashamed of herself. "That you could ever hurt a suspect deliberately. You could have beaten TRK, could've killed him."

"Believe me, I was tempted."

"But you didn't. You showed far more self-control than I would have in your shoes. I'm sorry I doubted you."

"How can I blame you? I never showed you that side of myself. Never let you into my world. Never explained anything."

"I understand that you're not used to opening up." Ignoring every hard question and putting her doubts on the back burner. She was aware he'd worked with black ops units as a ranger doing highly classified stuff. Volunteered for joint terrorism task forces with the FBI. Things that required him to be secretive. Hardened. She knew that a certain sort—an alpha, lone wolf, protector—was well-suited for that type of work. "But I need you to confide in me. Not all at once. When you're ready."

"The truth is I have kept you at a distance when you wanted to get closer because... I was afraid."

Her heart stammered. Nash Garner afraid? "Of what?"

"Rejection," he said, and the air caught in her throat. "That you'd see me as damaged. Something to fix. Not someone you could love."

He wasn't Humpty Dumpty. He was a man, with flaws, like everyone else. Her job wasn't about fixing people, it was about helping them, but he wasn't a client.

Nash was the man she already loved.

She pulled back. Not entirely, just enough to see him better. "You're so good at listening," she said, putting her hand on his chest. "At asking me the right questions. At making me feel seen. Like you truly know me. That's all I want to do for you in return. For you to know that you have a safe space with me. I promise you that I will never seek to fix you."

Some of the unease left his face. "I don't talk about my past because it sucked. It wasn't happy like yours." He covered her hand that was pressed to his chest with his own. "My mom died when I was really young. My father was a good man. But a hard man. Strict. He ended up having a heart attack."

"How old were you?"

"Twelve. Too old, too far past the peak of cuteness, with too much of a nervous stutter for people to consider for adoption. Unlike my brothers, who found stable families that wanted them. Unfortunately, not together."

She knew that he was the eldest. That there were six years between him and the twins.

"I felt guilty for a long time over not being able to keep us together," he said.

"It wasn't your fault. You were a child."

"Still. The reason I joined the army was to have a solid job with health benefits so I could be their guardian, but by then it was too late. They had adjusted and were happy."

The weight of it was visible in his eyes, the sudden strained tension in his shoulders. He had never let it go. She couldn't begin to imagine what it must've been like for him, or his brothers. Twins, separated and raised by different families.

"How was the foster care system for you?" It was a toss of the dice. Some kids found nurturing placements. Others didn't fare so well.

His jaw clenched. He was silent for a moment, as if gathering his thoughts. "What do you want to know?" His tone sharpened. "About the beatings at some homes? How they made sure not to leave bruises?" The strain of their discussion was evident on his face. "About the state facilities that were like prisons where I had to fight other kids for food, for a warm blanket? Fight to make sure I wasn't the one getting injured?"

Her heart bled for him. She was furious at the system and sick for him. "Why didn't you tell me?" She had asked about his childhood so many times, fished around for stories, and had only been given clues, fragments of information. Not enough to form a complete picture.

"Because it's hard." His gaze fell from hers. "I packed it all away with everything else painful. It's better to move on. Leave that stuff in the past."

"Oh, Nash."

"See, that's exactly what I don't want." Tension pulled at his mouth. "You feeling sorry for me. It made me strong. Tough. It drove me to the army. Where I found a different kind of family."

He was a survivor. Nash had made it through the unspeakable loss of both parents at a young age, the foster care system, violence, psychological trauma.

"I want you to trust me the way you trusted your army unit." It wasn't a direct correlation, but the understanding that gleamed in his eyes told her it was a relevant one that struck a chord. "I admire your strength," she said. "That's what saved me. That's what was needed, your drive, your intestinal fortitude, to capture that man who was hell-bent on killing me."

The world could be a scary place. As she recently

learned, much more frightening than she ever imagined. Men like Nash leveled the playing field, giving those demons, like TRK, something bigger and mightier to be afraid of.

"I don't talk about my work because it takes me to a dark place," he said. "My job requires me to shut down my emotions, but not my conscience. When I'm with you, I'm happy, and that's what I want to focus on. Not replaying the worst parts of my day. The ugly, horrible things that I've seen." Pain crossed his face. "If I could change for you, be the man that you want, that you deserve, I would." He let out a haggard breath.

"Don't say such a thing. I never wanted you to change. Only to share. I'm lucky to have you. *All* of you. Because you are *not* broken." He was beautiful. Perfect just as he was. "You're amazing. The most spectacular and hottest man I've ever seen."

The tension in him lifted. He rubbed his thumb over her bottom lip, making her pulse quiver right along with her thighs. "You give me a reason to look forward to the future. I want everything with you. House. Kids. All of it. I never had that desire before I met you. Lynn…" His caress dipped to her chin and ran along her throat, sending a shiver of pleasure through her. "Lola, I love you."

Her heart squeezed at those precious words she'd always hoped to hear. He was the kind of man who would never say such a thing unless he meant it. Tears of joy welled in her eyes. "I never stopped loving you from the moment I first admitted it."

Lowering his head, he brushed his lips over hers. A rush of hot desire ran through her veins, melting her against him.

And they were back in their bubble. That sacred place where nothing else existed. Nothing else mattered other than being together.

She surrendered to his kiss as his arms came around her,

holding her so close until the beat of his heart thrummed through her chest, falling in sync with her own.

No longer wrestling her feelings, she opened to him. She breathed easier, sinking against him, but kissed him harder, letting her hunger for him slide into every stroke of her tongue over his.

Desire flared white-hot, his touch fanning the flames. She lost herself in him, in the strength of his body, in the harsh moan that rumbled up his throat.

This was everything she had wanted. His vulnerability. His warmth.

His love.

For him to be all hers.

Doubt still lingered. She hoped this wasn't a case of onetime sharing. It might be all too easy for him to put up a wall between them again come tomorrow. She couldn't go back to that no matter how much she loved him. They had to be able to grow together for this to work. Only time would tell.

With a groan, he broke the kiss. "If we don't stop, one of us might bust stitches." His body pressed against the length of hers, and she could feel he wanted her as desperately as she wanted him. "Possibly both of us."

She ran her hand down the ridges and valleys of the muscles in his torso and unbuckled his belt. "I'm willing to risk it if you are. Besides, we're in a hospital. They can easily replace them."

"I know I haven't always shown the most restraint in the bedroom where you're concerned." He kissed her again before drawing his mouth away with a tender smile. "I can wait. Until we're out of here and you're feeling better."

How admirable.

She drew down his zipper. "But I can't."

Chapter Eighteen

In the observation room that had one-way glass overlooking the adjacent interrogation room, Nash grabbed a chair for Lynn. "Sit."

"I'm fine," she said, holding on to a cane for support.

"Sit," he said, this time more firmly, and she compiled. Nash turned to Holden. "I'm surprised you're here for this. I thought you'd be knocking down the Crombies' door."

Holden sighed. "Don't get me started. The judge said since I told him I wouldn't need the warrant and he didn't have anything on the docket this morning that he wasn't coming in until this afternoon."

"Do you want me to give him a call?" the sheriff asked. "See what I can do?"

"No, sir." Holden shook his head. "I made my bed. Now I've got to lie in it. I'll have the warrant later today."

The door to the interrogation room opened. The two officers from the Laramie Police Department hauled in Lynn's assailant. He wore chains between the cuffs on his wrists and ankles. Jangling into the room, he took short steps to the chair and plopped down. The officers attached the chain to the bar on the table that was bolted to the floor. He leaned forward, bringing his head to his hands, and brushed his reddish-brown hair from his face,

Lynn gasped. "I know him."

"You do?" the sheriff asked.

"No, I mean I've seen him before."

"At the Silver Springs center," Nash said. "The last time you went to visit your aunt Miriam. I didn't get a chance to tell you. There's video footage of him marking your vehicle right before he spoke to you."

Nash looked over the man. He was doing a good job of hiding his discomfort from the bullet wounds in his shoulder, forearm and thigh. The hospital had been instructed not to give him any pain meds this morning.

"Yes, I remember," she said slowly, nodding. "He told me he was considering the facility for his mother and asked me what I thought of the place. He was so nice. Charming. Even funny."

"Are you sure you're up for watching the interrogation?" Nash asked her.

"I can't bury my head in the sand. I need to be a part of this process, not lying at home in bed watching television. It's important."

He agreed. This would help her heal faster, but he didn't want to push her to do something she wasn't ready for.

"Are you sure you're not too close to this to handle the interrogation?" Daniel asked. "Agent Hammond is one phone call away."

"No, I've got it." Nash wanted to throttle that man until he was no longer breathing but he would never let emotion interfere with his job.

"This might be personal for him," Lynn said, her voice confident and strong, "but he's capable of being a consummate professional."

Nash put a hand of thanks on her shoulder. It was nice having her fully in his corner. Having a partner who knew the darkest things about him and believed in him nonetheless.

"Okay." The sheriff nodded. "I had to ask."

The two officers left the interrogation room. After a

knock on the observation door, one stuck his head inside. "We're going to take off now, Sheriff, unless you need something else from us."

"No, we're good. Thank you. Tell Chief Nelson I appreciate the assistance."

"Sure. No problem." The officer nodded and left.

"I owe her a phone call to tell her myself," Daniel said. "I'm still surprised she helped. She's been so brusque with me since I took over."

"It's not you," Holden said. "It's her. She's got a bit of a chip on her shoulder."

"You wouldn't say that about her if she was a man in a difficult leadership position," Lynn pointed out.

Holden conceded with a one-shoulder shrug.

"Whatever the reason for the assistance," Daniel said, "I want to keep the good will flowing between our departments."

Nash gave Lynn's shoulder a little squeeze, and she responded with a supportive smile. Then he went into the tiny interrogation room. Meeting the man's dark brown eyes, he unbuttoned his suit jacket and took the chair opposite him at the small, battered table.

"Special agent Nash Garner," the man said. "I'm surprised they're letting you conduct this interview. Considering the conflict of interest."

Nash swallowed, taken aback. This was the first time he'd started an interrogation feeling as though he was out of his depth. How did he know his name? How did he know there was a conflict of interest because of Lynn?

Keeping his features bland, Nash refused to be thrown off-kilter.

Maybe one of the officers had mentioned Nash's name. It was possible the implied conflict was regarding the fact that Nash had been the one to shoot him.

"Would you like a cup of coffee before we begin?" Nash offered.

"No."

"You've been read your rights," Nash said, to make it clear on playback of the recording of the interrogation. "Do you understand the charges?"

"I do." He was calm and collected for a man facing three counts of murder and one count attempted.

It was disturbing.

"Cooperating now will only help you later." Any moment, he could invoke his right to have a lawyer and clam up. That was the last thing they wanted. Regardless, he had to ask the question. "Do you want your attorney present during this interview?"

"No."

Again, unsettling. "Please state your name for the record," Nash said.

They still didn't know who this guy was. No identification had been found on him. The DNA search had failed to turn up a match. At this point, they were running his picture against DMV records.

"There's one problem," the guy said, "with the charges."

"And what's that?"

"I'm not TRK. I didn't kill anyone. In Colorado," he said, adding the last two words after a slight pause, his eyes narrowing, a devious smile playing at the corner of his mouth.

"We have video footage of you marking Lynn Delgado's car with TRK's calling card."

"Because I did," he said, lightly.

"Yet you're claiming *not* to be TRK?"

"Correct," he said, and Nash wondered what game this guy was playing. "Before this day is over, you're going to come to realize two things."

"Enlighten me. What are they?"

"I wasn't in Colorado when those women were murdered. I was three states away for one of them and out of the country when the last one was killed."

"Great," Nash said incredulously. "Then giving us your name will help us to corroborate that sooner."

"Which brings me to the second thing. You and I are the same."

Nash sat back in his chair ramrod straight. "We are nothing alike."

"We'll see if your response changes by the end of the day."

"What's next?" Nash let his voice sound amused. "Are you going to deny trying to kill Ms. Delgado?"

"Nope."

Narrowing his eyes in suspicion, Nash didn't like this.

"But here's the thing," the guy said, "she seems like a nice woman. I didn't want to hurt her."

Okay. He was going to go with the insanity defense. Voices told him to do it. He had no control over stalking and stabbing her. "So you admit to trying to kill her?" Nash asked.

"Sure. Why not? You've got me red-handed on that one."

Nash should have been jumping for joy that the guy had confessed, on the record, but instead his gut was churning with warning.

"This is the part where I ask for a lawyer," he said, rattling his chains.

"You're a little late. Should have asked for one before you confessed."

"Oh, no, you misunderstand." The guy laughed. Had the audacity to laugh like this was all one big joke. "The lawyer isn't for me. It's for you and the sheriff." He gestured at the one-way glass with his chin. "I want the district attorney involved."

"The DA already is. She filed the formal charges." Or at least she would later today.

"This time she's needed to authorize my immunity deal."

Now Nash was the one laughing, though there wasn't anything funny about the situation. "You've given us a confession. You're not getting immunity."

The guy placed both palms down on the table. His hands were rock steady. Then he gave a long exhale as if he was bored. "You never asked me *why* I tried to kill her."

Nash's gut twisted into a greasy knot of tension, but he kept his gaze cool and hard. "All right, I'll play along. Why did you do it?"

"Because I was hired to."

IF LYNN HADN'T been sitting, she would've keeled over from the shock.

At first, she wanted to reject what she had heard. Call the man a liar.

"Hired by who?" Nash asked.

A wicked smile spread across the man's lips. "I couldn't simply kill her," he said, avoiding the question. "It had to be done in a way that would never point back to the person who wants her dead. It was my clever idea to make it look like TRK. Complicated things, though, because TRK stabbed his victims. Do you know how many times I could've shot her and been done with it?"

Lynn recalled with horrifying clarity how in the valley he had shot at the snow to make her stop moving when he could have easily put a bullet in her. And he had also said something about intending to make it quick.

This was really happening.

It wasn't over.

"You need a name," said the man chained to the table in the other room. "Right? Without it, how do you keep Lynn Delgado safe? How do you stop the person who paid me from hiring a replacement to finish the job?"

The thought hadn't occurred to her. That someone else might be sent to kill her.

Her mind was reeling. Who wanted her dead so badly that they would hire a contract killer?

Both Holden and the sheriff glanced at her with concern before turning their attention back to the interrogation room.

"To get what you need," that vile man said, "you've got to give me what I need. Immunity from all crimes I've committed. Feel free to throw in a clause excluding any crimes related to the real TRK since I'm not him, okay, my friend."

Nash jumped to his feet, his chair scraping back against the floor. "I'm not your friend."

"Figure of speech, but it doesn't change the fact that we're the same."

Nash clenched a hand into a fist. "We can't give immunity to a ghost. What's your name?"

Lynn looked between the sheriff and Holden. "Is he really going to get that monster immunity? Let him get away with everything he's done?" That was so unlike Nash.

The sheriff raised a palm, signaling her to hold on a minute.

The guy shook his head. "No name until the DA is here and prepared to agree to the deal."

"Why are you stalling?" Nash asked.

"Let's just say it's in the interest of self-preservation. The DA might choose to hem and haw for a few days, mulling things over. For Ms. Delgado's sake, I would advise against that. But as for me, you can't move me until you know my name. Once I'm transferred to the county detention center, I'm as good as dead."

"Why?"

"They'll make sure I can't talk."

They?

"You have proof of the contract?" Nash asked.

"Irrefutable. I'll get off as a result of the deal but the person responsible, the one who hired me, won't."

Nash stalked to the door and grabbed the knob.

"Hey, buddy," the guy said, causing Nash to hesitate, and she could practically feel his burning irritation. "Can I get that coffee now while I wait? Black is fine."

Slamming the door behind him, Nash left and entered the observation room.

Using her cane for support, Lynn stood and faced him. She was surprised how fragile her legs felt, like thin glass that could be shattered with the careless brush of a hand. "You can't seriously be considering this. Are you?"

Taking a breath, Nash grasped both her shoulders. His grip firm yet loving. "This is not a game we can win. I knew something was off the minute he opened his mouth. I wasn't in charge in there. He was. Because he's holding all the cards."

"He watched me for days. Held me at gunpoint. Stalked me. Stabbed me. Tried to kill me and you." The distress flooding his face silenced her.

"I'm painfully aware. But we need his cooperation to learn who is behind this. He'll only give it in exchange for immunity."

"There has to be another way." She wanted justice. To hell with that, she wanted vengeance. On the person who was behind this and on the contract killer.

"It has to be Todd Burk," Holden said. "The Iron Warriors have that kind of money from the drugs they traffic and the resources to do this."

"Allegedly," the sheriff said. "As far as I know, this department has never been able to prove anything."

"They have guys sitting in county lockup as we speak," Holden said, "capable of silencing that man. I'm telling you it has to be them. He said *they*."

"Sometimes your instincts seem to be right on the

money," the sheriff said. "And sometimes they're way off base. From the old reports I read, any time someone from the Iron Warriors is brought in for questioning, instead of talking, they lawyer up."

Holden straightened. "We can't be afraid to pursue this."

The sheriff put his hands on his hips. "I'm not afraid to do my job. I just don't see the point of prematurely riling a hornet's nest."

Nash stepped between them, throwing Holden a look that Lynn couldn't read. Whatever it conveyed, Holden backed down and backpedaled.

"You're the sheriff," Holden said. "Not me. You're right. We need evidence, not me jumping to conclusions. I'm going to go check and see if there's been any progress with ID'ing that fellow." He excused himself from the room.

"Does Todd Burk have any reason to want you dead?" the sheriff asked her.

"He's not happy with me or the mandatory domestic violence program he was court-instructed to take. He believes I'm trying to destroy his relationship with his girlfriend. But is that enough to want to kill me?"

She couldn't think of any reason that anyone in town would have to justify her murder.

"People have killed over less," Nash said.

"And killing for love ranks high as a motive. Even if Todd Burk is responsible, our hands are tied without evidence."

"If I have to choose between that man," Nash said, pointing at her assailant, "doing jail time and the one who took out the contract, then I choose the latter. Without the deal, he won't talk. He will probably never make it out of county lockup alive if he's telling the truth. And you'll still be in danger."

The idea of letting that monster, who had most assuredly

killed others, walk away scot-free made her want to retch. "This isn't right. At least try to question Burk."

"The second we do," the sheriff said, "it tips our hand, letting him know the contract killer failed and is in our custody. If it is him, that might spur Burk to hire a replacement to finish the job that much sooner."

Her stomach pitched and rolled. Bile rose in Lynn's throat.

Nash came to her side, putting an arm around her. "I won't gamble with your life." His voice was rough and raw. "We need to get the DA in here to talk."

The sheriff put his hands in his pockets. "You know blanket immunity might not be our only option."

"What are you thinking?" Nash asked.

"That fellow wants to live. Which means getting him released. I say we get immunity only for the charge of attempted murder. Then we let him give us enough rope to hang him on something else before he leaves the state."

"The execution of that idea might be tricky." Nash's jaw clenched. "But it could work."

Chapter Nineteen

What had he been thinking to mouth off at the sheriff like that?

Holden tended to be self-critical, but he also recognized when he had hit a home run. Lately, he had been striking out. All the time.

Tightening his hands on the steering wheel, Holden continued to berate himself. Something that had been made all the easier to do after he went back to Judge Don Rumpke, with hat in hand, and more or less said *pretty please with sugar on top*.

It had definitely been more, not less.

Gritting his teeth, Holden grumbled.

"Everything all right?" Mitch asked from the passenger's seat while eyeing him.

"Yeah. Everything's peachy." His behavior earlier had not been the right approach to bolster the sheriff's confidence in his judgment. Next week, Daniel was leaving town on vacation through the new year. The sheriff was trusting Holden enough to put him in charge. And he almost ruined it. A demotion would be the straw that broke the camel's back. More humiliation than Holden could bear.

He slapped the steering wheel.

"If this is peachy, I'd hate to see lousy," Mitch said.

"I'm upset we weren't able to turn up anything on that contract killer's identity and had to hand it off to the FBI."

Once the sheriff's office had turned up nothing it was passed on to Agent Hammond. Twenty-one states currently allowed federal agencies such as the FBI to run searches of driver's license and identification photo databases. "I prefer it when we can take care of it ourselves."

"Yeah, sure. Whatever you say."

Holden pulled up to the Crombie place and parked. The vehicle following with Livingston and Russo did likewise.

They got out of the SUV and met up with the others.

Holden slipped on his cowboy hat. "Do you see that?" He gestured to the front of the house.

"What are we looking at?" Livingston asked.

"That cleared path from the door and down the stairs," Holden said, watching as someone drew all the curtains in the front windows. "Same with the driveway. The Crombies are in their seventies and George has problems with his back. I don't reckon either of them shoveled that snow. But someone did."

The four of them made their way up the stairs to the porch. A scuttling sound came from inside as if one or two individuals were moving in a hurry.

Before knocking, he turned to deputy Ashley Russo. "When I give you the signal, I want you to take Mrs. Crombie to the kitchen. Keep her there and out of the way." He chose Russo because Shirley was capable of accusing a male officer of inappropriate contact if left alone with no witnesses. Hell, she might do the same with Russo, but Holden figured the odds were substantially lower. "If she loses it, goes for a knife or a frying pan or something, put her in cuffs."

"You think it'll come to that?" she asked.

With Shirley Crombie it was best to expect the unexpected. "Never know. Be prepared."

She gave a curt nod. "Got it."

Holden opened the screen door and banged his fist on the

main one with authority. The pounding made it clear they were not there to ask a few questions. "Laramie County Sheriff's Department! Open up!" They waited. Thirty seconds ticked by. He banged again. "If you don't open the door, I'll be forced to kick it in!"

More shuffling inside.

The door swung open. Shirley Crombie stood, wearing a seersucker housedress that harkened from the 1960s along with slippers, blocking the entryway. Her wide-eyed gaze washed over the cluster of deputies. Anxiety coated her like sweat. "What do you want?"

Holden held up the official document. "We have a warrant to search the premises." He handed it over and shoved past her, entering the house before she could protest. The deputies followed.

The last one in was Russo. She spotted a shotgun near the doorjamb and snatched it.

Inside there was only dim natural light that filtered in through the curtains.

"Get out of my house," Mrs. Crombie snapped. "You-you-you can't do this."

Holden leveled his gaze at her. "That document you're holding states we can."

Mrs. Crombie tore up the warrant and threw the pieces at him. "Get. Out." She pointed to the front door.

Holden made eye contact with Russo, gave her a slight nod and hiked his thumb in what he presumed was the direction of the kitchen.

Holding the shotgun upright by the barrel, the deputy turned to the older woman. "Mrs. Crombie, I need you to come with me," she said in a firm voice. She extended her other arm and eased forward in a way that forced Shirley to move.

"I want my lawyer," Mrs. Crombie said.

Russo kept walking with her arm extended, herding the

woman out of the way. "That's fine, ma'am. Call him from the kitchen."

"I—I—I got to get his number," Mrs. Crombie said. "It's upstairs."

Russo didn't hesitate. "Then the call will have to wait, ma'am."

"No! You can't do this."

"It's legal." The deputy didn't back down, making Holden proud. "Take it up with your lawyer. Later."

Once Mrs. Crombie was sequestered in the kitchen, Holden exhaled.

"Where do you want us to start?" Mitch asked.

Holden guessed it would be upstairs since Mrs. Crombie was so hot to get up there, but they had an attic and bedrooms and no telling what else.

So he said, "In here." Crossing the foyer, he looked around.

The house had seen better days. Wallpaper was peeling, dust covered knickknacks, and the floor looked as if it could use a good scrubbing.

In the sitting room, Holden found Mr. Crombie watching television. There were rumors that there was no love lost between George Crombie and Phil Pace. It was time to see if that was true.

He stepped in front of the TV and captured the man's gaze. "Did you hear all that? Do you understand why we're here?"

The gray-haired man nodded. His eyes solemn, his posture hunched.

"I need Phil," Holden said. "Then we can leave you be. We know he's here."

Mr. Crombie's gaze fell, and his mouth twisted like he was chewing on something.

Holden took a knee, forcing the other man to meet his eyes. "I hate interrupting your programs. I know how much you enjoy watching your shows. The sooner we find Phil, the sooner we can be out of your hair. But we're not leaving until we have him. Even if that means we have to pull up every floorboard to find him," Holden said, and Mr. Crombie started wringing his hands. "It's probably difficult dealing with Shirley *and* Phil every day. We can take one burden away for you. Where is he?"

George Crombie adjusted his glasses and looked up at the ceiling. Then met Holden's gaze again.

"He's upstairs." A statement, not a question. It was as Holden suspected.

A nod.

"Which room?"

"Master." Crombie's voice was low, weary. "False wall in the closet."

"Is he armed?" Holden asked.

"Rushing, he forgot to take it." Crombie pointed to a 9mm on the end table next to the remote.

Holden looked at the other two deputies in the room. "Search a secondary bedroom first. So it's not too obvious. Go, get him. Be careful." They nodded in response and left the room, heading up the stairs. He turned back to Mr. Crombie. "Does Phil have a laptop and printer here?"

"Laptop." He gestured to the dining room table across the hall. "No printer."

"Maybe he has one at his apartment that he's been using. Has he left the house since the bench warrant was issued?"

"He was hiding somewhere else the first week. Don't know where. Then he came here. Hasn't left since."

"Not at all? Not to get food or beer or cigarettes?"

"Shirley wouldn't allow it. Too afraid he'd get caught. She goes shopping once a week. Gets what he needs."

"Do you know if Phil has been writing any harassing letters to Dr. Delgado? Maybe Shirley has been getting them printed and mailing them for him."

The old man's eyes turned glassy with tears. "Phil has done enough to Dr. Delgado. He's not interested in doing anything else."

"Are you okay?" Holden asked. "What did Phil do?"

"That no-good boy got my son killed."

"What do you mean?"

Mr. Crombie pinched his lips together, his gaze lifting across the house. Toward the kitchen.

Holden looked in the same direction. His wife wasn't in sight at that moment. Deputy Russo had probably gotten her to take a seat. "You can tell me," Holden said, his tone gentle yet coaxing. "How did he get Andy killed?"

"Phil was angry at Dr. Delgado because she wouldn't let him shirk his responsibility to attend those classes. He set Andy against her. Poured poisoned words into his ears. Later I found out that he'd taken Andy's medicine. Convinced him that he didn't need those pills. But the doctor had said it was important he took 'em and didn't go off his meds. That rotten boy, Phil, was such a coward. He turned my son into a weapon. To hurt the doctor. Rotten. No-good." Tears leaked from his eyes. "My only son. Dead."

"I'm so sorry." Holden put a hand on his arm.

Scuffling and shouting came from upstairs. Something was knocked over. Glass broke.

"Don't hurt him!" Mrs. Crombie said from the kitchen. "Please, don't hurt him."

"George," Holden said in a softer voice, "would you be willing to make an official statement regarding what you told me? If you did, we could charge him. What Phil did is a crime."

The deputies hauled Phil down the stairs in handcuffs. He was kicking and struggling.

"Mama! Don't let them take me, Mama!"

Mrs. Crombie was doing her darnedest to get out of the kitchen, and Russo showed true grit blocking her. "Don't worry, baby. I'll call the lawyer. Mama will fix this." Then she shrieked foul words at the deputy. Had the nerve to spit in her face.

But Russo handled it with impeccable decorum, not letting the woman pass.

"I can't," George said, his voice a hoarse whisper.

"Why not? We can make him pay for what he did."

"Because…" George stared across the house at Shirley, who was ranting and raving about injustice in between her bouts of screaming like a banshee. "I've got to live with that. Besides, it won't bring my boy back. Nothing will."

Holden was sorry for the old man. Truly, he was.

But if Phil hadn't written the letters to Lynn, then who did?

Was this all connected to Todd Burk after all?

"I'M NOT SURE about this plan," Deputy District Attorney Melanie Merritt said, sitting in a chair in the sheriff's office. She wore a pantsuit and snow boots. With her intelligent eyes and severe bun, she looked as though she deserved her reputation as a shark in the courtroom.

"If we don't do this," Nash said, "then we can't neutralize the threat. Lynn will still be in danger."

"I understand that. I do. But a bird in the hand is worth more than two in the bush," Melanie said. "Even if the evidence turns out to be irrefutable as you say, you're asking me to give up a contract killer in exchange for what? Potentially a gang member?"

"I'm sorry if 'Contract Killer Apprehended' works better in the headlines, but the fact remains that someone hired him." Nash folded his arms, ensuring his face and tone remained neutral despite his mounting frustration. "We need to know who it is."

Lynn sat in the other chair with a look of disgust on her face.

"Let's call a spade a spade," the sheriff said, seated behind his desk. "This is political. You're thinking about what's going to look better for your career."

"I'm doing my job, considering this as my boss would and how it will affect his career. Not mine." Melanie crossed her legs. "When we're finished here, I have to go to his home, brief him, and convince him whether or not to do this. And yes, the DA is elected just as you are, Sheriff. Oh, wait, you were appointed because of the scandal and haven't faced the blistering heat of an election yet, so please spare me your self-righteousness."

"We're talking about a woman's life here," Nash said. "Her life." Everyone in the room looked at Lynn. "If our plan works, you'll have whoever hired the contractor and the killer. That's a double win. Worst case the DA gets one. This must be worth the risk to your boss."

Uncertainty hung heavy as a curtain on Melanie's face.

"This is the right call," Daniel said. "You have to persuade him. Heaven forbid that something happens to Lynn. Then the headline will read 'DA's Dereliction of Duty Results in Death.'"

"Nice alliteration." Nash nodded. "Readers and voters would eat it up. Bet the headline would sell a lot of newspapers."

Not so easily manipulated, Melanie folded her hands in her lap, looking unflappable. "I need to be one hundred percent about the best course of action when I speak to the DA. I'm not there yet. From everything I've heard about this contractor, he's clever. He might accept an immunity deal that's less than blanket, but he will most assuredly want it to cover any murders he has committed. Right now, I don't see how he doesn't walk."

A groan rumbled up Nash's throat as his cell phone rang. Taking it from his pocket, he spotted Holden and several other deputies hauling in who he presumed was Phil Pace.

Nash glanced at his screen and answered. "Becca, I'm going to put you on speaker. I'm here with the sheriff, the deputy district attorney Melanie Merritt and Lynn." He hit the icon so everyone would be on the same page. "Please tell me we know who this guy is."

"Sorry. We don't."

"We didn't get any hits from the DMV?" Nash asked.

"That's the problem. We got three. All in different states with different names. Same picture. Same man."

"It's the sheriff speaking. One of them must be his real identity."

"That's what I thought, too," Becca said. "But when I dug into each background, I found deceased people."

"Are you sure?" Melanie asked.

"Of course. I wouldn't report it unless I was certain."

Nash swore under his breath. "We needed this."

Smiling, Melanie uncrossed her legs and scooted to the edge of her seat. "Actually, we don't. This works to our benefit."

"How?" Lynn asked, speaking for the first time since they entered the sheriff's office.

"Previously, we were hoping that our contractor would let something slip about another crime he committed. Some other murder so he would do jail time for it. I say we offer an immunity deal. Not blanket. But one that covers any murders, excluding those related to TRK, in case we're wrong on that front."

"Then what do they arrest him on?" Lynn asked.

"Fraud. In the application for a license."

"But that's only a Class 1 misdemeanor," the sheriff said.

"Correct." Melanie's smile widened. "Unless the license was used with the intent to purchase a firearm or used as proof of residency. Then it becomes a Class 4 felony, punishable by up to ten years in prison. For each act. We're talking about thirty years. If he did use it to buy a gun, then we're talking additional charges. Class 6 felony. This will be a federal case. A big one."

Nash let out a little breath of relief. "Becca, I need you to—"

"I know. Verify he's purchased weapons under the assumed names. Then I'll check to see if there are residences in each state also under those names, because it never hurts to double down."

"Thank you," Nash said.

"No problem. I'm on it." Becca disconnected.

Standing, Melanie straightened her suit jacket. "Now I'm a hundred percent certain the DA will agree to this. It'll take some time to draw up the paperwork."

"How much?" Nash asked.

"A few hours. But I'll need his name. His real name for the document to be legal."

"He may want a personal assurance from you." Unfolding his arms, Nash stepped toward the door and opened it. "That the DA's office is on board with giving him immunity."

"I'd be happy to give it," Melanie said.

She followed him to the interrogation room, where they had him chained and waiting. He stepped inside and she was right behind him.

"This is the deputy district attorney, Melanie Merritt."

Narrowing his eyes, the contractor looked her over. "I'm not important enough to warrant the attention of the DA? All I get is the deputy?"

"I'm the DA's right-hand person. I've given Agent Garner and Sheriff Clark my assurance that you'll have your immunity deal. My next stop is the DA's house to update him. Then I'll get the deal written up. To do so, I'll need your legal name."

"I'll tell you my name, but if you don't hold up your end of the bargain and bring me a deal, remember that pretty little Lynn will pay the price. Because I won't tell you who hired me."

The words made Nash's gut burn.

"You'll have a deal," Melanie said. "I give you my word."

"She needs your name," Nash reminded him.

"Ian. Ellis." He also gave them his Social Security number.

"I'll be back in a few hours." Melanie turned and stepped into the hall.

With one last glance at the man, at Ian, Nash left, shutting the door behind him.

He walked her down the corridor. "Please try to hurry."

"I will."

"And when you're writing up the deal, keep in mind that he's going to look for loopholes."

"Do you know what the biggest part of my job is?"

"Going to trial and getting convictions?"

"No," she said, shaking her head with a smirk. "It's getting criminals to take undesirable plea deals. Bargaining. Ninety percent of cases don't make it to trial. Don't worry, I'm very good at what I do. The deal will be extremely attractive. An offer he won't refuse. But in the end, we're going to send that man to prison for a very long time."

Chapter Twenty

The sun had set, and night had fallen. Pacing in Holden's office, Lynn wished she had something to do other than wait. Melanie was out writing up the immunity deal. The sheriff was taking care of other things in town. It wasn't as if everything in Laramie revolved around her. Becca had gotten proof of the firearm purchases under the aliases and was tracking down evidence of the residencies next.

Nash was on the phone. He'd gotten as far as he could online, digging into Ian Ellis. Now he was making some calls.

She had no idea to whom and quite frankly, didn't care. All she wanted to know was the name of the person who wanted her dead.

Holden came in. "Hey, Lynn, how are you holding up?"

"I need this to be done. Until then?" She shook her head, not knowing the answer. "Did you find out if Phil was responsible for sending the letters?"

Hanging up the phone, Nash stood and joined them.

"Phil isn't behind the letters," Holden said. "We confiscated and searched his laptop to be sure."

They still had no clue who had been harassing her through the mail. Suddenly light-headed, she became unsteady on her feet.

"Sit down." Nash guided her to a chair. "Try to stay off the leg."

"I spoke to George Crombie." Holden leaned against the edge of his desk. "Apparently, Phil instigated what happened to you that night at Turning Point. He took Andy's medication and convinced him you were the devil. George said that he turned his son into a weapon. To hurt you."

"What? How could he? Being off his medication would have caused Andy to suffer a relapse of his symptoms. Delusions. Paranoia. Hallucinations." Recalling how Andy had looked and sounded that night, Lynn pressed a palm to her forehead. "It would explain why he appeared ill." Pale. Sweaty. The tremors. "His aggressive behavior. Especially if he had been led to believe that I was the problem."

How could Phil have been so petty, so manipulative? So cruel to his own brother?

Nash knelt in front of her and held her other hand. "Phil Pace is responsible for Andy's death. Do you hear me?"

She nodded, but she was overwhelmed by sadness. For poor Andy. For Mr. and Mrs. Crombie.

"Some things are beyond our control," Nash continued. "It's time you let this go. It's time to forgive yourself."

"All right," she said sincerely. Maybe it was exhaustion from the past two days. Maybe it was hearing about Phil's culpability. Or maybe she was ready for the first time to finally have the weight lifted. Letting her eyes close a moment, she took a cleansing breath. "All right." Looking at Nash, she caressed his cheek and kissed him because it would've hurt not to. She loved him so much. "Thank you."

"For what?"

"For being stubborn. For not giving up on us. On me."

"I'll always fight like hell. Remember that."

"I will." She kissed him once more until Holden cleared his throat. Honestly, she'd forgotten he was standing there. "Did you find out anything more about Ian Ellis?" she asked Nash.

"I did after a few calls." He sat in the chair adjacent to hers.

"To who?" Holden asked.

"The Pentagon."

Lynn exchanged a surprised glance with Holden.

"It looks as if Ian was telling the truth," Nash said. "We're the same. In a manner of speaking. He was once in the army. Special Forces. Worked on high-value black ops missions taking out targets."

"But how would Ian know about your background?" Holden asked.

"We weren't together that week he watched me," Lynn said. "Why would he look into you?"

"I've considered that and came up with two possibilities. One, he read that article the paper wrote on you when he was researching how to make it look like TRK was responsible. In it, that journalist mentioned I was your boyfriend."

Her cheeks heated thinking about it. The article had implied that she had been protected by law enforcement because her boyfriend was an FBI agent.

"The other possibility I'm ashamed to admit."

"Why?" Holden asked.

"Because it's possible that he may have seen me watching you."

"Oh." Lynn wasn't sure how she felt about that. "Why were you watching me?"

"I was worried about you. My patience was wearing thin. I went to your house a couple of nights that week. Sat out front. For a while. Debated whether to knock. But never did. That's how I know you had been parking your car in the garage and that he couldn't have marked it there. That it had to have been somewhere else."

"Ian could've thought you two had a lover's spat," Holden said, "but weren't entirely out of the picture. If that's the case, I imagine a good contract killer would thoroughly research all factors."

"Anyway, he was discharged seven years ago. That's when Ian Ellis became a ghost."

Looking out through the window of his office, Holden pushed off his desk and stood. "It's game time."

Lynn turned in her seat. Melanie Merritt was back.

"I should call the sheriff," Holden said. "Let him know."

"Go ahead." Nash marched toward the door. "But we're not waiting on him."

Leaning on her cane, Lynn limped out into the hall.

Melanie held up the document. "The DA has already signed off."

"The verbiage?" Nash asked.

"It's some of my finest work. I'll do the talking in there and I'll get him to sign. I may have to say some tough things, but trust me."

"Okay."

On the way to the interrogation room, Nash ensured Lynn was sitting in the observation room and not putting weight on her injured leg. The wound throbbed, but she was riveted to the scene in the next room.

Melanie slid the deal across the table to Ian Ellis. "All we need is your signature for it to be official."

Ian scrutinized the document, examining every line. "This is not what I asked for. I said immunity from all crimes."

"This is the best deal you're going to get," Melanie said. "You're a contract killer. You have immunity from any homicides you may have committed. Excluding, of course, those of TRK, in case you do turn out to be him."

"I'm not." Ian shook his head.

"Then we don't have a problem," Melanie said.

"But—"

"You want to live, don't you?" Melanie asked.

Ian scoffed at the rhetorical question.

"This offer expires at midnight." Melanie looked at her watch. "Five hours from now." She set down a pen. "After that, you'll be sent to county lockup."

"If you do that, you'll never get the name of who hired me. Lynn Delgado's life will still be in danger."

"That's not my problem," Melanie said without a drop of remorse. "Because it's not the DA's problem."

Nash glanced at Melanie with a look of horror.

"Tell him," she said to Nash. "Our offices have already conferred and after hours of discussion, this is as good as it gets."

Nash lowered his head. "Please. Take this deal. They won't give us anything else."

Melanie set the pen down on top of the document.

Glancing between them, Ian seemed to be weighing his choices. Then he picked up the pen, turned to the last page, and signed.

"Who hired you to kill Lynn?" Nash asked.

"Richard Jennings."

NASH ROCKED BACK on his heels in disbelief. "No." It didn't make any sense. "Rich wouldn't even know how to hire someone like you."

"If that were true, I wouldn't be sitting here."

"How did he find you?" Nash asked.

"Explaining that part is the reason I needed the immunity deal to cover more than the attempted murder of Delgado. I do freelance work for Trident Security," Ian said, and it rang a bell for Nash. "Usually, it entails making problems disappear."

"You mean you've killed people for them," Melanie said.

"When necessary. One of the cofounders, the vice president, Devin Jennings, gave his father my phone number."

The magazine cover flashed through Nash's mind like

lightning. "Five Minutes with Devin Jennings: Mitigating Artificial Intelligence Concerns."

"Devin paid for it."

"Cash? Check? Direct deposit?" Melanie asked.

"Same method we've used in the past. Bitcoin."

Nash groaned. Every transaction could be traced on the blockchain, a permanent digital record, linking one address to another. The problem was if someone was transferring money for a nefarious purpose, the address would be anonymous. They would be able to see the money and track it, but not link it to a specific person.

"That better not be your evidence," Melanie said, "or your deal will be null and void."

"I recorded the call, with Richard asking me to kill Lynn Delgado. He insisted that it had to be done before Christmas, and in such a way that would never lead back to him."

That's why Ian tried to make it look like a serial killer was after Lynn.

Melanie folded her hands in front of her. "How do we get our hands on the recording?"

Ian flipped over the document. On the back, he scribbled something. "That's my account and password for Google Drive. There's quite a few video files."

"Related to other murders?" Nash asked.

"Yes."

Melanie stepped closer to the table. "Will any of those files directly link to Trident Security?"

"Some will," Ian said, and Melanie looked like Christmas had come early for the DA's office. "But you should start with the digital file labeled 'Laramie Xmas.' You'll hear everything. Including Rich warning me to watch out for Special Agent Garner. Former ranger. Still in love. Still sniffing around her. There's also copies of texts we exchanged. The last one was after I failed to kill her in the car. He provided me the details of her vacation to the Red Tail

Lodge. He was very clear that I wasn't to hurt her friend and to avoid any collateral damage if possible. Lynn was supposed to be the only casualty."

"But why?" Nash asked. "Why on earth would he want her dead?" And why a deadline of Christmas?

Ian shrugged. "I don't ask such things. The why isn't my business. Only the how and when. If you want to know, you'd have to ask Delgado or Jennings."

Lynn.

Nash spun around and flew out into the hall. By the time he crossed the threshold of the observation room, Lynn was making her way to the door. "What's Rich's reason?"

Her face was pale and shocked. She was shaking her head as if this couldn't be true.

He cupped her arms. "I need you to tell me his reason."

She squeezed her eyes shut. "This all goes back to that night. At Turning Point. With Andy."

"What does Andy Crombie have to do with this? I don't understand."

Lynn looked up at him. Tears glistened in her eyes. "Because of Andy I walked in on Rich. With Cindy Morris. I got the feeling that something inappropriate was going on between them. After I visited my family in Fort Collins and came back to town, I went to see Cindy. She admitted that they had been having an affair."

"So what?"

"He was treating her. She was a client. It was unethical and illegal. But it also got me thinking."

"About what?"

"Whether he'd done this before. Our offices are sound-proofed. He said it was to ensure patient privacy and to limit distractions. But what if he had a different motive?"

To have sex with his clients in the office?

Nash had never thought of Rich as a sleazeball before, and now it was hard to think anything else.

"Talking to some of his previous clients," Lynn said, "another woman admitted that he had started an inappropriate relationship with her. After he began treating her."

"Did you report him?"

"No. That's why I don't understand this. I confronted him, of course. Told him it was unacceptable. I gave him a choice. To retire or to be reported. He agreed to change the status of his license to inactive, which I'm able to track to ensure it never reverted back to active, and when the expiration date came, he was supposed to let it expire."

"Did you give him a deadline of Christmas to retire?"

With a shudder, she nodded. "What he did is considered psychological abuse, even though the sex was consensual. I spared him criminal charges by giving him a choice. I promised him I wouldn't tell anyone and that I'd keep it to myself. Why? Why would he hire that man to kill me?"

Nash brought Lynn into his arms and held her, close and tight. "I don't know. But we're damn well going to find out when we arrest him."

Chapter Twenty-One

The drive to Rich's house was surreal.

A man she had once called a friend and considered to be a mentor had hired a contract killer to murder her. After she had done everything possible not to ruin his reputation while fulfilling her ethical obligations.

The convoy hit the old two-lane bridge that ran over the Laramie River, dragging her from her thoughts. They were close now but had just missed a shortcut. There was a frontage road that provided access to the driveway at the rear of the house, where his garage was located.

The shortcut would've saved them five minutes.

It was too late to turn back now.

Nash led the way in his truck. A red-and-blue flashing strobe light sat on the dashboard. Behind them were Holden and Mitch in one vehicle. Livingston and Russo in the other.

Shaken, sick, Lynn wrapped her arms around herself. Even after listening to the audio recording and hearing Rich's voice—irrefutable evidence—she still found it hard to believe.

"Back at the hospital," Nash said, dragging her from her thoughts, "I thought it went without saying that things will be different. That I won't be afraid anymore. Even when it comes to the hard stuff. Like sharing. But I realize now, you need to hear me say it. Your concerns are mine. Any issues we have, we can work through it. We just have to be willing to try."

Time was what he needed. And her love. And her almost dying. But he was finally willing to take down the wall. Permanently.

"You're right. I did need to hear it," she said. "As long as we're open with each other, honest, I can see a future for us." A bright, happy one.

They only had to get to the other side of this dark tunnel first.

Nash and the others pulled into the U-shaped driveway at the front of the house.

"Are you sure you want to come inside?" he asked.

"Yes. I don't want to hear his answer secondhand. I need to see his face when he tries to explain."

Nash put a hand on her knee, giving it a little squeeze. "All right. It goes against protocol to have you in there, but you might be useful in helping to get a full confession out of him for everything. Hopefully, we'll wrap this up, putting an end to it once and for all. Just stay behind me and Holden."

She was glad to have him at her side through this. So she didn't have to face it alone. No matter what, she would always be able to count on him. To have her back. To fight for her.

That kind of certainty and the strength of his love was more than she had ever dreamed of. Neither of them was perfect, each beautifully flawed, but she had discovered that they were perfect together.

Getting out of the truck, Lynn had a sense of conviction and finality.

Walking up the front steps, Nash said, "Rich lied. About selling his house. There's no for-sale sign. That bastard never bothered because he thought you'd be dead by now."

The notion sickened her.

Nash knocked as the others gathered behind them, the red-and-blue flashing lights washing over them.

It didn't take long for Rich to open the door. His startled gaze took them in. "Good evening. Is there something I can do for you?"

"As a matter of fact, there is," Nash said. "May we come inside?"

"Certainly." Rich stepped aside, letting them all in. Then he shut the door. "Is there a case you'd like me to consult on?" He looked at Holden. "Like I did for you yesterday."

"Something like that," Holden said.

"Maybe we should go into the living room and sit down." Rich gestured to the room off the foyer.

"We don't need to go to the trouble." Nash pulled out the arrest warrant and handed it to him.

"What's this?" Rich took his reading glasses from his pocket and put them on. As he began reading, a frown pulled at his mouth.

"It's a warrant for your arrest," Nash said. "For the attempted murder of Lynn Delgado."

"There must be some mistake," Rich stammered. "I'm a pillar of the community. I would never do such a thing. Where did you get such a preposterous idea?"

"From Ian Ellis." Nash stepped up to Rich. "The contract killer sitting in a holding room in the sheriff's department."

"Well, he must be lying." Rich's cheeks reddened. "For some sick, twisted reason. This is some kind of awful mistake."

Nash shook his head. "The only mistake was the one you made. Trusting a hired killer not to record your phone call. You're going to go to prison."

Rich blanched.

"I heard the call," Lynn said. "Between you and Ellis." Her nerves were rubbed raw, but her voice was solid and strong. "Giving him details about me. My life. Telling him that you wanted me dead before Christmas. We were friends. I helped you. I protected you. Why would you do this?"

Straightening, Rich's entire demeanor changed. Gone was the appearance of an innocent victim. "Why?" There was so much venom laced into that one word. "I am the one who helped you after you moved to town. I took pity on you because of your aunt. Do you think I wanted or needed a partner in my practice? I ensured you had plenty of clients. I was *your* friend. And when Andy came there, dead set on killing you, I put myself between him and you." Rich stabbed the air in her direction. "I got shot, took a bullet," he said, holding up the arm that was in a sling, "trying to protect *you*. How do you repay me? By threatening to ruin me. By forcing me into an early retirement. By stealing my practice!"

Dropping the warrant, Rich lunged at Lynn, going for her throat. Her heart jolted as she stumbled backward.

Nash and Holden grabbed him by the arms, restraining him.

The other deputies closed in around her, forming a barricade of bodies and badges.

Reciting his Miranda rights, Holden removed the sling and handcuffed Rich with his wrists in front of him.

"Hiring Ian Ellis wasn't enough?" Nash asked. "Why did you have to terrorize her with those letters? Do you have any idea how sick it was to torment her with the idea that harm was going to come to her before you sent that killer after her?"

"I don't know what you're talking about." Bewilderment washed over Rich's face. "Why would I send her letters advertising the fact that I intended to kill her? I was desperate. Not daft." Then the contours of his expression slowly shifted, changing as though something had dawned on him.

"You didn't send the letters?" Lynn asked.

"No." His voice dropped to a contemplative whisper. "I didn't." Rich swore under his breath.

"But you know who did, don't you?" Nash asked.

"No," Rich snapped, glaring at him. "I don't."

"Cindy." The name left Lynn's mouth on instinct. "She sent the letters. Didn't she?" Lynn recalled that Cindy was originally from Jackson. She went to visit her family often. It would have been easy for her to make stops on the route and send the letters from various mailboxes.

The hot air in Rich deflated and he crumpled inward on himself. "She joked around with the idea. I told her not to. I warned her not to. She understood how you hurt me. The depths of the betrayal. And she wanted to hurt you back."

"You're still seeing her?" Lynn asked, appalled. "Did she know you were planning to kill me?"

Rich straightened, regaining his vigor. "I shouldn't have intervened that night. I should've let Andy kill you!" he spat.

"Get him out of here and down to the station." Holden handed him over to Livingston and Russo.

The two deputies hauled Rich out the door and loaded him into their vehicle.

Coming to her side, Nash curled a protective arm around her shoulder. Together, they watched him being driven away.

Nash kissed the top of her head. "He can't hurt you anymore."

"I know." She put her head on his chest. "But I'll feel better once Cindy is brought in."

"Don't worry," Nash said. "We'll get her and prove that she was behind the letters. Justice will be served."

ONCE NASH AND Lynn left the house, Holden tugged on a pair of latex gloves and took out an evidence bag. "Ready to do this?" he asked Mitch.

"Yeah, the sooner we get this done and get out of here, the sooner I can have a beer."

"I'll start down here. You take upstairs. Bag and tag anything that might support the case."

"Okay." Pulling on gloves, Mitch bounded up the stairs.

Heading down the hall, Holden looked in the dining room. Candles were burning. Two dirty napkins were on the table. One had red lipstick smeared on it.

He went deeper into the house. In the kitchen, he spotted two wineglasses on the counter. Neither was empty. Two dirty plates were in the sink.

A cold breeze cut through the room, drawing his attention to the back door. It was cracked. As if someone hadn't shut it all the way, perhaps leaving in a hurry.

Had Cindy Morris been here?

The back light was on. He stepped outside and looked around.

Jennings's Mercedes was parked in front of the garage. Beside it were fresh vehicle tracks. Looked like the doctor's dinner companion skedaddled when they arrived. He followed the tracks away from the house down an incline.

Where did it lead? Was there a side road?

HOLDING THE STEERING wheel with his left hand, Nash reached over and took Lynn's hand with his other one. "You did Rich a favor. I'm sorry he didn't see it that way."

"So am I." She sighed, tightening her fingers around his. "I can't believe Cindy Morris is complicit in all this."

He hated the worry on her face. She needed a break from thinking about it. Needed to focus on happy things to come once they made it to the other side. "After we get Cindy, we'll celebrate."

"That sounds nice. I can't wait."

The material of the road shifted as they hit the bridge.

"Do you ever wish I made you laugh more? Or took you dancing?"

"What? Where did that come from?"

Your brother. "Something I've been thinking about."

"If I wanted a comedian, I'd be with one. But dancing sounds good."

"Really?"

"Yeah," she said, her spirits lightening. "We could go to the Stagecoach. They have live music. Or we could do some slow dancing at home."

"Now you're talking." Smiling, he looked over at her.

She leaned in to kiss him. Then her gaze veered. "Nash! Look out!"

High beams flashed in front of them, blinding him.

The truck came out of nowhere, bearing down on them at twice their speed, heading straight for them. Nash swerved to the right to avoid a head-on collision. His only thought was to get away from the danger. In those few split seconds, he hadn't considered the consequences of making such a sharp, sudden turn. The tires skidded, the rear end fish-tailing. But it was too late. The other truck smashed into his left side. The jarring *bang* of the impact knocked the breath from him, sending a shock wave through his body as they were rammed into the guardrail.

A piercing scrape of metal on metal wailed in the air.

Then the driver accelerated, adding deliberate force that pushed his truck. The smell of burning rubber filled his nose. He yanked on the wheel, trying to turn them in the opposite direction. But they were pinned between the guardrail and the front end of the other truck.

Slamming on the brakes, he hoped that might stop them from being shoved sideways.

Steel whined and screeched. His door groaned as it was crushed inward. The old guardrail on Lynn's side buckled and snapped, giving way.

On pure instinct, he thrust his right arm out over Lynn to protect her from the inevitable fall. He braced himself for the impact.

She screamed, frantic. Her face pale with terror. There was nothing Nash could do to stop them from sliding as they were thrust over the edge. The grille of the other vehicle was locked to his door, dragging it with them. His truck tipped onto the right side and plummeted straight down, crashing into the Laramie River.

A gunshot sound followed as the airbags deployed. The impact sent a horrendous jolt through his body, the seat belt tightening, digging into his flesh. Lynn's screams stopped.

It felt as if somebody had slapped his face as hard as they could. Chalky dust clogged the air.

While the bags deflated, he noticed the windshield was cracked.

Gravity had separated the vehicles. The other truck had flipped and rolled away from them.

His truck was stuck at an awkward angle. Lynn's door was pressed against the river floor. His side was turned up, skyward, but this section of the river was deep enough to cover the truck with water.

"Lynn, can you move?"

She was dazed. Until the icy water flooding into the cabin sharpened her senses, soaking her right side. "Oh God."

Nash released his seat belt and eased down to help her. She screamed as the water rose, closing her mouth just before it covered her head.

He depressed the button on her seat belt, freeing her. Scooping her up, he lifted her from the water. Tilting his head back, he looked at his door. It was the fastest way out. He flipped the switch, unlocking the door, and pulled on the handle as he pushed up. Metal groaned, sticking together. Pain ripped through his wounded biceps. Frigid water rushed up their legs to their waists. He tugged harder, but it wouldn't budge.

The door was jammed shut.

Keep calm. Succumb to panic, you'll never get out.

His gaze fell to the webbed cracks in the windshield. He had to break through it.

Drawing his weapon, he took aim. Pumped three bullets into various spots in the windshield to weaken the glass. The holes poured more water inside, flooding the cabin faster.

Lynn was panting. Soon she'd hyperventilate if she didn't control her breathing. She stared at him with eyes filled with fear.

Desperation to keep her safe overwhelmed everything else. He kicked at the windshield, over and over. Bashing at it, he threw his weight behind every thrust. The water had reached Lynn's neck.

"After everything we've already been through," she said, wet and shivering, "we're going to drown in here."

Like hell they were. "No, we're not." Another kick with his boot heel and the windshield popped out.

Grasping Lynn by her waist, he guided her through the opening first. She swam out and up. He was right behind her. They didn't have far to go to reach the surface.

They popped out of the water. Both of them drawing in a lungful of air. Red-and-blue flashing lights caught his eye. Holden was there. He was climbing down the embankment, and they began swimming toward him.

Seeing that they were all right, Holden took off toward the other vehicle. The rear end of truck was in the water. The front end had managed to hit a tree on land.

Pain radiated through his bad arm with every stroke he took with it.

By the time they had made it to the bank, Mitch was waiting for them with wool blankets.

Nash helped Lynn out of the water, bearing her weight because of her bad leg as they made their way up on to land. He sat her down.

"Are you two okay?" Mitch asked, wrapping a blanket around Lynn.

Teeth chattering, shivering down to the bone, Nash nodded, taking the other blanket and throwing it around himself. "How...did you know?" he asked between sharp breaths. "To come?"

"Holden was following a hunch," Mitch said. "He realized someone else had been at the house. They left when we arrived, taking a back road."

"The sh-sh-shortc-c-cut," Lynn said, trembling, her hair plastered to her head.

Holden jogged back over to them. "The driver is dead. Broken neck from the crash. It was Cindy Morris."

Lynn lowered her head, her shoulders slumping. Another life lost in this madness.

"That could've been us," she said in a low voice. "Necks broken. Or drowned. I hate how close I've come to losing you."

Nash put an arm around her, relieved the circle was now closed and there was no one else to worry about. She leaned into him, resting her head on his shoulder.

"Rich is going to get what he deserves for setting all this in motion," Nash said. "Ian Ellis will go to prison for a long time. And even Rich's son will have his day in court. Melanie will see to it that Trident Security doesn't get away with the things they've done. You're safe. No one is going to hurt you ever again." He'd make sure of it.

"I want to put all of this behind us. No more darkness and death."

He couldn't agree more. This nightmare was over. Once and for all.

And he was ready to focus on the future right now. "Move in with me," Nash blurted out.

Sitting upright, she stared at him. "Did you hit your head in the crash?"

Laughing as his jaw trembled from the cold, he rose to his feet. Then he reached out for her. She took his hand and he pulled her up, facing him. "I didn't hit my head. I know what I want, and that's you, Lola. I'm in this for the long haul."

"You realize part of that haul will be the occasional family dinner in Fort Collins."

More Jake. Wonderful. Nash wasn't going to jump for joy about that, but he was willing to jump through any hoops for her. "I do. And it also means you have to meet my brothers."

They checked in on each other over the phone, but it had been some time since they'd seen one another. It was long overdue, and he couldn't think of a better reason than to introduce the woman he loved.

He stepped closer, erasing the gap between them, letting her lean on him. Regardless of what trials and tribulations might be ahead of them, he wanted to be there to support her. To love her.

She searched his eyes. "You're serious."

"I've never been more so in my life." Lowering his mouth to hers, he kissed her. Through the cold wetness of their skin, their love burned, warming him from the inside out. "Provided you think you can handle having me around all the time," he said.

"I can definitely handle you."

For better or worse, she certainly could.

After they moved in together, he'd make sure she was

happy and ready for the next step. Then he'd propose. The two of them being together was right. She was his forever.

"We need to get out of these clothes and warm up." Lynn smiled at him. "Take me home. *Our* home."

* * * * *

SHIELDING COLTON'S WITNESS

LINDA O. JOHNSTON

Yet again and as always, this story is dedicated to my dear husband, Fred. I also once more want to thank all the other authors in this enjoyable series, as well as Carly Silver, our wonderful editor for the Colton books.

Chapter One

Alexa Colton sat down at her desk at the Blue Lark-spur, Colorado, office of the US Marshals Service. Before putting her purse into a drawer, she pulled out her phone and checked the time. It was not yet eight o'clock.

She smiled, stuck her phone on her desktop and swiped her short blond hair back from her face. Time to get busy.

Following her usual routine, she had arrived early that day, said good morning to the few other marshals, deputies and support staff she'd seen, then hurried up the stairs to her office on the third floor and shut the door behind her.

Her own office. This room, with space enough only for her desk, two chairs facing it and a couple of file cabinets off to the side, was an accomplishment. She'd shared a large space before when she was a deputy marshal. But now she was a marshal working in witness protection and had her own workplace at twenty-six.

She booted up her computer on the right side of her desk.

Her phone rang at the same time she saw she'd received an email from her boss, Marshal Vince Cudahy. He wanted to see her first thing.

She wasn't surprised that he was the person calling but was a bit concerned that he was both calling and emailing at the same time. What was on his mind? It had to be something important, with that kind of urgency.

Answering her phone, she said, "Hi, Vince. What's going on? I just sat down and saw your email."

"Good," said his deep, scratchy voice. "You're here. I'll be right there."

He hung up before she could offer to join him in his office instead. Whatever he wanted to talk to her about must be important.

She stood and took a quick look at herself. She wore what was standard around here—a black, long-sleeved shirt with metallic buttons and a badge on the front pocket, tucked into black pants. Her tied shoes were black, too, the thick tread on the soles for safety if she ever had to run while on the job.

She didn't have much time to make sure she appeared appropriate since her door was flung open almost immediately.

Vince must have headed over quickly, although it wouldn't have taken long to get here from his office at the end of the hall.

"Hi, Alexa," he said hurriedly. "Got an important assignment for you, starting tomorrow."

"Great," she said. "Tell me about it."

Fiftysomething Vince was at least twice Alexa's age. He had neither facial hair nor hair on his head, and his features were loose and wrinkled. But there was a shine to his light brown eyes beneath his pale brows that suggested he was passionate about what he said and did. Right now, he held a file folder in his thick hand.

"Sure," he said. "Sit down."

She obeyed, leaning forward in her chair as he took a seat at the other side of her desk.

He clasped his hands together and stared. "So are you ready to take on another assignment?" His voice remained scratchy but almost harsh, as if he expected her to say no—which was unlikely to happen. Alexa was proud of what she did.

Another person in trouble she could take care of, to help bring criminals to justice? *Bring it on*, she thought. "Absolutely," she replied. Over the past year, since she'd begun working in witness protection, she'd helped four women stay safe, shielding them from people they ultimately testified against in court. Every situation had gone well, and she loved helping victims in need. Her subjects had seemed relieved to have another woman in charge of guarding them. In her custody, none of the witnesses had been harmed; those they'd testified against had all been found guilty of the crimes they'd been charged with.

"Okay, here are the basics. I'll explain more, but to do this you'll be heading to Arizona tomorrow with the man under your protection, who is currently living here. He has had several of our marshals taking care of him over the past months. He'll be testifying against another law enforcement officer in Phoenix at the end of this week."

Wow, even with no details yet, Alexa was somewhat floored. She would be defending a man this time?

If so, that would be a first. And another law enforcement officer?

Plus, Phoenix, Arizona, was a substantial drive from Blue Larkspur—at least a day away.

Oh yeah. This could be a real challenge.

Was she up for it? Especially since she'd be watching over a man, who might not feel a woman could handle it? Of course! Sure, the situation could feel uncomfortable, driving a distance alone with a guy needing protection, but so what? She'd handle it as well as she had the others.

She had questions but let Vince take the lead in describing more about the situation.

Her subject, who'd been given the name Daniel Brennan, had been in the program for a while. Alexa wondered why he'd had so many different marshals protecting him but didn't ask; she assumed the danger he was in was the reason. He would be testifying as the key witness against a police chief in a murder trial. "You're to take over watching him first thing tomorrow, so you'd better get ready today."

"Will do," she said earnestly. "Is it okay if I take the rest of the day off to get ready?"

She had something in mind to do that afternoon to bring any anxiety under control before it even began— ride her favorite horse at the nearby dude ranch owned by a couple of her siblings.

"Sure thing. You should get in touch with your subject soon to let him know your schedule, though. He'll be expecting your call. I've given him your phone number to confirm your identity when you contact him."

"Of course."

"And be sure to stay in touch with me and let me know any questions that come to mind and if you have any concerns." Her boss was standing now, regarding her with those intense eyes as if attempting to see inside her head to make sure she was okay with this new assignment. He shoved the file folder toward her, and she glanced inside as she accepted it. It contained at least a couple of printed pages. "It's highly classified," Vince said, "so be careful with it."

"Of course. And this sounds like one interesting and important assignment. Thanks for giving it to me." Alexa stood, too. She felt proud. She hadn't been in this job that long, and her boss was trusting her with something that sounded highly significant. But she worked hard and was glad to see her efforts were paying off.

"Yeah, I know it's a bit different," he said. "And it's definitely important." He leaned his large body toward her slightly and said, "Now make me happy that I decided to give it to you by succeeding at it. Got it?"

"I definitely do." This time Alexa gave her boss a genuine salute.

His grin turned the creases on his face upward. He saluted back, pivoted officially and, after opening the door again, stomped out of the office, closing the door behind him.

Wow. Alexa felt her heart race but took a deep breath and then another. First thing, she needed to learn as much as she could about Daniel Brennan.

She sat back down and opened the file, studied it for a few minutes, then researched the situation both in the secure department files and online. She'd heard of the underlying case since it had dominated the news a few months ago, but she hadn't heard of any local connection internally—like, having one of the victims and a witness, who remained alive, under witness protection. Those other marshals who'd taken care of him had apparently been appropriately discreet.

The police chief defendant at the upcoming trial, from Tempe, Arizona, was named Samuel Swanson. He was not only accused of murdering a cop who'd been a subordinate but also had been under investigation for running a prostitution ring.

That cop's partner, who'd also been working on the investigation, had also been shot, and had disappeared, according to the media—but Alexa knew he really was the one in protective custody, the man she was about to guard.

Daniel Brennan was that cop. His real name was Dane Beaulieu. His picture had been made public earlier, and Alexa suspected there'd be a lot more in the news about him, and the case, as the trial began.

Dane Beaulieu. Alexa couldn't help blinking when she saw his photos. As an important witness, and a victim of a shooting who'd survived and wanted to get justice for his brother officer, he sounded like a possible hero. And he certainly was one handsome guy.

But that was irrelevant.

She would call Daniel Brennan on the secure phone supplied to him by the department and let him know she would see him tomorrow.

DANE BEAULIEU SAT on the cheap sofa in the living room in the tiny apartment he'd called home for the past few months. No, the apartment *Daniel Brennan* had rented, he reminded himself.

The apartment rented for him by the US Marshals Service, of all things. Him. A law enforcement officer. Under witness protection.

Absurd. But necessary. His preference was to stay alive, and there were those who wanted to do away with him and had the knowledge and ability to accomplish that much too easily.

It was midmorning. He'd just gotten a text message from Marshal Vince Cudahy, letting him know he would soon be hearing from the marshal who was to take over his protection, and giving him a name and phone number to watch for.

The name Vince had texted him was Alexa Colton, which was interesting, too. Dane knew the name Colton. There were quite a few family members in law enforcement across the country.

Plus, here in Blue Larkspur, he'd heard that a member of the Colton family, a judge, had gotten into trouble with the law himself years ago by making extra money while convicting some innocent people, and that had led to other family members starting an organization to help other people, in an attempt to atone for it.

And a woman? Well, in his experience, it wasn't only men who did well in law enforcement. He hoped this one excelled, as the five marshals previously assigned his case had done.

Vince had also noted he'd sent an email. Dane checked it out on his secure laptop, also acquired from the Marshals Service. The email didn't include much information, but it did provide some background.

Not that there was much info there, though.

Well, it sounded like, over the next day or so, he'd have a lot of time to talk with Alexa Colton and find out more.

It was almost time to leave. To go home. To do what he'd wanted—no, needed—to, for his own peace of mind, as well as to now accomplish the very little he could for his dead friend and partner, Alvin O'Reilly.

And to do his own job, on hold now and maybe forever, as a vice detective for the Tempe Police Department. Which he missed. He didn't like being in hiding. He didn't like having to go against the man who'd been his chief. But it all had become necessary, thanks to that chief.

He rose and started pacing, glancing at himself in the mirror over the fireplace with false logs that glowed when a button was pushed. His mind had been working on jokes about that from the moment he'd first seen it.

He loved jokes; the cornier, the better. And these days, getting a laugh about anything was a good thing.

He made himself smile as he looked into that mirror, though he felt no humor at the moment.

He'd pretended to be a real human being named Daniel a few days ago when he'd left this apartment to get his dark hair trimmed into its usual conservative cut. He'd had Marshal Paul with him at the time, acting as a buddy but watching the world around them for Dane's protection. They'd also stopped at a grocery store before coming back here. Even knowing he would need to leave this place soon for the trial, he'd bought a bunch of stuff that shouldn't go bad—frozen food and otherwise.

But he missed even being able to shop when he chose, along with everything else in a normal life.

So when would he hear from this Alexa? They needed to head for Phoenix tomorrow to get him settled in and prepared to testify when the trial began in a couple of days.

The homicide had occurred in Tempe, which was in Maricopa County, Arizona. The trial would therefore be held at the Maricopa County Superior Court, which was located in Phoenix.

He wasn't clearing out this apartment yet, though. He'd wait till things were over, hopefully successfully, and then return to—

The burner phone he'd recently been given rang. He looked at the screen before answering, having already memorized the number with the Colorado area code Vince had sent, and this was it.

He swiped the screen to answer and made sure his voice was firm. "Hello?"

"Hello, Daniel," said an equally firm female voice— a bit deep and somehow sexy, though that didn't make any sense given the circumstances. "This is Alexa Colton. I believe Vince Cudahy let you know I'd be in touch."

"Yes," Dane confirmed, "he did." He waited for her to continue.

"You and I should have an interesting time ahead of us," she said. "We'll drive to our destination tomorrow. I'll pick you up at 8:00 a.m. Does that work for you?"

"Definitely. See you then."

She hung up immediately, which was fine with Dane.

No need to draw things out now. They'd have a lot of time together to learn more about each other soon.

The drive to Phoenix should take around nine hours but, knowing the situation, he figured they would make some preplanned stops for security purposes. Worst case, they could figure out a locale to stay overnight since the trial didn't start till Thursday, three days from now.

How would it all work out? Would he need Alexa's protection? It was certainly likely.

He'd no doubt have opportunities to determine Alexa's competence after they met up tomorrow. He would protect himself as much as possible, too.

For now, he decided to chill as much as he could for the rest of the day, here in his small apartment. He'd make a sandwich for lunch, and have a dinner of leftovers later.

He checked his fridge. He had plenty of food.

Even better, he had a couple of bottles of beer.

He figured that, as he drank one, he'd ponder how things might go starting tomorrow as he hoped to get justice for his friend and partner. With the help of a US Marshal—with one sexy voice.

He wondered what she looked like…and knew he'd soon find out.

ALEXA LEFT THE office a short while after the phone call. Her subject had sounded nice, professional, ready to proceed and, hopefully, to listen to her instructions as they headed for Phoenix.

She would find out how nice, and how respectful, starting early tomorrow.

Right now, as she headed for the Gemini Ranch, she called Kayla St. James. She'd rather bother one of the ranch hands than either of her twin siblings Jasper and Aubrey, who were four years older than her. As ranch owners, they tended to be fairly busy most of the time and would most likely refer her to Kayla anyway to saddle up her favorite horse, Reina. Sweet people that they were, the twins always tried to accommodate Alexa as long as Reina wasn't busy with dude ranch guests of the day.

Fortunately, according to Kayla, Reina was available, which made Alexa smile.

When she arrived, she parked her white SUV, an imported hybrid that served her well, in the open lot in front of the ranch's vast and attractive main lodge. She grabbed a backpack from the floor behind her seat and headed toward the door, calling Kayla again. "I'm here," Alexa said. "I'll go change then meet you at the barn, okay?"

"Sounds good."

The inside of the main lodge entry was crowded, filled with the buzz of a lot of conversations. Alexa smiled, glad for Aubrey and Jasper's success. They always seemed to be busy, and she was proud of them, even though she didn't see either of them in the large room lined with multipaned windows and decorated with a lot of dark-shaded wood.

It didn't take Alexa long to wind her way through the lobby to the restroom, where she changed into clothes a lot more amenable to horseback riding than a marshal's uniform. The long-sleeved denim shirt should be comfortable enough in the October coolness since it wasn't raining. Her dark blue jeans and Western-styled boots completed the outfit—along with her official weapon, a gun she always carried but kept hidden in a pocket.

Still not seeing anyone she knew, she returned outside to place her uniform in a secure area in her SUV, not visible from the outside, then locked it. Finally, it was time. She hurried back through the main lodge and out the rear door, then along the paved pathway to the barn.

The empty corral told her that any guests taking rides late this morning were already out on the trails. She was happy to find Kayla near the stall door, apparently finishing up with securing the saddle onto Reina's back. Reina was lovely and sweet, a pale bay horse with a white face. Jasper and Aubrey had indicated she was at least part Arabian.

At five foot seven, Alexa wasn't a particularly short woman, but the ranch hand was a couple of inches taller. The way Kayla handled horses and their feed made it clear that her muscular physique wasn't just for show. She wore casual clothes, too; jeans and a green sweatshirt this day. Her long, dark brown hair was in its usual ponytail down her back.

"Hi, Alexa," she said right away, her smile broad beneath her arched brows.

"Hi, Kayla." Alexa approached and ran her hand down Reina's face, enjoying the warmth and feel of the short coat and the way the mare snorted and nodded her head.

"Looks like your friend is glad to see you. So am I."

Alexa laughed. "Well, I don't think I have to tell you how glad I am to see both of you. I need a ride."

"Job giving you a hard time?" Kayla knew that Alexa was a US Marshal who protected people for a living. They'd talked about it often—or at least the generalities Alexa could discuss—whenever Kayla accompanied Alexa on her rides. Kayla also knew not to ask specific questions about what Alexa was up to.

Before Alexa could ask if she was going to have human company that day as well as equine, Jasper came into the barn. Like the women here, he was dressed casually. He moseyed forward, smiling broadly. "Hi, sis," he said as he reached them. He wore his strawberry-blond hair on the long side and his dark blue eyes glittered as he shared a brief hug with Alexa.

But as he stepped back and looked at his ranch hand, Kayla moved away. "Sorry I won't be riding with you," she told Alexa. Holding her hand up in a wave goodbye, she headed for the door. Alexa had noticed that she seemed to walk away often whenever Jasper approached, and had always wondered why, though neither of them talked about it.

When Jasper offered to ride along with her, she decided that today she would use the opportunity to be pushy about it.

He rode beside her on Shadow, a gorgeous black horse with a somewhat aggressive personality. Few of their guests were permitted to ride on a steed so assertive, but he was one of Jasper's favorites.

This was far from the first time that Jasper had joined Alexa when she wasn't with Kayla. Sometimes Aubrey rode with her or she rode with both of them. But things appeared to be too busy for Aubrey to be her sister's company today. From what Alexa had heard, a

TV show was recently shot on the ranch. Plus, Aubrey had to be planning her wedding. Yes, she'd met the right guy and was getting married. Alexa was even a teeny bit jealous.

"So what's going on, Alexa?" Jasper asked. "You've got some time off?"

"Only this afternoon. I'm starting a major project tomorrow."

Jasper knew better than to ask for details.

Alexa's own mind kept circling around what she would be doing the next day. The potential danger she'd face. How she'd handle protecting a fellow law enforcement officer who happened to be a man.

For this afternoon, she forced herself not to focus on it.

They rode across the narrow stream behind the barn and along a path into the woods, discussing how active the dude ranch was and future promotional plans.

Alexa loved this route. The woods contained mostly leafless trees, yet the brisk October air and crunching under the horses' hooves somehow made her feel happy. Even more enjoyable was the feel of Reina's wide, warm body walking slowly but determinedly ahead. This was a wonderful trail ride.

Still, the question always inside Alexa whenever she saw Jasper and Kayla's interactions, or lack thereof, surfaced once more.

"So," she blurted. "Tell me. At last. Why does Kayla act that way around you?"

She looked at her brother astride Shadow and he shrugged a broad shoulder. "Okay. I guess I should finally let you know. You can thank our dad for it."

"What!"

Ben Colton had been dead for many years. He'd been a judge—and, as it turned out, a corrupt one. To support his twelve children and their mother, he'd taken bribes and kickbacks from owners of private prisons and juvenile detention centers to sentence adults and kids, guilty or not, to their facilities. He had died before suffering any consequences.

And as a result of his misdeeds, their family had begun a very special organization, The Truth Foundation, to help clear the innocent. Some had also gone into law enforcement—like Alexa.

"What do you mean?" Alexa prodded.

Jasper then told her that Kayla's dad had been one of the people their father had put away for life. "I've no idea if he was guilty or innocent. Kayla knows my issues with our dad, so she's at least civil to me as one of her bosses, and Aubrey, too. But we're definitely not friends, even though we're civil co-workers."

"Wow." Alexa shook her head slightly. "Another thing to blame our dad for." She felt a bit choked up, so she pressed her heels into Reina's side slightly harder. "Let's go!" she said, and Reina began galloping, with Jasper and Shadow following.

It wasn't long before Alexa decided to enjoy her time with Jasper more, so she slowed and started asking her brother questions about what was going on with their other siblings—anything he knew about all ten of them, including Aubrey and her engagement. And then the conversation turned to their mom, Isadora, who preferred being called Isa.

"Far as I can tell she's dating someone," Jasper said.

"Yeah, and if I'm right that person may be the local police chief," Alexa responded.

They talked and rode a short while longer, but Alexa recognized at last that it was time to go and start getting ready for the next day. Her mind had already begun to wander away from their conversation.

"This has been great, bro," she finally said to Jasper as they walked their horses side by side along a wider portion of the trail.

"I hear a 'but' in that. Time for you to leave?"

"Afraid so. But I'll want to do this again. Soon."

And that, she would look forward to, though she wasn't sure how long she'd be involved in her upcoming assignment.

They soon turned a corner in the path and headed back to the barn. On the way they saw several other sets of horses being ridden by visitors and led by mounted ranch hands—including, at one point, Kayla.

Alexa chose not to wave. She'd see Kayla again, maybe even have her join her on another ride sometime soon.

But at the moment, Alexa's thoughts had turned to wondering about how things would go tomorrow with the man she would be protecting. How much danger was he in? How perilous would it be for her?

But she hoped that her charge, who'd sounded okay, at least, in their brief phone call, would be cooperative.

Chapter Two

Several hours had passed since Dane had spoken with Alexa.

He would therefore soon be leaving this apartment. This small hangout he'd lived in for months. Would he remain safe? Who knew? But at least so far, no one had come after him here.

Not that he wasn't prepared for something, whether or not he was under protection. What mattered was that he would do all he could to get justice for Alvin and make sure his rat of a former boss paid.

He just wished his life hadn't changed so dramatically. But he would deal with it in the best way he could, danger or not.

He looked around the place yet again as he sat on the cheap blue-upholstered sofa, leaning back in his T-shirt and jeans and holding the bottle of beer he'd lifted from the coffee table in front of him.

He would work along with the marshal protecting him to ensure both of them remained safe and healthy. The sexy-sounding lady marshal who would be officially in charge of taking care of him.

Well, whatever it took for him to be able to return to his real life was a good thing.

Away from this tiny hellhole.

Oh, it was okay. The living room walls were smooth and white, and they contained a collection of photos of the Colorado Rockies, mostly in the winter, since the mountains were decorated with gleaming white snow.

The TV on the wall worked well with a remote control, and Dane used it often to try to keep from being bored. At least there was a cable system so he could watch anything from news to true crime to comedy, if he ever wanted to do that. And yeah, there were a few shows hosted by comedians who thrived on corny humor. His favorites.

But was he bored? Hell yes. A lot of the time. He wanted to be out there, working his job, checking out evidence, following leads, doing…something. Anything besides waiting.

And thinking. Overthinking. Again. Like now. About what had happened to drag him here. About being shot. And, worse, about the loss of his good friend and partner, Alvin.

But Dane wanted to survive, to testify at the murderer's trial. And so he'd do as he was told.

For now.

The kitchen had all the necessary amenities.

He wondered what that Alexa, his protector, had eaten to start preparing for their journey. Hopefully, something a lot better than he'd had.

His thoughts wandered now to what it would be like when she arrived tomorrow. She was picking him up here early in the morning. He couldn't stop thinking about her deep, sensual voice…

As a US Marshal on witness protection duty, she'd be armed. And him? Yes, he still had his gun. He'd wondered, when he'd first entered WITSEC, if they'd try to take it from him to ensure he wouldn't shoot the marshals assigned to him. But, considering he had been in law enforcement for years, too, they'd likely realized that he knew better. That he'd only attack to defend himself.

Although if the person assigned to protect him attacked him… Unlikely.

Putting his beer down, he settled back on the sofa and stared at the TV remote control on the table in front of him. He didn't necessarily want to watch anything. Not even silly humor.

How was he going to sleep tonight? He needed to be rested in the morning.

What might relax him now?

An idea occurred to him. Oh, it was unlikely to relax him, but it shouldn't hurt, and it worked well with his sense of humor.

He grabbed his burner phone and checked the screen for recent phone calls. The number he was looking for came up right away.

He pressed the number and was pleased when the call was answered immediately. "Daniel?" demanded a sexy female voice. "Is everything okay?"

Daniel of course. Dane hopefully wouldn't have to answer to Daniel Brennan much longer, but he did now. "Yes," he said, "with me. I'm ready to go. But I'm calling to confirm that all's okay from your end, too."

"Yes, of course." Her voice wasn't so sexy with that grumble in it. "I'd have let you know if there were any problems."

"I figured. I'm tickled to know there aren't any. In fact, I'm so tickled, I'm wiggling about it and laughing." Dane couldn't help smiling, even though that might be corny and it wasn't much of a joke.

Apparently, Alexa didn't think so, either. "Whatever. Don't call again, though, unless you do have a problem. We both need to get our rest now. See you in the morning."

Dane made himself calm down and drop any attempt at joking. "Right," he said. "See you in the morning. I assume we're both to eat breakfast first."

"Exactly. We'll want to get on our way fast."

"Fast it'll be," Dane said, wondering how it would be to ride in the car for a long period of time with this woman whose voice he enjoyed hearing, but who'd not given any indication she had a sense of humor.

Well, he'd find out tomorrow.

"Good night," he said and hung up.

IT WAS MORNING, and Alexa was driving along the wide streets of Blue Larkspur toward the large apartment complex to pick up Daniel.

Daniel. She fortunately hadn't lost any sleep after their phone call last night. What had it really been about, though? she wondered for far from the first time as she stopped at a traffic light.

The witness who was now the subject of her protection duties had sounded a bit strange—and yet there was something about him that she'd appreciated. Maybe it was his attempt to keep things light as he'd checked on the status of an outing that would be anything but light, even though she didn't think what he'd said had been particularly funny.

She wondered what their conversation would be a short while from now, as they drove to the city where his life was likely to be in danger. Danger she would handle.

The light changed, and Alexa drove the plain gray SUV the Marshals Service had obtained for her for this assignment, rented with a license that couldn't be traced to her or her employer and shouldn't draw the attention of anyone looking to stop Daniel from arriving in Phoenix. She'd had it washed, and the inside still held the slight scent of a floral cleaner. She inhaled, concentrating on the clean smell for a moment to get her mind off what she was doing.

But then, she had to get back to it. As if she'd ever really left.

Only another few blocks to go.

She could have stayed overnight in the extra apartment leased by the marshals in the complex where they'd rented an apartment for Daniel, but she had decided to stay at home. From what she'd understood from Vince, things seemed calm here in Blue Larkspur and although there were some criminal activities in her hometown that her family wanted to stop, she hadn't heard of anything going on lately.

While she drove, Alexa let her mind wander—for now. She couldn't help thinking about the last telephone call she'd had before dropping off to sleep last night from the person she always spoke to at least once a day: her fraternal twin sister, Naomi.

They remained dear buddies, despite the fact they lived in different towns. They were the youngest of the dozen Colton kids, and they'd always been close to one another.

"Now, you be careful tomorrow," Naomi had said after they'd finished talking about what they would be doing for the rest of the week. Naomi was a reality TV show producer, of all things. And *she* thought it odd that Alexa had become a US Marshal, despite the fact that so many of their siblings were involved in law enforcement.

Alexa hadn't told her any details about her current assignment, only that she was off on a job for the next week or so, starting today.

And given the fact that she worked in witness protection, she wasn't surprised that her sister had warned her to stay safe.

There. Alexa saw the sign for The Village, the largest apartment complex in town. She drove along the wide entry with its pillars on both sides, and soon turned left. She pulled over and checked her phone. Vince had sent her a map of the area, indicating where Daniel's apartment was located. It was the last building on the left, and at the end of the ground floor.

Okay, it was time. She got out of the car and scrutinized the area. She noticed two women exit through a door in the next building over and kept her eyes on them. They headed the opposite direction from her and into the closest parking lot. Probably just residents leaving for the day. She'd glance at them often anyway.

She got to the door to the subject's building. It had small glass panes but was mostly thick wood. Good. A phone hung on the wall near the entrance, the apartment numbers listed.

Alexa chose Daniel's number from those programmed into her phone.

"Hello, Alexa," he answered immediately. "You here?"

"Yep. Buzz me in." She wanted to take a quick scan of his unit to ensure nothing looked wrong before they took off.

"Right," Daniel said, and she heard a buzz then a click at the door.

She turned briefly to reexamine the area. She no longer saw those women, or anyone else. Good. She pulled the door open and entered the hallway.

She'd entered through the door closest to Daniel's unit. Even so, she took a quick stroll down the corridor, passing half a dozen closed doors, watching and listening. Though she heard what might have been TVs or radios inside some of the units, she didn't find anything abnormal about the place.

She returned to Daniel's apartment and tapped on the door, which opened immediately. She hurried inside and shut it behind her.

And there he was, the man whose photo she'd looked at often during the past twenty-four hours. He was tall, maybe six feet, and definitely good-looking, although that didn't matter. He was the subject of her protection. That was all. But it didn't hurt to study him, to ensure she knew all she could about him.

Okay, dark brown hair, slightly long but in a conservative cut. Green eyes that stared at her, and she hoped she wasn't blushing. A handsome, angular face, with a well-shaped nose and slightly full lips.

Oh yeah. *Definitely* good-looking.

"Hello, Daniel," she said, nodding at him. "Are you ready to go?"

"Of course. I'm more than ready. I've been waiting for today for a long time."

Alexa understood what he was saying. And now she hoped to talk to him about what he'd gone through, what she had read about him and the events that had led to his being in witness protection.

She noticed a carryon suitcase on the floor behind him. "I assume that's coming with us?" She nodded toward it.

"Yeah. And I hope to return here for everything else that's mine really soon."

"In other words, you want the court decision to happen fast and well."

"Exactly. So— Let's go."

HE COULDN'T HELP glancing at her often. Her hair was light blond. Short, with side bangs. Framing a face that was lovely, highlighted by gorgeous, intense blue eyes.

Dane wasn't biased professionally. He'd always liked women. Respected them. Knew they could excel at whatever men did, too. And he'd worked with some really skilled female cops and investigators in his own offices. No reason to think any less of them than the men he worked with.

But maybe he did have prejudices hidden so deep inside that he didn't really know about them. Till now, maybe, and he certainly wasn't proud of the way his mind was going.

Still— Could a woman do a great job at protecting him?

Well, sure. She had to—to keep him safe. He'd find out. He'd help to the extent he needed to, wanted to, but for her to have been picked for this particular assignment, making sure he got to testify against the guy who'd murdered his partner, who'd also injured him, who'd led to him feeling so damned sad and angry... Well, her superiors had to think a lot of her.

As Dane settled in the passenger seat of her car, watching Alexa start driving away from his apartment complex toward Interstate 70, he assumed she would head in the best direction toward Phoenix that he'd found online.

But she was a local. He wasn't. He'd leave the route determination to her.

Still— "Would you like me to drive?" he asked. She'd gotten right into the driver's seat while he'd loaded his suitcase, his laptop inside, into the rear portion of the vehicle, so he hadn't been able to ask her before.

She glanced at him, then turned her eyes back to the busy city road they were on. "Why? Are you one of those men who assumes women aren't capable of driving? Or maybe not capable of witness protection?"

"Hey, I'm one of those men who enjoys being taken care of well by whoever does it, and if it happens to be a woman, so much the better. I just thought, since you're supposed to coddle me, protect me, make sure I get to our destination alive, that as a US Marshal you would want to be able to check out the roads we're on, our surroundings, to ensure you take perfect care of me." He'd said it seriously.

"Okay, consider yourself my kid for now. Yes, I'll protect you. Get you to our destination safely, or at least as safely as possible. But I've done this before. I know how to scan our surroundings to make sure everything's okay. So, you can just sit back and enjoy the ride. For now, at least. It's a long drive, so I might ask you to take over some of it, although I've already scheduled a few stops along the way."

He figured she had. She seemed professional. Efficient. Prepared to do her job. Never mind how beautiful she was.

And she considered him her kid? No way. She was younger than he was, for one thing. He assumed she was around twenty-five or twenty-six, young to be in charge of a subject in witness protection, so that was something impressive about her, too. And he was thirty.

He looked out the window, figuring he'd start a conversation soon to help them enjoy the drive more than if they stayed silent...or argued. And he didn't only want to think about her skills or looks or anything else that was personal. Like her sexiness.

They had a professional relationship, after all. He was relying on her. And—

"Are you armed?" she asked.

"Yes," he said, and patted his side pocket where he'd placed his weapon.

"Good. Me, too. And soon, I'll want to hear your side of what happened."

"Sure." He'd planned to do that, if it made sense. Not

quite yet, though. Once they got on the first highway, the first step toward their goal.

Only— They apparently were already there. As he'd been watching, they'd driven around several Blue Larkspur streets, sometimes even circling a block, he believed, before getting back onto a main drag.

She had evidently been maneuvering to make sure they weren't being followed. He'd been watching, too, and appreciated her professionalism as well.

She pulled onto a ramp that would head them northwest through Colorado, where they'd then turn south into Utah.

So he'd been right in his assumption. And she seemed right in having picked the best route.

He nodded to himself and settled his shoulders back on his seat. "Okay," he said. "Let's talk about what happened."

Chapter Three

Alexa was eager to hear it, but she had something to tell Daniel before she learned those details.

It was important that he knew the plans for this trip.

"Great," she said. "But first, I want to tell you how this journey to Phoenix will proceed. You're aware, aren't you, that the trial will take place there, even though the homicide occurred in Tempe?"

"Yeah," he said, "I am. The Maricopa County Superior Court is in Phoenix. But they're not that far apart."

"That's right."

"So, do you plan to drive us there right now, on this—what?—nine-hour trip, O Wonderful Chauffeur?"

She couldn't help glancing at him as the car ran smoothly over the current road. His tone was sarcastic enough that she had a desire to shout right back in his face, which she couldn't do.

He watched her with his dark brows raised and a hint of a grin on that face that shouldn't be so handsome, considering the irritating personality lying beneath.

"Nope," she finally said. "Yes, I'm starting us on this expedition, but you're going to help. Got it?"

"Got what? You haven't told me anything."

"I'm about to," she said.

"Hey," he said. "I want to hear all about those plans. How are we getting to Phoenix? And what are you going to do to keep me safe?"

Tie him up on the floor of the back seat, was the wish that circulated through her mind. Why was this guy so annoying?

And yet so darned sexy?

"I'm going to make several stops in towns along the way, at locations I already discussed with Vince. He'll have deputies or other law enforcement officers available at some, but not all, and I don't know which. But, of course, neither will anyone who might be after you."

And who did he think that would be? Not likely to be the ex-police chief he would be testifying against, who was in custody, but Alexa figured the guy might have hired others to help him. Daniel might know. And he'd already agreed to tell her more about what had happened to put him in the position of needing witness protection. Pointing at more specific enemies should be part of that, or at least she hoped so.

"Sounds good," he said. "What's our first stop—or should I guess?"

"Go ahead and guess," she said, shaking her head. This guy was a know-it-all on top of everything else... although maybe he wasn't just a smart aleck. Maybe he did know a bit.

That would make him an interesting subject of her witness protection. An interesting assistant who could help take care of himself.

"Let's see. The first noteworthy place I saw on the map was... How about Moab?"

He was right. It was the first town of any substance they'd get to after turning south.

But she had to ask. "Was that the last town you got to when you were first brought to Blue Larkspur from Tempe by one of my predecessors?"

"No. We flew to Grand Junction with me in disguise, then drove to Blue Larkspur from there," he said. "And in case you're wondering, I felt fairly comfortable in witness protection that soon, even though that marshal had just taken over. I'd never been under anyone's guardianship like that before. I suspected the marshal had info on everyone on that plane, including the pilots and flight attendants. That's what you witness protectors do, right?"

Alexa couldn't help feeling a little proud as she answered him. "Yep, that's what we do. And more. In case you're wondering, I've spent some time checking out the route and places we'll be stopping, as well as the facilities we'll have in Phoenix. Am I sure you'll be completely safe? Well, I'll make certain of it."

"Hey," Daniel said. "You're my marshal now. Thanks."

She was cruising in the slow lane on the four-lane road and managed another glance at her passenger. He was smiling at her—and what a smile. Large and apparently serious and—well, it couldn't be grateful, could it?

"Yeah," she said in response. "I am." Should she demand that he tell her his underlying story right away? Maybe soon. To get started, and learn more, she asked, "Do you live in Tempe?"

"Yes. And I really appreciated my home until…until what happened. But with the local police chief involved in the shooting that killed my partner and wounded me, I was glad when some good cops showed up and prevented me from getting hurt any worse. Fortunately, they determined I needed federal help and called the FBI while I was being treated in the hospital. The FBI put me in touch with the marshals, and I was glad when they said they'd help me. And move me to safety in witness protection, at least temporarily."

She'd wondered about that. She'd wondered a lot about the details of his situation.

"So they're the ones who brought you to Blue Larkspur?" she asked.

"Exactly." Daniel's voice sounded grim, uncharacteristic during the short time she'd known him, and she glanced at him. He was looking at her and, yes, he appeared even more than grim. Furious, maybe. But that still didn't minimize his good looks. "I might as well tell you the whole story now," he said, "since you asked, and we'll be on this road for a while."

"Good," she said, and she really was glad she would hear his side of what had happened.

Still, she had to be careful. She scanned the highway around them and saw nothing out of the ordinary. There weren't many cars on the road, but a couple of semis drove the other direction. The barren land was fairly flat with a few rises here and there, probably no place anyone could lie in wait without being seen.

Not that anyone was likely to know where they were or how they were getting to their destination, although they might be able to guess the timing somewhat thanks to the upcoming trial.

Still, she glanced in the rearview and side mirrors as well. Nothing looked in the least menacing.

She would keep watch, nonetheless.

"So here it is," Daniel began. "And by the way, yes, I know I'm Daniel to the world right now. But I'd appreciate it if you'd call me Dane while we're alone. I'd like to be myself as much as possible. And I'm hoping once the trial is over, I can return to my real life."

"Got it," she said, and gave herself a strong mental reminder to be careful which name she used for him, at least when they were around other people. "Okay, Dane. Tell me everything."

"It all began a few months back when I was my regular self, a vice detective in Tempe, Arizona." His tone was strong yet husky, and came across well despite the hum of the car tires on the pavement beneath them. Alexa looked over at him. He was leaning against the seat, arms folded and hands behind his head, as if he wanted to appear relaxed, but he didn't. "My partner, Alvin O'Reilly, and I were close friends and were used to getting difficult assignments—and succeeding in solving whatever crime they involved."

So he'd been a successful cop, or at least he believed so. Why was Alexa not surprised? He exuded confidence and competence. "Sounds like a career all of us in law enforcement strive for," she said to encourage him to go on.

"Yeah, sounds that way," he said dryly. "Our assignment at that time was to uncover a major prostitution ring in Tempe. Sounded like an interesting task, even as we got right down to work and did our usual good job of researching the situation till we learned who all the major players were. And that was when the shock hit us."

He became silent, and Alexa glanced at him. His arms were down now, and his expression as he stared out the windshield suggested he was reliving the emotion he had just described. Or attempting to shove it out of his mind.

"Who were they?" she asked quietly even though she knew the answer from her research.

He turned his head to look at her, though she couldn't go on watching him. She planted her gaze back on the road in front of them.

"We didn't believe it at first. We didn't want to believe it, even though the evidence was solid. But the guy in charge of the prostitution ring was none other than our boss, Chief of Police Samuel Swanson."

"How awful," Alexa said. "And I suppose he thought that, considering his position, he'd be able to get away with it."

"Yeah, that's what he thought."

Dane just sat there for a few moments, still looking forward. Alexa wondered what he was thinking but didn't ask. Not yet. He'd surely continue.

"Alvin and I just collected all the evidence we could. In silence. Without telling anyone in the department since, with the chief so involved, we didn't know who we could trust."

"Got it." Alexa's mind started swirling about what she would do if she ever found herself in a similar position.

She couldn't imagine Marshal Vince Cudahy running a prostitution ring, though Swanson had clearly proved anything was possible. But if anything like that ever happened, she knew she would do all she could to bring down whoever was committing such crimes, Vince or otherwise. Thanks to her own family situation, that was who she was.

Even more fortunate was the fact that as a Colton she had relatives she could trust who were also in law enforcement. At least she would have people to discuss the situation with, get their take on what she should do.

She didn't mention that to Dane.

Alexa had questions, though, about what had happened, but for the moment, she had to concentrate on her driving since a midsized green sedan was about to pass them, and she needed to make sure it didn't get too close. And that no one inside was paying any attention to Dane and her. That no one in the sedan was someone she needed to protect Dane from.

The car just rolled by in the passing lane. Only a driver inside, and though he glanced over, it seemed he only wanted to make sure he was passing safely. He didn't appear to try to look inside Alexa's vehicle.

Soon, he was ahead of them, and Alexa's breathing returned to normal.

"So what did you do?" she coaxed, wanting Dane to continue.

"We tried to stay discreet, although the chief, of course, knew what our assignment was. Maybe he thought we weren't smart enough, or brave enough, to out him even if we learned he was our target. Or maybe he thought we weren't even clever enough to figure out his connection, or would ask to become his ally. Well, he was wrong on all counts—and his revenge was to set us up.

"Alvin and I saw some things online about an upcoming evening of fun at an all-night club connected with a hotel. We also got a tip that some of the women there might be connected to a ring of exploited sex workers. So, of course, we had to go to the party undercover. And then, as we approached the door, the chief walked outside, hailed us, his left hand raised, smiling and calling out that we were invited, too, although since we'd come in disguise, he might not have recognized who we were at first."

"Really?" Alexa had to ask.

"That's what I figured, although we did have our phones out and were covertly taking pictures as part of our surveillance. Swanson, as he got closer, held his hand out, clearly wanting us to hand him our phones. And, no surprise, we refused. That was when he drew his gun. Maybe he knew by then who we were. Alvin was closer and…our boss shot him, grabbed his phone, then turned and fired at me. He hit me, but his shooting Alvin was enough of a warning and so I fled, bleeding and all.

"I was damned fortunate to get out of there. My wounds weren't exactly light, surface injuries, but I still managed to run and hide—and call 9-1-1."

He paused then, although he was breathing hard, and Alexa figured it was difficult for him to talk about it. "I'm glad you were okay enough to do that," she said.

"Me, too. And some uncorrupt cops arrived quickly, fortunately, so Swanson had to stand down. I learned later that he'd been smart enough to pretend to others that he'd had my back and that the shooter had run off. I didn't know where or how he'd hidden his gun, but I did know I was momentarily safe with the cops who'd showed up, and probably others."

Alexa could only nod, picturing the mayhem. Picturing a dying, or dead, cop on the ground. Picturing the handsome, strong, smart detective—currently off the job, but planning to return—beside her shot as well.

She shuddered, glad she was driving. Otherwise, she might want to hug him.

"Swanson visited me in the hospital," Dane continued. "Apparently at least some of the others in charge believed his story that he'd been helping rather than being the guilty party, so he was able to come see me. But my colleagues who knew the truth had already called the FBI for help and they'd sent some agents to keep an eye on me. Did they believe me? Apparently so, considering their getting me into witness protection, as soon as Swanson was arrested."

"Do you know if Swanson had any collaborators on the police force?"

"I assume so and so apparently did the FBI, since they put me in WITSEC, but so far no one else has been arrested, so there must not be sufficient evidence to point to any particular individuals, despite threats against me. Anyway, now you have the facts about why I'm in witness protection. My side of it, at least. And apparently others in law enforcement believe me, and whatever evidence there was, enough to have taken Swanson into custody for Alvin's murder and for heading the prostitution ring, too. I was the only other one outside at the crime scene at the time, so I'll be the main witness at his trial."

That didn't mean Swanson didn't have allies who would do all they could to prevent Alexa's charge from testifying.

Well, Alexa would do all she could to ensure he remained safe and able to testify at the police chief's murder trial. Not to mention running an illegal prostitution ring.

Why did some cops go bad like that? Especially one at the head of his department. He surely made enough money as chief of police.

But maybe he didn't think so.

Others who shouldn't went bad, too, like her father the judge...

Ugh. Alexa had to turn her mind in another direction. She had an idea of what Swanson's situation was, thanks to the police files she'd read.

She knew he'd been running the prostitution ring. He had to make money in commissions, or whatever. And maybe getting to enjoy the sex on the side. Or helping other men have sex anyway. Or—

Enough. She needed to keep her mind on her driving, not illegal acts.

And she had to watch the road and what was around them...

Her cell phone rang. Fortunately, this car had Bluetooth. She answered it. It was Naomi.

"Hi, sis," Naomi said.

"Hi back," replied Alexa. "How—"

"Are you on your road trip?" demanded her twin.

"It's my sister Naomi," Alexa told Dane, then said to Naomi, "Yes, I'm on my road trip and—"

"Just be careful, okay? I have a very bad feeling and need you to be extra cautious. Got it?"

The best Alexa could do under the circumstances, without revealing to Naomi what she was up to, was to assure her twin that all would be well.

But when she ended the call, she felt uneasy. Her sister sometimes got an eerily accurate sense of foreboding.

Well, that just meant Alexa had to keep a more watchful eye out.

For now, she'd already noticed that the earth around the road looked different. They were reaching the Colorado/Utah border and Arches National Park. That very special area where the natural red rock landscape appeared almost planned, in tall, carved-looking arches.

Amazing.

And it was a good way to hopefully distract Dane from his pain, and to distract her from her concern about her sister's call.

At least for a while.

"Hey, Dane, are you watching our surroundings?"

He hadn't been. Not really. He'd been too wrapped up in his thoughts, his recollections, his anger and what he hoped to accomplish in the next few days. Plus, he'd wondered why Alexa's sister had warned her to be extra cautious. Did she know where Alexa was, and who she was with? Alexa seemed very concerned, if her frown was any indication. But at least she didn't appear distracted.

At her question, he looked around at their surroundings. "Wow!" he couldn't help exclaiming. "I've heard of this kind of astonishing landscape, even saw photos, but I haven't seen anything like it in person before. Have you?"

"No, but it's definitely remarkable," Alexa said, her voice sounding awed. "It lives up to its reputation."

For the next part of the drive, Dane couldn't help smiling as they both gawked at the scenery surrounding them and talked about it. Dane had a passing thought that it would have been fun just to visit this location with the beautiful woman beside him whose company he enjoyed, view the landscape, discuss it as if they were merely sightseers, not a witness to a murder under witness protection and the marshal assigned to protect him.

They grew quiet for a while as they took in their surroundings even more.

Dane was somewhat amused as they started talking again, discussing other places they each had traveled, and the unique things they had seen and done.

Alexa made it clear that one of her favorite activities, when she wasn't on duty, was to visit the Gemini Ranch in Blue Larkspur—owned by two of her eleven siblings—and go horseback riding. She even had a favorite horse.

He was being driven by a cowgirl. Or so it appeared.

Although the scenery changed, he was glad when he started to see signs along the highway that they were approaching Moab. He knew Alexa wanted to stop there for a while.

A short while, he hoped. But it wouldn't hurt to get

a break. Buy some more gas if they needed it. Get a drink. Find a restroom.

And maybe change drivers if it made sense, so Alexa could observe what was around them even more carefully as he drove.

Only, as they got nearer, he felt the car slow a bit. He eyed Alexa.

She seemed to be looking a lot into the rearview mirror, and the side mirrors.

Her lovely face seemed…well, more than uneasy. Maybe apprehensive.

Maybe even disturbed.

"Is something wrong?" Dane asked, also looking into the side mirror nearest him.

A couple car lengths behind them was a large silver SUV. He'd seen the same vehicle, or one like it, just a short while ago when he'd been checking out the appealing terrain around them.

It was traveling at the same speed as they were, slower than the traffic had been.

"I think," Alexa said, "that we're being followed."

"Damn." Dane knew his voice came out as a rough whisper. What was his protector going to do?

What was *he* going to do?

He hoped Alexa would pull over, maybe, and let that SUV pass.

And if it didn't, they both could do their best to evade their pursuer. They would pull their weapons at the occupant as a last resort.

Alexa changed lanes, without pulling over. She sped up a little.

As far as Dane could tell, the SUV followed without getting closer.

"I'm calling Vince on my Bluetooth," Alexa told him. "Letting him know. Hopefully, this is one of the scheduled stops where he's got backup waiting."

"What's up, Alexa?" boomed the voice of Marshal Cudahy. "Everything okay?"

"I don't think so," she said. She related to Vince her—*their*—concern about the SUV following them. "But we haven't been able to see the license plate."

"And you're just outside Moab?" Vince's tone was brusque.

"Right, maybe ten minutes away."

"You're a little early, but the deputies I sent should be there by now. And I've also contacted local law enforcement. You still planning on heading for that shopping center to gas up and rest for a little while?"

"That's right." She looked over at Dane. "I'd already chosen our pit stop, in case we did need backup. That's where we'll still go."

"Sounds okay to me," Dane said, wondering if it really did.

Alexa continued her conversation with Cudahy for a short while longer. Dane kept checking the mirrors. That silver SUV was still there, even though Alexa sped up again, changed lanes, then slowed down a couple of times.

Soon they reached the Moab exit and Alexa drove off the highway. "We'll be there in a few minutes," she told Dane. The GPS on the dashboard designated where they were heading. Dane knew nothing about the shopping center but he figured it would be a good place to go, thanks to the backup Cudahy had promised.

They'd arrived. It was called The Moab Place, and a large gas station lined its west side.

Alexa pulled up to a pump and looked around, even as she started the process of pumping gas.

Dane got out of the car, too, to help, or at least to watch. "Get back inside," she hissed at him angrily.

Right. She was supposed to be protecting him, and they'd no idea if the person, or persons, following them were here, too.

"Okay," he said. "But I'm driving next."

"Fine." Her tone suggested it wasn't fine at all, but he nevertheless entered via the driver's door.

While she stood there, Alexa put the phone to her ear again. In just a few seconds, she was back in the car.

"Damn it all!" she said. "I called Vince again and he confirmed our backup was to be here by now, like he'd said. There's supposed to be at least one unmarked car containing deputies, but also a local police vehicle, or more. I don't see anyone who appears to be looking for us."

"I do," Dane said through clenched teeth. "Isn't that the SUV that was following us on the highway?" He nodded toward the next row of gas pumps.

That sure appeared to be the same SUV that had been behind them.

"Damn!" Alexa said again. "I shouldn't have gotten off the highway. Where's our backup?"

"Looks like we can't count on it." Dane wasn't the kind to panic, but he certainly didn't feel happy.

What were they going to do now?

Chapter Four

Alexa wasn't sure how she felt about Dane driving the
car now, though she'd been okay with the idea initially.

Oh, he'd seemed from the first like a good presence
behind the wheel, staying in lanes and going with the
flow of traffic in the downtown Moab area between the
tourist-attracting stores and occasional office buildings,
none of which was particularly tall.

Dane didn't signal when he was going to turn,
though. Normally, that would annoy her. Not now. Assuming they were still being followed despite not seeing
anyone, why give whoever it was any more advance information about their route than necessary? And hopefully they wouldn't be pulled over for a ticket, since that
could also put them in danger.

Alexa sat in the passenger's seat, her phone in her
hand. She'd tried to call Vince again but only got his
voicemail.

Had he neglected after all to send backup to help
them on this path to Dane's trial testimony?

That wasn't like Vince. But maybe his equipment
had been hacked somehow. That might mean all the
Marshals Service equipment had been hacked. Or not.

But she wished she knew. She especially hoped her phone hadn't been.

Or maybe there'd been no hacking. Maybe it was simpler, yet more complicated. Maybe Swanson had gotten to someone inside the marshals' office to elicit inside information about Dane's path.

In either case, or even if it had been something else, Alexa had ideas about what to do, but she also wished she had some expert advice within the service. Sure, the guy she was protecting was in law enforcement, too, but she didn't want to rely on him for answers. No, he was to rely on her.

Though she might ask him some questions, depending on how things went from now on…

A thought occurred to her. Several members of her family might have suggestions, and she quickly decided which one to call: her brother Dominic. He was one of the fraternal triplets who were now thirty-six years old.

More important, he was with the FBI's International Corruption Unit. She wasn't certain where he was located at the moment. Although he had an apartment in Denver near his FBI headquarters, he went undercover a lot and lived wherever his job took him.

Alexa had all her siblings' numbers programmed into her phone. Another good reason for Dane to be driving right now, since it took her a moment of looking away from the road to scan her contacts and find Dom.

She pressed his number, using neither Bluetooth nor her speaker. Not while she was talking with her FBI brother about something requiring his expertise.

Although Dane would hear her end of the conversation, he didn't need to hear Dominic's.

"Hey, sis," her brother answered immediately. "What are you up to?" Dom was fully aware of Alexa's position with the marshals, just as she knew of his with the FBI.

"That's why I'm calling, bro." She could picture her good-looking brother with his shaggy blond hair and dark blue eyes standing…well, somewhere. And she also pictured him with his lovely fiancée, Sami, though this wasn't a good time to talk about her. Even so, Alexa's usual tinge of envy that they'd found true love that way slipped into her mind, and she immediately thrust it out. "I don't know whether you can help at all, but I'm on a witness protection assignment, and I've got a dilemma or two."

She quickly explained that she was in the process of getting one of the people she was guarding from one town to another, without explaining who, why or where. He'd understand her need for discretion.

"We saw a car along the way that appeared to be following us. That was dilemma number one."

"I'd say so," Dom agreed. "Were you able to shake him off?"

"Not sure. I'm going to take the position he's still around, since I don't know otherwise. And things are even worse than that."

"How?" her brother demanded.

"I was advised by the marshal I report to that I should stop in towns along the way, and he'd have backup at the places we discussed, so I'd have assistance there if anyone appeared to be following us or I otherwise felt we needed support. We just stopped in one of those places, though, and no one was there—no deputies, and no local law enforcement, either, although they were supposed to be informed and assist us as well. I'd even confirmed it with my boss, but now I can't reach him." She hesitated for only a second. No more needed to be described except... "So what would the FBI say? Any idea what I should do now?"

She assumed he would tell her to call the local police, even without knowing who her boss's contact was. But instead—

"Yeah," Dom said immediately. "Change your plans right away. Whatever you agreed to do with your marshal in charge, figure out a way to reach the same result, the same location, but use a different route or vehicle or whatever to make it harder for whoever's after your person under protection to find you. And don't contact anyone else yet, since you don't know who to trust."

"Great idea. Will do. Thanks, bro." Alexa didn't ask for any specifics. Her mind was already whirling in that direction, as it had been before. Dominic hadn't said anything she hadn't already considered, but she appreciated his confirmation. She had to ask before hanging up, "Is everything okay with you?"

"It's fine. Now, you take care of your charge, but be sure to take care of yourself, too. And if there's anything else you need from me, advice or even FBI support if your own remains lacking, be sure to let me know. It's not the best idea, though, to continue to call one person, so try not to do it often if you can avoid it."

"Got it. Thanks again. And you take care."

"You too, little sis."

They hung up, and Alexa found herself smiling grimly down at her lap, where she now held her phone again. Dominic understood her issues and her dilemma.

He'd undoubtedly given her the best advice possible under the circumstances.

Now she had to run with it. And ignore the unease that swept through her.

"So, what did your brother say?" Dane asked. Alexa looked at him. He was driving just above the speed limit, watching the road, passing a car now and then—and keeping watch in the rearview and side mirrors. Just as he should be. Like a cop would be driving while not after a suspect. "I gathered he's with the FBI. Did he make any useful suggestions?"

She'd already started pondering what she could do to disappear from whatever radar their follower might have on them. She'd come up with some ideas and needed to focus on them even more closely to determine which way to go.

True, it would have been more convenient if Dom had suggested more specifics. But she purposely hadn't been specific with him, either. That was the way she was supposed to handle cases, even when she talked with law enforcement family members.

Secrecy was vital—not just to protect Dane, but also herself.

"Yes," she said. "I think he did. But now I have to figure out the best way to follow those suggestions—safely and in a way that will ensure our ability to get to Phoenix as planned."

"Let me know what I can do to help."

Good guy, Alexa thought. But of course he'd want to help, since it was his life that was in danger.

Hers, too, since she was protecting him…

"Just keep driving for now," she said. "I need to do a

little research." Once more, she pulled her phone from her lap.

She looked at the map to Phoenix again, and began researching the metropolises, big and small, along the way.

She decided they would stop in the next town, though she hadn't planned it before, with Vince or otherwise.

That town was Monticello, Utah. It appeared to have the limited kinds of facilities she'd be looking for. And so, once more scanning the road behind them both through the side-view mirror and turning around to look, she said, "I don't see anyone following us at the moment. That doesn't mean we're not on someone's radar. But I want you to get off the highway at the next town. That's Monticello." Even though that could be obvious to whomever might be following them. But if it seemed appropriate, they could zigzag through various streets while they were there.

"Okay," he said. "What's in Monticello that'll help us? Any indication there'll be backup from the marshals, or local cops?"

"No. But if all goes as I'm beginning to plan, we'll still be okay."

"Fine. Care to tell me about it?"

"Sure, Dane. Er, Daniel. Er… Whoever you are. And whoever I am."

"What does that mean? Are we both changing identities there?"

"You'll see."

It didn't take much longer to reach the Monticello exit. "We're here," Dane told her unnecessarily. "I assume I'm to get off now."

"Good assumption," Alexa agreed. Then she had to ask, "Do you see our buddies who seemed to be following us before? Or anyone else I should be aware of?"

"Not now. But that doesn't mean—"

"Got it." And she did. Could be those who'd been following had changed places with others, and even more cohorts of former police chief Swanson could be in on this game. Chasing them. Planning to stop them, in whatever way they chose.

Not if Alexa could help it.

Dane drove carefully. Alexa watched her phone and what she'd been researching on it, as well as the road around them.

In a short while, she had Dane drive into a two-story parking structure and stop on the first level amid a bunch more vehicles, backing in so the car's trunk was facing the wall but not close to it. She kept watching the entrance but saw no other car drive inside. Good.

She hadn't told Dane about what was in the backpacks and suitcase she had stashed in their vehicle's trunk along with the stuff he'd brought, but everything was geared for her job. She was the one to extract them, digging first for herself; she pulled out a man's wig and hid her head under the trunk lid while putting it on. She also extracted a black hoodie that she pulled on over her head. Plus, she removed a face wipe and quickly rubbed off all her eye makeup, then, using a small mirror she brought out, too, daubed on some darker stuff in lines that should hopefully make her appear more angular and masculine.

Still hiding behind the car, she looked herself over.

With the jeans and athletic shoes she'd already been wearing, she now resembled a man. She hoped.

She'd insisted that Dane stay in the car, and, ignoring his amazed stare, now brought him a bag from the trunk that contained what she wanted him to wear, handing it to him as she settled in the passenger seat. No, he wouldn't look like a woman, but hopefully an overweight man. Too bad she couldn't inflate him, but she did tell him to slouch and keep the front of his new sweatshirt pulled out. His hairpiece? Well, it made him appear partially bald, with his hairline swept back.

It didn't make him look any less handsome, though. And who'd have thought she would consider that sexy?

She told him to move to the passenger seat to change, since he'd have a harder time with the steering wheel over him. Besides, they wouldn't be in this car much longer, so it didn't matter which seat he was in now.

She'd also brought his suitcase out of the trunk. She figured he wouldn't want to leave its contents here.

"Interesting that you have all this disguise stuff along," Dane told her as he pulled off his shirt, revealing his muscular body beneath his T-shirt.

Alexa tried unsuccessfully to make herself glance away.

"Some of it's what we're taught as part of witness protection," she said, "although I added to it. I liked the idea but wasn't sure it went far enough. My own change of wardrobe is essential, too, for example."

He fluffed out the large shirt that would make him look heavier when he stood. "Got it. And you definitely look like someone else. Me, too. In fact, if you tell me to lose some weight, be sure not to sugarcoat it or I'll eat that, too."

Really? A corny joke? She tried to ignore it.

When he was done changing, she said, "Okay, now. Here's what we'll do." First, she exited the car briefly, removed some of Dane's belongings from his suitcase and stowed them in the empty backpack she'd kept their new clothes in.

Getting in on the driver's side, she told him they would each exit the parking structure alone, via separate doors—and stay alert. Individuals, both males, were not as likely to attract whoever was stalking Dane, she said, since he had already been spotted that day with her. His appreciative expression when he said he agreed made Alexa blush—or at least she felt slightly warmer for a moment.

She then gave him detailed directions to where she intended to go and told him to walk there directly. She'd take a more circuitous route, and she would be in charge of the bags with his stuff, including his suitcase, while he took care of hers. If they were spotted, his stalkers would most likely assume she was him.

"That way," she told Dane, "we definitely won't look like we're together. Hopefully, Swanson's accomplices are aware you're in witness protection and will assume you'll have your protector with you at all times. And that means—"

"That means while we're separated, I'll need to be particularly careful." Dane nodded toward her. "Staying in shadows or behind buildings or whatever seems to work. So far, I like your plan. But what is the place you're directing me to?"

"A car rental agency. I've already texted them and they have vehicles available."

"Another thing to like about your plan," he said, nodding. His eyes captured hers, and she felt like blushing even more at his approving—and alluring—look.

"Thanks," she said almost brusquely. She needed to get any inappropriate thoughts about this man far away from her consciousness. Too distracting. She had to concentrate. And keep him safe.

That meant they had to join up at the car rental agency really quickly, and she told him so.

"You want me—Daniel Brennan—to rent the car?"

"No, I've got some alternate credentials to use," she said. "Are you ready to head that way? You'll go first and wait inside a store near the office. I'll take a nearby route where I should be able to keep an eye on you and your surroundings. But put your own figurative cop hat on and be damn careful. Got it?"

"Sure do," he said.

They both exited the car she'd been assigned. She locked it, wondering when she'd be able to let her superiors know where it was.

Alexa watched as Dane started in the direction she'd told him, first to the parking lot door. She couldn't help grinning. He did walk fast but hunched forward a bit as though following an enlarged stomach beneath his oversized sweatshirt. He must have been a good undercover cop, she thought, then set out.

The car rental place was a block away, and she headed that way, watching all the while for someone attempting to find him—or who had already been successful.

She saw no one except a few faraway pedestrians.

But she was relieved when she reached the rental place and saw Dane duck inside the bookstore beside it.

She soon got a car rented—under an assumed name and with assumed credentials she'd been given. For the moment, she was Bradley Brown.

The car was a light blue midsized sedan from a US manufacturer. Finding it in the filled rental shop parking lot, she quickly stuffed the backpacks, along with Dane's suitcase, into the trunk.

She didn't need to go get Dane. He'd apparently been keeping watch, and he was soon with her. She put her suitcase into the trunk, too.

Her turn to drive again, she'd decided. She motioned for him to enter via the passenger door and half expected him to object.

Fortunately, he didn't.

She soon pulled out of the rental car lot, telling Dane to crouch down in his seat, which he did, though he didn't look thrilled. She figured it was because anyone looking their way would see her. She'd be the potential target.

But that, too, was part of her job. She would just remain watchful. And careful.

OKAY, HERE HE WAS, Dane thought as Alexa pulled the car onto the small-town street. Being driven by this gorgeous woman who now resembled a not-so-good-looking guy. Following her orders in the hope he'd get to Phoenix, testify against Swanson, then return to his own life where he was in charge.

And Alexa, too, would regain her usual appearance—and her life. And they'd go their separate ways, probably never meeting again.

He knew that her precautions were in his best interests. Maybe the only way he could do what he needed, to get Alvin's killer into prison for the rest of his life.

But Dane wasn't used to following instructions this way. Sure, till recently he'd done what his superiors in the Tempe PD told him to. That was his job. Although those superiors weren't all that great, he admitted, given Swanson's crimes.

But he at least worked in concert with other law enforcement agents—he wasn't the one being protected. Usually, he was the protector. Now things were different. This was his life, for the moment. And he didn't like it.

Not even he could come up with a corny joke or two to ease his tensions. Not now, at least.

"So what's next?" he asked Alexa. Despite how early they'd started, a lot had occurred that day. In fact, it was late enough that he doubted she'd try to make it all the way to Phoenix.

He was right. "My research suggested we not try to get to Phoenix tonight," Alexa said. "Our followers might assume that's what we're doing, since they know our destination. But we can spend the night in an upcoming Utah town. It's small but has several motels and other amenities. It's not far from here, and we can keep an eye out for anyone following us on the road—or when we get off it."

"Fine with me," he said, though his mind glommed on to the fact they'd be spending the night together. In the same space, at least. They were both disguised for the moment, he reminded himself. But that wouldn't necessarily be for any longer than until they got into their room. Maybe two rooms would be better—except for the whole thing about keeping him safe. That meant they needed to be close to one another—and he didn't mind it one bit.

"Okay, then," Alexa said. "Bluff, Utah, here we come."

Chapter Five

Alexa had heard of Bluff and had researched it previously along with the rest of their route. It was a bit of a tourist haven, since it was near a variety of state and national parks and other sightseeing attractions such as Bears Ears National Monument and Natural Bridges National Monument.

Not that she'd get to see them on this trip, but maybe someday she could come back and check them out.

With Dane? He might appreciate them, too.

But by the time she could return he would most likely no longer be in her life.

That made her frown as she watched the road in front of her. Not that they had a romantic connection. Romantic connections? Not her. Not really, although she'd been involved with a few men, one almost seriously, but she'd never found a guy she really felt she could spend the rest of her life with.

She pulled onto the highway once more and headed south toward Bluff.

Maybe she'd been better off when all those she'd been guarding in witness protection had been women. There'd been no emotional overload then. She'd liked them. She'd taken care of them. She'd helped to get them through whatever crisis they'd each been in—which, most often, had been getting them to trials where they testified.

That was all this situation could be, too.

Never mind that she found Dane handsome, charming, sexy and more. Oh, and brave. And a bit silly at times, though in a surprisingly appealing way.

But he was her assignment. That was all.

To convince herself of that, she looked over at the passenger seat, where he appeared to be viewing something on his phone. He was still dressed like the portly guy she'd helped to manufacture while they were still in Monticello. But now that they were on their way, he had removed the head covering that had suggested he was going bald.

That made him look a lot better.

She glanced at him as often as felt safe, enjoying his appearance of concentration as he studied his phone.

Phone. Just in case, she figured it wouldn't hurt to send a text or two to her boss to protect them.

No one needed to know they intended to stop as soon as Bluff.

She pulled her phone from her lap and handed it to Dane, who seemed rather surprised but took it from her anyway. "I'd like you to use my phone to text Vince in a little while, after you do some research," she said, "and tell him we're stopping before Phoenix for the night. But since we don't know what's happened, why he didn't have the backup he'd promised when we got to Monticello, let's assume there's an issue and deal with it. We'll give him a town, but we won't tell him where we're really stopping."

Dane turned to look at her, a sly smile on his face. "You mean, you want me to lie to your boss."

"Exactly." She grinned back. "In a manner that he'll think it's me, but won't know it's a lie, at least not at first. So, please figure out a town along this route that's closer to Phoenix that we can mention."

"Okay," Dane said, then began concentrating on his phone again.

As he did his research, she watched the road. Listened to the car's tires on the asphalt below. They hummed, but she didn't find it as pleasant as her own car that she'd left at home.

Oh well. They were safer for now. Not as obvious as they'd apparently been before.

She hoped.

She snuck a peek at Dane, continuing to enjoy the look of concentration on his handsome face. She had an urge to stroke his cheek.

Good thing she was driving. Touching anything but the steering wheel and, occasionally, her phone, wasn't a good idea.

A short while later Dane looked up from his phone and suggested, "How about Kayenta, Arizona? It's farther toward Phoenix than Bluff, part of the Navajo Nation, and it has some facilities like hotels."

"Sounds fine with me, if you're happy suggesting it. Now, use my phone and text Vince as if you're me, telling him that's where we'll be overnight. Let him know I'm still concerned about the lack of backup before but want to keep him informed about how we're doing."

"You think he'll respond now?" Dane asked. "He didn't before, right?"

"Yes, and I don't know if he received my correspondence then. He didn't answer his phone or any texts for a while. But time has passed, and we're in a different location, which might affect the phone's cell reception and all. Let's just give it a try."

"Whatever you say, Madam Protector."

When Alexa glanced at him this time, Dane's dark brows were raised and his smile was challenging, as if he figured her response would be irritated.

Instead, she said, "Glad you recognize I'm in charge, Mr. Protectee."

He laughed then looked down and got to work texting, while Alexa kept her eyes on the road around them, including, via the mirrors, behind them. A few semis rolled by, again heading in the opposite direction, and a car or two going in their direction passed them.

Nothing to make her worry about whether she and Dane were currently under observation. But she knew better than to assume they weren't.

"Okay," Dane said after a minute. "The text is on its way."

But there was no immediate response. And after five minutes, Alexa requested that Dane try again. "Maybe we were in another location with no service."

"You sure your office has service?"

She sent a quick glare at him. "What do you think?"

"Then—maybe it's your phone."

She shrugged, though she concentrated even more when the car bumped a bit on the road. She wasn't sure what that meant, but she judged it wasn't serious. "Why don't you try your phone?" she asked then.

"Sure." But Vince didn't respond to him, either. And when Alexa suggested the cell number of one of her other colleagues in the office, there was no response to that as well.

The road turned gradually toward the left. Alexa started seeing signs to Bluff. Good. But she did want to let the world erroneously know that they were headed for—what was the place's name? Oh yeah. Kayenta.

"Tell you what. Please call my brother Dominic. His number's the last one called on my phone before your latest attempts to reach Vince."

"Got it."

"And put it on speaker so we both can hear him."

It only took an instant before Dom answered. "Everything okay, sis?" he demanded.

Alexa glanced at Dane, who'd raised his brows again as if he was ready to join in, so she hurriedly said, "I think so. My charge and I are on our way. But I'm glad to talk to you since no one in my office is apparently getting my texts, and my boss doesn't answer my calls."

A moment of silence. "For how long?" he finally said.

"Quite a while." She didn't get into what had happened before. "That might have been the cause of the lack of backup I mentioned previously. And they couldn't be reached on my charge's phone, either."

"Ditch your damn phone," Dom commanded loudly. "Your charge's, too. Replace them with burners when you can, but assume now that they've been compromised. Make sure you get rid of them in a way you can't be followed. Can't say for sure they're causing a problem, but you need to make sure they aren't."

"Thanks, bro," Alexa said. "You're probably right."

"And be sure to contact me and let me know how things are going once you get your burners, you hear?"

"I hear." Alexa hung up.

"I'd wondered about that," Dane said. "But I figured your marshals' people would have control of such things."

Alexa snorted. "I figured they would, too. But Dom is right. We shouldn't take any chances." She paused then shot a quick look at Dane. "Know what I'd like you to research now?"

"Hmm. How about whether there are places in Bluff to buy a burner phone?"

"You read my mind," she said with a slight smile. It wasn't a surprise that he knew what she wanted. He'd want it, too, if they wound up ditching their phones.

It didn't take Dane long to find the answers. "Bluff's got it," he said. "In fact, there are several stores where people can buy techy stuff."

"Good," Alexa said. "We'll pick a couple up tonight or tomorrow. Oh, and please figure out a good, dumpy motel we can stay in, one anyone following us would assume is too much of a hellhole for smart officers of the law to hole up in."

"Excellent idea, although we'll only need one new phone. I'm carrying an extra burner that I've never used yet. Oh, and one more thing we need to do, and I've got an idea how to do it."

"What's that?" Alexa asked.

"The best way to dump our current cells."

ALEXA EXITED THE HIGHWAY, though not at the first sign for Bluff, which made Dane smile. She'd already warned him to keep his eyes open when they did get off to see if anyone else had gotten off at the same exit.

Fortunately, no one did.

He told Alexa to pull into a large service station just off the major road. It contained several rows of pumps, indicating lots of drivers must stop there on their way to wherever they were going. He indicated a parking spot behind the convenience store off to the side, and Alexa pulled into it.

"Okay," she said. "Now what?"

"Now you do what I tell you," he riposted. "If there are any phone numbers you care about or other info you'll need in the near future, I suggest you jot them down. I just happen to have a couple pens and pads of paper, in case my phone's not handy and I need to make sure I remember a joke I hear." That was somewhat true, he thought as he met Alexa's exasperated yet lovely expression with a smug one of his own. He mostly wanted to be prepared for anything.

Like having to ditch his usual phone...

She pulled a small, spiral-bound memo book out of her purse as well as a pen, and started making notes.

Him? He didn't have to. As part of his witness protection program—and his own practices as a detective—he carried that extra burner all the time, plus a charger. Although it was almost always turned off, it had all the info he'd need to call those he wanted to stay in contact with.

He'd have to change the number he'd added to it

as Alexa's, though, once she obtained a new phone of her own.

When she was finished, she turned to him again. "Okay, what do we do next?"

"Next, go into your contacts again and delete them all."

She grimaced but appeared to do as he said, even as he did the same himself on his regular phone.

When they both were through, he said, "Just watch what I do next. First, say good-bye and hand it to me."

Her expression grew glum, as if she really did regret saying good-bye to her high-tech possession, but she did reach out with it. "Here," she said. "Oh, and good-bye, my phone."

He took it from her, amused by what she'd said. But surely she wasn't developing a sense of humor.

Fortunately, this service station was as busy as he'd anticipated. Lots of cars and a number of big rigs.

Dane quickly exited the car, both phones in his hand, and sidled along to the nearest semi. There, he looked around to make sure the driver wasn't watching, or anyone else. Then he wedged both phones between two prongs of the metal connector fastening the cab to the trailer.

Finally, he returned to the car. Good timing, since the driver of that truck approached and got inside. In moments, he left.

So did their phones.

"Now," he said, "if anyone happens to be monitoring our location via those phones, they'll assume we're going the opposite direction, for now at least." For, happily, and as he'd anticipated, judging by the way the big rig had been facing at the station, it embarked on the route from which they'd come.

"That was a good idea," Alexa said. "I've worked out leaving phones and other electronics before, after deleting potentially damaging info, at various places for the people I'm protecting, or tossing them in the trash, but I've never actually sent them and us in different directions. I'll definitely do that again."

"Good. And here's the extra burner I mentioned." He pulled it from his pocket and turned it on. "There. Since I haven't used it, no one should be able to follow me because of it. Now, next step. We need to figure out where we'll stay tonight. I want to check out all possibilities, but I've pretty well narrowed them down to a couple places that look absolutely horrible online."

"Sounds perfect. Let's drive by them."

ALEXA FOLLOWED THE directions Dane gave her, forcing herself not to shudder.

For the most part, she enjoyed seeing the small town of Bluff. Some of its areas appeared better than others, and some of the motels and inns also looked nicer than their rivals. Alexa was glad that Dane and she, in their discussion as they cruised the various districts and neighborhoods, soon narrowed their potential choices down to a couple—the rattiest-looking ones.

On their route, they stopped at a fast-food place to pick up their dinner plus some water, then got going again.

As they were on their way, Dane said, "Pull over here for a second." He gestured to the curb on a narrow street.

Alexa noted an option about a block away. She assumed Dane had, too, and was checking it out. A sign indicated it was the Stone Motel. No indication why that was its name. Alexa saw few stones around, mostly paving and enclosures of small gardens with grass and a few flowers.

"Is that place our goal?" Alexa asked.

"The first we'll look at," Dane replied, "and hopefully it'll work out. I checked out some of the local reviews on a couple popular online sites. That one has some of the worst."

"Perfect." Alexa grinned as if she really meant it. In some ways, she did. "I assume whoever is after you will figure that, if we don't make it all the way to Phoenix tonight, we would only stay in a nice, secure place. Which does make the most sense. Except—"

"Except that we're better off staying in a place they wouldn't be looking for us."

Alexa nodded. "Exactly. So…" She turned the key in the ignition, starting the car again. "Let's just hope this delightful place has a room available for us."

A room where they would stay together. A room in which she would be close to Dane, overnight…

Okay, she could admit to herself she was attracted to the guy, and the idea of that kind of closeness shot surges of heat inside her. But she would of course keep things cool and professional.

She had to.

"Do you really have any doubts that kind of place has rooms available?" Dane asked.

Alexa did, though just a few. The town hadn't seemed especially busy, so there might not be much overflow from the nicer motels to the dumps. But people some-times chose accommodations based on cost instead of convenience and cleanliness.

They'd find out in a few minutes, she thought as she parked the rental car on the rutted paving of the park-ing lot just outside the two-story motel with the equally rutted walls. The windows, presumably one or more per room, were unbroken, but the caulking around the frames appeared uneven and damaged.

Oh yeah. If they stayed here this night, sleep wouldn't be highest on Alexa's agenda. Nor would it be anywhere else.

Staying aware and awake, and protective of Dane, would be her top priorities.

And the fact they'd be alone together? Irrelevant.

First, though, she had to book the room, if possible. She considered telling Dane to wait in the car. But al-though she was hopeful, she couldn't know whether they'd been followed here. And the only way she'd truly be able to protect him was to remain in his presence.

"Okay," she said. "Give me a minute, then we'll go to the reception area and see if they've got a place for us to stay."

"Fine. Are you—"

She assumed he was going to ask what she needed the minute for, but she figured it became clear pretty quickly since he shut up. She'd turned and knelt on the seat, then brought a backpack up from where she'd laid it on the back seat and put it on the center console.

She extracted her wig and some makeup.

"You're becoming a guy again?" Dane asked.

"Since we'll be seeing other people, yes. It makes

more sense for us to remain in disguise so we can't be recognized. So, here." She reached into the bag again and pulled out Dane's bald wig from where she'd stowed it before, handing it to him. He wouldn't need makeup. He already looked like a man.

Quite a man.

She nevertheless also extracted the big, bulky sweatshirt that would help him appear overweight that he'd taken off as they continued this direction.

No sense in either of them looking like who they really were.

Alexa next unzipped a pocket inside that bag and pulled out an envelope. She wasn't merely looking like a man. She was taking on the persona, too, at least for certain purposes.

Like paying for their room that night.

She had several different identities she could use, including other women. Too bad neither of her male IDs had the last name of Brennan. That way, she could turn herself miraculously into Daniel Brennan's brother.

But when she'd gotten set up with these additional identities, she hadn't known who she would be protecting. And so she'd had to decide between being Roger Jones or Bradley Brown, or a different woman tonight.

She extracted an appropriate driver's license and credit card from the envelope. "You ready to go inside?" she asked.

"Sure," he said. He'd already turned to look at her. "Since I see you have cards there, I assume my protector is going to attempt to pay, but—"

"But nothing. As you know, I'm in charge. And if

you talk to me at all with anyone else around, I'm Roger Jones."

She wasn't surprised when his dark eyebrows rose and his head tilted slightly. "Roger?"

"You got it."

His laugh sent a ripple of pleasure up her spine, which she recognized was absurd. "Okay, Roger. You're in charge…sort of. And Daniel is ready to prepare for our night here in Bluff." He turned and reached for the door handle, then stopped and swiveled back to her. "Question, though. I know we're both men, guys who are buddies, right?"

She nodded. "That's right."

"Are we staying in the same room together? I mean, guys don't always take each other on as roommates while on the road. I still could pay for my own."

"Nope. We're staying together. Yes, we're good friends. We'll have lots to discuss about our road trip before we drop off to sleep, after all. Or that's what we'll allow whatever clerk who's there to believe."

"I got it. But—"

Alexa wasn't finished talking, so she interrupted Dane. "But dropping off to sleep is only on my schedule now and then. Even though staying in this hellhole, not as close to Phoenix as we should have been by now, isn't what I would have preferred, it should work best under the circumstances since we were followed before—and there's a good possibility our now-disappeared phones were hacked. I still really like what you did with them, by the way. And before we head off tomorrow, we'll stop in one of the local stores to get me a new one."

"Fine, but—"

"Let's get going," she said, interrupting him again. She'd heard the additional irritation in Dane's—no, Daniel's—voice. She'd better not forget that. As far as she knew, WITSEC had even given him official-looking ID with that name. Maybe he needed yet another name now, in case the people after him knew this one, but she couldn't be the one to work that out—not here, and not now.

And she couldn't allow herself to worry about his being annoyed.

She would do all she had to, to protect him. If that annoyed him, tough.

Alexa turned her back on him in the car and opened the driver's door, reaching back inside for the bag she'd been removing items from. Time to put it in the trunk and take out the small suitcases that would make them appear to be checking in to this motel.

She hadn't seen any other people around, so maybe the place's façade and reputation would mean they would be alone.

She would be damned careful in any case.

As Alexa walked around and opened the trunk, behaving in all manner the best she could as a guy around her age, she was glad to see that Daniel had exited the passenger's side and now approached her at the rear of the vehicle.

She liked that he was bent forward a bit, to help emphasize his appearance as a lot bigger than he was.

She didn't like his scowl, but she would live with that.

Although she always seemed to enjoy it when he smiled... Enough of that.

As he joined her, she made herself smile in as masculine a manner as she could, even as she looked around his shoulder at a few other cars parked in the lot.

Still no people, but the other vehicles' presence did indicate some rooms in the place might be occupied.

She let Daniel pull out the handle for the suitcase containing some of his belongings, and she did the same with her own.

"Under other circumstances," he grumbled as they started forward, "I'd offer to handle both pieces of luggage."

Because, no matter what she looked like at the moment, she was a woman. "Glad you recognize the current circumstances," she said, deepening her voice, in case anyone was listening, although she didn't think so. "You need to remember that no matter what I look like, I'm in charge."

"Yeah. I get it."

"Good."

"Not many cars here, so I assume they'll have room for us." Daniel had modified his voice, too, making it gravellier.

"We'll soon see." They strolled at a leisurely pace toward the ground-level, glass-fronted door labeled "Office."

Inside, the place was as grungy as it appeared from the outside. The decorative tiled floor looked ancient, edges worn off. There were a couple of chairs where people could sit, but they both appeared sunken and likely to scratch anyone on them. Two vending machines looked like the best part of the place, where people could buy water and soft drinks from one, and candy from the other.

The girl behind the reception counter, with shaggy brown hair and thick glasses, looked to be in her late teens, and her sweatshirt and jeans were both torn, highly in fashion, Alexa thought. She seemed fairly young for this position, but Alexa assumed the place was family owned and run. Or maybe the owners had just hired anyone who'd applied for a job.

They did have a room. The girl hardly talked to them but got them to sign some paperwork—and Alexa signed everything as Roger Jones, paying for the room with cash. Never mind that she had a credit card in Roger's name and also a false driver's license. It would be preferable for whoever was after Daniel not to know the identity Alexa had taken on for this case, but if they did find out by tracking them to this motel, at least they'd only have a name.

Soon the receptionist handed them a couple of actual keys in a small envelope that had the number 16 on it.

"Thanks," Alexa said in her disguised voice, a much lower register than her normal tone. "Where is it?"

"Floor right above us." The girl then started doing something on the computer on top of the counter, ignoring them.

Time to go to their room. Together. Alone.

And Alexa again resolved to herself to remain professional, no matter how sexy the man with her appeared once undressed for the night.

Chapter Six

She'd paid for their room with cash. Dane had figured
that the marshals providing witness protection must
carry a lot, as well as alternate identifications. That
made sense.

He carried quite a bit, too. He'd had to keep all the
assets he could with him since he couldn't exactly show
up at a bank or anywhere else using his real identity to
get cash. He had a credit card with his current ID but
didn't want to use it unless he had to since it would be
paid by the Marshals Service.

Well, when this was over, he'd reimburse Alexa, or
the Marshals Service, for all his expenses.

Now, as Alexa and he left the office and started up
the uneven paved stairs to the second floor, Dane—no,
Daniel again for now, he reminded himself—couldn't
help wanting to grab the suitcase from Alexa, even
though it was carryon size.

But that was simply a masculine urge to help a
woman. And she was a he for now, he reminded himself unnecessarily, considering not only her neutral outfit but also her masculine hairpiece and makeup. She'd
undoubtedly get damned mad at him if he attempted to

act like a polite guy, let alone protective of her. But he had to admit he was drawn to her, despite their circumstances, and wanted to make sure she stayed safe, too.

At least for the moment, when neither of them appeared to be in danger.

He preceded her up the stairs. At least, along with his own suitcase, he carried the paper bag that contained the dinner they'd picked up. Alexa—Roger—lagged behind a little, apparently glancing around to make sure they remained alone. Protecting him.

Although if there was anyone after them here, that person could be on the motel's upper level, waiting for them. For *him*. He was the one under witness protection, and for good reason.

Dane was completely aware that Swanson was likely to do anything to keep him from testifying at the murder trial. Swanson knew full well that Dane had been a firsthand witness of the killing, as well as a victim of his shooting rage. And Dane felt certain Swanson was furious he had survived and had most likely hired assassins to go after him.

They reached the top level. It was also paved, with a railing along the steps and the perimeter of the balcony walkway. He stopped and looked around again.

He heard voices from inside one of the nearest rooms, maybe a parent and child. If so, it was unlikely it was anyone waiting for him, although he would still remain alert in case it was a ploy to fool him.

Alexa caught up to him. "Okay, Roger," he told her, "I'll go open our room." He didn't bother telling her why he'd stopped, what he'd heard or how he felt about not helping with her luggage.

Their footsteps shuffled along the balcony paving. The room nearest them at the top of the stairs was number 14. It didn't take long to pass that one and number 15, then reach 16.

Dane pulled the envelope from his pants pocket and used the key to open the door. No problems there.

He wasn't surprised when Alexa, leaving her suitcase just outside, edged her way past him and entered the room first. He watched her check out every inch of it, including opening up the doors to the bathroom and closet, her hand on that hip bulge beneath her shirt. That had to be where her weapon was, where she kept it a lot of the time.

Then she knelt on the floor and checked under the two twin-size beds across the room. She coughed a little, and he figured that was an indication of how unclean the place was. He'd noticed right away that it smelled rather musty.

But Alexa didn't do anything to suggest there was anyone or anything under there that shouldn't be.

He wondered, though, how he'd be anticipating their night together if they'd had only one bed to share, no matter what size…

"Okay," she said. "You can come in now."

He already had, though not very far. He'd wheeled both their suitcases in, too, and shut the door behind him.

He'd also been prepared to grab his gun, at his hip beneath his bulky sweatshirt. He'd hoped it wouldn't be necessary. He doubted anyone could have anticipated they'd be here. They hadn't anticipated before where they'd stay the night, either, other than to hopefully find the kind of place no one would figure they'd hang out in.

Like this motel.

Even though Alexa had checked out the entire room, Dane scrutinized it again, from the beds he'd been studying to the TV hung on the wall across from them and the dresser with a scratched mirror on the wall across from the bathroom. He walked to the closet and looked inside, too. It was small, and the hangers on the rod at the top were of many kinds, from bent wire to plastics of several colors. There was a luggage rack at the bottom that he pulled out, intending to put his suitcase on it, unless Alexa preferred that to placing hers on the dresser.

"Guess we're staying the night," she said unnecessarily, but he figured she was in her way asking him if he was all right with it.

He was. "Guess we are," he said.

He asked her preference for the suitcase. The dresser worked for her, so he put her bag up there. They both entered the bathroom and washed their hands. They each then sat on one of the beds, facing each other, as they ate their dinners. He'd gotten a burger and fries, and Alexa had a chicken sandwich. His tasted okay, but he wasn't very hungry. He had too much on his mind.

Including how things would go in a short while when they got ready for bed, then lay down in their respective places.

Heck, this woman shouldn't be getting into his thoughts the way she was. He didn't want to seduce her, no matter how she was dressed now or would be later. He wanted to get his time in her presence over quickly. Safely. For both of them.

And yet... When they were finished eating, it was only about six o'clock, and even at that they had taken a bit of extra time to drive there. Alexa said nevertheless, "I know it's early, but I suggest we get to bed soon, since tomorrow will be a big day."

Yeah! Dane's hormones cheered, but he of course tamped them down.

Getting to bed individually, to sleep, was what she'd meant. He knew that, even as every fiber of him wanted to hold her.

"Good idea," he said. "We'll want to get on our way early tomorrow."

"Right."

"I usually like to take my shower at night," Alexa said, "but I figure the sheets aren't likely to be that clean, so I'll wait till morning to remove any added dirt. How about you?"

"Yeah, that sounds like a better idea to me, too."

"I'll go change now, then you can." She meant she'd run through the bathroom first, which was fine with him.

While she was in there, he put the TV on, which was likely how they'd spend their time that night till they fell asleep. There was apparently a cable connection, and he found a news station right away.

It provided national updates as he watched, not local. And certainly not Tempe's news. Or Phoenix's.

He wondered what was going on in Phoenix, in preparation for the trial. They'd arrive there tomorrow, so he'd find out...and he'd say goodbye to being on the road with Alexa.

She soon exited the bathroom. She no longer had her hairpiece on, but her pajamas appeared unisex: nothing feminine about them.

Even so, there she was, in his motel room with him, in pj's. With her lovely blond hair framing her face that was again highly feminine now that she no longer wore her wig or any masculine makeup.

He hurriedly grabbed his own pajamas and toiletries kit and went into the bathroom.

When he came out again, Alexa was under the covers of the bed she'd chosen, sitting up. She appeared wide awake, but he wasn't sure.

The news was still on, and they watched it for a while longer. And Alexa rose, pulled the draperies back a bit and looked out the window several times before returning to her bed.

"You ready to turn off the TV?" Dane eventually asked.

"Sure. I'll set the clock radio here for seven o'clock since we don't have our phones now. We can go out and grab breakfast at one of the fast-food places. I assume the shops here open around nine, but if they don't open earlier, we can continue on and stop somewhere else for my new burner."

"I figure I'll wake up early on my own, but setting the alarm is fine," Dane said.

In a few minutes, she was done fussing with the alarm. "Good night, Daniel," Alexa said.

"Good night, Roger," he said, and swallowed his laugh.

It was a good thing to think of her as Roger right

now, he realized. He'd found his protector much too sexy a woman.

He'd remain aware of her presence not far from him that night. He wasn't sure he'd sleep, but at least he wouldn't make any attempt to seduce her.

Darn it.

Only... Well, it wouldn't hurt to thank her. The light on the nightstand remained on, very dim. Was that okay? Apparently, Alexa thought so. But if someone was looking for them, and tried peeking into the room despite the closed curtains...

At least it gave him an excuse. He got out of his bed on the side nearest Alexa's and reached for the light switch.

"Are you uncomfortable leaving it on?" she asked. "I've got a flashlight, so we don't need to keep it lit."

"I think that would be better," he said. But before he turned it off, he bent down and gave Alexa a deep kiss, tasting her mouth, her tongue... And was delighted that she responded passionately. Wow.

Too bad they couldn't do anything more. That would be unprofessional on both their parts. Plus, it would be too distracting if anyone was around here pursuing them.

Still... Well, when that kiss was over, he started another. And Alexa put her arms around his neck to tug him down even more. The kiss continued, and he felt Alexa stroke his back, then downward, which caused his penis to become erect.

He debated stroking her as well and did let his hand touch her buttocks.

But before he could do more, she was the one to

pull away. "Okay, we've gotten that out of the way," she said. "And I, for one, enjoyed it. But that's all. Go to bed, Daniel." She reached around him and turned out the light. "And I hope I don't bother you too much when I get up and check our surroundings a lot tonight."

SLEEP? AFTER THAT, and knowing sexy Dane was just across the room from her?

Alexa knew she shouldn't have participated in those kisses, let alone encouraged them—and more. She'd anticipated…something. And was glad they had done what they had done.

But she'd been serious when she said it was a good thing they'd gotten them out of the way.

Never mind that she'd become so sexually aroused that it was damn difficult to move away.

Well, it was over now. One less thing to worry about this night.

Except that she'd have to force herself to focus on her real reason to be there.

Fortunately, Alexa hadn't intended to get a good night's sleep.

Her intent was to doze, off and on, and listen while awake for anything going on outside their room. Walk around inside it, too, a few times and check out the window some more. Maybe even throw on a shirt and her hairpiece, go outside onto the upper area of this motel and look around a bit, but she'd only do that if she felt they'd been compromised at all, and so far she didn't.

She lay awake a lot, listening for sounds indicating trouble, but that wasn't all.

She listened to the sounds from the other bed. Dane

sleeping deeply, shifting around sometimes, maybe even snoring.

She heard that briefly a couple of times though not particularly loudly. She otherwise became aware of his deep breathing that might indicate he was asleep—or just resting.

Maybe even keeping track of her late-night noises as well. She considered getting into his bed with him and snuggling—but forced herself not to.

Did she snore? She wouldn't be surprised if she did on other nights. But that night she didn't ever sleep deeply.

She might not have slept at all.

And not just because she was doing her job.

She kept thinking of the two of them together for the night, in the same motel room. Especially after those kisses.

Sure, during the day right now she was just another guy accompanying him, appearing to the world, she hoped, like a buddy, and that was all.

But even in disguise Dane was one good-looking guy. She couldn't help thinking of him sexually, at least a bit…well, maybe more than a bit. Especially since she knew he'd taken his clothes off to change into pj's, as she had. Only a few feet from one another, though separated by the bathroom door.

And then those good-night kisses…

Cut it out! her mind kept yelling at her. But for now, she hadn't been able to get those thoughts about Dane out of her mind.

She wondered what it would have been like if they'd actually made love. She'd had sex with other men, of course, but nothing that had made her want to keep any of those guys in her life for long.

Would it be different with Dane? No matter. Wasn't going to happen.

But he was one attractive, brave, sexy guy...

Good thing he mostly stayed in his bed, even when she got up to check that the room was secure, which probably woke him at least sometimes. As she'd mentioned, she had a flashlight in her overnight bag, just as she carried extra weapons, to go along with her job.

She'd wanted to keep the room lamp on a little longer, but Dane had been right. It had been time to shut it off.

She'd have been glad to use the light on her cell phone, but that object was probably in Grand Junction or Blue Larkspur, or that far away at least, right now.

Okay. She was thinking too much. Again. She glanced toward the clock radio on the nightstand between the two beds. The night was passing more quickly than she'd figured, considering the fact she hadn't slept through it. The time was nearly five o'clock. They hadn't planned to get up for another couple hours, which was fine.

But Alexa once more itched to get out of bed. She pulled the flashlight from the nightstand and turned it on, planning to check the perimeter yet again.

"You're awake again." The voice from the other bed startled her.

Even when she'd wondered previously if Dane was awake, he hadn't said anything.

"So, apparently, are you," she responded.

"Yeah. Everything okay?"

"Seems that way."

"Good." Dane sat up a bit, putting his back against the wall at the head of the bed. "Need any help making sure this time?"

"No. You can go back to sleep for a little while," Alexa told him. She intended to get back in bed, even though she doubted she would sleep any more.

"Oh, but I'm a little chilly. Care to join me to help me warm up? A kiss might help."

She hadn't really heard that, had she? He wanted her to join him in his bed? Kiss passionately again?

He was right, it was a little cool in the room. This was a desert area, but it was October. They hadn't put on the air conditioning, but neither had they turned on any heat.

She figured that wasn't the reason for his unexpected invitation.

An invitation that made her shiver a little, and not because of any coolness.

But this time she had to stay professional. Aware of their surroundings. Aware of how to protect this man under her observation and care.

"I think you can warm up on your own," she said. "Just burrow down under your sheet and blanket. And think about the day we're going to embark on soon. I think that'll take any chilliness away."

Alexa no longer had any desire to nestle back down in her bed. Not the way her thoughts were going. She thrust her sheet and blanket aside and stood up.

"You sure you won't come over here?" Dane's voice suggested he was smiling.

"Is this another one of your corny jokes?" Alexa retorted, even though on some level she hoped he was serious.

"Who, me? Joke?" Dane got out of bed, too. He stood across the room from her now, and she aimed her flashlight in his direction. "Gee," he said then. "Guess you're getting better at figuring out when I'm teasing."

That made Alexa deflate inside.

What? Had she hoped, on some level, that he *was* serious?

Hell yes.

But she'd never admit that to him. Instead, she decided to respond with a dry word or two of her own. "Damn. I was hoping you were going to say no, that it wasn't a joke, that you really wanted me to jump into bed with you and have some hot sex. After all, I'm not the guy I look like during the day right now. And you've already tested that with those kisses."

"Those kisses. Hey, I wouldn't mind some more. After all, we're both dressed. We're wearing pj's, both of us. We're protected and—"

"You know, Daniel," Alexa made herself say drolly, "this is getting out of hand. A little more sleep—sleep, and nothing else in our beds—will probably be a good thing for both of us. And—"

"And you're right." This time Dane started walking around the room, pulling back the curtains on the windows just a bit before passing them, then walking close to the other walls. "Maybe this isn't the best of hours to kid around. No more kisses. Just a little more sleep."

"Right." Alexa also made sure no one was lingering outside their room, then snuggled back down in her bed. Alone. Of course.

Even realizing this guy was too clownish at off times like now, she couldn't help wondering what it would be like if they were sharing a motel room for other reasons and weren't both alert for trouble.

You'll never know, she told herself, forcing her eyes to close despite knowing she wouldn't sleep. *Stay professional. Don't even think about it.*

DANE GOT OUT of bed a while after that conversation of sorts with Alexa. He knew he wouldn't be able to sleep any more that night. Time to take his shower. Without saying a word, he went to the stand holding his suitcase and, using his own flashlight that he'd brought along, he pulled out underwear and the clothing he intended to wear that day as Daniel.

Sure, he was well aware that the danger to him was likely about to multiply, especially when he reached Phoenix, and even, potentially, on the way, in spite of his being in witness protection. His insomnia was largely based on concern.

And remembering those kisses.

Damn. He never should have started that. But he had. And he had to put it behind him.

It was critical that he get to court in time—and in one piece. He had to testify.

He had to do all he could to get justice, for Alvin's sake—and to bring down that murderous Swanson.

He'd shut the bathroom door. Time to strip and shower. But the idea of being naked now and for the next few minutes, with Alexa—not her alternate persona Roger—in the next room, made him think all the more about what he'd been kidding about before when he'd spoken with her. Teased her about their spending some time together in the same bed.

Kissed her last night…

Only, on some level, he hadn't been kidding or teasing. The idea of being that close to her in bed… Okay, he needed to direct his thoughts another way.

He hurriedly took a few steps on the dirty, cold vinyl bathroom floor and turned on the water. He let it run cold for a minute as he stepped inside. Ah. That helped him cool down in many ways.

He turned up the heat a bit then and completed his shower.

After drying himself, using a towel that actually appeared clean, he shaved then dressed.

Only then was he ready to face Alexa again.

She, too, had awakened and left her bed. She had turned on the TV. "My turn for the bathroom?" she asked.

"Sure."

While she was in there, Dane watched television again, trying damn hard not to imagine what she looked like in the shower and after…

She emerged from the room fairly quickly, smashing his imagination since she had definitely morphed into Roger again. "Okay, are we ready to go grab breakfast?" Damn, but her wig, covering her lovely hair, appeared to be real.

That was okay under the circumstances.

"Fast food, yes?" he asked. "I figure it should be fast, since we're hurrying today."

"Right. But our next stop after eating will be—"

"A store where we can grab you a burner."

"Exactly. And we'll get you another one, too, to make sure your extra one isn't compromised. You should keep it turned off. Let's check to see when the stores open around here, then decide whether to shop or continue on."

He obediently allowed Alexa, carrying her own bag, to go check them out of the ratty place.

She returned to their room after apparently leaving her suitcase in the car. "I think we're okay to leave, but let's be careful."

"When am I not careful?" he asked, raising his brows as he talked to the guy in front of him who was his supposed buddy.

"Don't get me started." She tried to grab his suitcase but he didn't let her, though she did take the backpack.

They were soon in the rental car, and she was letting him drive. They were learning to compromise, he observed. "I'll want you to drive a lot today," she said, "so I can be as observant on our route as possible."

"Got it," he said.

He drove them into a better part of town so they could more likely assume their breakfast would be sanitary. He was glad to see they passed a couple of stores that might sell cell phones.

They reached a family restaurant and agreed to eat there since they had time before the stores opened. Fortunately, that early, it wasn't very busy. They sat at a booth near the back. He ordered pancakes and coffee from their middle-aged server, and Alexa got a breakfast sandwich, also with coffee.

And as they ate, he appreciated how alert Alexa/ Roger appeared to be.

"Which store do you think we should head for when we're done?" she asked him.

"Not sure, but I have an idea." He asked their server where the nearest shopping center was that had a name-brand discount chain store. He figured they'd carry phones. He'd seen some possibilities as they had driven here, but someplace close would be better.

She told them. Fortunately, it wasn't far away. And that kind of retailer should open early.

It did, they learned a short while later after driving there. And also fortunately, it had an electronics section that included prepaid smartphones.

"I'll buy them," Alexa told him. "I'll register both in my assumed name of Roger, too." She'd kept her voice low, and he understood what she meant.

This was another way to keep even his new identity secret.

It was her job, sure. But Dane really appreciated all this beautiful woman—no, this frumpy, short-haired guy—was doing for him. Even if he knew that whatever was developing between them couldn't last.

Chapter Seven

She hadn't needed to set one up before, but Alexa was aware of the procedure her department used to get numbers for burner phones obtained for those under their protection. Soon, she was back in the car with the man she now always thought of as Dane but referred to as Daniel when they were out with others around, as they'd just been. Only then did she download the app that she recalled from her training days.

Fortunately, she remembered how to do it well enough, and she followed the procedure to obtain temporary numbers for each of them. And, surprisingly, these were free for a week or so.

They were both using their new identities, of course, not just him, and Dane was driving once more. She checked the phone again and set up the GPS so she could direct him how to get back on their way toward their destination. That would be Route 191 till they reached the Arizona border, then Route 160 for around two and a half hours, and they'd still have a distance to go.

Alexa was glad to see there weren't many other vehicles on the road around them. Since the landscape was mostly flat or rolling desert, places where anyone could hide were rare.

For now, at least, they could travel their route in peace, as long as no other cars seemed to hang around them.

"Okay, we have phones again," she soon told him, letting him know what his new number was. It had the Bluff, Utah, area code of 435, as did hers. "I'll write it down for you later."

"Good." He glanced at her then back at the road. "I'll probably need to let the prosecutor know as we get near Phoenix."

"Good," Alexa said, although she would handle communications as much as possible. His former ties were with Tempe, and that was where the crime had been committed, but, as they'd discussed, the court in Phoenix would be in charge of the prosecution. "Have you been in touch with the prosecutor before?"

"Not directly. Since I'm in WITSEC, I was told by your predecessors to let them handle any contacts, to try to ensure no one learns my identity or whereabouts by sneaking around using that angle."

"Glad you're aware of that." She would give him more info later, maybe even this evening, assuming they reached their destination tonight. And that looked quite feasible now.

That would be good, since the trial started tomorrow.

But for now? She didn't want to just sit observing the scenery, which wasn't changing much. She considered discussing last night, the fact they'd seemed safe in that motel.

Even more, she had an urge to mention those kisses—

No. They'd been impulsive, a mistake. She didn't want to think about them again.

As if she'd really be able to get them completely out of her mind...

So what should they talk about now?

An idea came to her: their respective backgrounds.

"Have you always lived in Tempe?" she asked him.

"Pretty much," he replied, glancing toward her again. "I got my degree at Arizona State University in Criminology and Criminal Justice and attended classes for that in Phoenix. But I came back home to take on my job as a vice detective with the Tempe PD."

"Got it. So is your family in Tempe?"

"That's right." At her urging, he went on to talk about them. His mom was a transactional attorney for a downtown Tempe law firm, and his dad worked in finance at the local headquarters of a national bank.

"Any siblings?" Alexa asked. She was looking forward to telling him about hers, assuming he wanted to hear about them.

"A brother, Max. He went into finance like our dad and got a job in Los Angeles at a different bank. He's married and has a couple of kids, so I'm Uncle Dane."

His tone suggested he was happy to be an uncle. Did that mean he liked kids? She thought about asking him if he wanted a family someday, but stopped herself. That didn't seem appropriate, even though she was interested.

"Why did you wind up in law enforcement?" Alexa couldn't help asking. She didn't gather that anyone else in his family was the stimulus. As she waited for his response, she turned to check behind them. There were a couple of cars in the distance, but nothing looked threatening. She set her eyes ahead again and scanned the horizon. She only saw one car coming toward them and had no reason to worry about it so far.

"Got interested in it while still in high school. The Tempe PD had some programs for familiarizing locals with the department and various programs, including for kids, and I was hooked."

"Sounds good." Alexa watched as that car coming toward them passed and kept going. She took a deep, calming breath. Nothing to worry about now. But that didn't keep her from staying alert. She wanted to know more about him and his personal life, but he started talking again first.

"How about you?" Dane asked. "How did you get into law enforcement?"

Ah, here it came. "It's pretty complicated," she said. "Family related."

"I figured, since you're a Colton and your family's reputation precedes you."

She knew he'd heard of the Coltons before—who hadn't? How much did he know?

"But we've got time. Tell me about it so I can make fun of you." Dane shot a glance filled with a smile toward her before looking back at the road.

Alexa couldn't help shaking her head. This was a serious discussion, and yet Dane made it clear he wanted to joke about it.

Why did she find that appealing? She knew she didn't have much of a sense of humor.

But this guy seemed to stimulate what little she had.

"Okay, what would you think if I told you I wanted to get into law enforcement because my father was a crook?" A bit much, but it was definitely true. And considering her family's reputation, he probably was aware of some of it.

Even so, he said, "Tell me about it."

That, she did. She explained that she had eleven siblings, and that she and Naomi were the youngest. "Most of us are trying to help others with our careers. We go about it in different ways, but we hate what our dad did and we hope to make things better for those he harmed and others in need of justice."

She kept it short and sweet. Their father had been a judge in Lark's County, Colorado. He'd apparently worried about supporting his large family. At least, that had been his excuse for his heinous criminal activities.

"His corruption was brought to light eventually by the family of one of those he convicted. But before he could be sent to jail himself—" Alexa felt her throat close up. No matter what he'd done, no matter how much she'd wanted to help those other people, she'd cared for her father though she had been too young to remember him well, except for the hugs he had given her and her siblings. And it had been so hard to grow up without a dad. "Anyway, there was a car accident on ice, and he died."

Dane glanced at her again. "I'm so sorry." He sounded serious this time. No joking in his tone.

"But the good thing was how his evil stuff spurred so many of us to do good things. Like me, in law enforcement. And among my eleven siblings, two are attorneys who started their own law firm and also created The Truth Foundation, which helps to get innocent people, like those our dad convicted, exonerated. One's a former sergeant in the army. Another, Dominic, the one I've been in touch with, is with the FBI's International Corruption Unit. And one's a district attorney in Lark's County, where Blue Larkspur is located."

"That all sounds really good," Dane said. "A bunch of you are doing all you can to atone for anything bad your father did."

"That's right."

She didn't mention, though, that her law enforcement family members were all after drug smuggler Ronald Spence. He had been thrown in prison thanks to their father, and The Truth Foundation had gotten him released after evidence had seemed to prove his innocence. Only it had since become apparent that Spence was actually guilty.

He needed to be thrown back into prison, and Alexa knew she would do all she could to help accomplish that—at least, once this latest case was complete.

She continued. "But would you like to know one of the careers a couple of my siblings have that's my favorite?"

"Sure," he said.

"They own the Gemini Ranch. I get there as often as I can. Maybe I'm a cowgirl at heart."

That caused Dane to laugh aloud. Alexa, too. Maybe she had a sense of humor after all.

Or at least she enjoyed talking about her family, and the strong—and fun—parts of it.

"Got it. I'd wondered about that. But that's not all of your siblings. What else do they do?"

"Well, my twin is in show business." She explained how Naomi's career differed from her own, and how

Naomi had fallen in love with an undercover cop recently while shooting a reality show at the Gemini. Her very lucky sister.

Naomi, Alexa couldn't help recalling, who seemed to know strange things sometimes, and who had expressed concern about what might happen on this journey.

Nothing bad had happened, though…so far at least.

But they still had several hours to drive.

"And the rest include a venture capitalist, a social worker and a journalist who's also a podcast host."

"That's quite a family," Dane said. "I'd like to meet them sometime."

Really? Alexa assumed that, after he testified against his former boss and hopefully helped to get him convicted of murder, he'd be out of witness protection—and out of her life.

But what if he wasn't?

She couldn't help recalling those kisses…

Fortunately, he started asking more questions about her family, including her widowed mother.

"Her name is Isadora. Isa. She's a freelance graphic designer, a really nice person."

And Alexa and her siblings had recently realized the depth of their mom's feelings for a new man—family friend and local police chief Theo Lawson. Alexa was happy for her.

Right now, Alexa was glad that they'd started seeing signs indicating they were getting close to the Arizona border. They were making progress. It would still be a few hours before they reached the Phoenix area, but not too long. She'd have to figure out where they'd stay that night.

Tempe, and anywhere near Dane's usual territory, would be a bad idea.

But now that she had her burner phone, she could try again to contact Vince for his take on what should come next.

She couldn't relax, of course. But at least for the moment she didn't have to feel stressed.

And she could enjoy Dane's presence for as long as they were together. Even as she made sure to protect him if any action to accomplish that became necessary.

THEY WERE APPROACHING ARIZONA, he realized by looking at the terrain. Signs along the roadway confirmed it. Soon, they'd cross the state line.

Dane resisted the urge to push down on the gas pedal. He'd seen no highway patrol, but that didn't mean they weren't around. He drove slightly faster than the speed limit, and that was good enough.

They remained a distance from Tempe. But Phoenix was a bit nearer on the route they were driving. And every minute they continued this way brought them closer to his testifying in Swanson's trial.

How did he feel about that?

Glad. Very glad. He would bring that dirty police chief down, help get him sent to prison for the rest of his life.

For Alvin's sake. But how would it feel to go his separate way from the marshal he'd come to like?

"Hey, we're making progress," he said to Alexa now. He figured she was well aware of it. She'd stopped talking about her family and seemed to be concentrating even more on their surroundings, glancing often around them.

Dane had found himself fascinated by what she'd said as they'd discussed their backgrounds. What a family she had! The Colton name was well known in law enforcement, so he had heard of them before, but it was interesting to learn how versatile they were, in so many areas of the law and peacekeeping. And bringing down bad guys, he figured.

As well as protecting witnesses in danger.

He'd been serious about wanting to meet some of her family. But he realized that once he was no longer the subject of Alexa's safeguarding, he would probably never see her again.

He was determined to move back home as soon as it was safe for him.

Like, hopefully, in another week or two.

Although, if there was any possibility of his getting together again, in some manner, with Alexa—

"You're awfully quiet." Alexa's soft voice brought Dane out of his reverie. "What are you thinking?"

Like, *Are you scared*? Dane figured that was what she meant.

And *heck*. He *was* somewhat scared. He'd have to be stupid to assume all was well, even with his own private protector with him.

But nerves wouldn't stop him.

Only another bullet…

Forget that. If nothing else, he would be prepared this time, or at least aware his life was in danger, which would keep him vigilant.

"I'm thinking about all I want to say tomorrow," he

said in response to Alexa's question. "I've no doubt the prosecutor will ask the right questions to get me to testify about what I saw, what I know."

"I've no doubt, either." Alexa's voice was soft and encouraging, and Dane had an urge to pull her quickly into his arms and kiss her again in thanks…and more.

That was wrong, especially now. He was concentrating on his driving, as he had to be.

And drawing them even closer to their destination— and where he would ultimately help bring Swanson to justice.

"Hopefully, you will have time to discuss the trial and your testimony in advance with the prosecutor," Alexa continued. "That's what they usually do. I've seen it a lot before, with the witnesses under my protection. But this situation… Well, it's a bit different."

"Like, the perpetrator being tried was my former boss, a police chief, and he has a lot of cohorts who just might be happy bringing down a bigmouth like me. He might even pay them for it." As he said that, he recalled what Alexa had said about her father.

He appreciated that Alexa, and apparently a bunch of her siblings, had been horrified by what he'd done, enough so that they'd chosen careers that could help the innocent and those in danger.

Like him.

He couldn't help it. He scanned the horizon in front of them and, via the rearview mirror, the area behind him. Again. As he did often. And as he was fully aware the amazing woman who accompanied him to protect him also did.

The woman he thought about often as the subject

of his protection as well, if it ever came down to that. Or at least he would be prepared to attack anyone who targeted her.

"Say," he said, "tell me a little more about your brother Dominic, the FBI guy you talked to. How did he decide to go that direction?"

"Well, he's in their International Corruption Unit. Oh, and he's a triplet, older than little twin me."

Dane laughed. He'd also thought that, of all the siblings she'd described, Dominic might be the one he'd like to meet most. But the two oldest were lawyers who had started that organization—The Truth Foundation, right?—to help the people their dad had hurt by sentencing innocents or recommending harsher sentences than crimes warranted. They also sounded pretty darned interesting.

Well, someday the trial would be behind him, and he could continue with his detective career, being even more observant of what was going on around him.

And by whom.

Plus, he would be able to follow up on anything he learned as a result of this situation, not only about how cops should or shouldn't act, but also about their families.

Having a chance to talk to some of Alexa's siblings might be damned interesting for that.

There. They were just about to reach the turnoff from Utah into part of Arizona.

They were getting closer.

The route they were on continued south, but the next veered west a short distance before heading southwest—mostly south, from what he recalled of the GPS.

He relied on Alexa to confirm the route as they continued, but for the moment he prepared to make the turn
onto the interstate.

Several signs prepared him for the intersection. He
slowed, flipped on the car's turn signal, and turned
left onto Route 160. Soon, he accelerated to reach the
speed limit.

That was when he saw an SUV come from the direction he hadn't taken.

It looked like a police car. Lights on top were flashing, but he heard no siren.

A police car. He was back in Arizona now. At least
some of his former colleagues were now his enemies,
if they believed whatever cockamamie story Swanson
had undoubtedly made up to protect himself and throw
blame for the situation that had resulted in Dane's in-
jury, and Alvin's death, on Dane.

Well, what could he do but pull over? Although—

He glanced at Alexa. She was looking in the side-
view mirror on the passenger side. She had already
seen their pursuer.

"Under other circumstances, I'd be glad to pull over,"
he told her. "And we've no reason to think that Swanson's got any state troopers in his pocket. But they'd be
in charge here on the highway, and—"

"Understood," she said curtly. "But for now, let's act
like obedient regular citizens. I'll make sure my weapon
is handy, though."

"Mine, too." Dane put on his turn signal as he started
to slow down, preparing to pull off the road.

"Okay, but be careful. I don't want to kill or injure a
law enforcement officer because we're nervous. Got it?"

"Yeah, I got it." Dane knew he sounded more than irritated—that was just his anxiety talking. But he genuinely agreed with her.

Nerves were one thing, though. Danger might be related, but that was what he needed to watch for. What *they* needed to watch for. For better or worse, he'd realized, they were partners in this adventure.

He stopped and put the car in Park, though he remained ready to accelerate again. He didn't turn off the engine.

An African American guy in a beige uniform, with a badge on his chest and loaded belt around his waist, exited the driver's-side door.

Dane rolled down his window as he waited. He also checked to see how easily accessible his gun was.

"I'll take care of that, if necessary," Roger, beside him, said in a gruff, masculine voice, and Daniel, back in his own undercover identity, chose not to smile.

Nothing funny about this. And he understood why Alexa—no, Roger—would want every precaution to be taken.

As the trooper reached the open window, Daniel turned his head to look at him. "Something wrong, Officer?"

Like, were you hired to look for me by that SOB I intend to bring down, maybe even kill me?

The guy appeared to be in his thirties, with short, black hair and a scowling expression. "You didn't signal as you turned onto this highway from 191," the trooper said. He pulled out a pad from one of his many pockets. "Time for a ticket."

"Oh, but this is a rental car," Roger/Alexa called in

his throaty, masculine voice from the other side of the car. "We just picked it up yesterday." He'd pulled the paperwork from the glove compartment and waved it. "See? And I saw Daniel flip the switch for the signal. It must be broken."

"Oh yeah?" the trooper said without asking to take a closer look at the rental lease or registration card. "Give it a try, and I'll take a look."

He did. Daniel flipped the blinker a couple of times, and the trooper checked it out from the rear. His partner exited the SUV, too, and the two of them talked for a minute.

The first officer came forward again. "We'll let you go this time since it appears to be defective, but you'd better report that to the rental company, maybe even pick up another car if they've got an office wherever you're heading."

Daniel felt relieved the trooper didn't even ask where that was. "I'll certainly do that, Officer. I'm really sorry. And thanks so much for being so understanding."

The trooper stomped off. Daniel gave a big sigh of relief as he glanced at Roger beside him.

"Maybe this is our lucky day after all," Roger/Alexa rasped.

"You, with your law enforcement background, know better than that. If we were really lucky, he wouldn't even have noticed." But despite his words, Dane—now feeling like himself again, rather than Daniel—felt at least a bit optimistic as he started off once more toward Phoenix.

The trooper's SUV passed them as Dane maintained

the speed limit. Soon, the state vehicle was out of sight ahead of them as the road turned a bit.

There were other cars around, though not many. More seemed to be going the other way, but a couple caught up with them from behind and then passed.

Dane had an urge to speed forward, and although he did increase his velocity a bit, he decided to behave for now.

He was well aware there were likely to be more troopers around.

He kept checking to make sure none of them, or anyone else, was following him, glancing often into the rearview mirror.

No one that he saw at first, but—

He was about to say something to Roger/Alexa but she spoke first in her usual voice, as she stared into the side-view mirror. "I appreciate how you've been staying near the speed limit and letting cars pass, but there's one back there—"

"That seems to be following at our speed."

"Right," Alexa said. "I'd like to get it to pass so I won't be worried about it, so please slow down a little more."

That, he did.

The vehicle appeared to decrease its speed, too.

And so Dane went even slower. A few other cars passed, but not that one. Snail's pace time.

Ah, the black sedan appeared to accelerate, maybe no longer wanting to stay behind a crawler. Only—

As it reached them and began to pass, it sped up. Someone on the passenger side glared at Dane; a young guy whose brown hair blew in the breeze of the open window. He had no facial hair, but there was a look of determination on his long, thin face.

He wore a dark shirt. It looked like it could be official, although Dane saw no badges from this angle. Even so, could he be a cop? If so, what jurisdiction? Tempe?

Dane stared farther inside and noted that the driver, too, appeared to be in uniform.

And that was when that passenger pulled a gun and aimed it at Dane.

Chapter Eight

"Speed up! Faster!" Alexa yelled, not even attempting to sound like Roger anymore. But she didn't really have to tell Daniel/Dane. They were already accelerating rapidly past the vehicle beside them, at least for the moment. Alexa had pulled her gun from her pocket but didn't have anywhere to aim it, for now.

She wasn't surprised that Dane had done the same thing, still holding the steering wheel with the other hand and moving his gaze from the road ahead to beside them.

But she did hear a sudden blast—clearly from a gun. Their pursuers must have caught up to them. Fortunately, with the way Dane was also swerving across the road, the bullet hadn't seemed to have hit anything. Not them at least, thank heavens. Alexa had no idea where it had gone.

There fortunately weren't any other vehicles close to them right now, so hopefully it hadn't hurt anyone.

But the shot had made a loud noise. Loud enough for the troopers who'd pulled way ahead to hear and come back and help them?

Apparently not.

Their car continued to race in that direction, though, thanks to Dane, who also kept zigzagging across the road to keep the other vehicle behind them. She knew his defensive driving was also designed to make the people in this front seat—namely, both him and Alexa—harder to hit.

She just hoped it worked.

For her own safety, Alexa figured she should have crouched down, or at least bent over to stay out of any line of fire. But that wasn't why she was there. Why she was with Dane. And so she remained sitting up, wishing she could throw herself between Dane and any weapon aimed at him, but in this car that wasn't possible.

She did keep an eye on the other vehicle, though. His safety was her responsibility.

And she would do everything she could to keep him safe—and not just because it was her job. She realized she really had begun to care for the man in her charge.

She kept her gun ready in case using it became practical.

And she additionally pulled her new phone from her pocket and pressed in the number for her boss, hoping it would work this time.

It did. Marshal Vince Cudahy answered his phone immediately. "Hello?" He didn't demand, in that one word, to know who was calling, but Alexa was sure that was what he meant. He didn't have her new number, so no identity would have showed up on his screen.

"Vince, it's…" She was about to identify herself as Alexa but didn't have to.

"Alexa? Where the hell have you been? What's going on? Is everything all right?"

"No," she said, and really meant it now. She used her shoulder to keep her phone at her ear. Their assailants had pulled up close behind them, the hood of the vehicle now very close to their bumper. "Turn!" she shouted to Dane, who obeyed by turning the wheel abruptly to prevent the other car from hitting them. He then braked suddenly, throwing them both forward into the dashboard.

The other car was now ahead of them again. A good thing? Probably not. Not when the occupants had taken a shot at them, and probably would again.

But Alexa resolved to take control of that angle, at least somewhat. She loosened her seat belt, kept her phone wedged where it was, crawled somewhat into the back seat, rolled down the left window and shot at the other car several times, aiming for the left rear tire, though missing it as they moved. She also memorized the Arizona license plate.

The car didn't brake immediately, but it did pull over to the right side of the road, then slowed a bit.

"Good! Now keep going. Fast."

"Yes, sir. Or ma'am."

"Tell me what's going on," came the order in Alexa's ear.

"I don't know why we haven't been able to communicate, Vince," Alexa responded. She put it on speaker so Dane could hear, too. "Maybe it was because the burners Daniel and I both had were hacked. We've sent them off in a different direction now. But we're still on the way from Blue Larkspur to Phoenix, and the occupants of a car just started shooting at us. And they could be cops. Here's the license plate information." She related it to him, figuring he'd have a way to jot it down. But she figured it was likely to be false or stolen.

"Damn!" Vince exploded. "Tell me where you are."

"Somewhere between—"

But before Alexa could say, Dane said, "Don't do it! Even if you're sure it's your boss, who knows if our burner phones are totally safe? Hope so, but just in case, don't give him any details."

"If I don't tell him, he won't be able to send help." Alexa knew she sounded desperate. But she was, in a way. Still, this was the kind of situation she'd known she might face while doing her job. She could handle it. She *would* handle it.

But having some assistance sounded damned good right about now.

Yet Dane and she were far enough from civilization out here that it would undoubtedly take forever before Vince could be of much help, unless he sent a helicopter. Or even drones.

And that apparently was his idea, too.

"Look. He's right." Apparently Vince had heard what Dane had said. "But you know it's me. And I understand that you don't want to give a lot of information under these circumstances. But I'm assuming you're at least in Arizona by now, right?"

Alexa looked to Dane, who shot an angry glance toward her as she said, "Yes. And we dumped my assigned car before and are in a rental car. It's a light blue sedan. The car we were shot at from is behind us."

"Okay, then. I'll get in touch with some of my contacts in the area you're probably driving in. You'll see helicopters overhead soon. Be careful in the meantime, stay as far as possible from the shooter, of course. And after help arrives— Well, I figure you'll determine the best course of action then. Got it?"

"Right," Alexa said. "Thanks, Vince. And I'll be in touch again as soon as it's feasible."

"At least I have your current number, for now. But do what you have to, to stay safe, even sending this phone…wherever."

"Got it." Alexa hung up.

But where were those guys now?

Behind them somewhere, since they'd pulled over and slowed. But Alexa didn't see them.

That, hopefully, was a good thing. She checked her phone's GPS.

Not far from a turnoff road. That might be good.

They had passed the town of Tsegi. Route 160 continued on, but Alexa had an urge to tell Dane to drive off the main road toward where the Peabody Kayenta Mine used to be.

Not too far, though. They needed to be near the primary roads when—or *if*—Vince was able to get helicopters headed in their direction.

"Drive south onto Route 41 here," she told Dane. "There's an old coal mine a little way off, but there are some local streets first that even have a few restaurants on them. Let's wait there for a short while."

"Sounds good," Dane said. "It might be easier for us to hide among crowds of people."

"My thoughts exactly."

They agreed not to spend much time here by getting food or anything else in this small town, but he parked and they continued to observe the roads around them.

Nothing.

Good, Alexa thought. But where were their attackers? Were they lying in wait, preparing to spring another deadly trap?

"Time to go back?" Dane made it a question after a few minutes, but he must have already decided the answer since he'd turned the engine on and headed the car back to Route 160.

Coincidentally—or not—Alexa saw a car a distance in front of them. It looked a lot like their pursuers' black sedan.

Damn. How had they gotten ahead?

She told Dane.

"Yeah, I saw it," he said through gritted teeth. "I don't want to turn back the way we were going to avoid them. We're losing too much time, and I need to be in court tomorrow."

"I understand. I think I'll call Vince again soon and find out if any copters are on the way. Oh, and he could call the prosecutor and let him or her know that you'll do your best to be there, but maybe not first thing in the morning, considering the situation."

"Good idea. I don't have to be the first witness to testify."

"And if they have any way of helping us, they should let us know." But Alexa doubted the prosecutors could do much.

They cruised along the road, letting others pass since Dane wisely didn't floor it to get closer to the car they'd pegged as possibly containing their enemies.

That was when Alexa first heard the sound of a helicopter's whirring blades. Or was it two? She looked up through the windshield and saw a couple approaching overhead from the south. That would still make sense, even if they'd been sent from Vince in Colorado, since he would undoubtedly have contacted law enforcement closer to where he knew Alexa and the subject of her witness protection were currently located.

"Could those have been sent by your Marshals Service?" Dane asked, also looking in that direction as he drove slowly toward them.

"I'm fairly sure they were." Alexa allowed herself to feel a slight sense of relief. But not much. Just because they now had help didn't mean their jeopardy was over.

"Good. We'll just stay nice and slow for now till we see how things go."

Quite a few other cars passed them as they kept their speed just below the limit. The car they'd been checking out did not appear to slow down. In fact, as the helicopters kept circling the area, Alexa lost sight of it; she figured it had sped up to get out of the way.

She didn't see anyone, or any vehicle, that particularly troubled her—but that fact itself wound up troubling her. She wanted to know where they'd gone.

But she figured she could rely on the choppers that still showed up overhead with frequency to, if nothing else, scare off their potential attackers, at least for now.

They continued driving for quite a while, veering off the main road and back on again to keep an eye out for anyone following—and no one was. Alexa made her call to Vince, thanked him for the help and requested that he contact the prosecutor in Phoenix, which he agreed to do.

Dane and she didn't talk a lot, at least not like before. Dane did ask Alexa if she had ever experienced anything similar, like helicopters swooping in to help keep her, and the witness she was then protecting, safe.

"No, but I'd heard of similar circumstances. Now I have another experience I can add to my list of things I've had happen while on the job."

"Ah, so that's why the other car came after us. You planned it to add to your experiences."

Alexa had been scanning the sky yet again, but now she looked over at her driver—and the subject of her current assignment.

And the man who thought he was funny sometimes when she didn't see the humor.

Like now.

"Oh exactly," she said dryly. "I called on some suspects in other cases who wanted some current fun and told them to come after us in our rented car. And then I contacted Vince to get him to protect us."

Dane laughed. "Hey, of us two, I thought I was the joker."

"So did I," Alexa grumbled. She was looking at her phone. It was getting late enough in this day that she thought it would be better to stop for the night, then get up early enough tomorrow to drive straight through to the courthouse.

Hopefully, with more protection from Vince's allies. But this way, Dane's enemies, with a bit of luck, wouldn't know where they were or be able to figure out their timing.

"Hey, you know what?" she said. "I think we're getting close to Flagstaff. And I think your pursuers are going to assume, with those helicopter escorts, that we'll roll into Phoenix tonight. I want us to find another dinky hotel, this time in or around Flagstaff, and stay there till very early tomorrow morning. And I'll let Vince know, too, in case we need any more help."

She thought about asking Dane's opinion. But she was in charge.

"Okay by me," he said anyway. "How soon do we reach a Flagstaff turnoff?"

"Not long. But here are my thoughts about that." Alexa suggested that they exit where it was clear that food and gasoline were available and stop for those services. That way, if anyone had been able to evade the copters and still follow them, Alexa and her charge would have an obvious and necessary reason to get off the route they were taking.

Only, then they would find a nearby hole-in-the-wall motel to stay the night, maybe even leaving the car parked near the gas station. They could use a ride share to get to the motel, as long as they remained careful and in disguise. And asked their driver to get them there by a circuitous route while they observed their surroundings.

"Sounds fine to me," Dane said. "Tell me the best place to get off this road."

DANE WAS PLEASED when Alexa told him where to exit the route they were on, then get back on the main road, then off again.

So she could watch even more for anyone following, he assumed. She really was thorough, he observed.

At the second exit there were billboards for a nearby

service station and convenience store. That was where they headed, at Alexa's suggestion.

So did the couple of helicopters that had continued to show up periodically and circle their area.

"I think this might be a good time for you to talk to Vince and see where we are if we stay somewhere near here overnight—and whether he has spoken with the prosecutor," Dane said as they reached the shop.

Smart and helpful witness protector that Alexa was, she not only did what he requested, but she also put her phone on speaker as they parked in one of the few vacant spaces just outside the convenience store. Dane felt he could participate if it seemed appropriate, although he didn't wind up saying anything.

"Oh, hi, Roger," Vince began as he answered. "Thanks for calling."

Dane—no, maybe Daniel at this moment—looked toward Roger/Alexa's slitted eyes. She appeared concerned. Did her boss's use of her pseudonym mean they were in trouble?

"No problem, Marshal Cudahy." Alexa used her deep, disguised voice, and Dane continued to be concerned. "But I had some questions."

"Let me guess. And in case you're wondering, I'm assuming you aren't reaching your destination this evening, so those copters will only circle for a couple more rounds today."

Alexa nodded. "Correct assumption," she agreed, still using her male voice. "But your pilots know in general where we are. I don't want them to know where we're staying, so maybe you should call them off now."

So they could find someplace to stay and no one would know where, Dane figured.

"Will do, but, so that you know, I've made sure there are copters circling in a few other places so it won't be obvious where you are."

"Excellent idea," Alexa said.

Dane continued to sit there as he listened, staring at people who entered and left the store, and others behind where they were parked who were pumping gas into their cars.

"And in case you're wondering," Vince said, "I did speak with the prosecutor, District Attorney Moe Francini, to let him know that his key witness was getting close but, for security reasons, would not reach Phoenix till sometime tomorrow. I'll give you his phone number. You should call first thing in the morning, early, to give him a status report. Otherwise, he'll be hammering at me, I figure, and I won't have all the answers."

"Fair enough. Did he give any parameters about what might be too late for us to arrive?"

"Only that the trial will begin around nine and he'd like to have Dane there no later than eleven so they can discuss his testimony before Moe begins questioning him that afternoon."

"I think we can do that."

"Good. Sounds like you're doing well with your alternate identity, by the way. And I'd like you to call me again after you talk with Moe tomorrow to keep me informed, too. That'll possibly inspire me to get more copters over your heads if it makes sense in the morning."

"Thanks, Vince," Roger/Alexa said, and they soon hung up.

She looked at Dane. "I assume you're okay with all we said, or even a jokester like you would jump in and tell us what was wrong."

"Who, me?" Dane spoke in the grittier voice he sometimes took on with his Daniel identity. "A jokester? Or a complainer?"

"Both sound just like the wonderful you I've come to know over the last couple days." Alexa/Roger sent him an irritated grin, then said, "Now, let's hurry into this place and grab some stuff for dinner tonight. Then, I have an idea where we can stay."

"Sounds good to me. Another hellhole like last night?"

"Maybe, but there's a place I saw online that might actually not only be in a somewhat safe location, but even possibly clean."

Dane gestured into the air with his fist. "Yay! Bring it on."

"Food first."

That was fine with him. He got himself back into the mode of being Daniel Brennan, big and bulky, with a lot less hair. He also appreciated that Alexa, already somewhat in disguise, went into thorough Roger mode.

Soon, they were both in the store. Each chose a sandwich from a refrigerator case. Daniel's? Ham and cheese. And Roger decided on tuna salad. They each additionally selected chips on the side, and they also bought a six-pack of bottled water.

There weren't a lot of other customers, but Dane wasn't surprised to see Roger shuffle along one side to stare down the couple of aisles at the other people there. He didn't appear concerned, and neither did Dane see anyone who particularly worried him. But he remained on high alert.

Soon, they were ready. He wasn't surprised when Roger pulled his wallet from his pocket—opposite side from the fortunately not especially noticeable bulge on the other side where the weapon was stuck in his pants—and paid cash for what they'd bought.

Another thing for which Dane would ultimately repay Alexa, or the Marshals Service, once everything was resolved.

Dane let Roger lope slowly in front of him as they left the store, acting as if he was the older man he looked to be, yet staying close enough to Dane to be the target if anyone tried to harm him. Yes, this was Alexa's job. Dane definitely knew that before and now found it even more obvious, even if the intent was that the limping senior appeared to find it too difficult to move away.

But now the other "man" accompanied Dane to the passenger side and watched as he got into the car, after Dane suggested leaving the car there and using a ride share service to head somewhere else. "That would just provide another possibility of someone unknown sneaking into our lives—one of those who's trying to find you," Alexa said. "I know I considered that before, but the idea began to worry me."

"Got it," Dane told her. And he did. He was getting used to having to second-guess every move he made.

But were they really out of the vision of whoever was after him?

In any case, it was Alexa's turn to drive. Dane didn't even ask.

Once they were both locked inside, Alexa started backing out of the parking space.

As she drove away, he asked, "So are we off to the place you found where we can stay tonight?"

"Exactly. But not directly."

Sure enough, she drove around the store and parked first at one of the gas pumps, where she insisted on getting the fuel into the car's tank.

Dane pretended to be looking at his phone but mostly kept an eye on Alexa. He couldn't help himself.

When she got back into the car, he had to ask. "Did you see anything worrisome?"

"Only the price of the gas."

Really? This woman who seemed to have little, if any, sense of humor was making a joke?

He, of all people, loved the idea but wasn't sure if she was actually being serious.

On the other hand, this gas station's prices were on the high side, maybe because of the location near the road and not too far of a distance into Flagstaff.

Maybe she wasn't joking.

He didn't ask. But he did say, "So how long will it take to reach our destination?"

"Not long."

And in fact, she was correct. She drove around the block again. Then she got onto a wider street that appeared to lead to downtown.

Except that she quickly edged into an alleyway between a couple of office buildings.

Nearby was a small but relatively nice-looking motel.

The motel faced another road and wasn't too close to any of the offices or any other structures.

But Alexa didn't park in the spaces surrounding the motel. Instead, she pulled into a three-story lot at the end of one of the office buildings.

"Let's assume we'll be staying here and get our stuff," she said. "And let's be careful."

They soon had their belongings out of the trunk. And yes, they were careful as they at first stayed near the offices, then crossed the parking lot to the motel— but only after Alexa insisted on walking that way first.

Alexa had also insisted on being the one to check them in.

Dane hoped this place would be much better than last night's. But even if it looked better, Dane couldn't help wondering, *Would they stay safe?*

And could he get away with kissing his protector good-night again?

Chapter Nine

Though she acted even older than she had before, Alexa felt she did just fine hobbling as Roger into the small but attractive lobby on the ground floor of the Welcome to AZ Flagstaff Motel, and rallying her huskiest, senior, masculine voice to ask the receptionist—a middle-aged lady in a fancy pantsuit—if they had a room available.

She certainly hoped so. She'd done some quick digging on her burner phone to find a motel in an area where there was nothing to particularly attract tourists or anyone else. This one had not only come to her attention quickly, in a business-oriented neighborhood with a few but not many similar accommodations, it had also stood out as a potentially okay location, despite its remoteness.

Pictures had showed it was a couple of stories high but not particularly large, with limited windows and a visible outdoor path to reach the rooms. Their website had indicated the rates were reasonable, and the photos had depicted rooms that were more than decent compared with the place they'd stayed the night before. Those rooms appeared clean, with a couple of beds in each, and other amenities, including free bottled water in the small refrigerators.

And it hadn't been far off their existing path. Although that might have been more of a problem than a plus if anyone following them had managed to elude the helicopter pilots and continued to surreptitiously shadow them.

"Do you have any rooms available for just tonight?" she asked.

Daniel was standing at the door, looking out as if he was fascinated by the neighborhood. They'd planned that. He stood back far enough that he wasn't particularly visible, nor was he at an angle where he was likely to be shot if any of his enemies turned up, assuming they'd recognize him in his disguise.

Smart guy. He was doing a good job of keeping an eye on things for his protection, and even hers. And despite his ugly disguise, he still appeared somewhat good-looking to her.

"Yes, we do," the receptionist said in a calm voice, nodding so her brown hair caressed her shoulders as she regarded Alexa through her large, black-rimmed glasses. Her ID pin said she was Bobbie. She turned to the computer beside her on the wooden counter and typed something in. Alexa wondered how many rooms were available. Maybe all of them, judging by the lack of parked cars or other activity in this location surrounded by businesses that apparently didn't otherwise include places to stay. Bobbie looked back at them. "One room for the two of you?"

"That's right," Alexa groused as Roger, wondering if they'd get any kind of argument. Could be the place was so empty that management hoped a pair of guests might rent out two rooms.

But Bobbie nodded, typed some more and said, "I have a room on the second floor for you. We don't have an elevator, though. Would you like me to send someone to carry your bags up there?"

"No thanks," Alexa said, still grumping. "We'll manage."

Of course. She was strong enough to manage her stuff, and with the help of Dane/Daniel there'd be no problem at all.

They hadn't requested it, but she was glad they were getting a room upstairs. Maybe the place wasn't as empty as it appeared. But it'd be easier to keep an eye on their surroundings from up there.

Alexa showed her special Roger ID and paid by cash again. She felt Daniel's glare—did he really manage to exude irritation at not being in control while hiding from potential killers?—but had already told him she had sufficient cash, and it was certainly less traceable than credit cards, even obtained with fake, protective names.

More likely, he wanted to pay, as he'd said before. Well, who ultimately got stuck with the bill wasn't up to her. She was simply following orders. And *she* was the one in charge—she'd thought he'd come to terms with that, but apparently not the way she'd hoped.

She got the receipt and two keycards from the receptionist. It all felt a bit like last night, although Alexa definitely hoped their room tonight wouldn't be as ratty.

But even if it was, this was where they would stay. It was only for one night, after all. And if she'd done a good job selecting the place, they'd hopefully remain safe. *But is he going to kiss me again?* she wondered.

"Thanks," Roger said deeply and politely.

Alexa led Daniel out of the reception area, both of them rolling their carryon bags behind them. Daniel held the plastic container with their dinner food and his backpack.

At the base of the concrete steps, Daniel said, "I'll carry both suitcases. One at a time, though."

Even though Alexa considered herself totally able to take care of her own things, the Roger she was acting like around here might not be able to, and it wouldn't be a great idea to indicate to the world that he could. As a result, she agreed with her companion. "Thanks," she said in a deep mutter. "Let me carry the backpack and food, at least."

She followed large Daniel as he carried her bag upstairs first. She walked slowly, balancing the backpack and holding on to the thin rail at the side of the steps, as if she needed to do so to maintain her steadiness. Since she still had both keycards, she opened the door to their room, which was the closest to the stairs.

She hurried in and, hand on her covered weapon, she checked the place out. Looked okay. No one was there. She went back outside to watch apparently overweight Daniel strain his way up the stairs with his own bag... and, even more important, to keep her eyes on their environment to make sure no one else was watching her charge.

Fortunately, the area, despite having taller buildings around it, appeared quiet. She saw no one looking at them either from below, or from any windows in those buildings.

At the top, Daniel grunted and moved around Roger into their room, where she joined him and closed and locked the door behind them, then checked to make sure it seemed secure.

"Not bad," Daniel said in his normal Dane voice, standing taller, ignoring his distended stomach.

"I agree," Alexa said.

As with the other place they'd stayed, this room had a window looking out onto the upper walkway, and Alexa was pleased that it had slatted blinds that were closed. It would most likely be easier to move a slat or two to look out than it had been to deal with drapes.

And when Alexa walked around to study the place, she was even more pleased. The room not only looked clean, but the furnishings gave it a higher-quality feel. Both beds had fluffy, attractively lacy beige coverlets, decorative area rugs sat on the wooden floor and there was an ornate wooden dresser along one wall. There were photos of buildings hung on the plain white walls, and a very large flat-screen TV on the wall facing the bed.

Very nice, she thought. At least as far as the décor. But was it safe?

Well, she wouldn't sleep much. She'd pace the room often instead of sleeping, and peek out those slats through the window. Maybe even go outside and look around, although if she did that, she would have to be Roger—an armed Roger, with his weapon still not visible if anyone happened to see the codger out and about in the middle of the night.

Didn't sound like fun. But there were always parts of her witness protection job that weren't enjoyable. It was about justice, not fun.

And those parts were overrun by the good stuff, like getting her subjects to their trials safely and allowing them to testify against whomever was threatening them.

That was what she would do tomorrow with Daniel/Dane. And she'd resist the temptation to kiss him while they were in this room together, she vowed.

Dane. He'd slipped into the bathroom, although the door was open. Even so, Alexa figured it wouldn't be appropriate for her to peer in while he was there.

She pulled off her hairpiece for now, which made her a lot more comfortable, and quickly changed her clothes.

He soon emerged. And it definitely was Dane who emerged. He'd removed the clothes that made Daniel seem large and ungainly. He still had a T-shirt on, and his somewhat baggy jeans, but he appeared a lot better than when she'd seen him last.

A whole lot better.

And now they were again about to spend the night in the same room.

"So what are our plans for tonight besides eating dinner?" he asked as he sat on top of the bed nearest the bathroom door. His voice was back to normal. So was he, she assumed, although that question didn't hold a bit of humor in it.

And she had no intention of doing anything funny.

She was going to do all she could to keep this man, her subject, safe. *And nothing else*, she added silently.

"Early to bed," she said.

"Early to rise," he added. "Makes a man healthy, wealthy and—"

"On his way to testify in court, as he is expected to do," Alexa broke in. Okay, maybe a little humor was called for after all. Although there was nothing particularly funny in her modified last line. Wise? Maybe. But they definitely would need to rise early tomorrow and get on their way.

"Sounds good to me," Dane said. The way he smiled at her, his rugged face back to its usual handsomeness now that he again looked like the Dane she was protecting, made her insides quiver.

Cut that out, she told herself.

But she couldn't completely ignore his sexiness.

Not that she would do anything about it.

"So," she said, "let's eat."

Each sat on a bed as they ate. Different beds, hers the one nearest the door.

She put the TV on and they watched some local news, although she kept the sound low. No items about the sudden appearance of helicopters over their route earlier in the day.

Alexa's tuna sandwich was fair, but she wasn't hungry.

Or maybe she simply didn't have an appetite because of her assignment.

Or because of her discomfort that evening being in a hotel room again with the man she was protecting.

The man she was much too attracted to.

They both were side by side somewhat, each sitting at the foot of their respective beds. Alexa glanced over at Dane—and saw he looked at her, too, as he ate.

Neither looked away, not immediately. And Alexa felt her insides flutter, as if they were there for a reason other than having someplace hopefully safe to stay the night.

But she forced herself to ignore that.

"The news here isn't too exciting," she said when she turned away, as if giving him an excuse for having stared at her instead of the TV. But the idea of him watching her that way… Surely he was wiser than she, had no particular interest in her except as his protector.

That was as it should be. She couldn't allow any kind of distraction from what she had to accomplish.

And tomorrow would be a day where her skills would undoubtedly be put to their highest test so far in this assignment.

She would take care of Dane. It was her job.

And, she admitted to herself, it was also something she had to do, for her own peace of mind, as someone who really liked a lot about her subject. He seemed smarter, more reliable, even sexier than any guy she had ever dated—never mind how inappropriate it was for her to even think about that.

"Yeah," Dane said. He was regarding the TV then, and obviously responding to what they'd already been talking about. "Doesn't sound as if they're excited about a certain trial that'll start tomorrow south of here. A murder trial. They haven't mentioned it, at least not since we started watching."

"Assuming the news people even know about it," said Alexa.

"Oh, they do," Dane said. "Or at least I saw, around the time of the murder, that the media anywhere near

Tempe ran stories about that situation, and Phoenix and the national media surely picked up on it, too. It isn't every day that a police chief is accused of murdering anyone, let alone one of his own subordinates, and shooting another. I kept looking for all the information I could at the time, even as I was taken into custody myself by the FBI, and then your marshals, for my protection."

"Still, that doesn't mean they necessarily kept up with what was happening." But Alexa realized that the media always glommed on to any exciting news they could.

And the upcoming trial was definitely, at least potentially, exciting for a local audience.

"Do you believe that?" Dane responded in a highly skeptical voice, even as he grinned at her.

If only she wasn't so enticed by that grin.

Or everything else about this man...

"No," she admitted, smiling back. "Not really. I assume you were a media star back then."

"Pretty much. And I'm prepared to get in the spotlight again now, although I hope it's because my testimony is a major factor in putting that miserable SOB who used to be my boss away for life."

"Great idea, as far as I'm concerned."

And Alexa found herself beaming under that still growing, intimate smile of her subject.

He was off-limits. How many times had she reminded herself of that? Did she really need to again?

She'd finished eating. So had he. She pulled out her phone and checked the time.

With all the care they'd taken and veering back and

forth to avoid being seen as much as possible, they'd eaten up a lot of the day before.

Now it was nearing nine o'clock. Good enough for bedtime tonight.

First, though… "I think this old man needs to take a quick walk outside to act nosy again. But the other man in this room should stay here. I'll be back soon. You could even start getting ready for bed."

"Not till my old man companion is back safely." Dane was standing now, almost glaring at Alexa as if he expected her to object.

She didn't, but his protectiveness made her glow inside. Not that she'd mention that, either. "Well, if anything goes wrong, you have Vince's number," she reminded him as she had before. "And if it goes really wrong, you can always call 9-1-1 first."

His glare deepened. How could that be so alluring at a time like this?

"Things had better not go wrong at all," he growled. "And if anything—"

"I know. You were in law enforcement, too. You'll want to come intervene." She glared at him, hoping he would be obedient, but figuring he would do what he wanted. "Well, don't do it. We checked this area out as well as we could, and I think we're okay. I just need to make sure."

"I get it. But—"

"I'll be back soon. I promise." And Alexa hoped it was a promise she could keep.

She grabbed her Roger clothes, and more. After going into the bathroom and dressing again as Roger, she stuck her weapon into her belt beneath her loose shirt. Back in the room, she glanced briefly at Dane.

He was watching her.

She picked up a keycard from where she had put them, on top of the dresser, and prepared to leave the room.

"I'm listening, in case anything's out there," Dane said. Alexa realized he had turned down the sound on the TV.

"So am I. And looking." She unbolted the door and limped outside, pulling the door shut behind her.

The sky was dark. The motel area was lit, though, by a series of streetlights along the parking lot. Alexa stayed close to the wall.

There were a couple more cars in the lot now.

Did either belong to someone after Dane?

Alexa saw no people outside, nor did she see any movement of the slats in windows of the upstairs rooms as she limped by, pretending to be fascinated by the sky above and the parking area below.

Well, she actually *was* interested in the parking area, though she spied no activity.

Still walking like Roger, she returned inside, then locked the dead bolt on the door behind her, glad there was one.

Dane was sitting on the same bed he'd sat on while they'd eaten dinner, his back against the headboard. The TV on the wall still had the news on, not a surprise. "Everything okay out there?" he asked.

"Far as I could tell."

He grinned. "That wasn't especially positive. Do you ever say anything definitive?"

"Only if I'm sure what I'm saying is correct. If you want me to tell you you're safe for the night, the best I can say, as I have before, is that I'll do everything in my power to make sure you are."

Dane laughed. "I got it. So, what are my protector's plans for the rest of this evening?"

"Evening? It's night. My plans are to shower now so I won't need to take the time to do so in the morning, and I suggest you do the same. Then it's bedtime." Alexa felt herself swallow as she said that. It was bedtime, but the idea of them going to sleep together, even in separate beds in this very nice room, crept into her mind.

Well, she shoved it out as she walked across the room and placed her carryon bag on one of the foldable stands after taking it from the closet. She removed her pj's and the case holding her travel paraphernalia and headed toward the bathroom. "I'll go first, since you seem wide awake. Your turn now to listen for anything out of line. If so, let me know. Knock on the door or whatever."

"Will do."

Alexa was soon in the bathroom, with its door closed. As she stripped to prepare for the shower, she felt her body react as if she was removing her clothes in front of Dane, to seduce him.

She quickly started running cold water in the shower, hoping that would cool her off and make her stupid body regain its senses instead of continuing that warm reaction in her most sensitive areas, though she doubted anything had changed.

She made it a quick shower, wanting only a short time from her protective detail. Soon, she dried herself, put on her pajamas and brushed her teeth.

Ready for bed? Yes. But also ready to go back into the room and take up where she'd left off in protecting her very handsome subject.

She opened the door and strode toward the far bed, the one where Dane wasn't. "Your turn," she said. "And as I said, I'd prefer if you shower tonight, too, so there'll be no delay for it in the morning."

"Yes, master. Or mistress."

"Ha, ha." Alexa forced herself to stop thinking of the alternate meanings to *mistress*. Or at least she tried to.

Dane had already placed his suitcase on another fold-able luggage stand and had put a small pile of clothing on top of his coverlet, as well as his masculine-looking travel case that most likely held a razor as well as toothbrush. Alexa hadn't noticed much of that last night as they'd attempted to deal with the filthy room they'd stayed in.

But this space was comparatively nice and welcoming. And clean.

Alexa just hoped she'd be able to get a little sleep while ensuring that Dane remained safe.

And also knowing he was across this special room from her…

She might wind up sleeping in a room with him for more nights once they arrived in Phoenix, although additional marshals could be sent by Vince to help out. Maybe one of the guys would instead stay with Dane then.

Alexa had mixed emotions about that possibility. It would be better. More practical. Maybe even safer.

But she'd miss being with him…

For now she grabbed the TV remote and turned up

the sound of the news. That way she wouldn't be as aware of what Dane was doing in the bathroom, when he showered and all.

Or at least she'd hoped she wouldn't be. But the idea led her to listen despite the droning of the TV newscasters talking about a robbery at a grocery store in downtown Flagstaff.

In a short while, Alexa no longer heard the shower running. Dane didn't emerge immediately, but he soon returned to the room.

Alexa glanced in that direction, ready to tell him good-night.

Only—where were his pj's? He had emerged from the bathroom with a large white bath towel around his private parts.

His muscular chest, with hair as dark as that on his head, was showing. So were his long, hard legs.

Last night in their room together, Dane had put on deep blue pajamas, nice enough looking but they covered everything, as they should.

But now— She had an urge to call out to him to go back into the bathroom and put his clothes on.

She doubted he'd do it, though. Not considering the way he had started looking at her with those suggestive green eyes of his. Smiling sensually.

Communicating with her without saying a word.

Well, she didn't have to do anything about it. She could ignore him. Turn off the TV and settle down under her covers, turning her back in his direction.

She could… Yes. But instead she first listened for any inappropriate sounds outside and, hearing none, found herself smiling back, as sexily as she could.

"You ready to go to sleep?" she asked, but she knew her tone suggested anything but sleep.

"Soon," was his reply. "First, though—well, I can't help thinking we should kiss good-night again, like we did last night."

Just kiss? She doubted it.

But— "Sure," she said. "Why not?"

She knew exactly why not.

Yet that didn't stop her from standing as he approached. He held on to his towel with one hand as his other arm went around her. She threw both her arms around him.

Their kiss made their prior embraces seem almost juvenile. This was hot, sensual, enticing—as intimate a kiss as Alexa had ever shared with a man. Maybe more. A lot more.

Dane growled as his lips pressed hard against hers. His tongue slid inside her mouth, drawing in and out in a way that suggested what might happen if they actually engaged in sex.

Would they? Oh yes, Alexa hoped so. No matter that it was inappropriate. This man's hot, hard body tempted hers in a way she had never felt before. His chest against hers was strong and muscular and hot and—naked.

She still had her pajamas on. He was still draped in his towel.

Alexa could do something about both. And did.

After checking the door again to ensure it was locked, she rejoined him, reached down and gently tugged the towel out of Dane's hand, then let it fall to the floor.

And felt, and heard herself, gasp as she glanced down to his rock-hard, large erection that pointed at her.

She didn't let herself touch him—yet. Instead, she started unbuttoning her pajama top but felt her hands pushed gently away as Dane took over.

In moments, her top was off, then her bottoms.

"Dane," she breathed. How did they get onto the bed—her bed, the closest? No matter. They were there. She now lay beneath Dane's naked body, feeling his hands caress her breasts as his legs wrapped around hers. Her shoulders rose as she moved upward to savor his touch, how he caressed her, smoothly rubbed her nipples, then moved to suck them gently.

She didn't just lie there, though. She reached up and grasped his erection, moving her hand to allow her to feel the hardness, stroke it in the way she'd like to have it move if it entered her.

No, *when* it entered her. Not immediately, though. His right hand slid downward to her most sensitive area, caressing it, moving a finger, then two, inside her. She nearly cried out—and did moan when he suddenly pulled away, got off the bed. Where was he going?

To his bed, where he'd left his pajamas. Also his night case. He extracted something from it, and Alexa realized it was a condom. Smart man, to come prepared for this—as well as bringing a weapon.

That thought brought her up short. She was supposed to be protecting him, not having sex with him. This was a terrible distraction.

But she heard nothing to make her stop.

"You ready?" his deep voice, rough and seductive,

asked. Good guy. He was giving her the opportunity to opt out.

She didn't. "Oh yes."

He stroked her again, and she reached around to hold his taut buttocks. In moments, he entered her. She felt her hips rise and then settle into the irregular but wonderful rhythm of his plunging in and out. She breathed fast, irregularly, and heard him do the same.

And then… She inhaled deeply as she reached her climax and heard Dane's deep groan at the same time.

All movement stopped. They held each other as Dane gently lay on top of her.

Wow. It was over. It was wonderful.

And no matter how wrong it had been, Alexa knew she wouldn't regret it.

As long as it hadn't prevented her from keeping him safe.

Chapter Ten

Concentrating on the heat of the soft and gorgeous skin beneath him, as well as the irregular, deep breathing beneath him, Dane continued to lie gently on top of an amazing woman.

She was clearly there for him in more ways than one.

Not that they'd planned what had just occurred. Well, not exactly. He'd thought about it a lot since she had first insinuated herself into his life, but he hadn't anticipated it could really happen.

It had. And he was pleased. No, more than pleased. He was delighted. And satiated.

For now.

"Wow," he said as he rolled off her. But that caused reality to reappear in his mind. "Do we need to check outside to make sure all's well now? Or—"

"Or not. I'll look through the blinds after we turn our lights out just to make sure I don't see or hear anything I need to deal with. And if all's well, we'll simply go to bed."

Dane couldn't help feeling somewhat sad and disappointed as he watched that sexy woman move her slender but curvaceous body off the bed and grab her pajamas, pulling them on again.

Highly appropriate, yes. But it made his immediate thoughts of having yet another enjoyable session, or several, that night rush out of his mind.

Well, no, the thoughts were there. But the likelihood of doing anything more about them? That was what disappeared. Fast.

"See or hear anything?" He kept his voice low in case someone was out there, or at least to make it evident to Alexa that he would do what he could to assist her.

"No. But I'll continue to check tonight. Let's get to bed."

Dane sighed. Good idea, but he figured he'd not get much sleep thinking about what they'd just done, and wishing the woman across the room from him was at least closer.

Hey, maybe he could convince her to share a bed. "You know..." he began, but she interrupted him.

"It might be a bad idea," she said, "but it wouldn't hurt to stay closer together tonight. I might be able to protect you better that way."

"You mean, sleep in the same bed?" He felt his grin grow wide at their matching thoughts.

"Why not?" Her lovely blue eyes were narrowed now, and she, too, smiled—although that expression evaporated as she looked at him. "As long as the operative word is *sleep*. With our pj's on. As much as I enjoyed what we did, we need to rest, not do it again. You should let me know, though, if my getting up periodically to check on things will prevent you from sleeping. If so, we shouldn't stay in the same bed."

"I'll be fine with it."

At least he thought so.

They soon settled under the coverlet on the bed that had sort of been designated as his, him on one side and Alexa on the other.

The room wasn't entirely dark, since Alexa had left the bathroom light on. She'd closed the door except for a slit that let a little light in, presumably to help her when she got up.

That allowed him to see her lovely face as, head propped on her pillow, she closed her eyes. He watched her, observing all he could of her beauty.

Memorizing it, since he probably would never have this opportunity again. And keeping his thoughts deep inside.

Difficult thoughts. Yes, he'd had women in his life, quite a few now and then. Enjoyed sex when he could. Nothing recently, though.

But his former lack of sex wasn't why this had felt so wonderful. This woman was amazing in so many ways, professionally, sure. But also…well, now this. Sure, he had been spending a lot of time with her during the last couple days, but this was something more than proximity. It was attraction and admiration and—well, he couldn't hope for a future with her. Not even any more sex.

But still…

When Dane couldn't fall asleep, yet heard Alexa's breathing grow deep enough that he assumed she was, in fact, asleep, he slowly moved his way over until he first felt her warmth.

She didn't move, so he edged a little closer so their arms touched.

Yes, they both wore their pajamas, but somehow Dane felt they were attached in a sensual way, nonetheless. Not that he would do anything about it...

Except fall asleep, too.

He figured he'd done so a while later when Alexa's slowly getting out of bed woke him. He considered joining her but figured she wouldn't like it.

And since she soon got back in bed, he figured all was well.

Except his own state of mind. He had an urge to at least put his arms around her and pull her close.

And maybe remove those pajamas of hers, as well as his own...

He didn't laugh aloud at himself, but he laughed inside. He knew better. Way better.

It took him a while to fall back to sleep. Or at least he assumed he did, since he felt his eyes pop open sometime later when Alexa once more arose and did her checking.

He considered telling her he'd do it next time but figured she'd say no, so he stayed where he was. And fell asleep again after her return. Or at least he believed so the next time, too.

When he next awoke, it was because Alexa had snuggled up against him. Really? He reached out and put his arms around her.

"Good. You're awake. It's time to get up and get going—nearly six o'clock."

"Got it," he said. Although she started moving away,

he couldn't help it. He pulled her close again. And, right or wrong, he gave her a big good-morning kiss.

Yes, a sexy one. Well, so what? She wanted them, rightly, to get going, so nothing else could result from it.

Not then. And probably not ever again.

He'd stay alive, at least, with her help. But he realized how much she was putting herself in danger to help him. He'd known, from the moment he got into witness protection, that those guarding him could be the ones to die while they took care of him.

He hated the idea. He'd considered it a lot with his former protectors but even more now with Alexa—the woman he'd just made love to, a woman he wanted to spend even more intimate time with.

He also wanted Alexa to stay alive and…well, and not get injured, or worse, as a result of protecting him.

He pulled away first. "Okay if I use the bathroom now?"

"Sure."

He found himself saying, "About last night…" He stood there looking down at her lovely face. Her eyelids remained low, as if she hadn't completely awakened. Or maybe the ensuing look was the result of his mentioning what they'd done… He finished by saying, "Do you want to talk about it?" Like, blame him for getting her involved in something so improper.

"No," she said, her tone abrupt. But she didn't look away. Maybe she was trying to figure out where he was going with this.

Well, so was he. "Do you want to do it again?"

Okay. It was inappropriate to ask that, too.

But he was glad he had.

She hesitated. Then laughed. "We'll see."

Yay! It wasn't an absolute no.

Wanting to end this conversation, wanting to do what he needed to now, he grabbed his travel kit, underwear and clothes, and hurried inside the bathroom. There, he washed his face—and observed it in the mirror. He still looked like himself, although there was an aura of sorts that suggested both satisfaction and frustration. Maybe he just imagined it, but it seemed to remain as he shaved. Even got worse.

He had to do something.

Last night had changed a lot inside him. And his mind had started focusing even more on today and the future, on the danger that remained out there.

He soon changed from his pajamas into his disguise, including the hairpiece. He felt a hint of amusement that that gorgeous woman had made love with him, while his usual appearance during the day was as such a big frump of a guy, and she'd been dressed similarly.

But she knew what he really looked like. Not that he thought himself to be a great-looking hunk…but apparently he was appealing enough to her. Maybe irresistible?

Even if they wanted to again—and he certainly did—the circumstances likely to transpire over the next few days could make that impossible.

But what would happen now? Yes, his mind had mostly focused on Alexa and their time together, yet not entirely so. Now he allowed the other vital thoughts he'd been repressing somewhat to take over while he prepared for the rest of this day.

Okay, where were they—the deadly killers who had come after him?

Did they know where he was? Were there more of them?

Had they really been turned away by those helicopters flitting around and around in the sky?

Right now, it all seemed easy. Too easy. When would they, or someone else, show up again?

For he was certain their attempts to stop him from testifying, Swanson's determination to shut him up, weren't over.

Would those who'd attacked before now stay away and hide wherever they'd gone yesterday, let him get to Phoenix and testify against Swanson?

He doubted it. They were most likely waiting for him, maybe somewhere near the courthouse.

Even so, he had to get there. And at the moment, it felt even more important to accomplish it without Alexa getting hurt.

Never mind that she was his designated protector. An idea had come to him, one in which she wouldn't accompany him there, no matter what her Marshals Service's plans were. He cared too much now to allow her to be harmed while protecting him.

He would get to the courthouse alone, so Alexa wouldn't be endangered if his foes caught up with him again. He had an idea how.

And it was time. He fortunately hadn't been in there long. He knew Alexa was eager to get going. Well, so was he—but not the way she intended.

He exited the bathroom and noted immediately that

Alexa had taken advantage of her alone time to get dressed, too. Roger/Alexa stood near his suitcase, organizing things within it. As soon as he saw Daniel, he grumbled, "About time," grabbed a toiletry bag and rushed past him into the bathroom. He stopped at the door, though, and looked back. "I'll be ready in a couple minutes. Meanwhile, just stay there. I'll check things out, then we can get on our way."

He used the opportunity to finish packing and unhook his phone from its charger, which he also packed. He then grabbed his backpack and suitcase, and exited the motel room.

He didn't intend to be foolish, though. He waited right outside the door, which he'd closed gently, ready to duck back inside if he saw anything of concern.

Fortunately, he didn't. He saw a couple people getting into a car at the level below, a senior man and woman. A disguise like his or Alexa's? Maybe, but it didn't appear that way.

Even so, he remained cautious as he carried the backpack and suitcase down the steps, one hand over the weapon thrust into his jeans beneath his long denim shirt. He limped a bit as if he was the big guy he appeared to be, but still managed to hurry. And look around. A lot.

When he reached the bottom, he couldn't help glancing up to the room where he'd stayed the night. The amazingly wonderful night, thanks to Alexa.

The woman, the witness protector, whom *he* now intended to protect.

He didn't see her. She must still be in the bathroom.

It was therefore time for him to hurry.

ALEXA HAD WASHED her face, put on makeup to ensure she resembled the man she was supposed to look like and was about to leave the bathroom when her phone, in her pocket, sounded to indicate an incoming text message.

She was a little surprised to see the message had come at this hour from her boss. Sending an unscheduled text around 7:00 a.m. seemed a bit strange, unless there was a problem.

In a way, there was. His message told her to call District Attorney Moe Francini immediately. It included a phone number with an area code that was probably Phoenix.

It seemed rather early to call a DA, especially one she didn't know, but Alexa was now under orders from her boss, and so she did it, holding her breath in case the guy hadn't been primed and got upset.

She also headed for the bathroom door. Depending on how the call went, she could put it on speaker and let Dane hear, too.

"Hello?" the male voice nearly shouted over the phone. "I'm assuming this is Marshal Alexa Colton, right? I was told you'd be calling now."

"That's right," Alexa said. "Marshal Vince Cudahy asked me to call you. My job is witness protection, and one of the witnesses in your trial of Samuel Swanson is my charge at the moment."

"Yeah, yeah, Vince told me that. He also told me my key witness, Detective Dane Beaulieu, isn't going to be there when the trial begins in a couple hours. What's going on? When will he appear? Is there something wrong?"

"Yes, there is something wrong," Alexa said, "so we're running later than planned." Since she'd been given his info by her boss, she assumed she could be at least somewhat specific in her description. "We started driving in plenty of time from the location where Detective Beaulieu had been living under an assumed name and in witness protection since the time of the homicide, but on the way we were attacked by unknown assailants." Maybe cops, but she didn't mention that. "We took some evasive maneuvers and got away. Local authorities directed helicopters to protect us and perhaps to capture the assailants, but as far as I know, they got away. As a result, we are still being highly cautious as we continue toward Phoenix."

A silence for a moment, while Alexa opened the bathroom door and stepped into the motel room.

The empty room.

Where was Dane?

Her heart pounded. Was he okay? She hadn't heard anything, so hopefully no one had grabbed him. But had he left on his own? Why? Suddenly terrified while also holding back any pending anger, she had to end this conversation as soon as possible and find him.

"So when do you anticipate getting to the courthouse?" Francini demanded.

"This afternoon," Alexa said, repeatedly scanning the room to make sure she hadn't missed anything. "Assuming we don't have to do any further time-consuming evasive maneuvers. If you can delay Detective Beaulieu's testimony until tomorrow, that might be best." She didn't attempt to explain her concern about time. Yes, they were close.

But she didn't know where her charge was.

Better to plan on his testimony tomorrow, after she found him.

And yes, she would find him.

"You'll be here for sure tomorrow, then?"

"Yes, although if anything else comes up I'll call to let you know." Like the disappearance of the witness, Alexa thought grimly. Had Dane simply started packing the rental car?

If only it was as simple as that. She could hope…

Well, damn it, he knew he had to stay with her so she could continue to protect him, even if he was wearing his disguise. He shouldn't even go out to load the car without her.

Oh, Daniel, she thought. *I'm about to ream you out for leaving my presence.*

Assuming that all was well, and she could find him now, and they could get on their way again.

"You do that," Francini said, apparently almost spitting into the phone. "Damn it, I was considering changing my original plans and opening with the star witness's testimony. But— Well, I get it. You be damned careful and get him here just as soon as you can. Got it?"

"Yes, sir," Alexa said, hating lying but resolving to fix the problem before Francini even knew something had gone wrong. She'd accomplish her goal, preferably today, but no later than tomorrow because of the weekend. "And now you have my number as well, so please keep me informed of anything we need to know."

"I'll do that." Francini hung up.

Good. Alexa dashed to the motel room's door and

opened it, almost leaping out—till she reminded herself she was in disguise, too. And disabled seniors like Roger couldn't exactly jump around like that.

Instead, she hobbled onto the balcony area and looked around, down toward the parking lot first. Not seeing Dane or Daniel, she began to scan the area, and—

There. Was that him in the distance, also in his disguise? If that was him, Daniel had reached the far end of the walkway in front of the motel, pulling his suitcase behind him and crossing the street, heading in the direction of the closest shopping area.

What, he was that eager for breakfast? He could have waited. They'd have stopped on their way.

Okay. Time to get out of here. Time to catch up with him. She was already pretty well packed, so she ducked inside only long enough to grab her bag, then hurried to get the rental car.

In moments, she was driving in the direction she had last seen Dane head. She would catch up with him.

She *had* to.

DANE HADN'T FOCUSED on it as much yesterday as he wished he had now, but when they'd been driving around deciding what motel to choose, he'd checked out what kinds of businesses were in the area, mostly out of curiosity. And concern over his safety, and Alexa's.

There appeared to be more offices than retail around here. Several motels besides theirs, though not many. Convenience stores and liquor stores and fast-food restaurants on nearby blocks.

And a rental car place.

Fortunately, he had noticed that. And that was what he needed now. That location was where he headed, albeit carefully. Keeping watch around him to attempt to be sure no one was paying attention to him.

And keeping watch around the motel he was leaving to make sure he didn't see Roger/Alexa. Or, more important, that she wasn't outside anywhere watching him.

Was that their rental car driving in that area? Could be, darn it. He'd have to be even more careful.

Was it foolish to ditch her at this point? Probably. But it had gotten personal. He appreciated her watching over him, sure. But even though they hadn't become close friends—exactly—as he'd done with Alvin, he really cared about her, especially now. He couldn't bear the idea that Alexa might get hurt, or worse, because of him. Even if he had been hurt in the line of duty, he was determined that she would not be.

So now he stayed as much in the shade as possible. Moved off the sidewalk to use parking lots of some of the stores nearby. Ducked around the block to get there a different way. Checked his GPS often to make sure he was ultimately heading in the right direction.

Fortunately, he was. It took about ten minutes, but he was soon outside the location.

Also fortunately, it was open, despite the hour. He saw someone coming out with a car key in his hand and heading into the parking lot in front.

And so, Daniel, patting his pocket to make sure he felt his wallet there, headed inside, dragging his carryon bag behind him, the backpack over his shoulder, and making it appear that every step was an ordeal. After all, not only was he Daniel at the moment, but he was the form of Daniel that Alexa had created, big and senior and bulky.

But he did want to hurry, or at least not be visible from the street much longer. Alexa was hunting for him, and he didn't want to be found by her.

He entered the room that mostly contained a reception stand. Two desks were located behind it, each occupied by a woman. The one closest to the door stood as he entered. "Can I help you, sir?" she called.

"Yes, please," he responded in Daniel's cracked voice, although he had removed his hairpiece since he'd need to resemble the photo on his fake driver's license. "I need to rent a car for a couple days. Do you have any available?" He didn't mention he would return it to one of their facilities in Phoenix. The fewer people who knew his destination, the better.

"Of course. Please join me over here. I'm Marcia."

"And I'm Daniel," he said.

Marcia shot him a big smile. She appeared to be just a kid, barely out of her teens. This could be her first job. Her brown hair was curly, and she wore a very short peach-colored dress with long sleeves.

She waited till he reached the counter, then walked a few steps away to pick up some paperwork from the desk she'd just left. "Are you okay with a small domestic sedan, or do you want something larger?"

"That sounds fine," he said. "I just need it to get around."

"Very good."

In a minute, he found himself entering information onto a contract form Marcia had put on top of the tall counter. No problem with Daniel Brennan filling the thing out. Yes, that was his name. His address was in Blue Larkspur, Colorado.

"Everything look okay?" Marcia asked.

"Sure." And, fortunately, it actually did, or so Dane believed. At her request, he signed the form.

"What credit card will you be using?" she asked next.

Dane told her. Though it was also mostly to be used for confirming who he supposedly was, he'd been told he would be able to charge things on it, although he might be required to repay at least some of those charges when he got his real identity back.

At her request, he also showed her his alternate driver's license.

"Okay, looks good, Daniel," she finally said. "The car's in our lot right out front, in the space designated as A-26. It's a red Chevy. And you'll be returning it here in two days, right?"

Unlikely that he would but he nodded.

He took the keys that Marcia handed him and made his way unevenly, as large Daniel, to the rental office's door. He looked out the glass for a moment. Except for the cars he saw there, the parking lot appeared empty. A good thing.

He headed toward the back of the row of cars parked near the office, where he could see the space numbers painted onto the cement. Number A-26 was several cars to the right.

In a few seconds, he pushed the button on the key fob to unlock the doors and was close enough to hear the low thump. Good. He reached out and opened the trunk, pretending to take a lot of effort to lift his small suitcase and place it inside, along with the backpack.

After he stuck his hairpiece back on and closed the trunk again, he walked to the driver's side.

He tried not to hurry too much, or at least not to get out of his character as large Daniel. In moments, he reached for the handle and started opening the door.

"Let's not be too hasty," growled a voice from behind him. A gruff, male voice that didn't sound like Alexa's, even in character as Roger.

Dane turned slowly and found himself facing a tall man whose black shirt and black pants could have been a cop uniform, although it had no patches or badges. The guy had short brown hair, wide ears and clenched teeth, visible as he scowled at Dane. He looked familiar, like the guy in the other car who'd shot at them. He held his weapon low so that anyone around would be unlikely to see it.

But Dane could definitely see it.

He considered his own weapon that remained at his hip beneath his large shirt. But he felt certain he wouldn't have time to draw it at the moment without getting shot.

"Hey," he said, keeping his voice husky to remain in character but trying to maintain a friendly—false—note in it. "Are you one of those cops who shot at me on the drive here?" He considered yelling at the guy instead but figured that acting friendly might buy him more time. What he wanted to do, though, was beat the crap out of his assailant. Better yet, shoot him first.

"What makes you think that?" The guy grinned slightly, clearly not denying it.

"Just a guess." Dane hesitated. Was there some way he could call this guy off? "Look, I'm assuming you're working with Samuel Swanson, or at least believe he's in the right and shouldn't be standing trial today. I get it. But I was one of those he shot. Now, if he's paying you to go after me, I'd be glad to—"

"Gee, are you about to try to bribe me?" his assailant drawled. "Don't bother. I know what happened, and I'm fine with it. But I need to make sure Swanson— Never mind. You don't need my opinion or anything else. I think we've talked enough, in fact. I don't think it'd help for me to try to get you to accompany me someplace else. In fact, that might let you think you may find a way to get the best of me. So—"

The guy glanced down at the gun he held and started manipulating it, apparently flipping the safety off.

Dane figured he didn't have time to draw his weapon out and ready it to fire. But if he ran—

Damn it. He grabbed for his own gun anyway but before he could get it out of his belt he heard a voice he'd hardly anticipated hearing so soon.

Alexa's. And she, still dressed as Roger and sounding like a man, stood behind the armed cop.

"Hey, you know I'm ready to shoot you in the back if you don't put that safety back on and place your gun on the ground. You can ignore me if you want, but I wouldn't suggest you do that. Or, you can turn to see whether I'm really armed, and how much time you might have to get me first—which is none."

"You son of a bitch," the guy blurted. "You were in that car, too, right?"

He did slowly turn around, although he didn't move his gun.

But when he saw Alexa aim her weapon, the guy swore again and knelt down, placing his gun on the ground.

"Atta boy," Alexa said in her Roger voice. "Now, you're coming with me." She directed a glare at Dane. "You, too."

She—Roger—winked at Dane as she stepped forward, pushed the guy onto his knees on the ground and began cuffing his arms behind his back.

Dane felt relieved. Definitely. And yet he felt embarrassed Alexa had figured out what he had done and caught up with him.

Well, he was safe now. And he would deal with her anger—and possibly gloating.

Chapter Eleven

Alexa had already determined what to do with this hit-man cop. She felt certain she would have recognized him, even if he hadn't been aiming a gun at Dane. He'd been the shooter from the car that had come after them near the Arizona border but had been chased off by the helicopters.

Where was his partner?

"Okay," she said to Dane as she pulled her prisoner back onto his feet and behind the car. She'd already grabbed his weapon, checked to make sure it wasn't ready to fire and stuck it inside the waist of her jeans. Plus, she'd taken a few pictures on her phone of his accosting Dane before jumping in so she would have evidence of his attack. "This guy's coming with me. I've already called Vince, and he's got some local authorities on the way. While I take our buddy the short distance to where he'll be picked up, you're staying right here. Got it, Mr. Brennan? I'm in charge. I was, and I still am."

Despite her appearance, she made no attempt to pretend that she was Roger just then. She needed her captive to follow her orders, too, and even though he might not like listening to a woman dressed like a guy and looking old, that was the way things were. She was the one with the gun now. She was in charge—just like she should have always been with Dane, who had tried and failed to sneak off on his own, terrifying and frustrating her. She'd have a stern talk with him later.

She was protecting the witness who'd soon be testifying against the man this cop—whether real or pseudo, whether paid specially by Swanson or just following orders given at his station—wanted to capture. Or worse, kill.

Alexa definitely was not going to allow that to happen.

"At least let me come along as your backup," Dane said. "I can—"

"What you can do, if you come along, is to follow my instructions. If you promise to do that, you can join me. Us."

She hadn't taken her eyes off her captive, so she saw the guy's expression change slightly at her words. He didn't look at all happy. Nor should he. But she recognized he was attempting to figure out what he could do to escape.

The answer? Nothing. As she'd told Dane, she was in charge. Of both of them. Of this situation.

And she expected that Vince would follow through and do what she'd discussed with him over the phone— sending local authorities.

Never mind that the subject was also her lover, or had been. Fun, yes. But irrelevant. And in the past now.

Dane used the key he held to lock the nearby car he'd apparently rented. Good. At least he wasn't attempting to slip inside now and drive away while she took care of this evil goon who wanted to kill him. Alexa would have figured out a way to deal with both at the same time, but fortunately didn't have to.

"So," Dane said in his Daniel voice, bending over. "What's next, boss?"

She knew he was trying to be funny, as Dane so often did. Under other circumstances, she'd make a point of responding in an official but perhaps humorous way.

Not now.

"We're going to walk to the end of this row of cars and cross the street to the parking lot of the office building there," she said softly in her normal voice. "There's a shed at one end of that parking lot, and we're going inside. I've already checked, and it's not locked."

"Got it," Dane said, although Alexa knew he couldn't be aware of the reason she intended for them to go there. But it sounded as if he was doing as he should for once: obeying her.

In any case, Alexa stood on one side of their captive, her left arm through the guy's right as his hands remained cuffed behind him. He was quite a bit taller than she, but she was the one who was armed and untethered. She maneuvered him somewhat in front of her so she could hide his wrists at least partially from any observers.

"Like this," she said, and Dane clearly understood.

"Got it." In seconds, he was standing at the man's other side, not far from Alexa, and also shielding the bound hands from view.

"Before we walk away, I'd like you to put the keys to your new rental car under its driver's seat," Alexa instructed him. "You're going to notify the company that you changed your mind and just left the car there for them to lock up again. And don't bother attempting to have them give you credit on your card for non-rental. That'll only complicate things further. Got it?"

"Of course." He shot her a sad grin from the other side of their captive. Yes, he looked ashamed, as he should be. But that didn't quell her anger with him—or her relief that he was okay.

He quickly removed his backpack from the back seat of the car and arranged it over his shoulder, then grabbed his suitcase. In a minute, after leaving the keys inside, he was back in the position he'd been in before.

"Now," Alexa said, "let's go."

They did, walking slowly behind the row of rental cars. One man stood near a driver's-side door, but fortunately he only glanced at them briefly then slipped inside. There was no one else around.

As they walked, Alexa looked up into the face of their captive. He glanced at her once then continued to stare straight ahead.

"So where is your partner?" Alexa asked, watching him carefully. But not only didn't he answer, he also didn't glance around as if searching in a direction that partner might now be hiding.

Alexa wasn't convinced another man wasn't around, but neither was she certain he'd stayed with this criminal to get at Dane.

It took several minutes to reach the end of the rental car parking lot, then dutifully await the green traffic light before crossing the street. No sense making themselves look like scofflaws, Alexa figured.

The lot on the corner there held two five-story buildings, and both appeared to contain offices. There could be people looking out the windows that they didn't see, but at least no one anywhere close seemed to be paying any attention to them.

As they reached the shed, she opened the door, and she and Dane ushered their detainee inside. "Sit down," Alexa commanded, pointing to a spot in the corner, on the floor. Since she waved her gun, the guy obeyed—notwithstanding his furious scowl.

"Now stay here with him while I check." She didn't say what she was checking, but Alexa ducked outside again, still looking like the old guy she'd pretended to be and once more limping in character.

There. A black SUV pulled up alongside the shed. An undercover cop car, Alexa hoped as it drew closer. A real one.

She approached the driver's door cautiously, though. And, as she'd hoped, a cop in uniform got out of the driver's side, and another from the passenger side.

"Marshal Colton?" the nearest man, who'd been driving, asked, his voice low. "Flagstaff police. We were sent here to help you as the result of a call from Marshal Cudahy." A badge on his shirt indicated his name was Williams.

"Yes," she said, allowing herself to feel a little relieved. He certainly sounded legit. "That's me." She didn't bother to explain she was a woman marshal in disguise as a man that day, but waited for him to continue talking. She still had to remain cautious. She couldn't be certain where they'd gotten Vince's name—or if they'd just been sent to attempt to grab, or kill, Dane.

"I understand you have someone in custody who needs to be taken to our nearby station and booked. Is that true?" Officer Williams said. He was short but seemed muscular beneath his cop shirt. His taller partner, Officer Shaler according to his badge, joined him.

"Yes, that's true. He's in the shed." So someone, hopefully Vince's local contact, had given them at least that much information. Unless that was just a guess.

Williams drew closer and leaned over, talking even more softly. "I was told you also have someone in witness protection. Correct?"

Someone who was setting Dane and her up would know that, too, though. She pulled her phone from her pocket and motioned for Officer Williams to join her as she walked a few feet away. Officer Shaler stayed where he was.

"Who told you that and directed you to come here?" she asked Williams.

His grin moved his dark facial hair. "I get it. Here, you can call our chief and check us out." He pulled his phone from his chest pocket and typed in Flagstaff PD. The online search came up with a site that appeared genuine, and Williams had her press in the number for Chief Sanchez.

"What's up, Williams?" was the immediate answer.

"This is Marshal Alexa Colton," Alexa began. "I'm—"

"You've got my team there grabbing your subject's attacker, right—Williams and Shaler? And you're on Williams's phone."

Alexa smiled. "Exactly. And you've made me feel more comfortable that your team here is actually your team. Thank you, Chief Sanchez."

"You can thank your boss, Marshal Cudahy, for contacting me about it."

Alexa did, silently and fervently. She would call Vince later.

For now, she answered a few questions, but she kept her responses brief, without giving details about what her subject and she were up to, where they were going or why. It was safer that way, if Sanchez didn't already know.

She led them into the shed where Dane was keeping an eye on their captive, who sat on the floor in one corner.

"That's our suspect, I assume," said Williams, and Alexa confirmed he was.

It was time to go. "Thank you, officers," Alexa said.

But she wanted to leave first, with Dane, in case someone was out there and saw what was happening, particularly the partner of the man who'd just been taken into custody.

"We'll get on our way now," she said, to notify both the cops and Dane, who stood leaning against one wall of the shed, arms crossed, watching all that was going on.

"Sounds good." He tossed his backpack over his shoulder, grabbed the handle of his suitcase and bent forward a little to resume his character. That made Alexa appreciate his efforts, despite the fact he had nearly fled her custody.

"Be careful," Shaler said. "And be sure to call us if you need any more help in our area." He pulled a stack of business cards out of his hip pocket and handed one to Alexa.

"Will do. And thanks again."

Alexa saw Dane drawing closer to where she stood by the door. She nodded to him, and both soon dragged and limped their way in character, with her pulling Dane's suitcase.

Alexa told Dane, "My rental car's in the lot on the other side."

"Got it."

They both headed that direction. Alexa stepped up her pace a little, despite resembling a geezer. Even seniors could sometimes go faster if they had a reason. And she noted happily that Dane followed her lead.

Nothing, and not one of the few people they saw, appeared out of the ordinary.

In a short while, they'd reached her blue rental car, in the middle of a row of other parked vehicles. She drew the key from her pocket.

"I'd like you to drive," she told Dane. "I want to make a couple of phone calls."

"Sure." Dane placed his bag on the back seat of the car, then got into the driver's seat. Alexa maneuvered the suitcase inside. Hers was in the trunk.

Soon, they were ready to go. Good.

It was definitely time to get to Phoenix so Dane could begin testifying at the trial.

FIRST THING, AS DANE started to drive, Alexa started to lambaste him, then apparently stopped herself. "Why on earth would you run away like that? To protect me? Never mind."

Before he could respond, she pressed a number into her phone and brought it to her ear. Dane felt a bit relieved that they weren't going to talk about what he had done.

"It all seemed to go fine, Vince," Alexa said in a moment. Her boss must have responded immediately. "Thanks for calling your Flagstaff contacts."

She put her phone on speaker apparently so Dane could participate, too, but for now he just listened as he watched the road, driving just over the speed limit. There weren't many other cars going either direction that day.

"But you said they only got one of your attackers," Vince continued.

Dane didn't know Vince, but the marshal definitely sounded miffed. "We don't know where the other one went," Alexa responded. "And the guy we got wasn't talking at all. But we're being as careful as we can be about watching around us. And if things look bad on the main road to Phoenix, we'll figure out another way to go."

That had been on Dane's mind, too. He had even attempted to find an alternate route, but nothing direct had popped up on his GPS. Any other way would take much longer to get there.

And if he wasn't likely to get there this afternoon, he'd need to let the district attorney know.

"Just be careful, damn it," Vince said. "I'm glad you got the one guy before he could hurt Dane—and you, too, for that matter. And I'm glad my contacts were able to help. But it isn't over till it's over. Stay in touch as much as you can, and if you need any further help, let me know right away. Got it?"

"Got it," Alexa confirmed.

Dane glanced over to see she was nodding her head—in its costume that included odd makeup and a wig with short hair.

That was a shame. He enjoyed the look of her lovely face, including her special blond hair. The feel of it when they'd made love…

Okay. Of course he would think about that now and then. It had been an amazing, memorable experience.

A one-time experience. He knew that. Even though his mind, his body, reacted to the very thought and kept reminding him of how wonderful it had been. And urged him to find a time and place to do it again.

No matter how impossible that was, if for no other reason than Alexa would most likely never want to be intimate again with him after his essentially fleeing her custody. His betrayal of her—even though he had done it in an attempt to protect her.

Dane listened as Vince and Alexa said good-bye to one another, and he added his own good-bye. Alexa ended the call and put her phone on the console between them.

So what were they going to talk about now? He wanted to start a conversation with her but figured things would be awkward between them.

Should he mention the time, to start something? Fortunately, since all had started early, it was only mid-morning. If all went well now, it should take less than three hours to reach Phoenix.

If all went well. That punched at his brain.

When, on this trip, had anything gone well? Or since the situation that had thrust him into witness protection, for that matter.

Although he'd had some good caretakers.

None better than Alexa…

At least it should be a scenic trip to Phoenix. Some of the terrain was mountainous. Some was forested.

He figured it might be useful to get Alexa's opinion on how his testimony should go, so he pondered what he should ask first to get the conversation going.

Only she began talking first.

"Okay," she said, staring at his face. He knew that because he glanced at her. And she wasn't smiling. "Maybe it's irrelevant now, but I want to talk about it anyway. I'm still really peeved that you tried to run off without me this morning. We already knew someone was after you. At least we caught him, or at least one of the two we're aware of. And if I hadn't been with you before—"

Not exactly what he wanted to discuss even now, but he could understand why she wanted to.

"I appreciate that you were there and helped out the way you did," he said, interrupting her.

"You're welcome. Sort of. But if you hadn't run off that way, we might be farther along toward Phoenix, and your treacherous buddy might not have caught up with you."

She was right. He knew that. But he'd had a good reason for doing what he had.

Only—she had put herself in danger before this situation. After all, she was trained to do so, and he'd tried to subvert that; he hadn't doubted her abilities, he'd just worried for her. She'd known she could be hurt or killed while protecting one of the people whose problems she took on.

And she'd done so again today when he'd put himself closer into harm's way, sort of. She was right. He might not have been attacked again if he hadn't tried to protect his protector by running off.

Maybe he should keep quiet about his rationale. It wasn't particularly rational, after all. Or she was bound to think it wasn't.

Still—

Okay, he had to say something. "Look, you know of my law enforcement background," he said. Out of the corner of his eye he saw her move, so he quickly continued. "I know about witness protection, of course, and what it's about. And why it occurs. Plus, as you know, you're not the first marshal to help me that way over the past weeks. But—"

"I've just been doing my job," she broke in.

That was true to a point, he realized.

But their time together went far and away above her call to duty.

And he couldn't be happier that they'd engaged in it.

"I know," he responded. "And you know I've just been doing my job, as well, preparing to help convict a murderer. But that doesn't have to include someone else getting hurt, as you might if you step in while I'm under attack. And—"

"And you're the one who'd have been hurt if I hadn't gotten there when I did." As if she had to remind him again. "You know that."

He prepared to interject a protest. But he realized, ultimately, she was right. She was plenty capable, and he knew it.

Before he said anything, Alexa continued, in a much

softer, more controlled voice. "I appreciate your concern for me, Dane. I really do. But I think it's at least partially the result of our inappropriate behavior by having sex."

Dane opened his mouth again. But Alexa didn't stop talking.

"Oh, I found it wonderful. I really did. And the idea of more…well, it's not going to happen, but I truly relish the thought. But if that's even part of the reason you ran off to try to protect me, knowing full well that my responsibility is to defend you no matter what the peril you face right now— Well, thanks but no thanks. Can you even imagine what I'd feel like if something happened to you on my watch like that? I'd be devastated. The fact I'd be out of a job is only part of it. I care about you, Dane. A lot. I think you know that. And right now…well, I need for you to promise you won't do that again. That you'll let me stay in charge and take care of your safety. Okay?"

He didn't want to admit that he wasn't *really* okay with it, no matter how much he appreciated it. And understood it. But he needed to come to terms with that.

And found himself glowing inside at her admission that she cared about him.

They had to stay together now, and he did have to allow Alexa to do her job. To protect him, even as he intended to protect her, too, no matter what she said.

For the moment, though, he had to concede, or at least appear to. And so he said, "I understand, Alexa. And appreciate it. So, yes, I promise I'll allow you to remain in charge. I'll listen to you despite whatever danger we come across." He shifted slightly to look into her eyes before turning quickly back to the road. "Thank you," he said, wishing he could hug her and kiss her in appreciation…and more.

"You're welcome," she replied.

Chapter Twelve

Despite his thanks, his verbal acknowledgment of her duties and his appreciation of how she was attempting to meet them, Alexa wanted to slug Dane.

No, she really wanted to hug him. Hold him tight now that he was safe again, at least for the moment. Or both?

But neither was going to happen.

She had every right to scold him for putting himself more directly into trouble that way, when he knew full well she had a duty to protect him. Because he thought he was protecting her instead, he'd indicated.

A swear word came to mind, but she thrust it out immediately. That kind of thought would do no good.

Reprimanding him the way she had, had been a good idea. He seemed to understand, agree with her. Maybe.

Or he at least knew better than to criticize her any more—for now. And he'd been sweet enough to even thank her.

Was his gratitude real, or had he just professed it to try to get her cooled down?

Drat. She was riding in a car with him and would be for a while—and she was thinking too much about this bad situation that, fortunately, had had an okay ending, mostly thanks to her calling Vince.

Vince. She looked around them again, as she'd been doing a lot, as always. But fortunately she still saw nothing that indicated she should have asked him to send copters again.

There was someone else she needed to call, though. Or at least text. Only, she figured that District Attorney Francini was most likely in the middle of the first morning of the trial now. Even if he wasn't conducting a witness examination at the moment, he probably wouldn't want to answer the phone, or even respond to a text message.

But he was the one most likely to know what was going on. Where she should take Dane when they arrived near the courthouse. How to keep him safe from anyone who might be watching for him. And if there were any local resources there who would help.

Plus, keeping Francini informed about Dane's progress in reaching the place would be appropriate. In fact, they might hear from him even if they didn't contact him first. But who knew when?

If all went well, they could arrive in a couple of hours. So, she had a little time, but she definitely needed instructions about the best way to handle things when they got there.

Should they park in the regular lot and just walk inside?

Had any efforts been made to ensure Dane would be protected as he entered the court, and not just by her?

Where were Swanson's peons now? Were any in custody, or at least under observation?

Okay, maybe calling Francini wasn't a great idea at the moment, and she'd no idea when he might try to contact her, if ever. But she knew who she could call again who would be able to tell her what to do: Vince.

"You're awfully quiet," Dane said, breaking into her thoughts. "What's on your mind? Is everything okay?" He took his eyes from the road for a moment to look into hers, and he appeared highly concerned.

"I hope so, but that's exactly what's on my mind," she responded, not even attempting to appease him. He knew what was going on. Trying to protect him mentally as well as physically wasn't exactly her job. In fact, he'd been wary before, even if he hadn't completely acted rationally, and she needed to remain careful now.

"So everything's not okay? What's wrong?" He sounded uneasy, as well he should.

"Nothing I know of now," she said. "And I want it to stay that way. I'm going to call Vince again and ask him a few questions. I'll put him on speaker as usual so you can join in if you want."

"Sounds good."

Before calling, Alexa scanned their surroundings yet again. Nothing seemed concerning. They were still headed in the right direction on a road with minimal traffic and no obvious threats.

Obvious being the key word in Alexa's thoughts. She could never assume there were no threats around.

The same somewhat mountainous landscape surrounded the route here. Attractive to look at, but also concerning since the bumps and curves could hide danger.

Right now, she grabbed her burner phone from where

she'd stuck it on the car's console and searched it again for Vince's name—not hard to do not only because of their prior conversation—but also because she hadn't added many contacts to this phone since she'd gotten it. Dane, of course, and Vince. And her sister Naomi and brother Dominic. She'd added Francini's number but didn't want to call it now.

She pushed the phone receiver symbol to start the call, then put it on speaker.

"Everything okay now, Alexa?" was Vince's greeting.

"Everything's fine right now, thanks," she replied. "But I need your advice. We're moving right along and hope to get to the courthouse in a couple hours. But I want to talk to Mr. Francini about what to do as we get near there, how best to park near the courthouse and get Dane inside, and—"

"Got it," Vince responded.

Dane, meanwhile, had aimed a quick grin toward Alexa. He didn't say anything just then but he blinked and tilted his head as he mouthed, *I didn't know you cared.*

That, of course, was absurd. Of course she cared. It was her job to care. *But not as much as I do...*

And the fact she cared beyond only wanting to ensure his safety? Well, that she would keep to herself.

"Okay, I just texted Moe's assistant DA. Her name is Cora Canfield, and I'll text you her phone number so you can confirm it's her. I've told her to give you a call in five minutes to discuss status. Moe gave me her contact info for just this kind of reason, in case we needed to get in touch with him at a time he was likely to be in court. She's probably there, too, but she can step out."

"Got it. That should be really helpful. Thanks, Vince."

"No problem. Oh, and by the way. I've talked to both Moe and Cora about how you've been handling Dane's protection so they'll know what to expect, although I assume Dane will want to look like a detective and not a witness in disguise when he's inside the court."

"I agree," Alexa said. She'd already been considering how they'd change back to themselves but figured they could determine that closer to the appropriate time.

"Anyway, glad you called," Vince said. "And keep me informed, like I said before."

"Will do."

"And, Dane?" Vince added, apparently recognizing he was on speaker. "Are you ready to testify?"

Silly question, Alexa thought. He'd better be. But his answer was definitely important.

"The sooner, the better," her driver replied. "I hope I get a chance to talk to Moe or the ADA beforehand, though, so we can go over what he'll ask and my best way of responding. Telling the truth, of course. But making sure I phrase it in the best way possible to convict Swanson."

"Amen," Vince said. "Talk to you both later."

And meanwhile, they'd get to talk to Assistant DA Cora Canfield, Alexa hoped.

For now she said, "We should get to the courthouse as fast as possible, and hopefully we'll soon have our questions answered."

My questions, she thought, but figured Dane desired

those answers, too—like how he could get into court most safely. But he was human. They both were. And so she felt compelled to ask, "Would you like to make a brief stop for coffee, or anything else? We'll be passing a few small towns before we get there." She'd checked the map on her phone and looked at the Arizona Veterans Highway, which was another designation for Interstate 17. They'd be going by some places such as Lake Montezuma, Flower Pot and Black Canyon City. They'd pass Sedona first, but it was farther from them than the others.

"Not unless we want to check out anyone around us to see if they're following," Dane said. "Still don't see anyone. But this seems too easy, especially after being attacked earlier. Something's got to happen before we arrive. Someone's got to try to stop me."

"Unfortunately, I'm sure you're right. But—"

Her phone made its noise indicating she'd gotten a text, and she checked. Vince had sent her a phone number, which he'd said was Cora's. Her phone rang then. She glanced at the number. It was Cora.

"It's her," she said to Dane, then swiped her phone to answer. "Hello?" she said in a serious, professional voice.

"Hello, Marshal Colton?" asked a female voice.

"That's right." She waited for the other person to identify herself, just in case something was off.

"This is Maricopa County Assistant District Attorney Cora Canfield. Marshal Vince Cudahy—your boss, I believe—gave me your phone number. I understand you're on your way here to court with our key witness in the *State vs. Samuel Swanson* murder trial, Dane Beaulieu, correct?"

"Definitely correct," Alexa replied.

"I understand you have some questions, which I'll be glad to answer if I can. But first—where are you? How close? I need to get an idea about when you'll arrive."

"Of course," Alexa said. She felt a little uncomfortable giving the information, but other than being professionally paranoid to keep her witnesses safe, she had no reason to disbelieve this woman was who she said she was. "I see some signs along the road." She'd been watching the roadside as well as the cars around them as she spoke. The area was somewhat hilly and dry around the road, with some green bushes and trees along the desert-like ground. "I believe we'll be at Camp Verde soon, and I assume it'll be an hour and a half or so after that when we arrive in Phoenix. We'll have to get to the court then."

"Which won't take too long. Good. And more questions from me. Vince indicated that you and your subject are both in disguise as senior men, correct?"

"That's right." Alexa was starting to feel a bit more uncomfortable again. Why did she need to know that?

But her next statement clarified why she'd wanted to know, and also made Alexa feel more at ease, at least a little.

"Good. The situation is potentially dangerous enough that we're going to assume that the people who are apparently attempting to save Mr. Swanson are aware of your disguises. I understand that you and Mr. Beaulieu have already been confronted on your way here, correct?"

"Yes," Alexa confirmed. "And I have an idea that should help protect us as we get there." She'd been considering it for a while, and now requested that they have a couple of Phoenix's law enforcement officers dress as Dane and she were disguised now and walk into the courthouse as a diversion. "That way, if anyone's out to stop us, they'll hopefully be caught first."

"Good idea," Cora said.

Alexa watched Dane's face, too, and he appeared pleased as he looked out the windshield, even smiling a little. "But what should we do when we arrive?"

"Are you driving?" Cora asked.

"Not at the moment," Alexa replied. "Dane is."

"Good. I assume you have something to write with. Here's the location we'll want you to park at. And we'll need the description of your car and its license. Other plainclothes officers will accompany you into the courthouse by using back doors and seldom-used stairways."

"Sounds good to me." The driver was talking. Well, that was fine. He was entitled to participate, Alexa thought. "This is Dane Beaulieu, Ms. Canfield," he said. "And I might be less obvious if I go in alone rather than with Marshal Colton. She's been great, taking care of me in witness protection, but—"

Alexa glared at him. Participate, yes. Modify the situation to comply with his own thoughts, no. She was the protector, not him. "Detective Beaulieu has been overstepping his limits in witness protection, Ms. Canfield—" she said.

"Just call me Cora already," she interrupted, sounding annoyed.

"Cora. It's my job to ensure he remains safe before,

during and after his testimony. And though I very much appreciate the help you're describing, I'm going to tag along, and more if necessary." She kept her voice strong, and her gaze on her charge, who only shot a glare back at her as he kept driving.

"I understand," Cora said. Did she sound amused? Alexa couldn't be sure.

"Glad to hear that," she said anyway.

"So your car info?" Cora pressed.

Alexa turned and pulled the tote bag with her rental car info in it. Was she comfortable giving the information to a stranger, even one who'd been vouched for by her boss?

Not really. But she had little choice.

And she'd be there to protect Dane anyway, no matter how hard he tried to get her out of that situation.

She provided the details to Cora.

She then jotted down the information Cora provided to her, including the location of a parking lot in the vicinity of the courthouse, though not its main one.

"Definitely call me when you park," Cora said. "I'll send those plainclothes cops to join you and ensure you get to the right place safely."

"Thank you," Alexa said.

"Let's get this thing done right," Cora replied. "We have potentially enough evidence to convict Swanson without Dane's testimony, but with Dane's story about watching his partner die and getting shot himself… Well, that should take care of the situation and ensure the conviction."

Alexa certainly hoped so. Otherwise, this entire journey might have been in vain.

THEY MIGHT ACTUALLY reach their goal of Phoenix, Dane observed to himself. And have backup so he could safely get into the courthouse. And testify.

Although considering how late they'd get there, he probably would not be able to finish his testimony today. Not with all he had to say about Swanson and what he had done.

"Look," Alexa said now into the phone. How could she still appear so attractive while she was disguised as a grungy old guy?

Maybe it was just because Dane knew who she was underneath all that.

Too bad he wouldn't get to see it again.

Or would he? Would she stay with him that night?

Maybe only if the local authorities turned out to be scum like Swanson, and Alexa and he had to disappear till the trial's next day.

"I appreciate all your efforts and ideas," Alexa continued. "And I'm sure you know how concerned I am about keeping my subject safe, both in court and otherwise. And—"

"And you don't know if you really can trust me. I get it. Well, though my preference would be for our cops to take over Mr. Beaulieu's protection as soon as you reach the courthouse, I figure you'll want to remain with us to ensure he really is safe. Right?"

"Yeah, you got it," Alexa said. Her cold, efficient voice somehow made him smile inside. Sure, she was just doing her job. But he didn't want to permanently part ways with her just yet.

"Fine with me, and with my boss, Moe, too. He and I talked this over before. And though he's in court examining a few introductory witnesses for now, he's dealt with people in WITSEC before and knows how paranoid they can be. Their protectors, too. For good reason."

Dane couldn't help glancing toward Alexa at that. Her grin was wry; she was also looking at him, nodding slowly.

"So how do you intend to make us feel better?" she asked.

"Well, for one thing, we did come up with that scenario about getting Mr. Beaulieu into the courthouse, with the support of plainclothes backup. But if there's something else you want us to add to it, just let me know."

"I will, of course."

Why wasn't Dane surprised about that?

Well, could be because this smart, determined woman was full of good ideas to protect him...

When he looked in the rearview mirror this time, he saw a large gray SUV passing everything behind him, barreling in their direction. Was this it?

Were the occupants after him?

He gestured to Alexa, using his thumb to point toward the rear of the car.

"Hold on a sec," she said to Cora.

She pulled her gun from her pocket and turned around—just as that SUV pulled up beside them.

Dane prepared to slam on the brakes and pull his own gun out as he bent sideways—but the SUV kept going. Fast. He didn't see whoever was inside, but that also indicated no one was particularly staring at them.

And in moments that potentially scary situation was over.

"Guess that was simply a speeder," Alexa said. She quickly explained the situation to Cora, who laughed a little.

"Glad that's all it was," she said.

"Me, too." Alexa took a deep breath as Dane again looked at her. Then she said, "Okay. Here's what I was going to say...

"I'm going to ask that Vince get the local authorities to have most of the plainclothes officers dress similarly, appearing like possibly disabled senior citizens, to throw off anyone who might know how we appear now, and potentially capture anyone who's out to harm Dane."

Dane liked what she'd said. It was another small but important step on the ladder of protection she was building around him.

"Interesting idea." Cora's tone suggested she was musing on it.

"Do I recognize that the villains could figure out what's going on, even potentially dress like older people, too?" Alexa said. "Of course. But we'll have to take that into consideration with everything else. And if it works out, it may help Dane get into the courtroom more smoothly and be able to testify and participate in the conviction of that particular murderer."

Chapter Thirteen

Alexa's heart rate was finally settling down as she continued to sit in the passenger seat, still anxious despite the more relaxed tone she was using with Cora.

Oh sure, she'd been fully aware that a fast SUV passing them didn't necessarily constitute, or contain, any danger. But she'd nevertheless tensed up as she'd prepared to take on any attackers, if necessary.

Thank heavens, it hadn't been. Right now, even with Cora still on the phone, she carefully eyed their surroundings,

"Okay," Alexa said. "I think it's time for me to call Vince and let him know my idea. He's a smart guy, and well connected, and I'm sure he'll know which authorities in your area to contact to ensure that lots of plainclothes cops dressed like us show up around the courthouse. He'll probably try to contact Mr. Francini, too, to confirm what's happening. I assume you'll also let him know."

"Of course," Cora said. "And if I didn't have to appear in the courtroom to help, maybe I'd dress up to look twice my age, too."

"Sounds good," Alexa said, smiling. "As it is, I hope

we see you in or around the courtroom so we can meet in person."

"I'll look forward to it," Cora said. "And I'll head back in to let Moe know what's happening whenever there's a break."

"Fine," Alexa said, and hoped that, and all other contacts Cora had, went well. She had no reason to mistrust the ADA, but she didn't completely trust anyone just then.

Except Dane.

She wished suddenly that she could hug him. Hold him tightly even as he drove.

Protect him with her body. And do even more than that with her body…

But that had to remain only in her thoughts. "I'm sure we'll speak again," Alexa said to Cora. "Hopefully soon. And please let us know if you, or anyone you speak with, has any other ideas about how best to get Dane inside the courtroom safely."

"Will do. I look forward to seeing you. Oh, and by the way, I have a good idea how Moe wants to approach questioning you, Dane, but I'd rather you and he have that conversation before you're put on the stand. Okay?"

"Fine with me," Alexa's driver said, nodding. He now looked serious again.

"You okay with all this?" she asked Dane after hanging up. In his senior's getup, he certainly wasn't as handsome as he really was, yet she still liked his looks. Liked him.

Too much…

"I'm more okay than I was before." He glanced toward her before returning his gaze to the road. "And

I'm looking forward to seeing all those geezers around the courthouse."

"Me, too." Alexa couldn't help grinning as she looked back down at her phone. She soon pressed in Vince's number again.

"Everything okay?" was Vince's immediate response as he answered.

"For now," Alexa said. "We're getting closer and being careful about other cars around us. But things are too quiet, I'm afraid." She told him about their conversation with Cora. "And of course I'm hoping no one's bugging you now to find us, burner phones or not."

"I've got our techs checking it constantly. Far as I know, all's well."

"Glad to hear that," Alexa said. "And to also help keep it that way, I have an idea I want to run by you." She told him about her plan.

"Hmm," Vince said. "I like the idea. But I've only talked to the local Phoenix authorities about having two enter the courthouse around the time you get there. Not sure they can grab enough other people and get them dressed like oldsters on time."

"I understand," Alexa said. "But Cora's on board with it, though she may need help getting oldsters in disguise there fast."

"Well, I'll get in touch with the DA and see if he can delay Dane's testimony so it can start first thing tomorrow, not later today. Meanwhile, we can try to get lots of young apparent senior citizens, with protective weapons, prepared to take care of any bad situations that might arise."

Alexa felt like cheering. "Sounds good to me," she said.

"It may take me a while to talk to Moe, since he's already in court. But I'll let Cora know I need to talk to him, which it sounds like she may already know."

"Right," Alexa said.

"Anyway, keep me informed how things go as you get closer Phoenix, and I'll also keep you informed about how my upcoming conversation progresses."

"Great," Alexa responded. "Cora gave us a detailed description of what we should do when we get near the courthouse today, but I can let her know we'll conform to what she said tomorrow instead."

"I'll do that," Vince said. "She can get back in touch with you if there are any questions." He paused. "You listening to all this, Dane? Are you okay with it?"

"I'm listening, and I like what I'm hearing," he said, leaning slightly from the driver's seat toward where Alexa held the phone.

"Excellent. I'll be in touch again soon." Vince hung up.

"Interesting," Alexa said. And maybe a little worrisome. She'd considered what they'd do that night anyway, after the court closed. But she'd also considered that the local authorities might take over protecting Dane.

Not that she'd drop out of the picture, but she might have less ability to make decisions. And she wasn't sure she wanted to give him up...

"So we might wind up avoiding the courthouse till tomorrow." Dane expressed some of what Alexa was thinking.

They'd have another night together. But where?

And would it be even more dangerous, since they

were going to be so close to where Dane would be testifying against the murderer? Swanson had apparently been able to get a lot of support from those who had formerly reported to him or whomever the people were who had come after Dane.

She saw Dane aim a brief glance in her direction. Oh yeah. She needed to respond to what he'd said.

"That's right. We'll be together another night, but one where your safety might be even more in jeopardy."

"So how are you going to take care of me, O Protector of Mine?"

He sounded sarcastic.

And yet Alexa did hear reality, and true questioning, in what he'd said.

"Unless I hear otherwise from Vince or someone else in charge here," she responded, "I'm going to find us a place to stay that's off the beaten path, close enough to downtown Phoenix to get to court early in the morning, but somewhere your enemies are highly unlikely to find us."

Sounded good, she thought. But how was she going to accomplish it?

"So where's that?" Dane's tone was serious now, and so was his expression beneath his elderly disguise.

Good question. And then a thought occurred to her.

"Not sure yet, but I've got some ideas. First, I've been thinking about another phone call I need to make, to my brother Dom. Maybe the FBI would have some suggestions."

"I'm all for getting as much backup as possible," Dane said. "And getting advice from your FBI brother? Why not?"

Why not indeed? Alexa thought. She'd keep her phone off the speaker, at least at first, though, to help keep Dom's privacy, but also to allow him to say whatever he wanted about protecting Alexa's subject without that subject chiming in.

What was going to happen?

Would it wait till they got to the courthouse either later today or early tomorrow?

Or had the confrontations they'd already had been all they'd face?

She wished. But for now, she would make that call.

She pressed Dom's number into her burner phone but kept it off the speaker.

Her brother answered right away. "You okay, Alexa?" Of course he recognized the burner phone's number since she'd used it before.

"Pretty much so, Dom." She wanted to act as cool as possible, even though she was going to request his assistance to help keep her subject, as well as herself, safe. And this also wasn't a good time to ask about his fiancée, Sami, though she hoped all was going well with them.

"What's not okay?" He leaped immediately on the negative part of what she'd said. Unsurprising. He was her big bro.

She chose not to tell him about Dane's inappropriate attempt to rent a car on his own and show up at the court without protection. But she did describe her conversation with Assistant DA Cora Canfield.

And also how far along they'd gotten, and not gotten, on their way there.

"If we arrive at the courthouse today, there won't be

much time, if any, for District Attorney Francini to talk to Dane and prep him for his questioning on the stand, let alone starting that testimony," Alexa told Dominic. "I'm thinking we should stay somewhere in town overnight, then show up first thing in the morning at the court. I can let our contact, ADA Canfield, know that. My boss, Vince, might already be doing that. And I did come up with a way to hopefully keep us a bit safer."

She next described her plan.

Dominic laughed. "Sounds like something you'd come up with, Marshal Colton," he said. But then he added more seriously, "And I'll be glad to request that a few of our Phoenix special agents show up there, too, though I can't promise they'll be in disguise as oldsters. But they can arrive armed and observe what's going on and step in if further protection is needed. I'm pretty sure the office there will be glad to send people, but I'll let you know if there's any problem."

"Great. Thanks." She could let Dane know about that. In fact, it wouldn't have hurt for him to be in on the conversation. But Alexa had more to ask Dom. "So how are things with you and the rest of the family?" Even though she'd seen Jasper and Aubrey at the Gemini Ranch recently and talked to Dom and Naomi over the past few days, there were always things going on.

"Far as I know, we're all doing fine. Only—well, if what you're asking about is if there's been any further progress that I'm aware of in releasing the innocents our dad got convicted, I haven't been working on that at the moment or staying in close touch with our Truth Foundation siblings. And that drug smuggler Spence, who should be back in prison? Oh yeah, my eyes and ears are open, but he's still on the loose, as far as I know."

"I figured. Anyway… One other question. I don't know if you know the Phoenix area well, but since it looks like we're not going to the courthouse tonight, we'll need a place to stay till tomorrow morning. Any ideas?"

"Let me check with one of my fellow agents there who's my buddy and text you some suggestions. Okay?"

"Sounds good," Alexa said.

Before they hung up, Dom said, "Now, I know you're on an assignment and you've been doing witness protection for a while, but now that you're getting down to the wire and about to deliver your subject—"

"I know where this is going, bro," Alexa said. "I'll appreciate any help you and the FBI can provide, as well as the local police and my marshals. And you can be sure I'll be damn careful."

"Yeah, be careful. That's exactly where I was going."

Alexa could almost see her dark blond, blue-eyed brother staring at her with his head tilted and his gaze insistent. She smiled.

"Talk soon, Dom," she said.

"Yes, talk soon."

Alexa pressed her phone to end the call. But her mind was racing a bit regarding her conversation with Dom.

The family was still concerned about Ronald Spence, also as always.

Dominic gave a damn about his US Marshal sister who was performing witness protection.

Good thing Alexa had such a wonderful, caring family, even as large as it was. She loved her siblings.

And wanted to stay alive and healthy and see them all again soon. Including the significant others some of her brothers and sisters had found, the people they intended to spend the rest of their lives with.

Now, if only she too could find true love—and she kept her mind far from the man with whom she shared this car. Or tried to. That certainly wouldn't work—even though she now was about to spend another night with him.

It would help if Dom found a place around Phoenix for them to stay, and she directed her mind that way.

But as much as she relied on her brother, she couldn't assume he'd find all the answers. He was still in Colorado, after all, at least as far as she knew. He'd be relying on his Arizona colleagues for their help.

That might be perfect, and keep Dane, and her, safe.

But perfection was hard to achieve.

"So how's your brother?" Dane interrupted her thoughts. "Is he going to get a bunch of FBI agents to the court tomorrow along with the local cops? I heard you tell him about what you planned and how you're getting your own boss to get some contacts together in Phoenix."

"Doing fine. And I'm not sure how many FBI agents might show up, but I gathered he'd make sure some are there, armed and ready, in case any additional federal protection is needed along with the local."

"Good guy, I gather."

"Yes, he is," Alexa said. A thought about the other part of their conversation shot through her mind. Her brother, and other siblings, were all good people. And though she still missed the idea of a loving father, it was really hard to realize that, despite what had been good about their dad, it was outweighed by the bad stuff that hurt quite a few people.

Too bad that actual crook Spence hadn't remained in jail, though.

Signs along the road indicated they were getting closer to Phoenix, a good thing since it was nearly three o'clock in the afternoon.

Dane said, "I think we're still doing fine, but I want to get off at one of these exits and just make sure no one follows us." He paused then added, "Things have seemed too safe and calm, under the circumstances. I'm waiting for the next shoe, or tire, to drop."

"You're reading my mind," Alexa told him. "So, yeah, go ahead and exit. And I'd be glad to take over driving, if you'd like."

"Maybe for a while," he said. "But I want to be the one at the wheel when we enter Phoenix. That'll give you more ability to concentrate on who and what's around us, O Wonderful Protector."

His tone was intended to be humorous, she was sure. But what he'd said made sense. Dane Beaulieu, aka Daniel Brennan, had apparently come around to relying on the US Marshals, most especially her, to keep him safe at last.

Or he wanted her to think so. Alexa had no doubt he'd jump into any fray to try to protect himself. And her. But she appreciated his attitude, feigned or not.

They sat in silence for a few minutes, Alexa's mind spinning on the topics she expected involving keeping Dane safe.

Getting to Phoenix.

Getting to the courthouse. Presumably, it closed around five, so even if they arrived before that, there wouldn't be much the DA or his assistant or Dane or Alexa could do to help convict the killer tonight. So forget that.

Tomorrow? Oh yeah, they'd potentially have a whole day for Dane to testify about what he'd seen and experienced.

So—what about tonight?

What about something near Phoenix Sky Harbor International Airport? There'd likely be so many visitors in those hotels that the people out to find them might get confused.

But then, so might they. And Alexa certainly wouldn't want to do anything that could get them lost, or stuck in traffic, in the morning.

Something downtown near the courthouse? She started looking for possibilities, even though her mind told her that wasn't a great idea, either. They might wind up being too obvious to anyone attempting to find them.

How about contacting Cora again and asking if Dane and she could sleep at her home that night, wherever it was? Was she married? Did she have kids? In case she did, that was another bad idea.

Alexa didn't want to endanger anyone else.

Still, contacting Cora again seemed like a wise choice. Alexa could ask her for her suggestions for a hotel, plus confirm the time they should arrive at the court tomorrow.

At least they already had Cora's plans for where Dane should head.

Just then she got a text from Dom with some suggestions, too, that his Phoenix FBI contacts must have provided.

"Hey," Dane said from beside her. "What was that text? And enough of the silence. What are you thinking?"

"I'm still attempting to figure out how to figure out where to stay tonight. The text was from my brother, with suggestions, but I'm not sure whether to follow what he says or figure something else out."

"Hey, a joke of sorts. I like it. And thanks to the joke, I'm getting off the highway at the next exit. We could use some gas, and I could use a rest for... Oh, say five minutes. I'm still driving into town, and I know we're getting close, but maybe I can help you figure out how to figure out—"

"Got it," Alexa said. Yes, she'd attempted to be a bit humorous, which was interesting. But despite believing she had hardly any sense of humor, being in this sexy jokester's presence somehow got her thinking about how to make him smile.

And how to get him into bed— *Stop that*, she shouted internally to herself. Yes, it appeared they were going to spend another night together, probably the last. Alexa was likely to be out of the picture once the local authorities took over Dane's protection.

That made it all the more tempting to consider what they could do together this night.

To consider what they'd done in last night's hotel...

"And maybe while we're stopped," Dane said, shooting a sideways glance toward her and a wink, "I can be the one to figure out a hotel or two in the area we're heading to. We need to get lots of rest tonight to prepare for tomorrow."

Alexa felt her heart sink. He was absolutely right. They needed to sleep tonight, in advance of his testimony tomorrow.

Although she would still have to be on guard to ensure Dane's safety tonight, more than ever.

But anything else...?

"Of course, we have to get some exercise before we attempt to drop off to sleep to ensure we sleep well," he added as he slowed to approach the off-ramp. "Now, I know you'll try to stay awake anyway. But I intend to do my best to wear you out so you actually do get some sleep, while I'm the main one of us who watches for anyone after us. My turn. Maybe my last turn. But I do intend for us to have fun first."

Really? She should brief him on reality. Tell him that wasn't going to happen.

But she stayed silent.

Chapter Fourteen

Dane needed a break. Oh, he was fine with his driving, but his state of mind needed some time out.

Reaching a ramp, he turned at the last moment after making certain no one else had a turn signal indicating they were going that way, too. He didn't use his signal, either.

No sense giving a hint of what he was up to if any of the cars that appeared in the moderate traffic contained someone following him.

Fortunately, no one appeared to follow, turn signal or not. He couldn't be certain all was well, but no danger was currently apparent.

"We're heading to Cordes Lakes?" Alexa asked.

"I saw some signs for travel stops off the interstate." He noted that she hadn't expressed delight at his suggestion of how to spend part of the night. But she hadn't told him to bug off, either. "We'll check out one of them and spend a few minutes there, maybe get some coffee and visit the facilities."

"Sounds good to me."

He glanced over and saw Alexa nodding, her phone

still clutched in her lap, but she wasn't talking to anyone at the moment but him.

They were only about an hour away from Phoenix now, as far as he could tell. Maybe they should head for the courthouse right now after all. But if they did, it was likely to be after four o'clock when they arrived. Sure, he could stop in and say hi—and potentially get attacked today rather than tomorrow—but it would certainly not be the grand entrance he hoped for.

Not that he intended to stride in as Dane Beaulieu in his Tempe police uniform or even a suit. No, he'd go along with the protection lovely, and smart, Alexa had been providing him, and stumble in as senior Daniel Brennan, hiding among whatever authorities or undercover geezers showed up.

And talk to the DA. And eventually have the fun of entering the courtroom—probably wearing the suit he'd brought—smiling at his enemy, and give his testimony to bring Swanson down forever for killing Alvin.

And, oh yeah. For shooting Dane himself, too.

"Looks like you're doing a good job of staying alert," said the geezer beside him. She, too, was scanning the area around them, as she always did. Apparently nothing concerned her, or she'd have said so.

Oh yes, Dane trusted the lovely, disguised woman. Knew she was smart.

Knew she was goal-driven. And her goal, at least for now, continued to be to protect him.

And not to head to bed with him again, most likely.

Not tonight, but sometime in the future? Could they have a life together after all this? Maybe. He could contemplate—well, something. But reality…

"Trying to," he responded to her. "And by the way, I'm feeling fine. I want to do some more driving, including into town. We'd discussed changing drivers before but I'm fine with the fact we didn't. And I do want you to be our official observer as we get to Phoenix and decide where to stop."

"Fine with me, if you're not too tired."

"Here we are," he said, still cleaning up the idea of another night with Alexa in his mind. Or trying to. He already felt pretty tense about what was going to be happening over the next few days.

That was a kind of tension he could control. At least, theoretically.

Although… Well, once he was done, once Swanson was done, the reality he was contemplating was that Dane would return to Tempe and hopefully get his job back. Alexa would be back in Colorado. Would they ever see each other again, let alone have another night together?

Oh, yes, he could hope so. He realized he *did* hope so. But he knew better. And the idea of no longer having Alexa in his life was more than depressing.

"Are you okay?" Alexa, beside him, was regarding him with concern. "Did you see—?"

"I see a gas station and a nice large convenience store. And cars, some SUVs and a couple of semis parked there. But did I see something alarming? Nope. Although I have to admit that worries me. We haven't seen much of anything or anyone coming after me, and I know Swanson wouldn't have made it easy for me to get to court to have him convicted, if he could help it."

"Maybe he couldn't help it," Alexa said. "I hope not.

We've already been confronted by at least one of his paid peons. And we'll be prepared, with help, when it's time for you to get to the court."

Dane nodded as he pulled up beside one of the self-serve gas pumps. "Ah, time for this old geezer to limp his way over and fill up this car. Unless the other senior citizen in this car, who's in charge of me, chooses to do it."

He watched Alexa's face as amusement eased her expression. "Oh, I think you're perfectly capable of pumping gas, Daniel. But this oldster will get out of the car, too, to stretch his legs…"

In less than a minute, Dane had inserted the credit card with his new identity into the dispenser and started pumping gas.

He had an urge to touch her, to rip off her disguise and see the real Alexa beneath. He didn't do it, of course. Certainly not here, in public, even though there weren't many people around.

But he still couldn't help hoping he'd at least have one more chance to do that while they were alone tonight.

He heard her phone ring. Roger pretended to have a hard time finding it in his pocket, but soon had it up to his ear. "Hello?"

Dane couldn't hear the rest of the conversation, but he watched as Alexa took a few steps away to concentrate on the call. It was short but appeared rather intense.

Who was it? Was everything all right? Worry surged through him. But if there was a problem, he—they—would deal with it.

When he finished pumping the gas, he approached her, just as she swiped her phone to hang up.

He made himself smile. "Hey, should I have been in on that conversation?" She'd mostly let him participate while they were together, although she hadn't when she'd spoken with her brother.

"Maybe, but I'll tell you all about it once we're back in the car. I want to go inside the store first, and you need to go with me."

He bought them some water as well as pretzels, to tide them over till dinner, once they decided where they'd stay and what takeout they'd bring to whatever room they had for the night.

At least now he felt his mind had recharged a bit despite his concern over what Alexa might reveal. He was ready to get back on the road.

And to ponder again about what would happen beyond tonight.

First, though, he carefully waited on the walkway near the store to get back into the driver's seat, partly because someone was getting out of the car beside theirs—a tall, muscular, young guy with an angry expression as he looked at the person getting out of his driver's seat, an older guy. His dad?

His boss?

His cohort in attempting to take down Dane?

Okay, he could allow his imagination to run wild—and suspect everyone of somehow being paid by Swanson and wanting to harm him. He'd be safer thinking that way.

Slipping the plastic bag with the items he'd bought over his arm, he put his hand on the outside of his shirt, where his weapon was hidden. But both men just turned and went into the convenience store.

Dane got back into the driver's seat, closed the door and locked them all, since Alexa had gotten in, too. Then he put the bag on the floor in the back and turned to look forward again, eyeing Alexa, who was also watching him.

He merely nodded as if saying hello again, turned the key, backed up and then put the car in Drive.

"So, are we okay?" she asked in her usual lovely female voice.

"Looks like we are," Dane allowed Daniel to grumble as he nodded and glanced at Alexa after pulling onto the road that would take them back to the interstate. He paused and asked, "So who were you talking to on the phone?" It could have been a friend or family member and have nothing to do with him. Maybe even a guy she was dating… Well, he hoped not. And she apparently hadn't been speaking to anyone like that during the earlier part of their trip. Hopefully, there wasn't such a guy, or at least nothing serious.

"It was Cora. She asked our progress and said even if we were close, there was no need for you to be in court today. Tomorrow morning first thing, though? Yes."

"I figured. Did she say anything else useful?"

"We went over the plans."

Dane couldn't help a quick laugh. "Everyone will be protecting each other, too, then."

"Exactly. And I did warn her it was possible that some FBI agents might be there as well, potentially also undercover."

"I wonder if this kind of thing happens a lot at that

courthouse." Dane had reached the on-ramp for Interstate 17, and he hesitated only a few seconds to check their surroundings before pulling on to it. He also glanced at Alexa, who nodded her okay.

"I don't know, but we can check with Cora and Moe tomorrow. I suspect this kind of thing is unusual for them, though."

"Me, too." He paused and asked, "Did Cora have anything else to say?"

"Well, yes," Alexa said. "She and I discussed where you and I are going tonight, and I think it might work. There's a downtown hotel, maybe the closest to the courthouse, that Cora said we should head for. The police chief she's been talking to is going to help send in the officers in disguise tomorrow, and he agreed to send two to that hotel tonight dressed that way, too. She'll keep us informed about their progress, and we're to remove parts of our disguise to look more like ourselves, though not entirely, as we check in to the hotel."

"So they're going to be us for the evening, or at least hopefully look that way to anyone who wants to find me. But will our IDs work that way?"

"She said she would have the local authorities give enough info to the hotel reservations staff to ensure we can get in. If we run into any problems, we're to call her."

"That's an excellent assistant DA we're working with," Dane said. Or at least she wanted them to think so.

Well, so far, there'd been no indication Cora was anything but the kind of person she was supposed to be, working hard to ensure that an important witness finally got into court to testify.

Alive and unharmed, if all went well.

And knowing Alexa, and himself, they'd stay safe to-night, even if what had been described didn't work out.

"Okay," Dane said, aiming a quick glance at Alexa. She wasn't exactly grinning or appearing full of relief. Still, she seemed a bit less stressed. Maybe... "So, are you going to give me directions?"

"Absolutely." She started fiddling with her phone again, probably looking for the hotel's address and how to get there.

Should Dane feel relieved? Maybe a little. At least they had a goal in mind, and if it worked out, they'd stay one more night together, at a minimum, before this ordeal ended.

Would it be enjoyable? Maybe, but it would be stress-ful, too. It would also be the last night Swanson could get someone to kill Dane to keep him from testifying.

Did he have the contacts and means to do that?

Dane definitely hoped not.

He'd never appreciated his protector more than he did this day.

And he intended to feel that way tomorrow morn-ing, after this important night together.

They both had to be doing well, no matter what they did or didn't do that night.

His intent was to do everything in his power to en-sure that Swanson paid for what he'd done.

ALEXA CONSIDERED CALLING Cora again.

The ride from the Cordes Lakes area had been nice and calm.

Even so, Alexa didn't allow herself to pay a lot of

attention to the areas off the highway that they went by except to watch for danger. Some areas remained scenic, but as they drew closer to Phoenix there were more buildings of various types around them—offices, retail areas, hotels, even some apartments and residential areas.

For the moment, the voice connected to the map was the only one speaking in the car. Alexa wasn't happy about the silence, but she had nothing to talk about that they hadn't already addressed.

Their future? Any possibility of their being together was so unlikely that she didn't even want to bring it up and heighten her disappointment.

More realistically, she considered discussing some potential scenarios in which Dane got attacked that night, or going to the courthouse tomorrow, and what they would do about them.

Not something Alexa wanted to bring up either, though, at least not right now. Even though all of that remained at the forefront of her mind.

"So what are you thinking about?" Dane interrupted her thoughts.

She wasn't about to tell him. "Just checking out my first views of Phoenix." That was true, even if it wasn't everything.

"Nice town." Dane obviously wasn't starting a conversation, either.

In a short while, the female voice from Alexa's phone told Dane to exit the highway, then the next turn he needed to take. And the next one.

"I'm going to call Cora again," Alexa told Dane. She remembered very well the scenario they'd discussed for her to check in at the hotel for her subject and herself, but she wanted to confirm that nothing had changed.

"Everything okay?" was Cora's greeting when she answered after Alexa put the phone on speaker so Dane could hear.

"You tell me," Alexa responded.

"Yes, as far as I know. I haven't heard from the couple undercover guys, but I figure they'd let me know if there was a problem. I'll contact them now and call you right back."

"Sounds good." As she pressed the phone to hang up, Alexa turned to Dane, who was also looking at her. "Dinner?" she asked.

"We passed a fast-food place a couple of blocks ago."

That, Alexa interpreted as a yes. That way they could just hang out at the hotel until morning, which seemed safest to her.

She hoped.

Dane pulled out of their space and maneuvered around a few blocks till they got to a restaurant that specialized in foot-long sandwiches. Alexa wasn't very hungry but she could always eat just part of a sandwich, and another bottle of water sounded good.

Even better, the place had a drive-through, so they would be in and out of there quickly.

Her phone rang as Dane pulled away after paying for their food with a credit card at the window. It was Cora.

"Everything okay?" Alexa attempted to keep any anxiety out of her voice. After all, she worked in a field in which things could go wrong at any moment. Why worry about them? If there was a problem, she'd simply have to deal with it.

But tonight certainly wouldn't be the best time.

Plus, Dane had stopped driving just before he was about to take the car back onto the road again, and he looked at her, his expression appearing worried, too.

"Far as I could tell, all's fine," Cora said. "Your temporary counterparts were just parking at the hotel when I reached them. They should be heading inside soon to check in as the two of you."

"Lucky them," Alexa said. "We'll be there soon so I can check in as well, in one of my alternate identities as we discussed."

"Good. Keep me posted." Cora said good-bye and hung up.

Alexa considered taking a bite of her meatball sandwich with veggies now, just to keep up her energy, but figured it would be better to wait until they were settled into their room. Dane had handed her the bag before he'd paid, and she'd put it on the floor by her feet.

She wondered what the staff at the sandwich place had thought of old people like they appeared to be ordering full foot-long sandwiches. Well, even oldsters could enjoy eating, or even putting leftovers away for another meal as long as they could find a fridge.

And now her phone began talking again. They were only a few blocks from the hotel. Alexa told Dane to head into the place's official parking lot since, if anyone was after him here and knew they were in disguise, they'd go after the other old men—well, younger undercover cops—instead of them.

"How about if I park here?" Dane said, driving into the parking structure they spotted across from the hotel.

The space he chose was near an exit. It made lots of sense to keep it easy for them to run, if necessary.

"Looks good to me."

So did the hotel. It was part of a major chain and appeared to be well kept up. She couldn't tell from here how full it was, but the parking lot they'd entered was only partly full, which suggested there might be plenty of rooms available.

"So now—I'm to get out and find someplace to hang out till you tell me to come back here, right?"

"That's the plan." Alexa was going to check them in, swapping into a different disguise.

She turned and dug into her small suitcase on the back seat. She then took off some of her clothes, whatever made her appear to be an old man. She pulled on a pair of workout leggings with pockets, adding a long vest over the same shirt she'd been wearing.

Then, after removing the hairpiece and makeup that made her look masculine, she put on a wig that hid her short blond hair with longer deep brown wavy locks.

She'd felt Dane's eyes on her as she'd pulled off the clothes. Too bad they didn't have time for her to tease him more.

Not now, at least.

"So who's that beside me?" Dane grumbled, keeping his identity as a geezer for now.

"Your protector, and don't you forget it," Alexa said. "Now let's get going."

They both exited the car. She stayed with him till they located a stairwell, and after Alexa checked to make sure the area was empty, Dane walked down it to wait for her. She ignored her urge to at least hug him as they parted ways, let alone kiss him. Never mind that he wasn't in a sensuous mood at the moment.

"Not many cars on this level," he called up to her after looking.

"Sounds good, but only stay there if there's no one around, got it?"

"You know I do." He chortled a bit as if she'd made a joke. And maybe she had.

He had been in law enforcement, too, after all. And he had a lot of good ideas about how to protect himself, even though he was in official witness protection.

But as she started crossing the walkway to where a valet stood near a kiosk, she heard something off to the side. A grunt? No one was shouting or complaining or anything, but considering who she was and what she was there for, she figured it wouldn't hurt to check it out.

She walked around the corner where a few bushes decorated the side of the building and saw one old geezer sort—maybe—in a fistfight with a tall, muscular man.

Was that one of the guys who'd gone undercover to pretend to be Dane and her? If so, where was the other one? If not, why was someone sparring with an apparent senior citizen?

And why wasn't the guy at the valet stand trying to help?

Alexa turned quickly and headed back to the parking structure, noticing then that someone had exited the hotel lobby and appeared to be heading in her direction.

She grabbed her weapon at the same time she grabbed her phone. She called Dane first.

"Be damned careful," she said as he answered. "And if you don't see anyone coming after you, get in the car and come pick me up right now. Head to the exit at the rear of the first floor of the parking structure, the one that leads to the street."

Chapter Fifteen

Damn.

Not that Dane had thought anything about this situation would be easy. But what was going on?

Why was Alexa demanding that he pick her up? She must not have checked in to the hotel. Why not?

He could guess.

Who was after him, and where were they now?

He had started out the moment Alexa had told him to come, and now he drove out of the parking structure at the exit she'd described.

She opened the passenger door the instant he unlocked it and flung herself inside. She looked mostly like herself now, her lovely self, despite that brown, wavy wig. "Go!" she said.

And he did.

But he couldn't help asking, as he headed onto the nearest street, "What's going on?"

"Not sure, but there was a fight near the hotel entrance between someone at least dressed like a senior, and someone else. I didn't see a second senior. I just figured it was time to go. And I need to call Cora."

She did. She didn't say much additional to the ADA,

but she'd put the phone on speaker so Dane heard Cora say, "Glad you're out of there. I'll get some authorities there to check it out. Where are you going now?"

Alexa looked at Dane. He had an idea, fortunately, but he wasn't going to mention it while anyone else was on the phone, even someone who was most likely trustworthy.

Most likely.

"Not sure," Dane said. "Do you have any suggestions?"

"No," Cora said as Alexa held the phone even closer to Dane's mouth. "And even if I did, I wouldn't pass them along. If whatever happened was intended to be an attack on you to prevent you from testifying, I don't have any idea how a third party would have known where you were. Or known that you were in disguise as a senior, which might be why Alexa saw a possible senior, or possible undercover cop, being attacked.

"Have we been hacked? I don't think so but— No, you're unfortunately on your own at least for now. I think getting more cops involved at the moment will only complicate things further—and make it more dangerous for you. I'll make sure the security and protection at the courthouse is ramped up even more than currently planned tomorrow, but right now please just be careful and figure out where to stay the night—in your car, even, if that seems best."

"Got it." Alexa pulled the phone back. "We'll see you tomorrow." She said good-bye and hung up.

It wasn't particularly dark out yet, but Dane nevertheless attempted to drive along the dimmest streets while he, too, observed their surroundings as well as he could.

"Any ideas where to go?" he asked. He actually had an idea, although he knew there were no guarantees it would be safe.

"Not yet, but I'm calling Vince."

"What the—!" the marshal shouted. "Damn. I've got further protection lined up tomorrow at the court-house but I thought local authorities had things under control tonight, even having a couple undercover guys pretending to be you as you checked in to your hotel."

"I thought so, too," Alexa said. "But at least one of them was probably who I saw fighting."

"Well—I don't really know what's best to tell you now, other than to trust no one. Except each other, of course. And to show up right on time at the courthouse, where you should be well protected. I'll even contact my sources again tonight including the local Phoenix Marshals Service office for any additional resources, maybe even get you to a safe house. But—"

"Please do let them know about us, but I don't want to rely on anyone else we don't know around here right now. We're just going to have to figure out how to spend tonight," Alexa said. "And we will. Thanks, Vince. And good night."

"So now what?" he asked as Alexa hung up on her boss. Maybe she had an idea.

If not, he'd let her know what he had in mind.

Only— He saw a silver SUV driving down the street behind them, from the direction of the hotel they'd left.

Could mean nothing, although the area he'd chosen to hang out in was pretty empty.

Even so… He decided just staying there was a bad idea.

And the silver SUV that had worried him sped up in an apparent attempt to catch up.

"Damn!" Alexa swore. He saw her reach into her pocket, pull out her weapon and hold it in her lap.

"You going to call anyone else here to help out?"

"No," Alexa said. "But I checked before and we're not far from the local Marshals Service headquarters Vince mentioned. Let's go there and hang out in their parking lot if it seems appropriate, and it'll be obvious to anyone following us where we are. I hope it won't be necessary, but I can even call Vince again to get the name and phone number of the local contact he speaks with while we're there to get them to send help if we still see that car or any other that might be a problem. The Marshals Service here might wind up being a better resource than the local police."

"Got it," Dane said.

She gave him directions. The subject vehicle followed at first, but the driver must have realized where they were going. It disappeared, and although Dane drove around the area of the courthouses and even the local police station for a while, they didn't see it again.

"Okay," he finally said, heaving a sigh of relief. "They may be hanging around, waiting us out, but let's get away from this area for now. I've an idea of a different hotel a little farther away to stay the night. We could just hang out in the car, but if possible I'd like to get at least a little rest to prepare for tomorrow."

He had glanced at Alexa as he'd talked. She looked furious. And determined.

And sexy as hell, somehow.

That wasn't the reason he wanted to spend the night in a hotel with her. Or not the main reason, at least.

He'd do whatever else it took to keep them both safe, even stay in the car as had been mentioned.

But Alexa said, "You're absolutely right. This isn't the way to spend this night. I'm glad you have an idea, at least. I could talk to Cora again and see if she could get local authorities to provide an escort to…somewhere, despite her telling us we were on our own. But that would only make us more obvious again. So—let's be careful, but let's go to whatever hotel you have in mind."

"Will do." Dane once more stopped along the street, this time about a block away from the police station. He saw a couple of patrol cars headed that way, but no silver vehicles or any others.

Were they safe? He could hope, but he doubted it.

But maybe, just maybe, they'd be able to find a hotel room and get a little sleep that night.

WAS ANYONE FOLLOWING them now? Alexa didn't see anyone.

And Dane appeared to know where he was going. Or at least he didn't hesitate when he turned onto one street after another.

Best she could tell, they were going backward on the route they had taken into town earlier but making some additional turns.

She had to ask. "So where are we headed?"

"A motel I noticed when we started driving into town. Couldn't tell for certain, but it appeared to be a bit better than the ones we've been staying at for the last couple nights, especially the first one. And since I knew we needed to be careful, I also looked and thought I saw a parking area in the back that seemed somewhat isolated."

"Which might be a good thing, or a bad thing," Alexa said. Right now she didn't know exactly what was best for them—unless they'd been able to rent a room in the marshals office or even the police station.

And even then, since Dane's enemy used to be a cop, who knew what authorities around here might be on Swanson's side?

Phoenix was a good-sized city. Alexa considered checking the internet on her phone to see where there were theaters, or other hotels, or places that were likely to have people hanging out at this hour on a weekday.

But even in those areas she couldn't be sure that anyone they saw was there for legitimate reasons of their own.

"Hey, we're here," he soon said, and Alexa saw the motel he must have been talking about. It was part of a large chain, like a lot of the places to stay overnight that they'd seen. It was relatively small, taking up only about a third of a city block, and a couple of stories high.

The time was after seven o'clock already. Would they be open to walk-ins? Or run-ins, since Alexa wouldn't want to stay there long.

And at this hour, and after the danger they'd just escaped, she'd bring Dane in with her so she could watch over him as she checked in.

No people visible on the street or in the glow of the illuminated sign. No other vehicles except those already parked there. No movement of any kind that Alexa could see.

Even so, she put her hand over the part of her shirt hiding her weapon. "Let me get out first," she said. "Then I'll want you to come in with me."

"Sounds good." But from what Alexa could see of the expression on the false geezer face beside her, Dane didn't appear thrilled.

She got out of the car and walked up to peer into the reception room. It was lit, and she saw a couple of guys playing cards at a table in the middle of the room.

Bad guys? Well, she wouldn't assume not, but she had no reason to suspect them except that she was worried about everyone around now.

She walked back to the driver's side, opening the door. "Let's go ahead in. But be careful."

"You, too, O Most Revered Protector." That kind of silly address to her again? But his voice was soft and his expression as he looked up at her appeared almost reverent, till he started making faces by lifting his brows.

She couldn't help laughing. "Okay, Not So Revered Protectee, come on."

THEY WERE FINALLY out of the car, in a motel room. Now out of his geezer disguise, Dane was pleased.

And concerned, as he stood by the front draperies, pulling them back just slightly. Keeping an eye on this area while Alexa organized her suitcase at the other end of the room. Looking down on the parking lot a bit. He'd decided to keep the car in the front since it was easier to see, easier for them to get to if necessary.

Hiding it in the back could be more dangerous.

He wanted to talk to Alexa, but his mind was racing. This wasn't a good time to start a discussion.

Not any more than it had been when they rented this room for the night.

Geezer Daniel had been with Alexa when, still in disguise as another woman with her wig and different makeup, she had gone into the motel's reception area and talked to the woman behind the front desk.

Alexa had decided on a room on the second floor, as she often did. She didn't ask her companion for his opinion, although she had made a couple of comments that suggested he was her stepfather.

Second floor was fine—again. In any case, they did get a room not far from the wooden stairway to this level. That could make it easier to flee, if necessary.

And easier for someone to sneak up to their room?

Heck, there was no perfect solution, except maybe someplace guarded by real cops not bought off by Swanson.

Assuming they could be certain that any people who were sent were honest.

In any case, tomorrow was coming up fast. This all would soon be over.

Or so Dane hoped.

Would his part of the trial only take a day? If not, tomorrow was Friday. The local authorities would need to ensure Dane remained safe over the weekend, until the trial resumed.

Would Alexa be helping with that security?

And after Dane testified…

Damn, but he would miss the beautiful woman who stood across the room from him now reorganizing things in her suitcase.

The sexy, protective, dedicated individual whom

he'd come to know, though not enough, over the past few days.

She appeared to be removing at least some items from his backpack and reorganizing the contents of her bag.

What was she up to?

"Can I help you with that?" he finally asked, wanting to break the silence and figuring she'd say no.

It was something else for which she appeared to be in charge.

"No, thanks." She turned to look at him. She was near the door, using a stand for her suitcase. "I'm just working on ways to get ready for tomorrow, and one of them is to make sure you don't need any luggage to carry into the courthouse. You'll need to go in dressed as you are now, but you'll have to change to look like a former law enforcement officer who's a witness—in other words, put your suit on. I know you have one with you. I checked."

That wasn't a surprise, that she'd violated his privacy and dug into his suitcase.

But he said, "Nosy, aren't you?"

"By career," she said. "And you should be glad."

"Hell yes," he said without thinking. And also without thinking, he found himself strolling across the room.

He took the backpack off the edge of the bed and placed it on the floor.

"Hey," she said. "What are you—?"

She didn't finish as he put his arms around her, pulling her away from the suitcase. And then he began kissing her.

She responded immediately. Her lips on his were

torrid and searching, as much as he had suddenly intended to do with her.

The kiss did not last nearly as long as he had hoped. She suddenly pulled away. "Let's check—"

He knew what she meant. She was right. They needed to check everything about the place so they then could hopefully indulge in what he had so carelessly, yet wonderfully, begun.

He was standing tall despite his disguise outfit as he checked their surroundings.

Meanwhile, he noticed Alexa had gone into the bathroom. He doubted she was in there for security reasons. It had a small window, but no one could sneak in there.

Assuming anyone after him could find them now. And he certainly hoped that wasn't the case.

She came back out again. Only—she looked different.

Wonderfully different.

She had removed her wig and her clothes down to her underwear.

As he scanned her with his eyes, then looked back up into her face, she said, "I figure we'd better take advantage of this opportunity. It could be our last, you know, and—"

"Oh yeah. I know only too well. But because of that…well, are you sure?" He definitely was. But he owed her a lot. The idea of having sex with her again, quite possibly for the last time, was doing wonderful, hardening things to his body, yet—

"Hey," she said in a soft voice. "I'm the one who just came out here with my clothes off. Doesn't that indicate I'm sure?"

She drew even closer, and Dane reached out to remove those clothes that still remained on her, even as she began unbuttoning his shirt.

Oh yeah, his body was reacting.

And he had every intention of them both enjoying what could be this final night together.

Chapter Sixteen

Was she wise?

Definitely not.

But she was certainly turned on, first by just the idea of having sex again with Dane, and now also because of the reality of his removal of her underwear. His warm, sensual touch on her most sensitive places.

Oh, but two could, and would, play that game. Mostly watching the carnal, heated look in his eyes as he scanned her body, Alexa began undressing him, starting with his hairpiece.

He looked fantastic once his dark brown hair was visible once more. She unbuttoned then removed his shirt next, enjoying the sight of his muscular chest with its smattering of dark hair, too.

But that wasn't enough. Far from it. She stepped away from his hands on her breasts so she could move toward him again and pull his jeans and shorts down. And maneuver them around the large bulge in front that she wanted so much to see.

And soon did.

She moaned then, both at what she viewed and the

feeling of Dane's hands back on her again, maneuvering them toward the bed.

She pulled away long enough, though, to turn out the lights and go stand by the window briefly, but long enough to listen and hear nothing outside, then peek out and also see nothing that made her worry.

This wasn't the first time she'd recognized that tonight could be the last opportunity she would get to have sex with Dane again. Who knew where he'd wind up the next night after at least starting his testimony at the trial? He might even need protective custody by more people than just her, once he had actually gotten into the presence of the murderer he hoped to see incarcerated for life.

Enough. She saw and heard nothing wrong. "Alexa," Dane whispered, looking her straight in the eye as if both challenging and inviting her to join him.

He was now as naked as she was. He'd followed her to the window but now he took her hand, led her away, and, after pulling back the coverlet and top sheet, helped her into bed.

In moments, they were in each other's arms, kissing. Then more. Dane stroked her all over, as she did him.

"Oh, Dane," she said softly against his mouth, and his lips soon encouraged her to be quiet again as he continued their kiss.

He undoubtedly had anticipated this moment, as he had put a condom on the nightstand. She had the pleasure of putting it on him. And that was only the beginning of the amazing pleasure she then experienced as soon as he slid inside. The warmth of his body on hers, his thrusting…

And it continued for a while, each moment making her feel more enthralled, wanting even more, thrilled that it continued, focusing on the pleasure he gave her below.

He reached around to touch her breasts, making her gasp, as he continued his sensual movements that she reacted to with her own. When he touched her buttocks, she did the same with him, enjoying the sounds of his pleasure as well.

And then—

She reached fulfillment, also hearing Dane's gasp as he, too, must have achieved satisfaction.

She lay beside him for a while, listening to his heavy breathing and her own.

Fantastic.

And a touch of hopefulness. This had been so wonderful... Could they ever do it again?

Forever? Would he be the partner she hoped for, for the rest of her life?

Oh, yes, she could hope. But she knew how unlikely it was that they'd ever be like this again.

But she was proud to be on duty. Watching.

"You okay?" Dane asked the first time she rose.

"I'll let you know," she responded.

Covering herself with a towel from the bathroom, she peered out from the drapes first. All seemed fine. She grabbed her weapon next just in case, pulled a long T-shirt on and opened the door slightly, placing herself in front of the opening and hiding her gun behind her.

Surely, if Swanson's fleet of assistants knew where they were and intended to come after them that night to keep them from court in the morning, they'd have been there by now.

Alexa would remain wary nonetheless.

Still, after locking the door behind her once more, she couldn't resist the enjoyment of getting back into bed with Dane—and the pleasure that again followed.

She didn't count how many times she got up, checked around—and came back to bed to find she'd awakened Dane, and he was ready to make love yet again.

So was she.

But morning arrived, too soon.

Alexa was awakened by her phone ringing. She had it charging on the nightstand on the side of the bed where she slept…when she slept. She glanced first at Dane, who'd also been awakened. Then she grabbed the phone and checked who the caller was.

Vince.

"Good morning," she said, hoping she didn't sound too groggy. It was six fifteen, and she'd set the alarm on her phone for six thirty.

"Good morning." Her boss didn't sound groggy at all. In fact, he sounded like—her boss. "Now, I know you intend to get to the courthouse with Dane before eight, but I want you to get there at seven thirty at the latest. And I want you to tell me exactly where you are now. I've been told there's some unrest around the court, so I'm having an escort sent to accompany you in."

"Unrest? What does that mean?" Alexa was sitting up now, her back against the headboard, and Dane had sat up as well. He was watching her. She hadn't put Vince on speaker before, but she did now.

"Just more people hanging around despite the early

hour. I called DA Francini to ask how things appeared to be going, and he said some of his staff who arrive early for preparation let him know there were more pedestrians around outside than they're used to seeing. No one could say for sure who they were or if they indicated a problem, but I want to make damn sure you get our witness inside safely before the trial begins again today."

"Got it. We'll get on our way soon. And that escort...?"

"Like I said, tell me where you are."

"I assume our phones are safe," Alexa said dryly.

She certainly didn't think Vince was asking while in someone's crosshairs. His voice sounded like Vince in charge. Still—

"Yeah, far as I know. But we'll be damn careful anyway. Now, tell me. And stay there till you've got at least a couple unmarked cop cars accompanying you."

Alexa couldn't help glancing at Dane for his opinion. He nodded. She was the one who knew Vince, but Dane had been under the protection of several of Vince's subordinates besides Alexa over the past months. He apparently trusted Vince, too.

"Okay. Here's our current info." She gave the name of the motel and its general location.

"High class," Vince said dryly. "Sounds good, under the circumstances. I'll call Moe again and he'll get some local cops there right away. Don't leave till they meet up with you, of course."

"Of course."

She soon hung up and then looked at Dane. "You ready for this?"

"I'm more than ready."

Alexa enjoyed the view briefly as Dane got out of bed naked. He let her shower first, quickly, then took over the bathroom.

Gee, they could have saved some time if they'd showered together, Alexa thought.

Or not. Could they have stayed out of bed after that?

Alexa dressed once more as herself with a wig, while Dane resumed his geezer Daniel appearance.

They both threw things in their respective bags, and Alexa wasn't surprised that Dane confirmed that his suit was now stuffed in the backpack they'd take into court. Alexa had noted before that the fabric was, fortunately, a kind that shouldn't wrinkle.

"Okay," Alexa said. "I'm going out first to check things out, probably wait for our escort. And—"

Her phone rang. She didn't recognize the number. She inhaled deeply as she answered, "Hello?"

"Marshal Colton? This is Officer Len Graben. I'm in one of the unmarked patrol cars that just pulled up to the motel. We were told you're in charge of a man in witness protection that we need to accompany now to the courthouse. Is that correct?"

"Yes, it is but— How can I be certain you're who you say you are?"

"I understand you've spoken with District Attorney Moe Francini and Assistant DA Cora Canfield. You can call them and check us out."

Alexa jotted down what the purported Officer Graben told her, including what his vehicle looked like and its license number, then called Cora's number and verified Graben's information.

"Okay, then," Alexa said after hanging up, turning

toward Dane, who stood near the door. "You ready to get to court?"

"After all this time and what we've gone through? Oh yeah."

Alexa called the cop back and said they were coming down, describing their rental car.

She also asked if one of the officers could stop at a fast-food place and grab them breakfast.

"Assuming you have enough other cars to take care of us," she said.

"I believe so," said Officer Graben. "We've got a half dozen. One of the cars can go through a takeout line and get us all a snack and coffee we can eat and drink at the courthouse."

"Sounds good," Alexa said. "We're on our way down."

SO FAR EVERYTHING that morning sounded good, Dane thought. And last night? Well, he couldn't get it out of his thoughts. Didn't want to. And it was more than sex. He was really falling for Alexa, and he knew it.

Now he did his thing of hobbling down the stairs, though anyone who'd been watching them would know who the frail but overweight senior really was.

He had his backpack over his shoulder as he hung on to the rail and let Alexa handle both carryon bags.

Three plainclothes cops met them at the bottom of the steps. One identified himself as Graben, and another got their room keycards to take into the office so they'd be adequately checked out.

Looked like the cops had thought of everything. Dane hoped so, at least.

He saw a few people apparently leave their rooms

in the motel. No one appeared to pay much attention to them.

And fortunately none of them appeared ready to attack him.

Alexa insisted on driving that morning, which was fine.

The cops almost formed a ring around the rental car, one regular-looking vehicle in front, one in back and a couple on each side until Alexa drove off. She drove slowly and insisted that Dane slump in his seat, just in case.

Fine with him. He was, after all, still under witness protection, and this was the day it would most likely matter the most.

Best he could tell, they didn't stop for traffic lights. It took only a few minutes to reach the courthouse.

The cars stopped on the street, and a bunch of people who also must be plainclothes officers, including women, surrounded their vehicle as they exited. Dane grabbed his backpack. Alexa locked the doors.

The officers also surrounded Alexa and him as they ventured up the walkway to a few outside steps. But then a whole lot of other older guys also surrounded them, some getting between them and the plainclothes cops accompanying Dane and Alexa. The officers just glanced at the newcomers and some nodded.

Dane figured they were the additional undercover cops and FBI agents that Alexa had told him about.

The whole group then walked the rest of the way into the tall courthouse building.

He had mixed emotions as they proceeded. He

wanted to get his testimony over with and wanted to stay safe. He worried about their surroundings.

He also worried about what it would be like when he potentially had to say goodbye to Alexa. The idea that it might be forever... Well, in addition to all his other swirling emotions, he felt sad.

Dane and Alexa passed through entrance security similar to what Dane had seen in airports.

Apparently, the courtroom where Swanson would be tried was on one of the middle floors. A cop got into the elevator with Alexa and him, and they got out on what he was told was the correct floor.

A lot of uniformed police officers were there, as were some of the geezer-looking law enforcement agents.

And some regular citizens? Looked that way, but some could be part of Swanson's party, so Dane appreciated the protection around them. At least they'd gotten inside safely and would hopefully stay that way.

The cops then ushered Alexa and him down the hall and into one of the courtrooms.

It'd be a lot harder for Dane to appear like anyone but himself there, although he still had to change clothes.

Dane hadn't been in many courtrooms in his career, but he saw the judge's bench, the jury box off to the side, and the area near the other side where witnesses would sit to be questioned by lawyers who had their own tables—the defense and prosecution—beyond the rail that kept the official area from the observers.

Another couple of tables sat just before the bench, and Dane knew they were for court reporters and maybe a clerk or two.

A few people already occupied the room, and Dane

figured the couple at a table near the front were the district attorney and his assistant.

But as they approached the rail, Alexa looked at a person who stood with those two. "Vince!" she exclaimed. "I didn't realize you'd be here."

"I didn't tell you," he said.

A smiling guy approached them. He was large, though not as big as the character Dane now looked like. He was closely shaved and actually bald, and his face had lots of wrinkles.

Dane had learned to trust Vince from a distance. He was glad to finally meet him in person.

"I assume this gentleman is Dane," he said. He held out his hand and Dane shook it.

"We'll be starting soon," Vince continued. "Let's go get you changed into a suit."

"Sounds good," Dane said, and he was soon accompanied to the men's room by Vince and a couple of cops.

Just after they entered, another man who'd been at the table at the front of the courtroom joined them. He was tall and thin, with black hair cut short, a mustache and small beard. "Dane Beaulieu?" he asked. "I'm District Attorney Moe Francini. We need to talk."

"Sounds good to me," Dane said. He went into one of the stalls to change clothes. And when he came out in his suit, holding his backpack, Francini led him to another room down the hall where they sat at a table, with Vince and the cops around them.

Alexa, who'd remained in the hall, joined them.

Another woman walked in. She looked highly professional, undoubtedly a lawyer, slim and tall, in a black suit, lacy white blouse and clipped brown hair.

Francini introduced her as Assistant District Attorney Cora Canfield.

In addition to the newcomers, one of the cops who joined them had the breakfast Alexa had asked for. He even got to sip some lukewarm coffee.

Inside the room, Francini asked questions as if Dane was then on the stand, all about how he'd known Swanson before, as his boss. About how he'd been assigned to look into a prostitution ring—and learned that his boss was the head of it.

And how that had led to Swanson's murder of Dane's partner, Alvin O'Reilly, and the attempted murder of Dane himself.

As they talked, Francini made suggestions now and then about how to address questions, or to counter the likely responses the defense attorney might have on cross-examination.

Cora participated, too, adding suggestions that Francini appeared to approve of.

Neither said anything that would alter Dane's testimony, fortunately. He didn't need to ignore them.

In fact, Dane felt fairly comfortable about the questions and his answers.

He glanced at Alexa now and then. Her wide eyes and pleased smile suggested she was happy with how their planning progressed.

Happy still being with him? If only that was true, and they could still be together in some capacity when all this was over.

And then, finally, it was time. They all rose and, cops surrounding them, headed back to the courtroom.

The hallway was somewhat crowded. Dane recognized that at least some of those hanging around must be from the media, since a few held cameras and others held microphones.

Still others, though, might just be curious members of the public. They just looked around as they stood there and milled among the plainclothes officers.

All seemed fine, though, as Dane, Alexa at his side and Francini ahead of him, entered the courtroom. Cora seemed to edge Alexa out as she told Dane to follow her past the rail and into the center of the front part of the room near the judge's bench.

"Please sit there," she told Dane.

No judge yet, but there were a couple guys in suits at the table beside theirs, where he assumed the defendant would sit.

The defendant. Where was—?

There. Dane recognized him immediately, despite his appearing a bit older and a lot more unhappy than he'd looked before. Samuel Swanson was escorted by three uniformed cops into the courtroom through a door off to one side of the judge's bench. They ushered him to the table where Dane had assumed he'd sit and gestured for him to be seated.

He did. But not before aiming an infuriated glower toward Dane.

Hell, he should be the one glaring at his former boss, the former chief of police of Tempe. A man who exploited vulnerable people.

The murderer of Dane's partner and friend, and shooter of Dane.

Instead, he decided to taunt Swanson, silently but in a way he figured would annoy the heck out of him.

He simply looked at the hefty guy with the large face and big brown eyes covered with glasses who he was more used to seeing in uniform than the navy blue suit he was wearing now, and smiled smugly, as if the trial was over and Swanson had already been convicted.

That was what Dane hoped, and figured, would soon be the case.

Swanson clenched his fists on the table, still staring at Dane. He showed his teeth as he appeared to snarl even more. Best Dane could tell, he was attempting a silent threat.

Given an opportunity, Dane would send him back a threatening look. Even more, if it was possible. The guy had not only murdered his friend and tried to kill him, but he'd continued to try to do so, and imperiled Alexa, too.

But Dane didn't really need to do anything menacing then.

His presence, and his knowledge, were enough of a threat.

Even so, he turned to look into the rows of onlookers on the other side of the rail.

Alexa was at the end of the front row nearest him. The angry expression on her face suggested she, too, wanted to show Swanson who was in charge.

He doubted she would ever get the opportunity to meet him. It was best that way. But—

He suddenly heard loud pops from outside the back end of the courtroom. Hell! Were those sounds gunshots? Before he ducked, his glance flew toward Alexa, but she was fine, just looking shocked and confused.

He felt scared though. He was undoubtedly the target. Was he about to be killed after all?

He spied a woman he hadn't noticed before at the back of the courtroom. She had a gun in her hand, and was aiming at Dane.

He knew her. She was short and somewhat pretty and dressed in jeans and a tight T-shirt. She'd sometimes come around the Tempe station, apparently flirting with Swanson.

And she wasn't alone. A man, also with a gun, had begun aiming his weapon as he turned one way, then back again, nearing Swanson with each step but apparently approaching Dane.

There was security downstairs. How had they gotten in here with guns?

"No!" Alexa shouted as the cops around Dane tried to shove him to the floor, while other officers burst through another door near the female shooter.

Alexa. The woman was near her now, though still looking toward Dane with her gun pointed—but she started waving it.

And Dane refused to allow Alexa to be hurt. He stood. Ignoring his own fear, he attempted to dodge all the people trying to protect him, but failed, desperately craning his neck to make sure Alexa was okay.

Chapter Seventeen

"No!" Alexa shouted to Dane. "Don't move!"

Fortunately, he had to stay there, under guard by the cops who surrounded him, protected as they grabbed him and thrust him beneath the table where he'd been sitting.

Alexa might not be in charge of his protection now, but she was still going to do her damnedest to ensure he wasn't hurt.

Even though she appreciated he'd probably thought he was going to save her.

She drew her own weapon but didn't have to use it. By then the two assailants had been swarmed by armed and uniformed officers. Alexa recognized some of them, even beneath disguises, as fellow marshals from Blue Larkspur.

The two were subdued immediately, their weapons seized, and they were taken into custody by some of the local cops.

When Alexa glanced toward the murderer at the center of it all, Samuel Swanson, she saw him glaring from one person to another, shaking his head, clearly furious.

Had he told some of his minions to come here and

shoot their way around to get him free? Or had they decided to try it themselves?

How the heck had they gotten inside with their guns? No matter. Whatever had spurred it, they'd failed. Swanson had failed.

Dane was safe. And Alexa could hardly feel more relieved, even though she wasn't currently protecting him.

She didn't see him at the moment, not with the crowd of cops around him. She'd seen him thrust down on the floor and he was still there, as far as she could tell. In any case, he was well protected.

And soon the courtroom had been cleared of anyone unnecessary to the trial.

Unfortunately, that included Alexa and the rest of the crowd. She understood, of course. But she would most likely not get to see Dane till the end of the day.

Only… "Well, that was entertaining." Vince had come up to her in the wide, starkly adorned hallway with beige walls and lots of recessed doorways, which was now nearly empty except for more cops and people dressed in security uniforms.

"I guess you could call it that," Alexa said sardonically. Then she said to her boss, "So not only are you here, but so are some other witness protectors in our group. Did you bring them all along?"

"Now what makes you think that?" The grin on his wrinkled face suggested he was holding back a laugh.

She felt like laughing, too. In relief. "Oh, maybe their presence and their jumping in to help protect my subject—our subject—when danger approached."

"Oh, danger more than approached. It jumped in, too. But fortunately, it was immediately caught." He took a few steps until he was right beside the wall, and Alexa joined him.

"A very good thing," she said. "Now…well, I'd love to get back in there to see the trial, but I suspect that won't happen. It's probably safest if they keep everyone who isn't necessary out of there, as long as they consider the cops necessary. But—well, witness protectors, too, couldn't hurt."

"As long as they were definitely witness protectors," Vince agreed. "But the more of us, or purportedly us, they have in there, the more time it'll take to verify who's who. Plus, I'm sure their preference would be locals. So—" He reached into his pocket and pulled out his phone. "I'll check with Cora anyway. I've been in touch with her quite a bit, and gather you were, too. And what I understood now was that she would turn her phone's sound off in the courtroom but check it for texts frequently."

He typed something on his phone, then looked at Alexa and said, "For now, we'll wait. I don't want to start going up and down the elevator. But—"

Alexa was surprised when the door to the courtroom, not far down the hall from them, opened. Cora exited and closed the door behind her.

She joined them. She appeared even more serious than Alexa had seen her before. "I just want to thank both of you, and your additional witness protection staff. The trial is now proceeding, and I feel like our security is good. Really good. But I'm sorry I still can't let you in, even though I know you're part of the solution, not the problem."

"Oh, that's okay," Vince said.

It wasn't necessarily okay with Alexa. She remained worried about Dane and frustrated that she couldn't remain part of his protection. But there was nothing she could think of to say that would change the situation.

"In fact," Vince continued, "it looks to me like you really do have things under control here now. Or if it's not, you've got enough people on the case to take care of any problems."

"Very true," Cora said. "I won't tell you what or where, but we've been talking in great depth with the local authorities and we have not only witness protectors available to take care of Mr. Beaulieu over the weekend, but a safe place to watch over him."

"I take it the trial won't end today," Alexa said, "and neither will Dane's testimony."

"That's right. But the little bit of examination that's gone on so far, with DA Francini in charge, has been going well. Oh, there've been objections on the other side, but nothing that stuck. Still, it's taking a while to get through the interrogation, so we assume we'll have to resume questioning on Monday, then go through cross-examination."

"Got it," Vince said. "Anyway, we're heading back to Colorado this afternoon."

Back to Colorado now? He sounded certain of it, so Alexa was, too. He was her boss. And she had no further obligations here, now that Dane was being taken care of by others. She tried not to let herself feel morose. She had done her duty, gotten him here safely. Dane was now testifying, and the others would ensure his safety from now on.

She hated the idea that she wouldn't have the opportunity to say good-bye to him. But it unfortunately made sense not to put anyone else in his presence now. Even her.

Damn, but she was going to miss him. A lot. Never mind that it was unprofessional to get involved with one of her protection subjects. She hoped Vince didn't find out about her secret trysts with Dane—she wouldn't want that to come back to jeopardize her career. But she had to admit that Dane was special.

Very special.

If only they could stay in touch somehow. But she knew that wasn't going to happen—and it made her very sad. She just had to ignore it.

She had to say something to Cora now, though. She had to learn how things went at the trial as it continued. She shot a serious glance toward the assistant DA and said, "I hope you'll keep in touch and let us know how it goes."

"Of course." She looked at Alexa then Vince. "And we can work things out so Dane and you can get a chance to talk and catch up after today."

"Sounds good," Alexa said. "But since we're leaving, although Dane does have a backpack with him, he's also got a carryon bag in my rental car. I can bring it up and—"

"Just wait a minute. I'll have someone go get it from you." With that, Cora headed back into the courtroom.

Alexa had little doubt about what would come next. She, and the others, would soon be on their way.

She did appreciate what Cora said, though.

She would at least have one more chance to talk to Dane.

If that worked out.

"So," Vince said, "as I'd hoped, looks like you and I and the rest of our gang can head back to Blue Larkspur this afternoon. We've got a team trying to find the partner of the guy who attacked you on the road, by the way. And we're still attempting to prove Swanson sent the assailants or figure out who did."

"Sounds good to me," Alexa said. "Please keep me informed."

"Will do. And in fact— Well, I've got a couple other possible witnesses in important cases in Colorado who'll be needing protection soon. And, well... I'm looking at giving you a lot of high-profile cases now. You've really showed yourself to be quite a badass."

Alexa laughed. Despite her internal sadness, she couldn't help but be amused. And she was proud. She was delighted at being recognized as skilled in her job. That was a very good thing.

But not so good was that she knew for certain she needed to head home this afternoon. And the fact she wouldn't get a chance to say good-bye to Dane in person kept disturbing her.

Vince and she left a few minutes later, accompanied by an officer in uniform and also followed by three plainclothes agents who had changed out of their disguises.

Others, locals, had apparently taken over everything necessary to make sure the trial proceeded safely for the witnesses.

Alexa led one cop to her rental car, got the bag out of the trunk and handed it to him. She hoped he was trustworthy, then realized that in her job she trusted no one—or not many people. But this guy certainly appeared to be trusted by the ADA.

She watched him walk off toward the courthouse, wheeling the bag behind him. She figured Dane would get it back sometime that afternoon.

Meanwhile, she knew, Vince was arranging for them to fly back to Colorado that afternoon, so Alexa would meet him at the local airport since her next step would be to return her rental car.

Back to Colorado. Away from Dane. She couldn't do anything to ensure his safety but hoped the local authorities would do it well. *Hoped* being the operative word, but there was nothing she could do about it but worry about him.

And she knew he would remain on her mind a lot. For many reasons.

She had never felt like this before about any man. But she had to leave him behind.

Well, she would soon be on a plane. And there would be no problem getting a ride share to pick her up at the Blue Larkspur airport and take her home once she arrived.

For now, she used her phone's GPS to head toward the rental car office. Vince called while she was on her way and told her he'd been able to get them all on a flight at three that afternoon.

She was going home! She loved her hometown and her family.

She might as well let Dominic know how things had gone.

She pulled over to the curb of the street she was

on then and pressed his number, then put the phone on speaker.

"Hey, little sis," he answered quickly. "How's your witness protection going? Do you need some more FBI assistance?"

"I'd wondered if I did, but right now things are just fine."

As she got back on the road again, she described to Dom what had happened since she'd reached Phoenix with her protection subject, the concerns, the danger, even the attack at the courthouse. She naturally told him how well her idea of law enforcement agents in disguise had gone. "It all seemed to work out. I'm on my way back to Blue Larkspur now, but my subject is now on the witness stand in court." She attempted to sound perky, so he'd believe she was thrilled to be heading home.

And she was, mostly.

But she just wished she'd had a chance to see Dane in person one more time...

"Good job!" her bro said.

"Thanks. So how are things with you?"

"Not bad," he said. "But there are some things going on with our buddy Ronald Spence, the drug smuggler."

"Oh yeah. Him again."

"Exactly. He's at it again. I'll tell you about it when you get home. No need to waste your time about it now. So—get home safely, and we'll talk again soon."

"Hope we can see each other again, too. Any chance you and Sami will get to Blue Larkspur anytime soon?"

"Maybe. I'm in Denver now. But I'm open to the idea of heading to Blue Larkspur for a visit."

"I hope so," Alexa said.

IT WAS LATE AFTERNOON. The trial had adjourned for the day.

Dane felt exhausted. He also felt jubilant. He believed things were going well in his testimony.

DA Francini had asked cogent questions about Dane's work as an investigator for the Tempe PD and his friendly relationship with his partner, Alvin. Their investigation of a solid prostitution ring, as assigned partly by their boss, Police Chief Samuel Swanson.

How Swanson had seemed reluctant to even have any of his detectives look into the criminal enterprise.

How they had discovered Swanson was in charge of that ring.

And what had happened after that.

The questions were phrased well, not leading him to make up answers but allowing him to testify about what he knew and how he knew it.

They hadn't finished by the end of the day, though. Surprisingly, not much yet about the actual murder, and his getting shot, as well as the way he'd been attacked by unknown thugs on his way to testify. That would come the next time court was in session.

He figured, with all the objections and questions raised by Swanson's counsel, that had been planned, so that the most telling information wouldn't be in the minds of the jurors over the weekend. The weekend. Without Alexa around. He knew she was on her way back to Blue Larkspur.

She wouldn't see how the trial progressed, though she could probably follow it in the media.

She wouldn't see him. Nor would he see her. And damn, but he would miss her.

He missed her already…

DANE WAS ACCOMPANIED out of the courtroom by Francini and Assistant DA Canfield, along with a number of uniformed cops. His suitcase had been left by the door, presumably brought there from Alexa's car.

So he didn't have to go get it. Or see her to get it, either.

Canfield had introduced him to a couple of plainclothes cops who she said were his next witness protectors. They were taking him to a place where they'd spend the weekend with him. Be in charge.

Protect him.

But neither was Alexa.

No one else could be. Oh yeah, he missed her.

Cora had told him Alexa and her gang, including her boss, Vince, were already on their way back to Colorado.

A couple of phone calls would be set up over the weekend so he could chat with them about how things were going and say good-bye.

He wondered if Alexa had missed saying good-bye to him here the way he missed saying it to her.

"Here we are," said one of the guys who'd accompanied him through the courthouse and out a rear exit. He looked nice and burly and protective, and Dane had no doubt he was armed. His name was John Angelo.

They'd reached a car, and John helped Dane into the rear seat on the passenger side. Officer Len Graben, who'd accompanied Alexa and his before, had now donned street clothes and slid into the other rear seat.

Soon, they were on their way. As they left the parking facility, Dane couldn't help wondering exactly where he'd spend the weekend.

Somewhere safe, he figured.

But though he would probably feel sheltered and secured, he was certain that neither of these guys, or anyone else he might be protected by here, would make him feel as safe—or as pleased—as Alexa had done. Or would light his heart and body on fire the way no other woman had ever done.

Chapter Eighteen

It was nine o'clock on Saturday morning. Alexa was just getting out of bed, quite a bit later than her norm, especially lately.

She had slept reasonably well last night. Surprisingly, her mind had cooperated with what she'd hoped for her body.

After all, she didn't have to try to sleep lightly, in case any danger caught up with her and the man she'd had under witness protection. Or get up several times during the night, to double-check that she hadn't missed hearing anything, also to protect Dane.

Or to make wonderful love with Dane. Multiple times.

Or even just once.

She missed it. A lot. But she missed his wonderful company even more. Even his silly sense of humor.

Dane. She wondered where he had spent the night. Somewhere in Phoenix obviously, with others now charged with his protection near him.

Not Alexa.

No, she was back home in her quaint ranch-style house in a fairly classic, but generally calm, Blue Larkspur suburb. The other homes around it appeared similar, and she knew most of them were also two-bedroom. A nice neighborhood.

Hey, she was back home now. She'd have to go visit the Gemini.

Get another ride on Reina, with one or both of those sibs along.

She needed someone to talk to, after all. Someone close to her. And—

A good idea occurred to her. Instead of heading straight to the shower, as she'd originally planned after taking off her pj's and throwing on a robe, she went back to where she'd left her cell phone on its charger, on the ornate nightstand beside her comfortable queen-size bed with its fluffy beige coverlet and pillows.

Yes, it was still the burner phone she'd gotten during her adventure over the past few days. She needed to get a new one that she could use forever, or at least for a good long time. In fact, that was one thing she hoped to do today or tomorrow.

She also hoped to be able to go back to her old phone number, since so many relatives and friends had that programmed into their phones. Even if Samuel Swanson wasn't convicted of murder—and she certainly hoped he would be—he would have no reason to look for her while she was no longer protecting his enemy. Not unless he was hell-bent on vengeance in a way she didn't anticipate. And even if he was, it wouldn't be that difficult, phone or not, for him to find her back at her home and back on her job in Blue Larkspur. No matter what, she'd have to be careful.

She pressed her mom's number into the burner phone

after unplugging it. It rang a couple of times, then Alexa heard a tentative, "Hello?"

"Hi, Mom," Alexa said. "It's me. I'm using a different phone thanks to work."

"Oh good! I'm so glad to hear from you. I know better than to ask many questions, but I got the impression from Dom that you were working on something important—and in your line of work that can also mean dangerous."

Alexa laughed. "You got it. But the good thing is I'm no longer on that job, and in fact I'm home. Can you join me for lunch today?"

"Absolutely!"

They arranged for a time and place, noon at one of her mother's favorites, Happy Dining, a family restaurant on the south side of Blue Larkspur. It was a place her mom particularly liked, and she was the one who'd suggested it.

Alexa was smiling as she got off the phone and headed for the shower. Would she get to speak to Dane today? That might make her smile even more. A lot more. Maybe he would even tell her one of his corny jokes if they talked.

And just the sound of his voice would cheer her so much…

Oh yeah. She had really fallen for the guy.

She thought she heard her phone ring as she was getting out of the shower in her nice-sized mostly lavender-tiled bathroom and so she grabbed her robe from its hook behind the door and ran back into her bedroom.

She hoped to see a phone number she didn't know,

as her mother had. But what she saw was good, too. Dominic's number.

"Hi, Dom," she said.

"Alexa. Hi. Where are you?"

"Home," she said. "I finished my latest assignment, even though the trial isn't over, so here I am."

"Excellent! I hope to come visit soon. Only— Well, I should let you know, as I have with others in the family, that Spence is making more threats against us."

"What? How? And where is he?"

"Wish I knew where he was, but I got the impression from the authorities I've been in touch with over the last few days that he's being more threatening in emails, as well as more discreet about his location. No one's been able to trace him or bring him in, but he's hinted at coming after members of our family since we've remained pretty obvious about wanting to get him arrested again."

"Wonderful. Well, thanks for the warning. But... Well, you be careful, too. Sure, I'm a marshal, and I'd do anything to bring him in, but—"

"But your name is out there like most of the rest of us, as nosing around about where the guy might be so he can be brought in. He'll know it... Plus, he knows a lot of members of the Colton family are after him now. So, yes, you need to be careful."

"Got it." And she did. She knew full well that Coltons and others in law enforcement had to assume there were bad things around, even outside whatever assignment they happened to be on. "Thanks, I guess. Anyway, I'll look forward to when you get a chance to visit, and Sami, too, if you can bring your fiancée."

Fiancée. Alexa liked Sami but at the moment she felt a tad jealous. Not that she wanted that kind of commitment. But she hadn't really considered getting into any kind of relationship…before.

Oh, dating and having fun, sure. But no one had been interesting enough to spur her to try for anything long-term.

Her time with Dane, though, had made her think about more, especially since all the relationships she'd had before had been brief and never very serious. But Dane? Their bond hadn't exactly been appropriate, given she'd been protecting him. But she realized now that somehow, deep inside, she'd begun hoping that the intensity of the feelings she had developed for him might evolve into something more.

"I'll also look forward to seeing you," Dom said, bringing her back to their conversation. "Anyway, got to get back to work now. Be careful—and I will be, too."

Interesting, Alexa thought after they'd hung up. She had always figured that law enforcement agents could always be in danger. But was that what she wanted for herself for the rest of her life?

Maybe she should consider finding a different, safer career.

Or not.

But if she settled down with someone, got married, had kids, it would be better to have a safer existence.

And if she actually developed a relationship with Dane…

Oh, yes, that sounded wonderful. But impossible.

For now, she headed to the closet in her bedroom to start looking for what to wear when she met her mom for lunch. She didn't need to get too dressed up, but she didn't want to look like a marshal on duty, either.

Maybe not a dress, but a dressy pants outfit.

She chose a lacy, black, long-sleeved blouse over a pair of sleek black slacks, and decided to wear low-heeled pumps with it. Good. She should look attractive enough for her mom to be proud of her, but not too posh to be at a family restaurant for lunch.

She didn't need to get dressed yet, though. It was only a bit after ten o'clock. She decided to throw on a pair of jeans and a T-shirt, then get on her computer and check any news available from Phoenix, particularly from yesterday.

She doubted any reporters had been permitted into the courtroom, either, but that didn't mean they wouldn't do whatever research they could and relate it in whatever media outlets they represented.

The T-shirt she chose had a logo on it for Blue Larkspur, a representation of the flower for which the town was named—bright blue with a group of attached blossoms.

But before she sat to start her research, her phone rang.

Dominic again? Or Vince, or Cora? Not too many people had this number.

And when she pulled her phone from the pocket of her jeans where she'd placed it, she didn't recognize the number.

Someone else's burner?

A bolt of hope shot through her. The person she knew right now who was most likely to have a burner phone was Dane.

But heck, it could even be a wrong number.

She swiped the screen to answer and lifted the phone to her ear. "Hello?" She kept her voice calm and a bit curious.

"Alexa? Hi. It's the subject of your excellent witness protection."

She smiled as she felt her body grow warm. She moved into her living room and sat on the plush lavender sofa. "Well, you don't sound like any of the women I worked with, so my best guess is that you're Daniel Brennan, although you sound a bit younger than he turned out to be."

A laugh. And then the voice that was clearly Dane said, "Hey, what happened to my protector who had no sense of humor?"

"Oh, *that* witness protector? She's around here somewhere."

Another laugh. "Then put her on the phone."

It was so good to hear his deep, sexy, wonderful voice. But Alexa couldn't tell him that. Instead, she put her professional hat back on and asked, "So how are things in Phoenix? Are you safe?"

"Things are fine and so am I, thanks. I'm sure you know the rules. I can't talk long, and I can't give even a hint of where I am, although your guess about Phoenix or somewhere around there can't be completely wrong since I'll be back in court on Monday. But—"

Dane stopped talking, and Alexa heard a stern voice in the background. Maybe his protector thought he'd gone too far in even mentioning the Phoenix area, no matter that she'd been his protector before, and she was bound to know full well he'd be back on Monday in the Phoenix court where he'd testified on Friday.

"Okay," she said. "Don't tell me anything else. What's important is that you're doing well, you're safe and you'll be back testifying on Monday. Right?"

"You got it. And how about you?"

"I'm fine, back at home in Blue Larkspur, having a good weekend and planning on going back to my office on Monday."

Oh, how she wanted to tell Dane how great it felt to talk with him. To know he was okay.

She also wanted to ask that they keep in touch... somehow. Maybe not get in contact again till he'd fully testified, but after that—

Well, she'd be back doing her job, and Vince had already told her he had people in need of witness protection in mind for her to take on as subjects. And presumably Detective Dane would return to his own job in Tempe as soon as he could.

So—staying in touch might sound like fun, but why bother? It might only make Alexa feel more miserable about not seeing him. Even if she desperately didn't want their association to end.

And so, when they ended their conversation soon thereafter, she said, "I'm sure I can find out on the news next week how the trial goes. I hope you really nail Swanson." But she didn't suggest he call again so they could talk about it.

When he said good-bye, she tried to ignore the stab of pain that went through her.

"Good-bye," she said in return, and hung up.

GOOD-BYE.

It sounded so final to Dane.

He looked around the bedroom where he was hanging out this weekend with his current witness protector, Officer Craig Geraina, a member of the Phoenix PD who'd sneaked Dane into his own home in Gilbert, Arizona, a small suburb of Phoenix.

Dane knew he'd hang out in this compact room—with its single bed, and, fortunately, a TV mounted on a desk across from it and a restroom next door—the entire weekend unless something bad happened here.

Craig had stayed with Dane while he'd made the call on a phone the cop had handed him. Then he'd taken it back and left the room after asking Dane what he wanted to have delivered for lunch from a nearby fast-food joint.

Dane had also been told there'd be a lot of patrol cars going by, though none would appear like a police vehicle. And if he happened to peek out the window in this room—only allowed occasionally, and not at all if Craig told him not to—he might see some civilian-appearing dog walkers going by, accompanied by official K-9s.

Oh yeah. Dane was still being well taken care of. He appreciated it.

He didn't appreciate, though, that he couldn't even talk to Alexa more, let alone see her.

Which hurt, damn it. A lot. He realized now, especially since they were apart and he missed her so much, how much he really cared for her.

Still, if all went well, he'd finish his testimony on Monday or Tuesday. He believed his examination on

Friday had gone well, despite lots of objections and interruptions by the defense.

Swanson should get convicted. And when he did, Dane would be released from protective custody—although he knew he'd have to be damn careful. Swanson's buddies who'd been willing to get arrested for attempting to shoot people in court probably had associates who'd be happy to continually pursue revenge. And whoever the captured would-be killer's ally was remained out there somewhere, although Dane understood the authorities were attempting to track him down, as well as anyone else Swanson had gotten to harm others to help him.

But Dane would soon be able to go home to Tempe. Return to his job as a detective, although it sounded a lot less appealing now, considering all he'd gone through recently.

Well, he'd be alone here in this room a lot this weekend. He had been given yet another burner phone, although he'd been directed to make no calls or texts, darn it, unless told to by his handler. No communication that way with Alexa, either.

But he would look forward to a time that he might be able to get in contact with Alexa again. Sure, they had behaved a bit too intimately, but he had enjoyed it. More than enjoyed it. He'd appreciated Alexa. A lot. Still did.

Okay, he had begun to care for her much too much, maybe even fallen in love with her. Loved how his corny jokes could just about crack her stern façade, how she felt in his arms, how she, like him, was relentless in her pursuit of justice.

He was glad she had left the area and was safe. But oh yeah, he missed her. Would he ever see her again?

He'd at least be able to talk to her again, eventually.

Hopefully soon.

And he definitely hoped that Alexa hadn't really meant good-bye.

Chapter Nineteen

Alexa was delighted that she was going to have some
alone time with her mom.

She needed something like that to help her out of
what felt a bit like depression. Not that it made sense,
but the idea she couldn't see Dane anytime soon was
making her feel bad.

But having some time with Isa Colton would certainly help that. Especially just the two of them. With
so many siblings, Alexa seldom got to see her mom
without additional company.

It was nearly noon. Alexa was in her car now, and
she'd reached the particularly nice part of town where
Happy Dining was located. Only a couple more blocks,
past a few more restaurants on the wide, well-main-
tained street, as well as some clothing stores and even
a wine shop. Driving slowly, she saw her mother walking briskly along the sidewalk toward Happy Dining.
Knowing Isa, she'd probably gotten here early and
wound up circling the block to find someplace to park.

Fortunately, Alexa saw two curbside spaces in front
of a jewelry store and immediately pulled into one. She

pushed the button to roll down the window on the passenger side, just as her mother got there.

"Hey," she called. "Would you like a walking companion?"

Her mom stopped, squinted as she looked inside and smiled broadly. "I'd love this particular walking companion."

Alexa quickly got out of the car and pushed the button to lock it. In moments, she, too, was on the sidewalk.

She and her mom hugged. Isa was around Alexa's height. Her hair was shoulder-length, which was longer than Alexa's, but was also blond. She had blue eyes, and her figure was amazing, sleek and attractive, particularly for her age. And she had thrown on a lovely, though not too elegant, pink dress for their meetup.

"So good to see you, dear," her mom said. Despite the other people passing them on the sidewalk, she stepped back and looked Alexa up and down as if assessing her. "You look good. Do you feel good? I heard that the assignment you were just on was dangerous. You didn't get hurt, did you?"

"Not at all," Alexa responded right away, waving her arms out as though wanting her mom to assess her even more. What she'd said was true—physically, at least.

Emotionally, she couldn't help thinking about Dane. About having had to leave him, with the understanding she might never see him again.

"You're sure you're okay, dear?" her mom persisted. "You're acting like—"

"Hey. Well, look at this. Just like I was hoping. Not just one Colton, but two."

Alexa immediately drew herself even farther from

her mother and spun around to look at who'd been speaking from behind her in that raspy voice.

Damn. She recognized the guy, of course. Ronald Spence.

What was he doing here?

He looked awful, with his stringy, uneven, uncombed brown hair and rather dead brown eyes that nevertheless stared toward Alexa and her mom. Plus he had a slight grin on his face. He had a cigarette in his hand and took a puff, causing his cheeks to move, emphasizing his dark, jaggedly cut hair.

"Hello, Ronald," Alexa said coldly. "I'm surprised you're out in public. Why are you here today?"

A few people slipped by them on the sidewalk, but Spence didn't look toward them. His gaze was intently focused on the two women.

"Oh, I've been just sort of wandering around town in areas where I know Coltons sometimes hang out. Don't you like that restaurant down the street? Anyway, there must be something you like around here, since here you are."

"Not for long. We were just leaving." Alexa had placed herself in front of her mom, and she now gestured with her head at her car. They hadn't yet moved away from it, which could be a good thing. "Let's go, Mom." Alexa pulled her key out of her pocket and pressed the button to unlock the doors.

"I don't think so," Spence snarled. "You're both coming with me." Running at them, he yanked a gun from under his denim shirt. Dashing around Alexa, he grabbed her mom. He aimed the gun at Isa, then Alexa, then Isa again.

Damn. Alexa was scared for her mom, and furious. She'd just gone through an ordeal in Arizona as part of her job and more, keeping Dane, and herself, safe. She didn't want to go through anything like that again.

And she would do anything to keep her mom safe.

Barely thinking, Alexa went into protection mode and leaped toward Spence, maneuvering so she could bend enough to kick the gun out of his hand. It flew sideways, toward the street, and Alexa dashed to pick it up, planning to use his own weapon to capture the attacker.

Only—as she grabbed the weapon, Alexa saw her mom gasp, breathe hard, clutch her chest. Oh no.

Alexa knew she had to do what was important: save her mother's life. Isa might be having a heart attack, and Alexa didn't want to leave her by chasing their assailant, who was now running. Someone else would have to catch Spence, much as she wanted to be the one to bring him to justice.

"I've called 9-1-1," said someone on the sidewalk near them, and Alexa glanced that way. A middle-aged woman had approached from the crowd that was now growing around them, and she held her phone up, though she justifiably stayed back.

"Thank you," Alexa said, feeling highly grateful—and frustrated.

Pointing the gun downward and holding on to her mother's arm to help keep her stable, Alexa couldn't help staring through the crowd in the direction Spence had gone.

One of the other women around them said, "Does she need CPR? I could give it a try," and proceeded to lower her mother to the ground. Not sure, Alexa felt grateful as she watched.

But she also continued to gaze after Spence. If she hadn't needed to stay there to take care of her mother, might she have been able to catch him and bring him in?

Don't go there, she told herself. She'd done what was important. Hopefully, cops would show up as well as an ambulance and—

There. She heard a siren. Apparently so did the rest of the crowd on the sidewalk.

The sirens grew louder. Multiple ones, in fact. In moments, Alexa saw both an ambulance and a police car arrive.

EMTs jumped out, and Alexa explained briefly that there had been some potential danger against her mother, who now appeared to be having a heart attack. As the woman who had been trying to help stepped away, medics began examining Isa. Some uniformed cops got out of the cruiser and also joined them on the sidewalk.

Alexa explained that a person believed to be a major drug smuggler, Ronald Spence, had threatened them. She still had the gun and handed it over to one of the officers by dropping it into a plastic bag he proffered. She also pointed in the direction Spence had fled—as well as getting the officer's ID information, in case she ever had to track down that weapon again.

"I doubt we'll be able to find him, Marshal," said the older of the two cops, "but we'll go see what we can find."

Alexa doubted Spence would be anywhere around now either, but she hoped the cops—who, after all, reported to her mother's longtime admirer, Chief Theodore Lawson, and he and Isa had been getting closer recently—would get identification of some of the observers still hanging around, as well as their versions of what had happened. Hopefully, the witnesses would describe how Spence's weapon had been aimed at the two Colton women.

She didn't care if anyone mentioned how she'd gotten the weapon from Spence. But she had made it clear, while describing her mother and herself, that she was a US Marshal, and had showed her own ID. That way, her version should be the one to stick, even if they found Spence and he claimed she'd attacked him. She wouldn't let him get away with any more crimes.

One of the EMTs approached and, at her invitation, Alexa got into the ambulance, too. They'd given her mother a preliminary exam. Though Isa appeared in no immediate danger and looked to be breathing more normally, they were still taking her to the hospital.

Once they arrived, med techs immediately wheeled her mother on a gurney to the emergency room, where an ER doctor took over her care. Alexa followed, then stayed in the waiting room nearby.

She sat on one of the stark wooden chairs along the sizeable room's perimeter and pulled her phone from her pocket. She was alone here while she waited, but she needed to let her siblings know what was going on.

It didn't make sense to call her emotionally closest sibling first, though. Naomi wasn't in town, and to learn what was happening would upset her, but she wouldn't be able to dash here to stay with them. Alexa would let her know later.

She instead considered calling Dom first, since she'd been in touch with him over the past few days. Not that what had happened had anything to do with what they'd been discussing. And he wasn't in Blue Larkspur, either.

No, she decided to call Jasper and Aubrey. They were local, and the Gemini Ranch was just out of town.

She called Jasper's number.

"Hi, sis," he said.

"Hi. Look, you need to know this." She quickly told him what had happened, and where she was. "I'd appreciate it if you'd call the rest of our sibs who are local. I don't know how Mom is doing now, but I hope to hear soon."

"Got it. I'll let everyone else know. And Aubrey and I will be there as soon as we can."

Good. That was necessary, though painful. Alexa hated waiting here alone. The idea of Dane being with her telling jokes crept into her head, but she thrust it out since it wasn't going to happen. But she could try to go bother someone here to find out what was going on with Isa.

But as soon as she reached the waiting room door to leave, she was joined by Chief Theodore Lawson. She'd met him before, mostly thanks to his friendship with her mother. He was tall, with silver hair, green eyes and an utterly polite personality.

Right now he stared down at Alexa as they both stood there, those eyes wide and his forehead puckered in obvious concern.

"How's Isa?" he asked immediately.

"Not sure." Alexa let the words out with a sigh, moving her glance so she wouldn't meet his eyes. "They've taken her into the emergency room for a checkup. She had symptoms of a possible heart attack, and—"

"No wonder. I have access to all emergency calls that come into the station, and I heard Spence attacked her. And you, too—right?"

"That's right." Alexa bit her lip. If he knew all the details, would the chief blame her?

But why? She'd done all she could to protect her mother. She hadn't led Spence there. She'd gotten his gun away from him and caused him to flee.

No, she just had a guilty conscience, for no reason except wishing she had done even more to prevent her mother from a possible heart attack.

And the chief? He obviously cared enough to dash right to the hospital when he'd heard Isa had been taken there. Alexa had already wondered if the two of them were in a potential relationship, and now she had more reason to believe it.

Theodore sat in the chair beside the one Alexa had previously occupied, and she slumped back down in that one.

"How long has she been in there?" Theodore asked, leaning forward and clasping his hands together over his knees.

"Not sure. Maybe twenty minutes." Alexa considered checking the time on her phone. How long after noon was it? That was approximately when she'd first seen her mother. But how long had the events with Spence taken? And the aftermath near her car, plus the ambulance ride here?

"Well, that doesn't matter. I'll stay here as long as necessary, and I assume you will, too."

"Absolutely."

Alexa watched Theodore's expression. He had gritted his teeth, and his breathing was fast.

She certainly didn't want him to have a heart attack, too. "Look," she said. "Since you're the police chief, let me tell you the details of what happened."

"Great idea."

And so she did, from the moment she'd heard Spence's voice, to his disappearance beyond the crowd after she'd gotten his gun.

But before Alexa could finish, a nurse in blue scrubs came into the room. Her name tag said Nurse Nelson. She looked older and matronly.

"Mrs. Colton seems to be doing better now," she said, approaching Alexa. "Best we can tell at the moment, she had a panic attack, not a heart attack as originally believed. Someone was threatening the two of you, right, when she started to have symptoms?"

"That's right," Alexa said, feeling somewhat relieved. A panic attack had to be a lot safer than a heart attack, didn't it?

"We want to keep an eye on her for now, though," the nurse continued, "so we're going to move her to one of the rooms down the hall. You can go there, too, to keep her company."

Her eyes moved from Alexa to Theodore, and Alexa said, "This is Chief Lawson. He's a friend of our family, and I'd like him to join us."

"That should be fine," the nurse said.

But there was more. "Oh, and I called some of my family members before," Alexa said, "and they may be joining us." She didn't ask if that was acceptable. She'd let them in a few at a time, if necessary. Anything to keep her mother safe and happy.

"That sounds all right, too," said the nurse. "Your mom will be on monitors, so we'll know if she's getting too stressed. And please don't overdo the number of people keeping her company."

"Of course," Alexa agreed. She followed the nurse out of the waiting room and down the open hall, busy with others mostly in scrubs, to one of the last doors, which she opened. Alexa also heard Theodore's determined footsteps behind her on the tiled floor.

Alexa's mom, in a private room, lay in a light green hospital gown, propped up by the back of her narrow bed. A lot of tubes and things appeared to be attached to her, and there were rhythmic beeping noises.

But she was awake, and called out in a slow, raspy voice, "Oh, Alexa, you're here." And then she stopped and looked beyond Alexa. "And Theodore. Why are you—?"

"Because I heard you were ill, Isa, and I wanted to make sure you were okay." The man who'd been behind Alexa moved quickly forward and bent over when he reached the bed, kissing Isadora's cheek.

Good guy, Alexa thought. So far she'd seen nothing to turn her against it if they had any kind of relationship.

There were chairs at the side of the room, and Alexa and Theodore each took one. "We'll be here with you, Mom," Alexa said. "We don't want to keep you awake or otherwise stir you up, but let us know if you need anything."

"I've got what I need right now with you both here," her mom whispered.

A knock sounded on the door then, and one of the nurses opened it. "Are you okay to have another couple of family members come in for a visit?" she asked, looking at Alexa's mom as she walked to the bed.

"Absolutely," Isa said.

Not surprising to Alexa, since she'd called them first, the visitors were Jasper and Aubrey.

And over the course of the next hour, a few other siblings who lived in or around Blue Larkspur also came to visit, thanks to Jasper or Audrey getting in touch. They included Dom, who'd obviously rushed here despite not living in town, as well as Caleb and Morgan. The rest of her siblings called.

But of those who were there, they all wanted to hear Alexa's story about what had happened, which she related to them when they joined her in the waiting room, always leaving Theodore in the room with their mother. Fortunately, no strangers joined them in the waiting area.

As Alexa told them how Spence had appeared on the sidewalk, out of the blue, Caleb stood from where he'd been seated and growled, "I'll bet he was following Mom. Or maybe you. Or maybe he really was just hanging out in areas he thought Coltons might appear, like good areas of town."

"However he did it," Dom said, also appearing furious, "we need to make sure he never does it again."

"I agree," Morgan said. "No matter how he found them, it's wrong. Very wrong. And—well, I know it's not our fault, but we should never have used The Truth Foundation and helped him get free, even though Clay Houseman copped to his crimes. But we didn't know that our father had been right this once in getting someone convicted and imprisoned for a long time. Well, Spence won't be free forever. I'm going to make sure of it. That's my primary goal right now, bringing Ronald Spence in. I'm working on locating him as fast as I can, and I won't stop."

"You're right," Alexa said, "but that's taking a lot of responsibility on yourself. I'll be looking for the guy, too, and please let me know if there's anything I can do to help."

"I will," Morgan said. "Thanks."

However it occurred, Alexa felt certain her siblings in law enforcement and involved in upholding the law would find the guy and get him arrested—again. She was glad, and proud, that the Colton family wasn't backing down and was out to get Spence.

The conversation slowed down, and Alexa returned to going in and out of their mother's room, trying to ensure there weren't too many people there at the same time. But she didn't even try to get Theodore to leave. Her mother seemed so happy and relaxed when the police chief sat beside her on the bed as they both talked to those of Isa's kids who came to visit.

Alexa was in the room, though, when a doctor in white scrubs, a stethoscope around his neck, came in. "Hi, I'm Dr. Carlo. I checked on Mrs. Colton before and would like to again."

"Do you want us to leave the room?" Alexa asked.

"Yes, please."

In a few minutes, Dr. Carlo came out. "Mrs. Colton is looking pretty good now. We're going to release her to go home, as long as someone can be there with her for the next twenty-four hours or so to make sure she remains stable."

"That would be me," Theodore said immediately. "I'm fine with taking some time off tomorrow."

The next few minutes turned into a bit of a blur after Alexa and a nurse got Isa dressed into her own clothes again, and the rest of them all helped her get ready to leave, while Theodore took a while on the phone to plan his upcoming time off, then left to get his car.

Soon, Isa was wheeled out to the curb in a wheelchair, then helped into Theodore's police SUV. "I'm taking her to her home now and will stay with her there, but any of you can feel free to visit tomorrow, of course, as long as she's left alone tonight to get a good night's sleep."

That sounded good to Alexa, and apparently to her siblings as well. The police chief had taken charge of the situation, and their mother's care, for now. Isa was clearly in good hands.

She had a new man in her life. One who really cared. Alexa felt happy for her.

But she couldn't help but think about the man who'd entered her own life, thanks to her profession, but was now out of it once more.

She couldn't help feeling sad, thinking of Dane. Maybe even heartbroken. She missed him. Might never see him again. Oh, yes, she had fallen for him, smart or not.

She only hoped all was going well with him now, and would continue to do so in the future, in court and otherwise.

Without her.

Chapter Twenty

It was almost over. There'd been a pause, though, in the trial this Tuesday morning. For the moment, Dane didn't have to concentrate on anything being said, and so he just sat there behind the rail, looking around at the many people in front of him, near the judge.

Watching the judge have a discussion with both the prosecutor and defense counsel as he leaned down from the bench.

Dane hadn't been permitted to be in the courtroom before he'd testified, which hadn't been surprising. Not that anything he might have heard would affect his testimony.

That had meant he'd been under guard in a small meeting room in the courthouse yesterday morning for a couple of hours. But his testimony had begun around 11:00 a.m. It had continued for the rest of the day.

It had been grueling, but oh so gratifying.

The defense counsel had done her darnedest to attempt to show he was lying or exaggerating, but he couldn't be shaken.

The facts were clear. Months ago, he had been looking into who was running a prostitution ring, thanks to

orders from his boss, Police Chief Samuel Swanson—
a big mistake on Swanson's part since it soon became
clear that the chief was the one they were after. Dane
and his partner, Alvin, had started investigating Swanson.

Swanson had unsurprisingly figured it out.

Dane had consequently watched Swanson shoot
Alvin. And he'd also watched the gun aim at him and
felt the bullet penetrate his arm.

His cross-examination had been even more arduous,
but his description was the truth. He hadn't hesitated.
He hadn't made even a tiny contradiction.

The defense had clearly not been happy.

And Swanson? He'd glared down at the table in front
of him, not directing his fury toward Dane—most likely
under orders from his attorney.

From what Dane understood, security in the courthouse had been ramped up enough that he doubted anyone else would show up with guns to attempt to shut
him up—even though the authorities apparently hadn't
found any of the others Swanson might have hired to
come after him. But even while he testified Dane wasn't
worried.

That was yesterday. And Dane been permitted to
watch the rest of the trial after his testimony, including
for a couple of hours this morning.

Not that there'd been much after that, although the
defense had managed to bring in a few witnesses. One
claimed he'd been with Swanson at the critical time,
but his testimony hadn't stood up to cross-examination.
And a couple this morning were character witnesses,
including a Tempe city councilman. But even acting

like a good guy to those he reported to didn't mean
Swanson was innocent.

At the moment, the warm courtroom, currently filled
with the low sounds of people conversing as they waited
for the trial to resume, seemed safe enough.

Dane had thought a lot about Alexa.

What would she have thought about his testimony?

What did she think about him now?

Did she think about him at all?

He hadn't been permitted to get in touch with her
again, just in case she was somehow under surveillance
by one of Swanson's cronies who were looking for him
when he was out of court while the trial continued, such
as the rest of the weekend, or last night.

And yeah, he missed her. A lot.

A whole lot. He had to talk to her again soon.

He realized how much he was in love with her.

RIGHT NOW, HE SAT behind the railing with a whole crowd
of onlookers, including members of the media, watching and listening as the trial got underway.

Good. Time to continue.

Now, Francini gave his closing arguments to the jury.
Defense counsel would be next.

Then the jury would be taken to another room to
conduct deliberations.

Who knew how long that would take?

No matter. He would be around here, waiting for
those results, which he certainly hoped would be correct.

It had seemed fairly short for a murder trial, but the
facts seemed pretty clear.

Dane would soon get whatever final backup he could from his protectors, then resume his life.

And would he talk to Alexa again then?

Oh yes.

And more, if possible.

A lot more. He would make sure of that.

TIME WAS PASSING. It was a Saturday morning, a week after her return home.

Alexa sat at her small kitchen table with her electric stove on one side and refrigerator on the other, all perched on a beige tiled floor. She liked this aspect of her house.

She liked most things about her home.

Even though, at the moment, she was considering how and for where to leave it for the day. She'd at least put on a casual cotton shirt over slim jeans. Nothing professional, but there were plenty of places she could go dressed that way.

Her mind slipped to Dane, as it always did. She missed him terribly.

But somehow she would need to learn to live with it.

No matter how much it hurt.

She was drinking a cup of coffee just brewed in a pot where she could grab seconds or thirds if she wished. She was home for the weekend. Her office was closed, except for emergencies, and so far she hadn't yet been assigned someone else for witness protection, although she'd had some detailed discussions with Vince about procedures she'd been using with Dane and others, as well as several possible assignments coming up soon.

Right now, she was pondering a way to get together

with family. Maybe her mother. Or maybe she could even arrange a dinner that night with her mom and Theodore, as well as some of her siblings and their romantic interests...

But that might feel painful, to be there on her own.

Not that Dane was really a romantic interest... Okay, who was she trying to kid? Of course he was. Or had been. But now he was out of her life.

She picked her cup off the table and took another sip. It was getting cold. Should she heat it, or just leave the house and go shopping somewhere?

Alexa had followed the Swanson trial in the media as much as she could from Blue Larkspur. The trial had ended on Tuesday.

The jury had deliberated for a couple of days, and Swanson had been found guilty. No surprise, and definitely a relief.

That meant Dane was most likely out of witness protection, since he was no longer a witness. Swanson was in prison now, or at least on his way.

His sentence had been life, with no chance for parole. Logical. He was guilty of murder.

Of course some of Swanson's colleagues could still be after Dane. But Dane had presumably resumed his job as a vice detective with the Tempe PD. He was in law enforcement. He'd be careful.

And even if Swanson's buddies were unhappy, why place themselves in the position once again of possibly going to prison, too, by harming, or killing, Dane?

No, she figured he was safe. Hoped he was, at least. He had to be back in Tempe. Who was the new police chief there? It didn't matter to Alexa, but she certainly hoped it was someone honest and straightforward, a good superior officer for Dane.

They had spoken once since Dane's testimony. He had called Alexa the next day, on Wednesday, but she'd been at work and hadn't been able to do much but trade hellos and a few good wishes. She'd appreciated hearing from him.

He'd sounded so sweet. Made her laugh a few times. Made her really miss him like she'd never missed another man. So— Well, it didn't matter. If what they'd said to one another before hadn't truly been good-bye, maybe that conversation was.

Even so, she'd pondered later that day, and after, if she dared call him back and talk more, maybe even about getting together again someday. They no longer had professional reasons to stay apart, after all. And he was constantly on her mind, in her thoughts, populating her dreams…

With that once more filling her mind, she slammed the cup back on the table, though not hard enough to break it. Time to do…something.

She rose, ready to go grab her purse and get in her car.

Except—the doorbell rang. Interesting. She wasn't expecting anyone, or even any deliveries. She pushed her chair back and left the kitchen, heading for the hallway leading to the carved wooden front door.

She peered out the side window—and gasped.

Dane stood there, and he clearly saw her.

He was grinning.

She pulled the door open. "Come in," she exclaimed and moved out of the way so he could.

What was he doing there?

And why did it make her feel so ecstatic? As if she didn't know. She had fallen for this jokester.

He brushed gently against her as he stepped into the wide hall. He was just as she remembered—not that they'd been apart very long. But he was tall, his dark hair combed perfectly to frame his angular, handsome, smooth-shaven face. He wore a nice blue buttoned shirt tucked into dark pants; he looked somewhat dressed up.

Why? Was he in Blue Larkspur for business?

Whatever his reason, she was delighted to see him.

She closed the door behind him. "Hey, it's early," she said. "When did you get here? How did you get here? And why—?"

"Why? Because I really wanted to see you, Alexa."

"Oh," she said. What were the answers to her other questions? Did they matter?

Should she tell him how happy she was to see him?

Should she tell him how she really felt about him?

Maybe… But not yet.

"Hey, have you had breakfast?" she asked. "Or how about some coffee? I have some fresh brewed in my kitchen. And—hey, how did you know where I lived?" The smile she'd been aiming at him turned into a frown. "You've never been here before, and I don't recall ever telling you."

"Hey, I'm in law enforcement, like you are. Your address wasn't hard for me to find, though I kept it as secure as possible on the source I used. Of course I didn't know for certain you'd be home, but I'm delighted you are." He put his arm around her, still grinning. "And yes, I'd love some coffee."

Good. A distraction of sorts. She could ponder what to say, what to do, while they spent a little downtime in the kitchen.

"Great. This way," she said, feeling a bit sorry as she pulled away but nevertheless led him down the hall.

She grabbed another empty cup from the wall cabinet near the sink and poured him some coffee, also refreshing her own.

She handed his to him.

Then she demanded, "Why haven't I heard from you since the one time we talked after your part of the trial?"

She almost wished she could take the question back, but he didn't look upset or offended.

"Because I was concerned about you. I wanted to make sure no one appeared to be after me in retribution to my helping to put Swanson away for life, since they might also go after my witness protector. I assume you know no one else has been caught."

"Yes, I'm aware of it."

He was still standing, but he put his coffee down on the table, and so did she.

They were suddenly in each other's arms.

"I'd do anything in the world to protect you, Alexa. Even stay away from you. I really care about you. A lot. In fact, I—"

Alexa put her finger over his mouth.

She'd been shocked just now, when he showed up on her doorstep. And now he admitted he'd stayed away from her for her protection.

Because he really cared about her.

Her mind pulsed with emotion already.

Was he now going to say he loved her?

If so, did she want to hear it?

Did she love him?

Oh yeah. But they couldn't be in each other's lives. She didn't want to move to Tempe. And him, near Blue Larkspur? And it was too soon for the "L" word—they'd only spent a few days on the move together. Or was it? After all, the heart wanted what the heart wanted.

She couldn't help it. She'd already put her coffee back on the table. Now she threw her arms around him again and pulled his head down toward hers.

Their kiss made her want to forget all her questions and just live in the moment.

With Dane.

OKAY, HE HAD to tell her why he was really here right now.

But not immediately. Not while he was enjoying, loving, their kiss.

Loving her.

He basked in their closeness a while longer. He drew out their kiss, using his tongue to tease her, his arms to keep her tight against him.

But then— Well, they had to talk. He pulled back, gave her another quick kiss on her gorgeous, inviting lips, then smiled and sat at her table.

He gestured to the chair across from him. Her lovely face appeared confused for an instant, but she did as he'd suggested.

"Okay," he said, taking a sip of coffee before digging into what he had to say. "How would you feel about seeing me more often here, in Blue Larkspur?"

Her expression grew even more puzzled. "You're

kidding, aren't you? What about your job with the Tempe police?"

"Well, I've enjoyed it—sort of. Until my superior turned out to be a murderer. And until my partner was killed. Oh, I could have taken on more and different responsibilities there now, but—"

He'd already considered different ways to approach this. One thing he hadn't said was that he had been in Blue Larkspur for a day, driving up here after the trial was over.

For a good reason. One that had made him delay attempting to see her.

Since, if it worked out, he would potentially get to see her a lot.

And it had.

"But what?" she encouraged him, her brow furrowed over those beautiful blue eyes.

"Well, I've just accepted a job with the Blue Larkspur PD, also as a vice detective—or I'm close to accepting it. The offer is hanging there for a few days. And I intend to accept it as long as you don't mind seeing me while I'm here. Maybe even entering into a relationship, particularly when things have calmed down after a while and our adrenaline isn't pumping any longer over me being a witness and you protecting me. Or my worrying about protecting you. What do you think?"

"I think— I'm not sure." She still looked confused, although was that hope he saw there, too? "But I believe I'd like to try it. Only, if it doesn't work out, you could be stuck here with a new job and all. How do you feel about that?"

He rose once more and put out his hand. She took it,

and again stood in front of him. Close to him. Tempting him.

"I think I love you, Alexa," he said, clasping her hand even more tightly.

"And I think I love you, Dane. But—"

Wow. That was certainly hoped for. And to hear it so soon…

"Hey," he said, "you know me. I can be serious—or not. This time, I'm serious. Only… Look. If I stay here and take this job, I may just have to arrest you."

"What? What are you talking about?"

"Well, I'm a cop. You know that. And I'll be here spending time with you. Sure, I'm a vice detective, but I can arrest people who commit crimes. And you're doing just that."

He'd been trying to keep his expression serious. But, heck, he was a jokester from way back. She knew that, even though they'd gone through some pretty nasty situations together.

And now? Well, if she went along with this joke, he'd feel even more in love with her.

"Tell me what you mean." She tried to pull her hand away, but he didn't let her. "Why would you possibly arrest me? What crime am I committing, or have I done something already, with my witness protection? Or—"

"Hey, I can arrest people for theft, you know. And you're in the process of stealing my heart."

"What! For a moment there, I thought you really were serious. But I should have known better." She started to laugh. Hard. So hard, he saw tears in her eyes.

Her giant smile was clearly driven by amusement.

"You law enforcement clown," she said, gasping as

her laughter slowed down. She tightened her grip on his hand this time. "Now kiss me."

And Dane knew he had won her over. Forever.

He took her into his arms and obeyed her command.

* * * * *

COMING SOON!

We really hope you enjoyed reading this book.
If you're looking for more romance, be sure to
head to the shops when new books are
available on

Thursday 10th November

To see which titles are coming soon, please visit
millsandboon.co.uk/nextmonth

MILLS & BOON

THE HEART OF ROMANCE

A ROMANCE FOR EVERY READER

MODERN

Prepare to be swept off your feet by sophisticated, sexy and seductive heroes, in some of the world's most glamorous and romantic locations, where power and passion collide.

HISTORICAL

Escape with historical heroes from time gone by. Whether your passion is for wicked Regency Rakes, muscled Vikings or rugged Highlanders, awake the romance of the past.

MEDICAL

Set your pulse racing with dedicated, delectable doctors in the high-pressure world of medicine, where emotions run high and passion, comfort and love are the best medicine.

True Love

Celebrate true love with tender stories of heartfelt romance, from the rush of falling in love to the joy a new baby can bring, and a focus on the emotional heart of a relationship.

Desire

Indulge in secrets and scandal, intense drama and plenty of sizzling hot action with powerful and passionate heroes who have it all: wealth, status, good looks...everything but the right woman.

HEROES

Experience all the excitement of a gripping thriller, with an intense romance at its heart. Resourceful, true-to-life women and strong, fearless men face danger and desire - a killer combination!

To see which titles are coming soon, please visit

millsandboon.co.uk/nextmonth

LET'S TALK

Romance

For exclusive extracts, competitions
and special offers, find us online:

- facebook.com/millsandboon
- @MillsandBoon
- @MillsandBoonUK

Get in touch on 01413 063232

For all the latest titles coming soon, visit
millsandboon.co.uk/nextmonth

JOIN US ON SOCIAL MEDIA!

Stay up to date with our latest releases, author news and gossip, special offers and discounts, and all the behind-the-scenes action from Mills & Boon...

 @millsandboon

 @millsandboonuk

 facebook.com/millsandboon

 @millsandboonuk

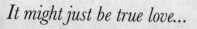 *It might just be true love...*

GET YOUR ROMANCE FIX!

Get the latest romance news,
exclusive author interviews, story
extracts and much more!

MILLS & BOON
Desire

Indulge in secrets and scandal, intense drama and plenty of sizzling hot action with powerful and passionate heroes who have it all: wealth, status, good looks…everything but the right woman.

MILLS & BOON
MODERN
Power and Passion

Prepare to be swept off your feet by
sophisticated, sexy and seductive heroes, in
some of the world's most glamourous and
romantic locations, where power and
passion collide.

Julia James
Heiress's
PREGNANCY SCANDAL
MILLS & BOON
MODERN

Jennie Lucas
Chosen as the
SHEIKH'S ROYAL BRIDE
MILLS & BOON
MODERN

Kim Lawrence
A WEDDING
at the
ITALIAN'S DEMAND
MILLS & BOON
MODERN

Sharon Kendrick
The
SHEIKH'S SECRET BABY
MILLS & BOON
MODERN

MILLS & BOON
MEDICAL
Pulse-Racing Passion

Set your pulse racing with dedicated, delectable doctors in the high-pressure world of medicine, where emotions run high and passion, comfort and love are the best medicine.

MILLS & BOON
True Love
Romance from the Heart

Celebrate true love with tender stories of heartfelt romance, from the rush of falling in love to the joy a new baby can bring, and a focus on the emotional heart of a relationship.